PRIMITIVE BEAUTY

AUTHOR'S SKETCHBOOK

VOLUME 1

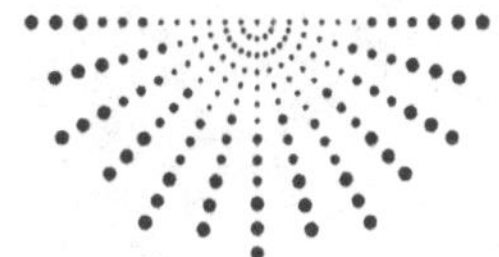

J.S. NATHANIEL

Published in
DENVER, COLORADO

Library of Congress Control Number Available

ISBN: e-book [978-1-967522-23-1]
ISBN: trade [978-1-967522-16-3]
ISBN: hardcover [978-1-967522-17-0]
ISBN: audiobook [978-1-967522-18-7]

ALSO BY J.S. NATHANIEL

Dominion of the Divine

Juliet + Juliette = Love in Mafia Land

Stardust Angel

Everything Spontaneous in the Land of Doll Parts

Narrator of Lies

CONTENTS

Part XXIV
RETURN OF INNOCENCE

For mother, who taught me the beauty of raw stories.

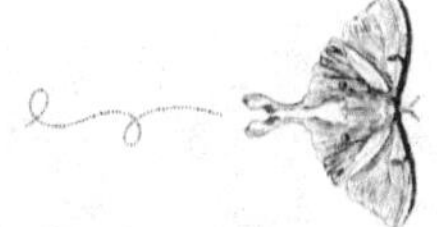

PREFACE

In the dim hours before dawn, with the taste of black coffee lingering and the smoke of her last cigarette curling toward the mountain peaks, my mother would lean in and whisper fragments of her untold stories. Tales of a life scraped raw by hardship. Dreams deferred like letters never sent. Those mornings bound us. Her words, a fragile bridge across the miles I later crossed, leaving behind the job, the home, the familiar ache of what was, for a meager existence in a new land where the lakes whisper secrets at three a.m. This book, Primitive Beauty, emerges from that crossing, a hybrid of our shared silences and the stories I carried away, evolving as I sifted through her journals, realizing her voice could only live through mine, imperfect and alive.

Every artist harbors a hidden sketchbook, a trove of half-formed ideas that strike in unlikely moments. On a train rumbling through shadowed lands, or beside a frozen Ottawa shore, where the cold sharpens the mind's feverish whirl. Writers compose ceaselessly in the quiet chambers of their heads, birthing narratives that may never see light. Short bursts of poetry or prose, riddles wrapped in everyday dread. Imagine the weight of those unseen words. The potential locked away, much like my mother's writings: a lifetime of raw hope, gathered but never shaped into the book she dreamed of sharing, not for acclaim, but to kindle resilience in others facing their own unrelenting storms.

I set out to weave her biography, to honor the best friend who knew my hidden fractures as I knew hers, but the truth unraveled differently. Her story, filtered through my lens, became ours—a memoir laced with the menace of loss, the subtext of reinvention, where quitting everything propelled me toward this raw craft. Primitive Beauty is no polished manual for artistry; it invites you into the writer's shadowed mind, to witness how imperfection forges timeless beauty amid a world that demands machine-like flawlessness. Tara, my wife of twenty-five years, often says she wishes she could glimpse the storms brewing inside me; here, I open that door, urging fellow creators to embrace their own turbulent dreams with unyielding courage.

INTRODUCTION

Primitive

Adjective

    i. (Literary) The base material of the universe; the fundamental substance or essence from which all things originate.

Beauty

Noun

    ii. (Literary) Things that are unspoiled by modern influence, characterized by ruggedness, honesty, and a direct connection to nature or early human expression.

PART I
PHANTOMS AND DOORWAYS

FRIDAY, JULY 26—
RESTLESS NIGHT

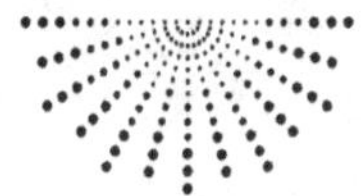

SHATTERED THOUGHTS

What if today was the turning point?

Loss is venomous.

—The agony of silence—

I remember the smell of white diamonds. Gone now.

I can still hear Patsy Cline's rich, achy tone singing somewhere in the house.

The wind rattles broken glass. I count each sharp edge

Why do we survive?

. . .

WHAT IF THE detective is the last person alive? Who does he interrogate—himself?

THEN I SEE

The white fox returns, nose to ground. I envy its certainty.

WHISPERS

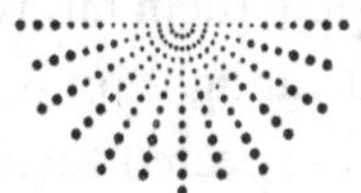

Patsy Cline kept haunting my Spotify—three times today, her songs played without me ever adding them. That rich, aching voice, the kind that knows hurt intimately, belonged to both. Same hurt, different decades. Patsy died at thirty. My mother, at sixty-eight.

Tara swears the kitchen light flickers every time I walk in. I'm so lost inside my head these days, I never notice the signs—never realize when mom visits.

Sea of Souls

SHE FELT the weight of those eyes bearing down on her—relentless, like ocean waves rolling in before her. They swept over her. Then receded, only to surge again. The ocean was so damn clamorous it rang her ears, the roar echoing long after the waves had pulled back. The weight of salty water tickled the back of her throat. Even the smell of seaweed lingered longer than she had hoped, the stench of rotting fish never far behind. Everything the sea brought these days washed up onto the smooth, shale-pebbled shore and turned to rot.

Her heart pounded, echoing the chaos that battered her ears. What puzzled her most was the sharp itch of barnacles stinging her nose—a sensation she could never quite get used to. But that was life. That was her life. The ocean's waves always brought things to her—mostly unwanted desires. Yet she could always count on the tide to take those unwanted things back, sweeping them far, far away, beyond the horizon, past the blinding shimmer of sunlight on water. Still, she knew someday they'd return, when she least expected them. Most likely when she was at her lowest. She could picture it now, her weary self, struggling to tackle, or at least face, those unwanted things.

But she'd make do, she tells herself. She always will. She always does. Not a day goes by without her managing the chaos of the ocean tide.

The ocean was faithful—punishing. Yet, without those barnacles stinging her nose daily, where would she be? More importantly, who would she be? The alternative frightened her most, that she'd be useless, even nothing, without that torturous ocean lying in wait. At least the waves gave her something, despite the headaches, the heartaches, and whatever else they decided to deliver each day. Still, she wondered, *Why, oh why, does life have to be this damn hard? This damn cruel?* Then she thinks, *if it was good enough for mother, then it must be good enough for me.* Her mother was her world. Then she, too, got swept away into that shimmering horizon. Someday, when it's her time, she'll meet the same fate. They all do, eventually. And when that day comes, she'll welcome the eyes of what comes after.

—*The Whisper*—

SHE FELT those eyes on her—unyielding, relentless—as if the weight of the ocean itself pressed down, wave after wave. Each surge swept over her, then retreated, only to return with renewed force. The sea's clamor echoed in her ears, so loud it nearly drowned out her thoughts. Salt stung the back of her throat. The sharp, briny scent of seaweed and fish clung to her skin, the odor of decay always lurking at the edge of the wind. Everything the tide delivered these days—memories, regrets, unwanted desires—washed up on the smooth, shale-pebbled shore and turned to rot.

Her heart pounded in her chest, its rhythm matching the ocean's unending assault. Sometimes, the sting of barnacles in her nose caught her off guard, a reminder of how the sea could wound as well as sustain. But this was her life, a constant negotiation with the tide, never knowing what it would bring or take away. She had learned to expect the unexpected, to brace herself for the return of things she wished would stay gone. She could already picture it, her weary self, facing those old burdens when she was at her lowest.

Still, she managed. She always did. Not a day passed without her wrestling the chaos the ocean hurled her way.

The sea was punishing, but faithful. Without the daily sting of barnacles, the relentless roar, she wondered who she would be. The thought unsettled her, that without struggle, she might become nothing at all. At least the ocean gave her something to fight against, even if it was only headaches, heartaches, and whatever else it chose to toss ashore. Sometimes she asked herself why life had to be so hard, so merciless. But then she remembered, if her mother could endure it, so could she. Her mother had been her anchor until the tide claimed her, too, sweeping her beyond the shimmering horizon. One day, she knew she would follow, and when that day came, she would welcome her mother's gaze.

PART II
LIZZIE

MARCH 19— A STORM OF DOUBT ERUPTS ON THE EVE OF LIZZIE'S (STARDUST ANGEL) RELEASE

I devoted myself completely to creating this list, driven by a deep need to honor Lizzie's story. Throughout it all, I felt my mom's presence beside me, even though she crossed the Lion's Gate last year.

Lizzie's decision to give the Polaroid camera to the other girl could be rooted in a complex mix of grief, guilt, hope, and a desperate need for closure.

—Here's a compelling reason for her actions—

LIZZIE HAD BEEN HAUNTED by the image of her sister ever since her tragic death. The Polaroid camera became both a torment and a lifeline. An object that tethered Lizzie to her sister's memory but also amplified her pain. Every time she saw her sister's face in its lens, it was as though the camera was whispering that she could never truly let go.

But then, one day, Lizzie saw something impossible: her sister standing beside another girl, not through the camera, but with her own eyes. It wasn't just an apparition, it felt real, tangible even. The way her sister looked at the girl was different, calm, almost protective. For the first time since her death, Lizzie didn't see sadness or regret in her sister's expression. Instead, she saw purpose.

Lizzie interpreted this as a sign that the camera wasn't meant for her anymore. Perhaps it had been a bridge between their worlds, but now it was time for someone else to carry it forward. The girl must need it more than Lizzie did—maybe to find answers of her own or to connect with something lost, just as Lizzie once had. In giving the camera away, Lizzie wasn't abandoning her sister's memory, she was trusting that this mysterious connection had a greater meaning.

It wasn't an easy decision. Letting go never is. But for the first time in a long while, Lizzie felt lighter. Her sister had found peace, and maybe now she could too.

This explanation ties Lizzie's action to themes of grief and healing while leaving room for mystery and interpretation about the camera's true purpose.

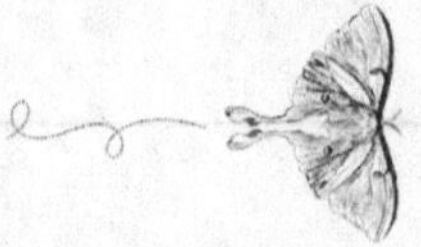

LIZZIE, in her imaginative musings, envisions each juror speaking in their unique voice, shaped by their personalities and motivations. Here's how she might imagine their statements:

a. **Juror 1** (The Foreman): "Let's keep this orderly. Everyone gets a turn to speak. We need to reach a decision, but we must do it properly."

b. **Juror 2** (The Meek Observer): "I'm not sure... but maybe we should consider that point again? I don't want to miss anything important."

c. **Juror 3** (The Biased Father): "She's guilty! You can't tell me otherwise. These kids today have no respect; they're all the same!"

d. **Juror 4** (The Rational Analyst): "Let's focus on the facts. Emotions have no place here. What does the evidence actually prove?"

e. **Juror 5** (The Empathetic Witness): "I grew up in a neighborhood like hers. I know what it's like. Maybe there's more to her story than we see."

f. **Juror 6** (The Honest Supporter): "I just want justice to be served right. If someone has doubts, we should hear them out."

g. **Juror 7** (The Impatient Salesman): "Can we wrap this up? I've got tickets to the game tonight. This is dragging on too long."

h. **Juror 8** (The Logical Advocate): "We owe it to her to discuss this thoroughly. A life is at stake, and doubt means we cannot convict."

i. **Juror 9** (The Wise Elder): "Sometimes, standing alone is the only way to do what's right. I see something worth reconsidering here."

j. **Juror 10** (The Prejudiced Cynic): "You people are soft! She's one of them. They're all criminals—it's just how they are."

k. **Juror 11** (The Idealistic Immigrant): "This jury is a privilege. We must respect the process and ensure fairness for all."

l. **Juror 12** (The Vacillating Executive): "I don't know... maybe she's guilty? Or not? Let's just decide already."

Lizzie imagines these voices clashing and converging in a confined room, each one representing a fragment of human nature (bias, logic, empathy, and apathy), all trapped within the weight of deciding another's fate.

PART III
SPLINTERS OF THE LOST

COSMIC D TRAIN—DENVER 2025

During those train rides to work from March through April, I poured my restless spirit into pages of raw, urgent writing and poetry. Each line forged in the clatter and sway of the rails. Every verse a testament to longing and transformation.

BRUNO'S SHAVING mirror might seem extravagant, but it's not actually the world's most expensive. That title belongs to a Russian masterpiece by Fabergé—crafted from solid gold and adorned with intricate enamel work.

GEOPOLITICAL TENSIONS (72) hours (Critical period) after a crisis

VOLATILE GLOBAL LANDSCAPES.

Interconnected threats

Cyber attacks

. . .

CLIMATE CHANGE

Disease outbreak

72 hours survival kits

NON-PERISHABLES that last twenty-five years (Everything Spontaneous).

EU Advisory?!

STRINGY ROAD FOR SURE.

WRITING IS AN ACT OF ARTISTRY. Any institution that claims otherwise aligns itself with the forces of authoritarianism. I write with unflinching courage, not to defy rules for the sake of rebellion, but because my imagination roams the cosmos, far beyond the confines of convention. To demand that I contain it within boundaries is to demand my extinction.

I KISS you like I'm pouring my soul into you.

FIRE Bender

I CAN'T HELP IT. My soul pours into you when I kiss you.

MY SOUL POURS into every kiss I give you, and I can't help it.

. . .

Your love is that strong for me to be unhappy being with...

—Archaeology of Words—

Your love gave me the universe. It was happy and sad and angry and melancholy. It was everything. We poured our universe into each other. It was a real love. Not perfect. But real.

Every day I fall in love with new words. Sometimes just one. Sometimes a cascade of nine at once. I can capture almost everything I experience in language, except for you. Each attempt to describe you ends in failure. Trying to define love feels as impossible as describing faith. Still, I'll spend my life trying, from this night onward, as your breath rises and falls beside me, your warmth seeping into my skin. I'll gather every word I cherish to express my love for you. Even after twenty-five years and countless new words, nothing compares to you.

I'm endlessly grateful you walked into Walgreens on a whim, because without that moment, I'd never have known real love or true happiness. No matter what life brings, I wouldn't trade a single day or share your heart with anyone else. That's what love means to me, devoting my life to finding the perfect sentence to capture what I feel. My only fear is that I might die before I find those words. Not out of pride or a need for recognition, but out of a longing to show you my whole heart. No, more than that. To invite you inside it. That's the only gift worth giving.

Level east

Resemble

Ludicrous

. . .

WHAT A WILD RIDE

The Knuckle Duster

RADIO SILENCE

Commodities

Open heart

A HINT of lavender

"THIS SALAD IS HOT."

"Hot? What do you mean?"

"The onions are hot."

"Oh, you mean like spicy?"

"No, I mean temperature wise."

STORIES THAT SHAPE water

PAGE TURNING opening lines in fiction:

LIP BALM OFFERINGS: for smooth lips in the afterlife.

THE BRAIN PLAYS our behaviors like a goddamn music box

I COULD SEE her cold breath swim in dewy light.

. . .

CHERRY SPOT

TREE OF SOULS

STAIN THE WORLD / spoil the world
So devout
To liberate

A LITTLE BLUE still shone through the crust.

"THE RIGHT WAY?"

"HOW WOULD you know if that was the right way?"

LOOK-SEE

I WILL SHOW this world a thing or two.

YOU GOT me all fucked up
Share secret knowledge and wisdom
Femininity
Erupted
Guineafowl
Lorikeet

Crowned

Waxwing

Spotted frosty moth

Cheetah

Spotted snow moth

Parasite

Assassin bees /mites

Dragon hoppers

Hoverflies

Big-eyed bug

Praying bugs

Viper

Boom flier

Banded

Sea/river/swamp/marsh/pond

Cooper/coral/ green

Leatherback darter

Raspberry darter

Baba-dawn

Braying cheetah mule

Copperhead newt

Vampire skippers

HORNLESS CAT FAWN

WALK HOT COALS

IN REVERSE

When I return to the same book again and again, it feels, in a way, like that book is my life. Or at least, it was. There's a message in those pages that keeps drawing me back. I'm not sure if it's a message of pain, redemption, or simply a way of putting things to rest. In my mind's eye, I hope it's the latter. But who can say? Maybe the reason I keep revisiting those same pages is a kind of self-deprecation—a sign that I can't let go of my past, my present, or maybe even my future.

Witches of Fortune

Her mind, her thoughts infested by evil thoughts of revenge.

Pure Latin stock

Hurtling dead things toward an invisible god in the sky.

GHOST FOREST

Things were finally looking up.

Akin

That murderous light

THE UNIVERSE GIVES

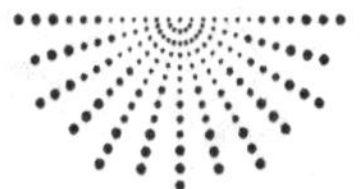

PEACE AT A TIME

The trees were gnarled and twisted, reaching toward the heavens like giant hands, as if crying out to God, "Why must we endure this pain every year on earth?" Their limbs stretched upward into a grayish, bluish nightmare. One only the sun could deliver them from.

THE VEINS in the smooth stone seemed eager to soak up all the blood scattered about, as if determined to grant Tetchy a second life.

DOWN TO A SCIENCE / perfected the process

CHRYSALIS—WORDS that seem impossible to speak, but sound beautiful. / ˈkrisələs /

Omnipotent

Primeval

Satiety—/ sə tiədē /

TREES OF BARREN

Single rarest thing

Deceased heart.

Death has lost all meaning.

I can't take my eyes off you.

I can't take my mind off you.

There is no hope in his eyes.

Hedonism.

Virile.

His skin has the texture of ancient scrolls.
Tissue paper. Parchment. Crepe.

His eyes were nothing but a film of
milkiness, with traces of blue still visible,
though bleached and eerie.

A BONY LITTLE FACE.

Ribs working overtime.

Benign.

A fine, warm, delicate face.

Silence swallowing her whole.

Deadness.

A flashlight seemed to live behind the pupil.

Ephemera.

Not well-to-do by any measure, in any country, but carefree when it
came to acquiring useless luxuries.

A SACRED ACT OF DEATH.

SKELETAL

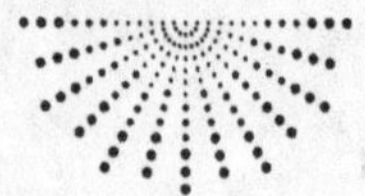

A brutal cold snap stripped the trees of their golden color,
leaving them naked and transforming the landscape into a
prison of skeletal forms. Creatures rising from the frozen
earth, a cemetery of the undead waiting to reanimate come
spring.

Moon face.

He would just melt into this adorable little creature—but beware.

Clouds of dander drifted in the morning light.

Let me carry your tears

I cannot be touched—ever. Not by the gentleness of a hand,
not even by the tickle of a feather. When the wind brushes against my

face on a breezy day, it feels as if my skin is on fire. I cannot be touched because my condition won't allow it. For five years, I have daydreamed about what it would feel like to be kissed.

True bliss is often found within the confines of poverty. When the world is yours, nothing holds value; but when you have nothing, you treasure every small thing within your reach. Only through humility can you truly love.

THE HEART IS in constant conflict with the mind. The heart is biological; the mind is not.

"SEND IN THE RATS, they'll detect those land mines."

A PORCELAIN-LIKE BIRD trapped inside a glob of hand-blown glass.

JILL

UNDONE

JILL WOKE WITH A PLAN. It was Thursday, nothing notable about the day except the overcast sky. When she opened the bathroom window, cool, moist air funneled through the screen and whistled softly.

She sat, staring at the metallic shower tile. Scum had clouded the glass barrier, making it look almost like sudsy waves, sweeping in and out.

Her latest social media post had crushed whatever was left in her. Her phone kept flashing on the counter. The harsh strobe bouncing off the golden snake wallpaper. She resisted the urge to pick it up.

She dumped the remaining pills into a lowball. Next to it sat another glass, filled with tap water. Bubbles crawled to the rim, the water was slightly cloudy. Calcium from the shower seemed to have infected the drinking glass, or maybe the apartment was plagued by hard water deposits.

She readied herself to down the pills when her cell phone rang. She set the glass down on the granite counter and waited for the ringing to stop. It never did.

She sighed and answered. "Hello." Even now, her voice retained that inviting, friendly tone.

She waited. Without a word, the caller hung up. Jill set the phone down, wondering who it could have been. It was an unknown number. Was it Racheal, calling to rub it in? Perhaps Ethan had a change of heart.

She stared at the phone, debating whether to call back.

As silence settled in, she lifted the glass of pills to her lips. Her phone chimed with a text.

She set the glass down, now aggravated, and picked up the phone to read:

My name is Jack. I accidentally dialed your number. When I realized my mistake, I was too embarrassed to speak. I apologize for any inconvenience. If it means anything, you seem like a really nice person. May you have a blessed day.

She immediately sent a thumbs-up emoji.

Jack replied with a sorry emoji.

Ok.

He sent nothing back.

She flushed the pills down the toilet, then peered at her phone.

She didn't recognize the number, but Jack had the same area code. She texted: Do you want to get coffee sometime?

I'm a stranger.

Ok, never mind.

Wait!

What?

How about today? It would be nice to talk to a kind person.

Me too.

How about Market Café on Larimer. Have you been?

Are you free now?

Yes.

OK.

Wait!

Yes?

How will I know it's you?

I'll text.

Ok.

We all must greet the grave. Our eyes turn the soil, digging down until we reach rock bottom. Our toes skirt the edge, fearful of the fall—even when our time has not yet come. We hover over death while reaching for life, our hearts plunging into the unthinkable. We remain here. But do we?

PITY WILL NOT SIT at my table. I will swallow the pain. The pain is delicious—it nourishes me more than judgment ever could.

FACIA

THIS ICY EVENING, I sat next to a man who was sleeping. Other passengers avoided him. He awoke from a dream as I took the seat beside him. I caught the scent of carbon monoxide drifting from him. Not from cigarettes, but from relentless exposure to traffic. A hint of sweltering asphalt began to settle in.

We both gazed out the window into the pitch-black night, as if our minds occupied the same place in life. Our stares mirrored each other.

But there was a difference: his eyes were not those of a lost man—mine were. There was certainty in his look. In that moment, I realized he was freer than I was. He had freed himself from the weight of the world, while I cracked beneath it.

It saddened me when he abruptly got off at the next stop. I desperately wanted to follow. To go wherever he was headed. But that's life, not enough courage to unlock the chains that bind.

> The monogram on the tracks was visible
> only under certain light. I saw "1975"
> inscribed there. Then I realized—the tracks
> are as old as I am.

THE SKY SPLIT into two worlds through the train window. On one side, a spotless blue afternoon stretched endlessly. On the other, snow-capped mountains rose, crowned with a halo of drifting clouds. The mountains lined up perfectly with the glass, holding my gaze captive, refusing to let me look away.

For a moment, the world felt turned upside down—or maybe, for the first time, right side up. I couldn't tell which.

DESOLATION COLLIDED WITH BEAUTY.

INDUSTRIAL CARNAGE PRESSED against tranquil splendor.

DOGS ROAMED THE BUSINESS DISTRICT—AN empire built of concrete and glass.

. . .

THE MOON CRAWLED BEHIND thin lip clouds to hide. Its ambient light spilled wondrous and would not erase. From where I stand, the earth is now a well. I'm on the bottom. The moon, my only way out. If I try to climb out.

TODAY I SAW a doctor walk out of a medical building, carrying a metal suitcase. He still wore his lab coat, stethoscope draped around his neck—glasses, the works. It made me think, *doesn't James Bond carry a metal briefcase?* I suppose doctors are heroes outside the office, too.

A cross on the side of the foothills at night levitates and glows as though it's God's Lite Brite

—Second Sight—

THE LEVITATING CROSS in darkness marks a summit indifferent to binaries of light or shadow—a symbol suspended between celestial aspiration and earthly denial. Below, a city discards its gods into neon-lit oblivion, where skyscrapers claw at smog-choked skies. Eight green doors glow like emerald portals on a monolithic building, while streets blur in dissonant velocities: cars, trains, and planes fracturing time.

The neon car wash sign had the word "car" burned out—or scrubbed away until it reached death. Does that mean anything can be washed to death?

THE NIGHT FEELS ominous as the light rail speeds past apartments and industrial lots. Parking lots lie in darkness all hollowed out, though the streetlights cast a faint glow. The pavement appears like inky glass.

Smooth, white lines frame death. As it always does. The mood warns: don't walk late at night—not in this neighborhood.

Need a house call? Dr. Fix-It fixes it all. If only such a creature truly existed. That's what the sign promised. Still, "God of Fix-It" has a nice ring to it—I'd dial that number in lickety-split.

WINTER HAD SCORCHED THE LAND, laying waste to everything it touched.

Concrete tubes and boxes were strewn across the landscape like Goliath's forgotten building blocks.

STERILE, stainless silos pierced the afternoon sky, almost erasing the heavens above.

Rails lay abandoned, weeds spidering over the tracks. The banks were overgrown—long past due for a haircut.

A STATELY BRIDGE LEADS—WHERE? Perhaps not to nowhere, but simply to the other side of the tracks. Then I think: Is nowhere everywhere. And if everywhere is nowhere, then where do I go next?

A pile of bird feathers lay on the asphalt, covering the double yellow line. The feathers were bleached and frayed, but the yellow lines remained sharp and clean, lending the feathers an odd vitality. It was a strange sight—as if the bird had plunged from the sky at lightning speed and crashed onto the road.

GEOMETRIC CONCRETE TILES were arranged in a herringbone pattern beneath the bridge. Creaturelike weeds stuck out their tongues between the cracks. In the tallest corner of darkness, a twig-like arm reached out as if to say, I know you're there—why can't I feel your rays raining down on me? What more must I do to bathe in your light?

BookTok— A social media execution—teenager-style.

—Removed Excerpt STARDUST ANGEL—

I was afraid to love Nodin. Afraid that I would eventually break
him. I stayed awake at night thinking, "It's only a matter of
time." The ghosts of Andrew and Abby would avenge their
deaths. Running wasn't sustainable in the long run. The
sins of the past are timeless. I am not.

IN THE DAYLIGHT, the train sped past dumpsters. One was spray-painted in white: "trash." Of course, dumpsters are designed to collect garbage. Then I noticed a man pushing a shopping cart near the dumpster. It dawned on me—maybe the sign is meant to keep people from sleeping inside the dumpster. Or worse, rummaging for something to eat. I got off at the next stop and went back. I had ten dollars in my wallet, but the man had vanished before I got there.

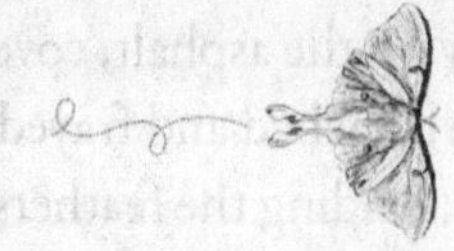

I NEVER WRITE dates on my work. But today is too striking to ignore —a crisp blue day in March 2025. America stands divided by a political civil war. On one side, those who worship a criminal; on the other, those who refuse. In Denver, the state capitol just raised a Canadian flag in protest, a silent rebuke against the criminal minds steering the country. But not a Mexican flag, despite our president's tariffs on Mexico. The symbolism is selective.

This is the world in a nutshell: the only time we come together is to hate. Denver raises a flag to spite the president; the other side raises one to spite the haters. No wonder nothing gets accomplished—we're too busy hating each other to build anything lasting.

True change isn't about raising flags in defiance. A flag is just a symbol; its meaning comes after the work is done. We raised a flag on the moon after we landed. We raised flags in victory after defeating the Nazis. Raising a flag before the struggle is over only breeds more division.

We live in a cushion world, insulated from the consequences of our own anger—mistaking gestures for progress, and pride for purpose. If we want to make the world better for the next generation, we need more than symbols. We need the courage to do the real work, together.

PART IV
EMPIRE OF GRANITE

PART IV
EMPIRE OF GRANITE

INVISIBLE SINS

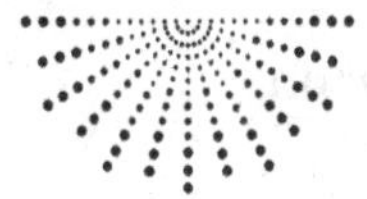

EVERY DAY, I watch this woman work tirelessly—hauling trash, scrubbing bathrooms. There are at least eight bathrooms in the building, maybe more, and I often see her emerging from one, toilet brush in hand, never pausing, always in motion. She seems to be everywhere at once, tending to a sprawling laboratory that must cover at least 40,000 square feet.

No matter what she's doing, she always greets me with a smile. I can't tell if she's truly content. Right now, I see her rubbing her sore neck, feet propped on a bargain chair, eyes fixed on her phone—her first real break of the day. I think it's lunchtime. If she's unhappy, a stranger would never know. Even those closest to her might not guess; she never lets it show.

Most people walk past her as if she's invisible. It's heartbreaking to watch someone care for so many and receive so little in return. She reminds me of my mother—always giving, rarely acknowledged. Why do we take our mothers for granted? They're here for such a short time, and once they're gone, they're gone. I know this pain firsthand. If I could do it over, I would.

Perhaps we're meant to live with this knowledge—that we could have done more. There's a punishment for that, quietly waiting somewhere in the future.

Next time I see her, I'm going to give her a gift card. I can't afford much, but I'll give what I can. Mothers deserve gratitude, even if it comes from a stranger.

A silky veil draped the moon

MOTHER MOUNTAIN

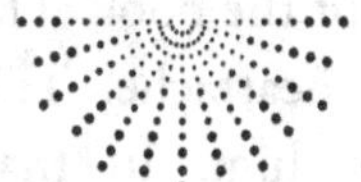

FLICKER IN THE PINES

The mountains and grief haunt me—a constant reminder of all I've lost and all I am forced to face. There is beauty in heartbreak and longing, a wild, aching splendor that cuts as deeply as the wind atop any summit.

But here's the truth: both mountains and memories refuse to let me rest. They loom, relentless and unmoving, casting their shadows over every attempt at peace. I am caught between awe and ache, knowing that neither the landscape nor the past will ever release their hold on me.

AT FIRST GLANCE, it wasn't evident he was reading a book. His hoodie fanned out, shadowing both his face and the book in his hand. From a distance, head slumped, he appeared to be napping through the bright afternoon. Yet he'd read each word too many times—enough to curl the paperback's spine. The pages had taken on a biblical texture, worn nearly transparent.

He does this faithfully—reads that same book and rides the D train from north to south, while the Rockies haunt the windows like silent apparitions. The mountains linger until the train descends into an empire of concrete and glass. Every day, he boards the D train, staying until the last one stops at midnight.

But he looks forward to the night, when the mountains sleep. As he gazes out the window and the world dissolves into a void, that's where he sees her—and thinks about the book. The darkness outside becomes a canvas for memory and heartache. The quiet of the mountains echoing the silence within him. In that emptiness, she appears, inseparable from the story he can't let go. Not the book. But her.

The D line runs north to south, not in a circle, roaring alongside the ever-reaching Rockies that soar beyond the city. The train's path is a straight shot between downtown Denver and Littleton, its windows offering fleeting glimpses of mountains that haunt the journey like distant guardians.

FAT OVER LEAN. Thick over thin.

We Must Purify the new world.

WHERE WHITE FIRE threads and flickers in the sun across the snowy peaks—not from heat, but from ice so pressurized and pure it glimmers like diamonds. Sunlight catches on the tiny, suspended crystals, making the mountains sparkle with a brilliance that seems almost otherworldly. This isn't warmth, but the cold transformed: diamond dust and snow sparkle, each facet reflecting the sun's rays, turning the high peaks into a living crown of light

. . .

Seldom,

among an empire,

apparel

made a pile.

In spite—Spite of—Despite

The light rail races past U-Haul. All the vegetation that surrounds it is skeletal, deflated, and dusty—like a business nestled in a void, or perhaps the Wild West. The OK Corral. A place where even a gunslinger might forgo a bounty. The sign reads: "Your Final Storage Place." I can't help but wonder—when did U-Haul start dealing in death?

> The woman in black—a true artist. I glanced at her sketchbook as she doodled, impressed by her masterful use of color and her carefully chosen subjects. Each detail was deliberate, every stroke well-crafted, revealing both skill and vision.

The man screamed madly, his words indecipherable. He could no longer contain the truth clouding his mind. I wanted to help him, but then I wondered—where would I even begin? And does he truly need help? Despite the distance between our worlds, perhaps through his eyes, it is my world that appears mad. Maybe both our worlds are mad. Then, the real question becomes: has he evolved? Freed himself from these worldly chains? And I am the slave—conformed and docile. Maybe his wild speech was not madness at all, but an attempt to free me.

We must plant. Harvest the crop. Then serve. But there's a problem: our society no longer works the fields. We don't rise in the dark cold to break our backs turning the soil. Today, we simply load flimsy plastic bags with fruits and vegetables, neatly displayed on irrigated shelves. Sometimes, while shopping, an automated sprayer mists everything—technology doing the work once done by hand.

Now, the only finger we lift is to tap a digital screen. That's a hard day's work: bag, buy, repeat. Two days later, the cycle begins again. We load the bag, carry it home, only to let the food spoil because we ate out all week. The groceries are tossed away.

The record keeps skipping in that same spot. Is it possible to smooth out worn grooves?

How could we ever know the difference? Society is a machine, and we are mere cogwheels—ineffective ones, with broken teeth, oblong and misshapen, wasteful in our function. We are broken teeth on a wheel that turns without end, warped yet still compelled to spin.

There's something elemental about working with your hands—smelling and breaking the earth between your fingers, feeling the silty clay glint in the sun. The smoldering breeze dries your eyes as you look west, and you sense the creatures living below the surface calling out when you dig, plant, or simply touch the soil. Maybe it's our ancestors, their voices woven into the land, crying at night, waiting for us to hear their call—to work the earth, to return home.

Perhaps we do hear them. Hear the spiritual veil. I wake at 3 a.m. every day, for no reason I can name. Each time, I feel there's something I must do, or have forgotten. I sit up, mind racing—Is the stove on? Did I forget to lock the door? But the feeling quickly slips away. I tire, and drift back to sleep.

Snow sifts down on the hillside with hourglass fashion /snow globe motion

Energy?

Vibe?

SNOW POWDERED THE HILLSIDE, sifting down hourglass-style—narrowing, then spilling wide, marking the slow passage of winter's time.

—Triple Distilled—

LUSH CLOUDS DOLLOPED THE MOUNTAINTOP, while snow dusted acres of conifers near the crown. Despite the wind burrowing through me, limb by limb, not a single pine bough fluttered. Each frozen droplet perched at the edge of a branch, illuminated and dazzling, clinking like crystal flutes. Why does the wind quicken me, and not them?

> The bearded man looks like a rabbi or a shaman, but he isn't—at least not in the traditional sense. His church is the train, and three disciples encircle him as it rumbles down the tracks. A thick, velvety blanket is draped around his neck, as if to shroud him or insulate him from the darkness that boards with every stop.

SHE WOULD HAVE none of those things—neither in life nor in death.

FORTNER ACTION / Straight pull

. . .

Dawn

Nightfall

Daylight

Nightlight

What about sunlight? Is it morning or dawn? Morninglight. Dawnlight. LightDawn?

Deprived lungs of precious oxygen

Winter clouds sifted/collapsed over the mountains and ushered total darkness

You must possess a zest for life. No matter the aim. Who said zest couldn't be violent or dark. Zest wears many colors. When in doubt, add zest.

Puking hot, locomotive steam.

There is a deep emptiness that resides in the soul, yet it is overcome by the fire of survival. Our basic human need to endure can purge the darkness. To be reborn, you must first die.

THE ART OF BECOMING

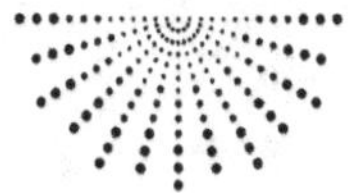

Endless Identities

Who do I want to be?

Journey through myself

Infinite Faces

DEATH WILL COME

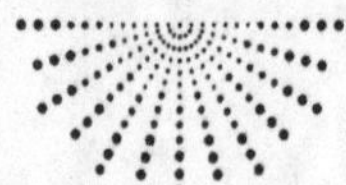

THE TRACK'S BONES STILL RATTLE

A DEFECTIVE TICKER could claim the man any day now. Everybody in town knew it. Yet, despite the deadly five-mile trail, where an ox-drawn traveler died every two weeks, the man volunteered anyway.

His wife was the first to object, her voice rising above the anxious crowd at the town hall. Many supported her protest. The man was ordinary in most ways, except for one; he was the mayor. The town trusted him, depended on him.

Still, the boy was too young. Unskilled and fragile. He'd die before the first mile marker. "Heed my warning," the mayor called out, trying to be heard over the crowd's unrest. "The boy will surely die, let that rest on your conscience."

The five-mile trek was nearly impassable. The town had no choice but to send their strongest to brave the subzero temperatures and reset the generator's timer. Without it, everyone would perish within days. First, the lights would go. Then the heat. Water would be the final nail in the coffin.

Despite the boy's inexperience, the man thought himself even less capable. His mind was clouded with frustration; he hadn't shared a bed with his wife in months, the passion between them long gone—physically impossible now.

Just yesterday, he'd seen the boy scuttle out of their bedroom window, half-dressed. Before that, the boy was a stranger.

He was not quick to anger. Deep down, he understood. He went about his duties, even kissing his wife goodnight.

He blamed himself. He could have tried harder, been more present. But he hadn't.

He didn't know his wife had stitched up the boy after a nasty cut from climbing into the chicken coop.

Her love never wavered; she hung on every word he spoke, even defending him during the town's unrest.

Most would never know the sacrifices, the tangled loyalties, the pain and endurance that kept the town alive. But the man did.

SHE HAD shades of foliage in her eyes, flecked with speckles of bark—her gaze like a forest, deep and alive.

An alien world—one that sparkled a light-year away from where they stood.

LATTICE—A thinning of the eye.

Holographic sight

Thermal vision

Night vision

AI vision?

MODERN CONDOS RISE, chiseled against a backdrop of poverty and the remnants of industry. Graffiti sprawls across pristine stucco and brick, dazzling and disrupting the buttoned-up world around it. In this decade, "buttoned-up" means home office—never leaving the comfort of your front door, tucking an eight-hour shift into your pocket. You never have to say hello to the neighbor above, below, or beside you. In fact, you never have to greet anyone at all. "That's today's world," she said.

The price for a decent living space has tripled, yet no one knows what the outside looks like, or if it needs tending. Years ago, the "dog houses" lining these industrial streets were alive with the affairs of the day, each one knowing every neighbor by name. Picket fences and tulips stretched from the city sidewalk to the front door, manicured and welcoming.

Somewhere along the way, commerce changed. Physical labor faded, brainpower became secondary—now, it's just bodies typing commands into the mainframe. Still, the graffiti spilling over the light rail tracks reminds us: no matter how many modern buildings rise, the world that came before will not be silenced. Human hands will never go out of style.

The bullet train barrels through—steel-clad car after steel-clad car—
while the train you ride speeds by on the opposing line. Everything is in
motion, a miniature city at lunch hour. The wind, meant to knock
everyone down onto the gravel below, is deflected by glass and welded
metal frames. When I close my eyes, I can feel the bullet pass through
my existence. I absorb its power, transforming stale wind and electricity
into constant motion now living inside my head. The noise of the wind
is enough to drown out the world I glimpse through frosted, tinted
windows—windows poked with pinholes that open onto the industrial
landscape beyond

PARTING FARTHER AND FARTHER AWAY—AN apparition of soul stretching from his grip, out and out, until the train leaves the station, but going the opposite way. I stretch from his grasp, out and out, until I am gone.

That billionaire obsessed with living forever—downing gallons of vitamins, swapping blood like a modern vampire, his entire existence turned upside down—seems absolutely insane. Then I remember: even Galileo was branded a devil in his time.
Maybe the craziest ideas aren't so crazy after all.
Though Galileo gave us the stars—he even gave us permission to dream of other worlds beyond our own. Humans already waste time with reckless abandon. I'm convinced people would squander immortality just like they do with one life.

PART V
CLOSURE ? DEATH

SATURDAY, FEBRUARY 27TH —3 A.M. WHAT I WRITE IN THE SPACE SHE LEFT BEHIND

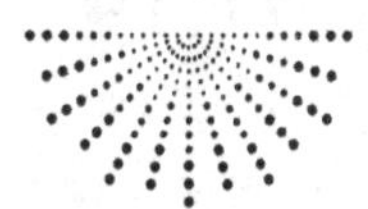

THE STORIES she'll never read.

When sleep forgets your name.

BREAD AND ROSES

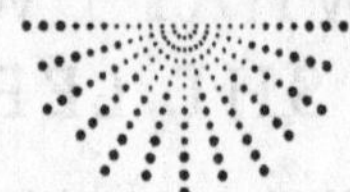

GOD SAID: man shall not live on bread alone. People used to call me Sam—short for Samantha. I just turned twenty-one, if my calculations are right.

For the last forty-eight days, I've survived on a slice of bread and eight ounces of water. It arrives once a day, when a sliver of light crawls from the east. I hope that's a guarantee—both the food and the light. For my survival shake.

But there may come a day when I resent the food, resent my own need to eat, to survive. Mostly, I resent my lack of courage to stop eating, to end this misery.

Day one shattered my soul. The isolation was that great. Here, you can't even hear a pin drop. Every sound is swallowed whole. The silence is subhuman.

But by day three, I began to anticipate the routine, the stillness. I depend on it now, like air.

On day four, my stomach hurt so badly I nearly passed out. Since then, hunger has possessed me. Now, I barely make it to supper before I double over and cry.

Still, I remain a coward. It's strange how the human body adapts to less, how easy it is to get used to confinement and scarcity. Do we really need so much space? Or food?

Whenever I wake, bread and water are placed in the center of the birdhouse. I don't know who delivers them. They're just there, like clockwork. The metal tray is just big enough for bread, water, and a single long-stemmed rose.

Strangely, the rose is always thornless, as if whoever brings it wants to spare me the pain. Some days, I snap off the stem and lay the rose across my nose, breathing in its perfume, its soul, until there's nothing left. That's the order of things, isn't it?

Some days, the rose feels more torturous than the bread and water. I imagine myself in a rose garden, far from here, and pretend this is all a nightmare I'll wake from. It's then I loathe the rose.

Still, like the food, I'm grateful for what little I have. Here, the little things become mighty.

I've had time to think. I still don't know how I got here. I've accepted that this may be my final resting place. But human instinct clings to hope, dwindling like embers.

A sliver of light is the only thing that shines in this place. It drags across the concrete from east to west, silent. Once darkness falls, I know another day has passed. That's how I keep track—scratching the days into the wall with a safety pin I found in a crack. What happens when there's nothing left to tighten?

Belt, don't fail me now.

What do the dead pass to the living? I am proof the dead can talk. The living are just hard of hearing. "That's all," she says.

I imagine this black, unobstructed view is a front-row seat for when the casket is lowered six feet below. From light to dark, and then back again. That's my life.

This place has no eyes to see my station in the outside world, no beating heart. If it did, I'm convinced it wouldn't care. The dark reduces everything to simple form. Once reduced, what's left to define?

Every day, when the sliver of light meets the center of the room, I feel the weight of unseen eyes on me. I get the strangest feeling someone is watching, studying how I survive on so little. When they sprinkle my seed there, center, how long will I last with so little nourishment? I am no longer Sam. I am no longer human. I am someone's little bird with clipped wings.

—The Cutting Floor Pieces—

For forty-eight days, I have lived on a single slice of bread and eight ounces of water. Each morning, a sliver of light crawls from the east, and with it, my survival arrives—bread, water, and a single long-stemmed rose, placed in the center of the birdhouse.

At first, the silence was unbearable—so thick it seemed to swallow even the memory of sound. But by the third day, I found myself craving the stillness, depending on it as much as the meager food.

Hunger gnaws at me, a constant companion. Sometimes I wonder if I resent the food more than the hunger, or if I simply lack the courage to let go.

I watch the rose, day after day, its petals fading. I wonder who brings it. I wonder why.

—Burned to Hell—

FOR FORTY-EIGHT DAYS, I have lived on a single slice of bread and eight ounces of water. Each morning, as a sliver of light crawls from the east, my survival arrives—bread, water, and a single long-stemmed rose, placed in the center of the birdhouse.

They used to call me Sam—short for Samantha. I just turned twenty-one, if my calculations are right. Time here is slippery. The silence is subhuman; every sound is swallowed whole. On the first day, the isolation shattered my soul. By the third, I began to anticipate the routine, the stillness. I depend on it now, as much as air.

Hunger has possessed me. On day four, my stomach hurt so badly I nearly passed out. Since then, I barely make it to supper before doubling over and crying. Still, I remain a coward. Sometimes, I resent the food, resent my own need to eat, to survive. Mostly, I resent my lack of courage to stop eating, to end this misery.

It's strange how the human body adapts to less, how easy it is to get used to confinement and scarcity. Do we really need so much space? Or food? Whenever I wake, bread and water are placed in the center of the birdhouse. I don't know who delivers them. They're just there, like clockwork. The metal tray is just big enough for bread, water, and a single long-stemmed rose.

The rose is always fresh. I watch it, day after day, its petals fading, replaced by another. I wonder who brings it. I wonder why.

PART VI
WHISPER YOUR PRAISE

SUBMISSION TO THE
ROCKY MOUNTAIN READER

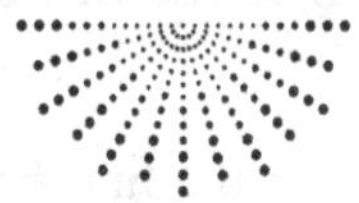

WHEN SILENCE BECOMES Your Standing Ovation.

Is it liberation?

Dark Room

Catalog of Life

Over the years, the backbreaking work had crippled him. Arthritis poisoned every inch of his knees. Whenever he mounted the stairs, everything from the waist down seized. He did his best to suppress the scream that begged for attention. His fingers, now malformed and curled, could neither extend nor grip a broom handle. Countless bulging discs along his spine made carrying anything up those stairs impossible. So he improvised—tying a barn rope around his waist and hauling whatever needed lifting to the second floor.

That upper floor was a world apart, dedicated to the overflow: boxes, gizmos, and whatever else had outlived its usefulness. Still, the man's sole purpose was to haul, catalog, and stack these relics in the dark room above.

That room mirrored the outside temperature. When it snowed, he froze. In August, he'd often wake on the floor, sweat soaking his button-up. The humidity was so thick it stole his breath. He spent countless hours there, sorting and stacking, every item cataloged, a marker of hours lost to labor.

The mountain of boxes that touched the ceiling claimed his knees. The endless shelves stole his fingers' dexterity. Those groaning plank stairs infected his toes with gout. A few snapped in half over the years, slicing his shins enough to send him to the ER. Still, the work continued. It always continued.

He couldn't recall anyone from the first floor ever visiting the second. No one ever asked him to retrieve anything from the catalog. Yet his job title never changed.

Even though not a soul visited the second floor, he built his life's work fit for a king's visit. Boxes aligned, everything positioned and saluting with soldierly precision. Dust blanketed everything—a creeping horror in its own right, as the century-old pine roof wept day and night.

At a moment's notice, he could entertain even the most distinguished guest. The second floor was a marvel to see. The first floor would never reach such heights.

Now, the man was winding down. Soon, nothing would remain of him. Who would continue the work? He lay awake at night, haunted by the question: Who would build upon his life's work long after he was gone?

He's barely a boy, and she's approaching sixty.

DOWN AT THE station every night, there's a young couple waiting for a bus or train to take them someplace. I find myself wondering where they're headed. Watching them takes me back to when I was young and in love, when the world seemed full of promise and I saw everything through crystal lenses—the kind that mask the truth.

But the young couple aren't hiding behind anything. They're living in their world, a little too hard. There's no promise in their eyes; they already know what reality is—something it took me years to learn. They don't hide their addictions, whatever it is that tethers them to this life and keeps them from floating away. Yet, they don't revel in it either. They simply hold hands and go about their way, letting the transit system carry them to the next stage, wherever that may be, with gusto.

Maybe that's what life really is: a vehicle in constant motion, shuffling us from one point to another, never letting us stand still for long.

—Excerpt Removed from EVERYTHING—

No pitter-patter of ticks tonight. Usually, they squeeze through
the spaces in the timber, inching along the windowsill,
hungry for blood—any kind. In a cabin made of cypress,
deep in the woods, ticks are drawn to their own kind. The
silence is unusual; in these woods, the absence of their tiny
feet is as telling as their presence. Like SHC, the cabin
attracts what thrives in shadow and grain.

LOVE IS EASY. The hard part is holding onto it.

Things needed for Juliet + Juliette

LIST OF DREAMS

BOWKER ISBN

Bookow

Library of Congress

KDP / KDP select

Apple Books

Kobo

Barnes & Nobel

Google Play book

Shopify selling direct

Draft2Digital / Smashwords—10%

Publishdrive—flat fee

Ingramspark / Lightning source

ACX

Findawayvoices / Spotify

. . .

BOOK MARKETING STRATEGY

The first launch window is actually (2) years?

MINDSET A WRITER NEEDS FOR MARKETING:

ONE SUCCESS STRATEGY that works universally—I wish.

GUMROAD

Storyorigin

Laterpress

PUBLISHER ROCKET OPTIMIZE my book landing page,
SEO optimization.

ATTICUS FORMATTING tool e-books and print books.

AUTOCRIT CONSTRUCTION LINE EDITING—THAT'S where
dreams go to die.

MIBLART BOOK COVERS

The Urban Writer

Dibbly

Affinity Publisher—optimal choice

Ashtrays were scattered throughout the house—fine crystal, industrial plastic, studio pottery. One of them was priceless.
As I began to warm to the house and its contents, I noticed each ashtray exhaled an elegant trail of white smoke. Half-lit cigarettes rested at the bottom, their tips glowing faintly. From a distance, they looked like tiny chimneys, warming whatever lived inside against the icy elements.

The best parts of life aren't about getting things right the first time—there are no other times except for now. Who would you be without your struggles and mistakes? What would you become without the lessons they bring?

STUFF YOUR BRAIN

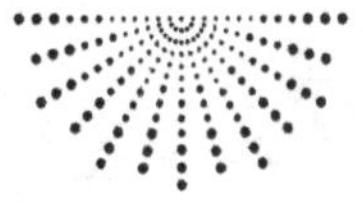

UNTIL IT EXPLODES

Coyote: A Subhuman Story

Philtrum

Paresthesia

Groak

Glabella

Crepuscular rays

Petrichor

Natiform

Overmorrow

Desire path

Collywobbles

Nibling

Dysania

Morton's toe

Phosphenes

Gnurr

Butt-load

Scurryfunge

Muntin

Low profile

Liath smoke

Ebony

Zinc-alloy

i. **Philtrum**: The vertical groove between the nose and upper lip in humans, a vestigial feature with no apparent function in people.
   - **Paresthesia**: A tingling, prickling, or numb sensation, often described as "pins and needles," usually painless but can indicate nerve issues if chronic.
   - **Groak**: To stare at someone longingly, especially when they are eating, hoping they'll share.
   - **Glabella**: The smooth area of skin between the eyebrows and above the nose, also a key anatomical landmark.
   - **Crepuscular rays**: Shafts of sunlight visible just after sunset, radiating across the sky from behind clouds or mountains.
   - **Petrichor**: The distinctive earthy scent released when rain falls on dry soil, produced by plant oils and compounds in the ground.
   - **Natiform**: Having the shape or form of the buttocks.
   - **Overmorrow**: An archaic word meaning "the day after tomorrow".
   - **Desire path**: An informal trail created by repeated foot

traffic, representing the most direct or convenient route people or animals take.

- **Collywobbles**: A fluttery, uncomfortable feeling in the stomach caused by nervousness or mild fear.
- **Nibling**: A gender-neutral term for a niece or nephew.
- **Dysania**: Difficulty or inability to get out of bed, often linked to exhaustion or mental health challenges.
- **Morton's toe**: A foot condition where the second toe is longer than the big toe, due to a short first metatarsal bone.
- **Phosphenes**: The spots or shapes of light seen when pressing on closed eyes or stimulating the visual system in ways other than by light.
- **Gnurr**: The lint or debris that accumulates in the bottoms of pockets or cuffs over time.
- **Butt-load**: Slang for a large amount or abundance of something.
- **Scurryfunge**: To hastily tidy up the house just before a visitor arrives.
- **Muntin**: A strip of wood or metal that separates and supports panes of glass in a window.
- **Low profile**: Deliberately avoiding attention or publicity.
- **Liath smoke**: Not defined in the search results; "liath" is Gaelic for "gray," so this may refer to gray smoke (inference).
- **Ebony**: A dense black hardwood, or the deep black color resembling the wood (general knowledge).
- **Zinc-alloy**: A metal made by combining zinc with other elements, often used for its strength and resistance to corrosion (general knowledge).

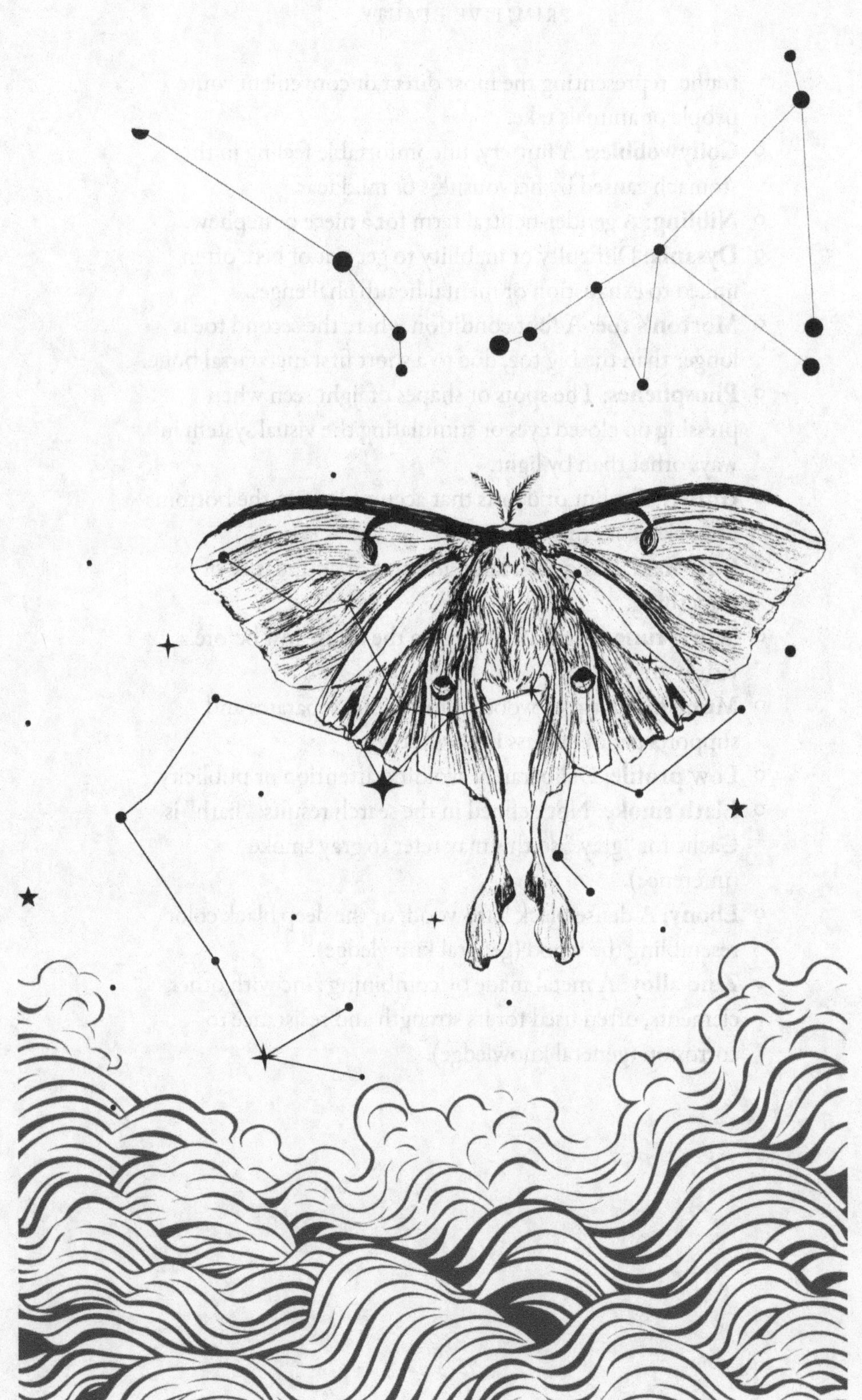

PART VII
THE MIRROR

FEBRUARY 25TH—
BROKEN PRETTIES

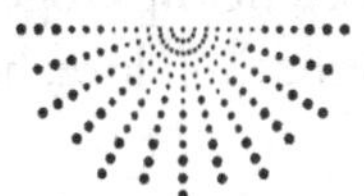

The Last Apartment—reminds me of our apartment when we were young.

Preconceived bias

IN AN ALTERNATE REALITY, fate traps two strangers from opposite worlds inside a cramped studio apartment—indefinitely. Cameron is a fiercely private recluse, rigid in her routines and wary of change. Dianne is her polar opposite: spontaneous, social, and unafraid to shake things up. As days blur into nights, a volatile, unexpected love story kindles between them—one that tests every boundary and belief they hold.

They clung to each other, desperate, as if their bodies could fuse in those fleeting seconds. Heartbeats hammered—a frantic, tangled rhythm pressed between ribs. The air thinned, each breath shallow, lungs rationing what little oxygen remained.

Cameron's skin carried the weight of weeks without soap and water, a film of sweat and memory. Yet the shower still roared with scalding heat, steam curling in the stagnant air. Every time Dianne twisted the tap, the water heater answered with a low, hungry hiss—natural gas feeding invisible flames. Lights flickered on command, appliances hummed. The world beyond had collapsed, but inside these walls, the machinery of daily life refused to die. That persistence unsettled more than silence ever could.

In the embrace, Dianne pressed her lips together, breath caught, fighting the sour tang of unwashed skin. Even love, here, demanded endurance.

THE TRAVELER

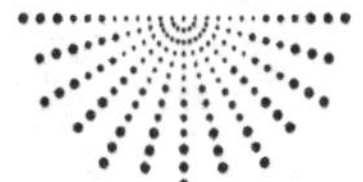

Used Book Store

SHE WORE the remnants of youth beneath a battered, ankle-length puffer. Her eyes, though, whispered a different story—something older, more distant. Frayed pant legs hovered above her ankles; sneakers, cracked along the knuckles, looked as brittle as parchment. The leather, creased and faded, recalled ancient paper left out in the sun.

Yet there was an effortless allure in her disarray—a beauty that made ruin look intentional, almost fashionable. Her pale blue eyes shone like beacons from a far-off country, a country she seemed to wear uneasily, as if she'd been assigned the wrong body at birth.

She paced the aisles, restless and uncertain, the way a child might wander lost through unfamiliar woods.

GIANTS AND FEATHERS

Survival and Scarcity in a collapsing world, my obsession these days. Perhaps it has everything to do with my heart and mother.

THE BOY WAS NOT ALONE on the barren plain. Shadows moved beyond the timberline. Something hunted him. Silent and patient. Around him, evergreens and aspens toppled in the darkness. Their collapse marked only by the hush of needles and the low murmur of wind.

His legs burned. Not with fatigue, but with a spreading fire that numbed his thighs, each step heavier than the last. Somewhere in the distance, twigs cracked, sharp and sudden. The sound barely reached him. The wind pressed cold against his ears, numbing them with its steady, frozen breath.

The scent of wet earth and pine sap thickened the air, clinging to his boots, until mud caked the worn leather and rubber soles. They offered no support, he might as well have been barefoot, stumbling over rocks and roots. Each attempt to climb higher left his ankles twisting, pain flaring and fading in the same instant.

It was late spring. April showers had swept through, quick and violent, leaving the land ruffled and raw. The rain had lasted only two days this year, last year, three. The barrels under the eaves barely filled a quarter. They would have to survive on less. He pictured the village: mothers pleading for water, infants wailing, men taking what they could by force. Some would endure, carrying on the work in fields that grew more barren each season. The harvest shrank. The tables emptied. And the little they had become enough. Until even that little felt abundant.

He stumbled upon an abandoned railcar, stranded in the wild with no tracks to anchor it. It looked as if some giant had hurled it from the sky, leaving it to rust and rot. Rivets bled orange streaks down the metal. Every window shattered, seats torn and crawling with mites. Bird nests filled the corners, most empty, a few littered with bloodied eggshells. Feathers plastered the floor and walls, a silent record of violence.

The car offered no promise of warmth, no guarantee of safety. If something chose to break in, he would be as defenseless as those birds. Still, he stepped closer, knowing it was all he could expect—next to nothing, and nothing more, except for the wind rattling broken glass.

MOTHER SHIP

Mother Universe

Mother World

A SCREAM TORE from the dinner bell—shrill, jarring, never warm, but always there. Lucinda flinched where she sat, heart hammering, nerves frayed raw. No one could grow used to that sound, not even in a house steeped in chaos.

That bell.

Never far from her mind.

The cork board displayed a graveyard of business cards, each one pinned with geometric precision—aligned in rows as if measured by laser. Even their ghosts lingered, dark rectangles etched into the sun-bleached surface, silent witnesses to what once was.

PART VIII
SCRABBLE POEM

D TRAIN

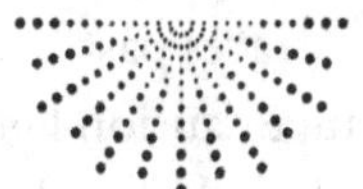

The air icy thick.
Harsh breeze bit through my
north face.
Razor burn skin.
Pitch-black encapsulates,
where I stand
near the tracks.
You can't see the summits.
Not even a pointy outline.
I climb three steps,
feet sore.
don't
Stand
for a living.
Then sit across
the man's nose whistles.
I pass
as his face slumps
into chest.
I look out

It's a blank screen.
Blank night.
Etch a sketch energy
The train turns the station
To
A neon car wash sign
framed in laser-blue pinstripe
Then a king Soopers semi
races past
Orange caution lights
outline the roofline
Erotic novelties on the corner.
Across
from
Exxon
where gas is 3.19
a gallon,
cheap gasoline.
No cars in sight.
On either side.
Slow night for love,
or hitch a ride
for love...

MENDED HEART

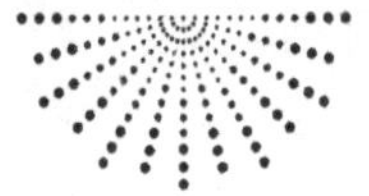

The air—icy, thick—
bites through my North Face,
razor-burns my skin.
Pitch-black swallows the platform
where I stand near the tracks.
No summits tonight,
not even a jagged outline.
I climb three steps—feet aching,
not made for standing.
I sit across from a man
whose nose whistles as
his face folds into his chest.
Outside, the window is a blank screen,
the night erased.
The train rounds the station,
neon car wash sign
framed in laser-blue pinstripes,
a King Soopers semi blurs past,
orange caution lights tracing its roof.
Erotic novelties glow across from Exxon,

gas at 3.19 a gallon—cheap.
No cars, no one moving.
A slow night for love,
or for hitching a ride
in search of it.

MOONLIGHT GLISTENS THE ROOTS

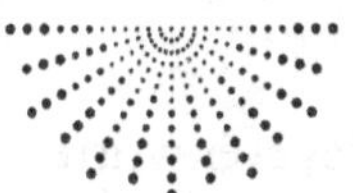

THE TRAIN GROANED TO A HALT, each car shuddering in sequence —like laundry pinned on a line, swaying in the stale air. Inside the dimly lit car, I spotted a couple huddled close, a thin ribbon of white smoke curling above them. Their movements were hidden, vague, so I slid into my seat and turned to the window, trying to disappear into the darkness outside.

But the smell gave them away—burned plastic, acrid and suffocating, settling over everything. My throat prickled. I glanced back. They were using, lost in their own world. For a moment, I froze, unsure whether to speak up or look away. Instead, I watched. The intimacy of their ritual drew me in—not out of malice or curiosity, but something quieter, more familiar. I have been here before. I realized I was a voyeur of the past, surprised by how naturally I slipped into the role.

Soon, the girl curled up against her partner, drifting into sleep. He stared out the window, face blank, eyes fixed on the black void beyond the glass. I couldn't stop watching them. I wondered what haunted him as the city blurred past—if he was counting hours until the next meal or just searching for something to hold onto.

I imagined his thoughts because, once, that was me: Tara pressed against my side, both of us staring into tomorrow, wondering what it would bring.

Their clothes clung to them, worn so long they'd become a second skin. Yet in that bleak car, with nothing but each other, they found a sliver of peace. No money, no home, nothing to their names. But they were rich in the things you can't put in a pocket—comfort, closeness, the fragile warmth of being together, if only for tonight.

SOME OF THE greatest stories ever written

Moonbeam

Clip art

Microtomes

Cryostats / mom

Ligament

Motorist

Goofy Motor Mania

Austere

Omnipotent

Malleable

Ubiquitous

Brevity

AMERICAN PLITE

TENDON

You can smell ketones

Or nerve damage

Localized infection

Bloodborne pathogen disease

Select hyperlink to learn more

Dirt Dust

Oxygen, fuel, and heat

Glass front sash

Obey the law

Cornucopia

Incel community

Pragmatic

Wanderlust

The brain's handiwork

Too eerie perfect.

Heterogeneous

The gold standard XX

The work of the gods

I died and went to hell

The high country looming somewhere over the gray horizon.

Dwarf elephant

Venomous cuties

Their deadly streak

Intricately cut

Fire flurries spitting like sleet.

Paramour

21st century misfit/ Ephemera Misfits

JAPANESE CYPRESS

ECHELONS

Lilac-breasted / Thunderbird

Immortal, they live so long.

Perigon

Throng of lilac-breasted

They were buried in shallow graves or not at all.

Poured herself into that string bikini

ORTHODOX IN HIS WAYS.

In retrospect

Over city

of which

Deserter

Zygote

Vanquished

Perversion

Procession

Agrivoltaics

Ammo synergy

Harmonic waves

Picaresque

Write with gusto, so says Bradbury. Okay, how about this:

Falling in love with a serial killer, a cannibal, or a demon from the underworld acts as wind resistance for stories—it creates friction, tension, and struggle that force the narrative to push harder, dig deeper, and fight for every moment of connection. This resistance amplifies emotional stakes and complexity, making the journey toward love more turbulent, unpredictable, and ultimately more compelling.

Put frosting on that cake.

Jump any distance

Pith

Pillow sconce

In reality

Has little to do with

Pleasure Circus / Future Circus

Amusement World / Circus World

. . .

THE HIPPODROME

SPECTACULAR WORLD

Neurolink

Mitochondria

THE AGE of Digital Sin

It struck me as odd, watching Shadow swipe a piece of cheese from my plate today. Honestly, I never wanted the cat in the first place. But with kids and a spouse, something—or someone—always ends up moving in, sometimes dragged across the threshold, claws out, yowling all the way. That's just family.

Now I can't help but wonder: do mice sweat cheese, tiny vapors seeping from their pores? Maybe the cat doesn't hunt them for the chase, but for the faint promise of cheddar beneath their fur. Maybe, in the end, it's always been about the cheese.

Bird in still air

Three-year fellowship

Child abuse pediatrics

Rich earthly smell of tobacco

to love books.

The guardian ad litem

Attorney appointed by the court to represent Lizzie's interest

Unencumbered

Stone icicle

. . .

Glowing

Overshadowed

Dwarfed

Ricocheted past the rib cage and pierced the heart.

What if the person who's supposed to hand deliver your prayer to heaven dies? You must deliver the message yourself.

Wind resistance

Idiosyncratic

Attirement: is a rare or archaic noun meaning "clothing" or "apparel."

Attired in exotic costumes?

Canopy

Some phantom tribe that lived and hunted in the most uninhabitable place on earth.

Her head was miles away, but her love, merely feet.

AUDIOBOOK

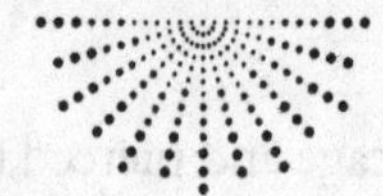

How to Record an Audio Book

Audacity

Studio One

Twisted Wave

Pro tools

FILTER

IZotope

FabFilter

Waves

Protectmywork.com

MIC AND POPFILTER

. . .

LARGE Diaphragm condenser mic

Mic book arm

Shock mount

Audio converter

iPad

Don't forget about the Narrator? Seriously?

Sound Effects

Freesound.org

Soundbible.com

YouTube audio library

99sounds.org

Sonniss.com / gameaudiogdc

BBC sounds

ROLLERCOASTER

Lots of little things built my love for you.
The biggest,
when I laid my head in your lap.
You stroked my hair.
Breath powdered my nose.
That was the first time we touched.
Our rollercoasters feared
to sink toes
past the sand.
And when we did,
the universe melted before my eyes.
I never felt love like yours.
Even at birth.
I closed my eyes and held my breath.
What else could I do?
The car is still in motion.
I was scared.
You held my hand.
Then I tasted your breath.

Our rollercoasters free fell. From universe to earth.
Then back up.
That is the day,
my rollercoaster
Only
hungered
for You.

—*Origination*—

Lots of pebbles built my love for you.
The biggest,
when I laid my head in your lap.
You stroked my hair.
Breath powdered my nose.
That was the first time we touched.
Our rollercoasters feared
to sink toes
past the sand.
And when we did,
the universe melted before my eyes.
I never felt love like yours.
Even at birth.
I closed my eyes and held a breath.
What else could I do?
The car was still in motion.
Fear overwhelmed me.
You held my hand.
Then I tasted your breath.
Our rollercoasters tumbled.
From universe to earth.
Then back up.
That is the day,
my rollercoaster
Only

**hungered
for
You**

ROLLERCOASTER

THE GHOST OF FUTURE

Many little things built my love for you.
But the greatest was when I laid my head in your lap.
You stroked my hair.
Your breath dusted softly across my face.
That was the first time we touched.
Our rollercoasters were afraid
to sink their toes past the sand.
And when we finally did,
the universe melted before my eyes.
I had never felt a love like yours—
not even at birth.
I closed my eyes and held my breath.
What else could I do?
The car was still in motion.
I was scared.
You held my hand.
Then I tasted your breath.
Our rollercoasters free fell—
from the universe to earth,
then soared back up again.

J.S. NATHANIEL

That was the day
my rollercoaster
hungered
only
for you.

PART IX
CANDLE AND MOTH

FOUR PLACES BEFORE DEATH

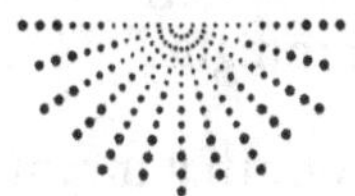

He could only read the first line before his vision blurred.

It read:

These are the places I want to visit before I die.

A tear slipped from his eye and crawled down his cheek. He wiped it away, irritated. Then he stared at the piece of paper for a long time—not reading the ballpoint words, but peering through them, lost in a strange world. The emptiness he'd felt as a child returned, something he'd spent a lifetime trying to outrun. Until he met Constantine. Constantine made all of that vanish.

The small bedroom they once shared seemed to expand, growing vast in seconds. John felt himself shrinking, reduced to the size of a pea at the edge of the bed. Soon, he'd disappear into the trenches of that shaggy carpet. The same one they'd argued about replacing last summer.

The argument had been simple, John found the carpet charming and romantic, and he was frugal to a fault. So frugal, in fact, that it often cost him twice as much in the end—a price he'd come to expect.

Constantine, on the other hand, was haunted by the thought that every night, when they climbed into bed, their feet carried forty years of bad luck with them.

It creeped him out, imagining how many strangers' feet had slept in their bed. He'd spend hours brushing the dead from their soles before they got in.

One night, before turning out the lights, Constantine said, "You might be sleeping with a serial killer tonight."

John gave him that look, the one that meant he didn't get it, then turned his back and fluffed his pillow. Constantine was talking about the dirty feet ground into that vintage shag. A serial killer might have walked across it many times before. "Who can say for sure," he said.

John even had the carpet shampooed three times, but nothing satisfied. Constantine was determined to rip it out. No reasoning could bridge the gap between John's thrift and Constantine's superstition.

What John failed to see was that Constantine wanted a fresh start—a new life. Free from whatever lingered in those walls before they signed the contract. He wanted to build a life of good fortune, to make a celestial nest and crawl inside for eternity. And all of it weighed heavily on that damn shag.

On this cloudy December day, as John's gaze shifted from the letter to the carpet, he wanted to crawl into those fibers and live with the dead. He was certain Constantine lived in those fibrous walls now.

They hadn't discussed such things after the diagnosis—Constantine's bucket list. John refused to debate it further, determined to keep things positive, hoping optimism might insulate them from the terminal disease devouring Constantine from the inside. "Doctors aren't always right," John would say over salmon and spinach dinner. "They're only human."

But Constantine knew better. He felt it deep in his gut. The disease would cut his life short. He'd been tired lately, no matter how much he slept. His energy was off. He knew something was wrong—had known for some time. Constantine could be dramatic, prone to jumping to conclusions, but this felt different.

All was forgiven though, because John adored his passion. That's how John put it, and he'd often defend Constantine at the round table.

John found the letter while searching for Constantine's favorite socks. He'd never hear the end of it if he forgot to bury him in them.

In truth, John had always loathed those socks. But now, he adored them. More than adored—he saw them as a key, a way to unlock a door.

Now he sat, dreaming of a life that had left the station without him. Just as his mother had, twenty years ago.

BLOOD, SWEAT, AND WHINES: MEMOIRS OF A MISERABLE VAMPIRE

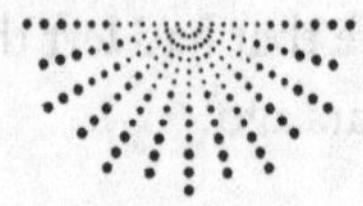

The Undead Are Over It: A Vampire's Guide to Modern Misery

Eternal Whine: Confessions of a Grumpy Vampire

EVERY MORTAL HAS A STORY. I've heard countless tales over the centuries, and I'm sick of mortals whining about every miserable detail of their lives. The truth is, mortals never stop complaining. It's exhausting. Worse, I think their habits have finally rubbed off on me a little too well.

Despite the fact that I'll never meet a tragic end or die of old age, unless, of course, the planet succumbs to some cataclysmic event and all life goes extinct, including me. I find myself depressed lately, with a splash of melancholy added to the mix. I have no love for this world right now, or anything in it. Honestly, I woke up in the wrong fucking century. Again. As I said, I'm complaining just like all those miserable mortals.

I have impeccable timing, or so my maker told me five centuries ago, though she was being sarcastic. To be blunt, she was right. The last time this happened was when I woke up in the Dark Ages.

Believe me, I never thought any century after that could come close to such a debacle. Don't get me started on the Black Plague. Not in my wildest dreams did I imagine anything worse. Yet, I was wrong. The twenty-first century has officially toppled the Dark Ages, and not in a good way. The debauchery and lack of shame are darker than anything I witnessed back then.

People say history repeats itself, and that's mostly true. The accuracy, however, is lacking. There's nothing like a fifty-year-old man getting the details wrong about certain events, or trying to convince someone who's been there, done that, that his version is correct. I've wasted countless breaths trying to set the record straight. But who would believe someone who looks to be in their twenties? That's certainly God's punishment. And yes, vampires can have faith in God—don't believe everything you read.

Last century, a gentleman tried to convince me the world was—well, never mind.

Why am I saying all this? It's simple. When a vampire wakes from a long slumber, they can't go back to sleep for another hundred years, give or take. It's impossible, biologically. Some have tried and failed. It's not an exact science, but it's all we have.

So, there you have it. I'm stuck in this century, and I'm not happy about it.

And since I'm miserable, it's time to stir things up. But before I do, I need to clear the air—right here, right now.

History got it wrong about vampires. Yes, we exist. That's the only thing they got right. We live among you. You pass us on the sidewalk more often than you realize.

But everything else is incorrect, and I want to set the record straight. Whenever I confide in a mortal and tell them I'm a vampire, one of three questions always comes up. Vampires don't drink blood. More to the point, we don't need blood to survive. Trust me, I've heard every variation before. So let's start from the beginning.

Vampires can do everything a human can do. We even look like humans —except we have the power of the gods.

Yes, vampires did drink blood at various times in history, and occasionally practiced cannibalism. Donner Pass was one such occasion, though that was for survival. The others, not so much.

But here's the truth: vampires never die. Never. The sun won't turn us to ash. A stake to the heart won't do it, either.

> For those who solve the riddle, may they embrace the road ahead,
>
> nor be tempted by the rearview.

Some children live in multiple dimensions—usually those eager to unlock the world's mysteries. Yet some may never discover those wonders, lost instead in introspection.

HE LEFT a cemetery in his wake,

from today to the grave.

IMMORTAL MISFIT

INCALCULABLE.

True love is choosing to join the person you love in hell.

He swiped the cobwebs of smoke from her face.

ETERNAL DARK

MEDLEY

NO ONE CAN FORCE the hand of God

Suburban sprawl

THE SEER/VISIONARY on Earth

When a society is built upon every accomplishment of man—right down to the god we praise—it's clear: man has ruled for thousands of years.

The mark of death upon you.

When death marks you.

You've got to change your crazy ways

Nymph

Sprite

Esprit

Fungus beetle

A forest of butterflies

People vs. nature

Lynx

Time crystal

Classics, because they are the best.

Luxurious

Punchy

Thorny blood zinger

To consummate: to boil things down for transactional purposes only.

The last of the visionaries.

He rubbed his chest, right above the heart.

Alchemy and sedition of the highest order.

PART X
STORY LABYRINTH

LUCINDA AND THE DEVIL

"I am your master in all things."

"But you're evil."

"Evil is subjective." He smirked. "Goodness has its own set of debacles, like everything else."

"I won't murder."

"Even after all I've shown you?"

"Let God deal with him."

"Who do you think sent me?"

Lucinda's face froze, stunned. She fumbled for words, unsure where to go from there. "I thought God cast you out?"

"Why do you think?"

"How should I know?" Her voice ricocheted off the grimy tile walls of the deserted subway station, midnight pressing in.

"Think, girl. Think."

"I don't know," she hissed through gritted teeth.

"You won't get another chance."

"I can't. He looks like Mr. Rogers."

"That's what the others thought, too—before he locked them in the basement."

She studied the man on the bench, his gaze fixed ahead, waiting for the train to Newark. He wore fine wool and expensive shoes. His skin glowed with the freshness of a newborn, yet his manicured gray hair suggested middle age. Still, he looked barely twenty-eight.

"You are not my master, but I'll do what's necessary."

"Check the pulse this time."

She didn't answer. Instead, she started the long walk toward the man. With each step, heat surged under her skin, threatening to boil her alive. She wanted to shed her layers before she collapsed, though frost billowed behind her like a ghostly train, the temperature outside plunging below zero.

The devil thrust his hips this way and that as "Return to Sender" blared —a song only Lucinda and the devil could hear.

"Mister," she called, voice sweet but eyes sharp. "Do you know what time the Newark train comes?"

He didn't respond, staring into some distant universe.

"Sir," she slipped her hand into her jacket pocket, fingers brushing the taser. "Newark?"

"I've been waiting for you."

She let go of the taser.

"He said you'd be here at midnight."

"What?"

"He said you were going to murder me at midnight."

A jolt of electricity shot through her. She began to back away. "You're crazy, mister. I just wanted to know what time the train—"

The man pointed to a shadowy figure beyond the tracks. "Do you see that thing over there?"

She knew better than to look away, but something compelled her. She glanced down the corridor.

"Do you see it?"

She saw nothing. Her instincts screamed, but she turned to check if the devil was still dancing. He was aiming finger guns at her, pretending to shoot. He blew out imaginary smoke and kept dancing as the music thundered.

She had taken her eyes off the target for a second too long and when she glanced again the tailored man had sprung lightning fast. He reached for something in his pocket. Lucinda tried to back away and reach for that taser hidden inside her jacket, but it had vanished. Her eyes were full of panic, as she scoured the floor thinking she may have dropped the taser near the bench.

Before she could find the taser, the tailored man snatched the collar of her jacket and reeled her in. Her blood curdling scream echoed and seemed to energize the devil into moonwalking like Micheal Jackson and grabbing his crotch.

"Help me!"

"You won't feel a thing," the tailored man sprayed something in her face that smelled of sweet perfume.

Lucinda inhaled the mist that seemed to steal her breath away. The solution in the rudimentary spray gun forced a sickly cough to spill from her. Then everything went black. Before Lucinda's body hit the floor, the tailored man gently guided her down. And situated her inky hair just so, as though she lay on a pillow made of the softest concrete imaginable.

The finely tailored man stood and peered in the direction of the music. He too could hear the music playing. Could see what Lucinda sees. He watched the devil dance to that dreaded *Return to Sender* tune.

He raised a hand, to flag the devil. "You were right."

The devil ignored him and continued to dance. Still hypnotized by Elvis's sweet voice. "Thank you, my allegiance for you."

The devil stopped dancing and cast haunting red eyes at the finely tailored man "I've got plenty of servants like you," the devil pointed at Lucinda with eyes that spoke to true evil. "This one's a real beauty."

He peered down at Lucinda's plain beauty. She lay on the cold concrete elegantly, as some fairy tale princess under a coma, waiting for rescue. He peered back up and shrugged. "I prefer blonds."

"Yes," the devil said, as though repulsed by the finely tailored man. "Your taste level isn't quite right my son. Isn't that what mommy used to say, Jonathan?"

"Don't talk about mother."

"If I'm not mistaken, she was blond too," The devil covered heart and slyly edged closer. "No heavy hearts here, my son. You'll get the reward you seek very soon. Now, pick up the girl before someone sees you."

The finely tailored man lifted her over his shoulder with ease and started to haul her from the subway station, but something inside compelled him to turn to face the devil once more. "Why her?"

"Why ask why, Jonathan," the devil instantly went face to face as though he wanted to devour him, and the music stopped. "Do my bidding and you will have your dessert."

"I want to know."

"Be mindful of this one, Jonathon, she's special. Now get to work before you screw this up too."

The music magically returned, and the devil danced even wilder than before. Somehow making his way out onto the street where the temperature registered below zero.

You know how people say, "the devil made me do it" when they take the witness stand after committing some horrific crime? Well, in my case, it's true. The devil made me kill. Not made me, exactly—he nudged me, with a very convincing argument.

Last night, he told me a young girl's life was at stake if I didn't get rid of Alexander Pitman. Now, Alexander Pitman isn't your garden-variety specialist. He's a doctor to the stars—or whatever cliché you want to use. The point is, the devil was right: Alexander Pitman has a very dark side he keeps hidden from the world. Calling him a "naughty little boy" doesn't even come close to the truth. Make no mistake, Alexander Pitman is a monster.

But none of that matters anymore, because I plan to kill him tonight.

Raw oysters served in chilled coconut shells with cognac—that's what Alexander served me the first night. On the second, it was liquefied wheatgrass, a single seared scallop, and a glass of 1990 pinot noir. My mouth felt furry after that. He emphasized the "1990" as if it should mean something to me. I'm no wine snob. I'm not even a wine person. Tequila straight from the bottle is more my style. If I used a glass, it'd sit in the sink for days before I'd bother to wash it. Not that I'm a total slob —I'd lie awake at night thinking about that dirty glass until I finally got up and cleaned it.

Honestly, I think Alexander could smell the lack of sophistication on me, like cheap perfume. But here's the strange part, he wines and dines his victims before filleting them whenever he pleases. Talk about your last rites. I imagine he'd even offer a condemned prisoner one last smoke before he gets to work. In that sense, he was a real gentleman.

"Close your mouth or you'll let the flies in," he'd say.

"I wasn't always like this, you know. I used to be just like—" he paused, reflecting, "well, not like you. I'm smarter. But let's just say, a citizen of society."

Lucinda watched his every move, making no attempt at small talk. She refused to appease him, even as death loomed. Her eyes said more than words ever could—she looked ready to bash his face in with a blunt object.

It was clear he was done with her. She could feel it in the air. His demeanor shifted in stages. First, he stopped preparing fine meals, serving only saltines and tins of herring. He no longer washed her clothes. He wouldn't even turn on the water so she could shower. But just as her eyes spoke the truth, so did his silence. He'd clean up after her only out of necessity, cramming the trash can without a flicker of emotion, as if he were standing outside himself, looking in.

Die for a cause

Feast of bones

THE GOOD WAY

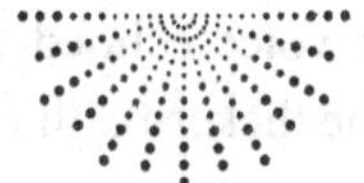

PERFECTION WILL NOT GRACE

Lucinda Umbra hadn't meant to become the devil's assassin. Yet here she stood in a deserted subway station at midnight, frost trailing her steps despite the summer heat, while Satan himself danced to Elvis in her peripheral vision.

"I am your master in all things." His voice carried the weight of ancient granite, though his face held the beauty of fallen stars.

"But you're evil incarnate, literally." Her fingers traced the outline of the taser in her jacket pocket, a habit from her former life as a social worker. Before the bargain. Before Sarah died.

"Evil is subjective." His smirk sent chills through her. "Goodness has its own set of debacles, like everything else."

"I told you, I won't kill again." The words felt hollow even as she spoke them. Three victims already. All monsters wearing human skin, he'd proven that much. But the weight of their deaths pressed against her chest like cold iron.

"After all that I've shown you."

"Let God deal with him."

"Who do you think sent me?"

Her eyes searched his burning pupils, wondering, not for the first time, if she'd finally lost her grip on reality. "I thought God cast you out."

"Why do you think?"

"God doesn't tell me." Her voice echoed against the slimy tile walls, decades of grime reflecting the flickering fluorescent lights above.

"Think, girl, think."

"I don't know," she squeezed the words through gritted teeth, the familiar heat beginning to build beneath her skin.

"You won't get another chance."

The target sat twenty feet away on a metal bench, waiting for the train to Newark. His fine wool suit and expensive shoes screamed old money, while his face held the innocent glow of a choir boy, despite the gray hair suggesting middle age. Nothing about him hinted at the horrors the devil claimed he'd committed.

"He looks like Mr. Rogers."

"That's what the others thought too, before he caged them and had his way with them." The devil's voice carried an edge she'd learned to recognize. The tone that meant he wasn't lying. Even the Prince of Lies played straight sometimes, especially when the truth cut deeper than any deception.

"Let's get something straight, you are not my master." The heat under her skin intensified, making her wish she could shed layers despite the visible frost that followed her movements.

"Check the pulse this time." The devil began thrusting his hips to "Return to Sender," a private concert only she could see and hear. The absurdity of it all did not unnerve her.

Lucinda approached the tailored man, each step careful and measured.

"Sir," she forced cheer into her voice despite the malice in her eyes. "Do you know what time the Newark train comes?"

He remained still, gaze fixed on some distant point. Then, "I've been waiting for you."

Her hand fell away from the taser.

"He said you'd meet me at midnight, and he was right." He checked an expensive watch. "He said you were going to murder me."

Electric tingles raced across her skin as she backed away. "You're crazy, mister. I just wanted to know about the train."

The man pointed toward the maze of tracks, into the darkness beyond. "Do you see it over there?"

Years of training screamed not to look away from a potential threat, but something pulled at her attention like a fishhook. "Do you see it?" His voice dropped to a whisper. "It's watching us."

She saw nothing in the shadows. When she turned back, the devil was aiming finger guns at her, blowing imaginary smoke from his fingers between dance moves.

That moment of distraction cost her everything.

The tailored man moved with impossible speed, reaching into his pocket. Lucinda grabbed for her taser, but it had vanished, along with all her careful planning. Her eyes darted to the floor, panic rising as she searched for the weapon.

His hand seized her jacket collar, yanking her close. Her scream echoed through the station, seeming to energize the devil into a full Michael Jackson moonwalk, complete with crotch-grab.

"Help me!"

"You won't feel a thing," the man whispered, spraying sweet perfume in her face.

The mist stole her breath. Her lungs seized. The world tilted sideways as darkness crept in from the edges. As she fell, the tailored man caught her with gentle hands, arranging her hair as though she were precious cargo rather than prey.

Through dimming vision, she watched him stand and turn toward the music. He could see it too, the devil dancing to that dreaded tune, proving once and for all that Lucinda wasn't crazy.

She just wished that knowledge could save her.

PART XI
CAR TO NOWHERE

JANUARY 11TH— THE WEIGHT OF EMPTY BOTTLES AND DEEP SORROW

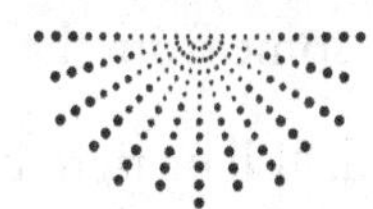

SHE STOLE my breath at first sight. Not pleasantly. There were no words. She was far from put together—her hair thin, wiry, and unwashed, her eyes sunken too deep for my liking. Her clothes carried the sharp smell of urine. I hadn't seen her in at least two years.

I wanted to cry but didn't. I wanted to shake that skeletal frame and demand, "Be stronger. Why have you let this wretched disease consume you?" But I did none of those things. We were worlds apart: I was forty-eight, healthy; she was sixty-eight, buckling under the weight of twenty more years of pain than I'd ever known.

I'm not sure where my head was. I didn't acknowledge the reality staring me in the face. In that moment, my mother needed me more than ever —she needed words of comfort, encouragement, the kind I was good at giving. I was the only one who could breathe strength into her. And yet, I failed to act. Another pivotal moment in my life when I did nothing.

If it were today, I'd shake myself and say, "Wake up, asshole. Do something. Say something. She doesn't have much time."

As I sat there, inspecting both of them, I knew in my gut that everything I had ever known was about to end. I didn't have the guts to face it.

Deep down, I knew I wouldn't survive it. But I had no other choice—my daughter was sitting beside me. I had to survive for her, and for everyone else counting on me.

We locked eyes, just for a moment. I think she saw the pain in mine. Like so many times before, she saved me. She cracked a joke, then said, "Can you get me something to drink?"

We both knew what that meant. I paused, not shocked by her request, just unsure. I looked to my brother for confirmation. His face was heavy with shame; he wouldn't meet my eyes. He was good at avoiding them. He, too, was in poor health—some from the booze, some from the pills.

So I did the only thing I could. "I'll be right back," I said.

I grabbed the keys and left.

Aquatic Glass Naked Sable Weasel

Glass frogs

The skin of a star-nosed glass newt

Feathers from a scarlet-breasted roller

A string of assassinations / a chain / a trail

Hunt Kill Eat

Even Imperfections are Beautiful

SWEEPING vistas

RUN of the mill

IT'S SO black it absorbs all light—ultra-black

VELVET beetle

A PARALLEL LIFE woken by a lamp.

CLICKBAIT
Hyperbolic
Feed lots
Pile up animals / foreign agents
Dossier
Acid
Aquatic mouse
The great green wall / important people
Food is a love language
How neat or sloppy they arrange the pieces on the board
What the inside of someone's house looks like
How they walk down the street
Eyes are windows to the soul—more windows to the brain
How they separate their trash

.   .   .

WHEN SHE WAS twelve

EARTH LIFE inside an asteroid

GALACTIC CHAIN

"YOU NEVER TRULY KNOW WHAT you're capable of until you're pushed to find out."

REENACT THE TRAUMA AND FEAR.

WRAPPED in greenery

DIE for a cause
Feast of bones

BEFORE YOU LEARN TO DOUBT YOUR VOICE

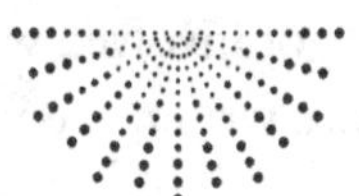

If I Could Reach Through Time and Hold Your Pen

CREATIVE WRITING TIPS

- **Forget the rules**. Throw out everything you learned in grammar school and college about writing. Those lessons can stifle your creativity.
- **No one can teach you creativity**. Creative writing is a skill you've developed by doing. If you want to write creatively, you have to write fearlessly.
- **Break old habits**. Your English teacher drilling dos and don'ts into your head. Those rules won't help you here—let them go.
- **Write fearlessly, write anything.** If you write without fear, you can make any subject compelling. Think about how documentaries can make even tree-cutting fascinating. The same is true for your stories—anything can be interesting if you approach it with curiosity and honesty.
- **Practice description**. Challenge yourself to describe anything you see, no matter how ordinary. You once wrote about a freshly planted tree knocked out by a winter storm. Fifteen

pages later, that tree was a full-fledged character who overcame a string of misfortunes.

- **Don't pressure yourself to be a genius**. You often get trapped inside your own head, chasing a "magnum opus." That pressure leads to self-doubt and, often, writer's block. Remember: not every page has to be perfect. Just write.
- **Respect the seasons of creativity**. There are seasons for everything—including writing. You suffered writer's block for a year, convinced you'd never write again. Once you stopped beating yourself up and got involved with daily life, the words returned. You are always a writer, even when you're not writing.
- **Capture inspiration immediately.** Creativity strikes at odd moments—often outside the house, while running errands or driving. Never leave home without something to write on. When inspiration hits, write it down right away. If you wait, the idea won't come back the same way. Let me say this again: NEVER LEAVE HOME WITHOUT SOMETHING TO WRITE ON.
- **There's no right way to write**. Writers come in a million forms. You can write anywhere, even at a crowded kitchen table for hours. When you're writing, the world disappears. So embrace that superpower.
- **Let your wildest ideas out**. Don't hide your "crazy" ideas. Write them boldly, without worrying about judgment. That's where originality lives. A few years from now, you'll meet a writer whose sci-fi characters had ordinary names—Jennifer, Bill, Henry. Some said it wasn't "sci-fi enough." You'll disagree with them and speak up. Who cares about the dirty looks they give. Something magical happens in that moment. Originality is what makes stories memorable. Every great writer has been rejected for being too radical at some point—Shirley Jackson and Sylvia Plath, your favs.
- **Stop worrying if you're good enough**. If you put in the work and write with honesty, your writing will find its audience. There's something for everyone. Trust your voice.

- **Be bold. Be honest**. Write what only you can write. The rest will follow.

> Horween leather—hand stitched
> Blocksy
> Jnews
> Phlox
> Truffle and singed leather
> Aromatics
> Decay
> Palate
> Fleshy
> Savory
> Meaty
> Feral
> Furry texture, mouth, mealy finish
> Flavonoids
> Coconut shells, and Cognac, oysters, botanical, mineral

WISE VILLAGE

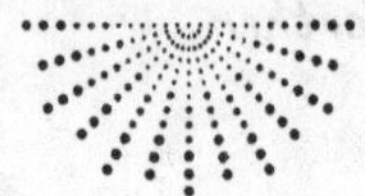

IN A SMALL FISHING village perched on the edge of the world, there lived a wise woman—though many whispered she was a necromancer dabbling in dark magic. It was a tight-knit place, prone to flooding during the monsoon season, but the waters had grown worse since the wise woman bought the old stilt house on the mountainside—a house that had stood empty for forty years.

The villagers had their reasons for avoiding the place. They gossiped in hushed tones about the tragedies that left the stilt house abandoned and did their best to dissuade the wise woman. "Why live up there in that abomination?" one villager pleaded. "There's a perfectly good home for sale down the road."

The wise woman, polite and reserved as wise women often are, thanked them for their concern. She was quietly surprised by their hospitality toward a stranger, but, despite their protests, she bought the house. The villagers watched with a mix of curiosity and dread as she moved in.

The floods came, right on schedule, every season after that. In just two years, four mothers drowned. One afternoon at the market, while the wise woman stocked up on provisions, she overheard a young woman boasting, "It was either save my mother or my husband. I chose my husband, of course." The merchant nodded in agreement, as if it were the only logical choice.

The wise woman's face fell at the young woman's words, disappointment flickering in her eyes. She lingered in the market, curiosity piqued, settling onto a bench to watch the flow of villagers.

Soon, a young woman entered with a boy at her side. The wise woman called out, "You there, may we speak for a moment?"

The young woman scowled. "What is it, old woman? Can't you see I'm busy?"

"It won't take long," the wise woman replied.

"Hurry, then. I've got plenty to do."

"When the floods come—and they always do—if you had to choose, would you save your husband or your mother?"

The young woman snorted. "What's wrong with you, old fart? I'd save my husband, of course."

The wise woman shook her head, saying nothing more.

Not long after, another woman appeared—older, perhaps in her thirties, her arms full of market goods.

"You there," the wise woman called.

The woman sighed, impatient. "What is it? I have much to do."

The wise woman didn't explain. "When the village floods, if you could save only one—your husband or your mother—who would you choose?"

The woman paused, puzzled, as if searching for a trick in the question. "My husband, foolish woman. My mother has lived her life."

Again, the wise woman shook her head, her disappointment deepening. She gathered her provisions and began the long walk up the mountain.

At the base, she crossed paths with another woman, this one with sharp eyes and a wary expression.

"You there," the wise woman called.

"Yes? Is something the matter?"

"If you had to choose—save your husband or your mother from the flood—who would it be?"

The woman didn't hesitate. "My mother, of course. I can always find another husband, but I'll only ever have one mother."

The wise woman studied her, a glimmer of relief softening her features. For the first time that day, she smiled—a small, knowing smile—then continued up the mountain, the murmur of the village fading behind her.

PART XII
EINSTEIN'S ZOO

EPHEMERA MISFITS

Zen played at being Zen.

They'd only synced for one day, she reminded herself. Maybe day two would be better. By day three, the greatest pleasure, perhaps.

She'd expected more from syncing with Trix. Instead, he just lay there—hands folded behind his head, eyes fixed on some far-off point, anywhere but her. Boredom seemed to gather in his gaze, as if he were stuck in a medical pod, irritated by a scan that took one second too long.

His body was flawless: brown skin, machine-smooth, not a hair out of place. Even his most intimate features were perfect—like every other man she'd synced with. That was the problem. Zen craved imperfection: a scar, a wrinkle, a single gray hair. Something real. Something human.

She straddled him, tired of always being on top. Every man before Trix had done the same—lying back, arms behind their heads, drifting off while she did the work. Warm skin against warm skin, a minute of mechanical movement, and it was over. Nothing thrilling. Nothing real.

Afterward, she kissed him—a gesture she hoped would mean something. Trix allowed it but didn't kiss back. No warmth, no taste, no scent. He was as clean as an android. Zen wanted to inhale his DNA, taste his flaws, swallow his essence. But there was nothing to taste.

She didn't crave the act of syncing itself, but the promise of connection—bare skin, salty sweat, the messiness of life. Even a hint of human imperfection would have satisfied her. But Trix, like all the others, offered only clinical emptiness.

She felt tears rising, her heart fluttering like a caged canary. She'd seen a canary in an iron cage once, in the archives—a memory that haunted her. Now, she understood its panic.

They dressed in silence. Zen broke it first. "Do I smell?"

Trix blinked, confused. "What?"

"Do my lips taste like anything?"

He looked almost horrified. "No... Well, what should they taste like?"

"Salty. Or... gum decay. Something."

"Gum decay?" He sneered. "Why would you want that?"

"I read about it in the archives. How do you know it's bad if you've never tasted it?"

He shook his head. "You don't need to taste something awful to know it's bad. Disease is disease. Like fossil fuels, atomic energy—barbaric. It's a miracle humanity survived."

Zen slumped onto the memory foam platform, chin in her hands. "I'm bored, Trix. Bored with you. Bored with sync. Even the sync celebrations are always the same."

Trix grinned. "Not tonight. We're not celebrating with the others. Our celebration will be... different."

Zen's eyes brightened, hope flickering. "A private celebration?"

"Sort of." He framed her with his hands, teasing. "Picture this, you and me, going to Planet Ephemera."

Zen frowned. "I'm not a level five."

"You are now."

"That's impossible. You're not a level five either."

"We are now." He tossed two digital bands onto the platform. "Here's your proof. You can taste all the gum decay you want."

Her hands trembled as she picked up the bands, inspecting them like rare butterflies. "But how?"

"Don't worry about how. Just take the win. Let's taste the real world together." He smiled, reckless and inviting.

Zen hesitated, turning the bands over in her hands. If they were fake, Trix was a master counterfeiter—and that could mean death. But the lure of the real world, of tasting, smelling, touching something unsanitized, was too strong.

Trix knelt before her. "This is our chance to see the human world. The real one. No synthesized water, no artificial air. The real stuff."

The sensor band blinked, counting down. In two minutes and thirty seconds, they'd know if they could be paired for offspring. Zen didn't expect her band to turn blue; it almost never did for women her age.

She gazed into Trix's eyes, anticipation radiating from him. The idea of the lost world—of tasting, touching, feeling—outweighed even the fear of death. After all, in their world, even death was painless. Clinical. Empty. What she wanted was a connection to the soul.

1

LOVELESS PAIR

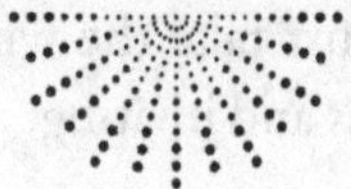

WITHIN MINUTES, a sky-link whisked Zen and Trix to Planet Ephemera. As they soared above the planet, Zen's pulse spiked to 115—her sensor band blinked three times, alerting her to the rush. Her stomach fluttered, a sensation she hadn't felt since she was eight, stepping onto the academy steps for the first time. Back then, she'd been the oldest child accepted into Zone 4, dropped off by a sky-link and eyed warily by children half her age. "You're too old for the academy. You won't make it," the four-year-olds had taunted, their words stinging with the certainty of youth.

They weren't wrong. Most candidates were under five; five was the cutoff. But PETM 4's democracy thrived on mathematical possibility—rules bent for promise, not precedent. Zen's test results had been exceptional, and that was enough. She remembered how, a decade later, a nine-year-old named Tatiana was accepted, won the Merit Prize, and revolutionized medical science. On Earth, possibility was everything.

Now, as the sky-link descended, Zen gazed out at the planet's edge—snow-dusted mountains, an orange glow pooling at their base, a crystal sky overhead. The view was almost enough to calm her nerves.

"Remove your sensor band," Trix said, nodding at her wrist. "Put on the digital band."

Zen hesitated. "Where do I hide it?"

Without a word, Trix tore a hole in her sleeve, slipped the sensor band inside, and let her jumpsuit's biofabricator knit the fabric shut. Tiny fibers wove together seamlessly, camouflaging the secret. Zen watched, impressed. "I'd never have thought of that."

"You have to take it off before we hit the wormhole," Trix warned, running his hand down her arm to check for lumps. "Don't forget. Otherwise…" He rolled his eyes back, playing dead.

Zen managed a nervous smile.

Planet Ephemera blazed ahead, neon colors painting the sky brighter than the Northern Lights. They slid the digital bands onto their wrists and, standing before the sterling arches, Zen closed her eyes and squeezed Trix's hands. She hoped the bands would work, melting the force shield at the entrance.

They stepped forward. The shield shimmered, then parted. A digital voice, bright and sprightly, greeted them, "Welcome to Planet Ephemera, 1001245 and 1001246. Please, enjoy your visit."

Inside, holograms flickered and danced—fantasy, advertisements, colors so bright they hurt the eyes. In the distance, a woman waited, rusty cowboy hat, red bandanna, boots with sterling spurs. Her jeans and shirt were stained with dirt, but her fuchsia hair and flawless skin gave her away as android. Indigo eyes locked on Zen and Trix. "Welcome to Planet Ephemera, 1001245 and 1001246," she said, arms wide. "I'm Aria, your host for the evening. As you can see, I'm dressed in genuine early twentieth-century attire—a cattleman's outfit."

Zen couldn't help but smile. The clothes looked so real, so worn. She had no idea what a cattleman was, but the authenticity spoke for itself. It must have been a hard life, she thought.

"Wearing century-appropriate attire is vital when traversing a wormhole to your destination," Aria explained, gesturing for them to follow. "Please, come to the measurement room."

Trix raised a hand. "How will we know what to wear?"

"The algorithm has already chosen the optimal look. Please follow me."

They were measured and fitted, still clueless about their destination—until Aria mentioned 1986. After the fitting, Zen pulled Trix aside. "I've never read anything about 1986 in the archives. Do you know anything about it?"

Trix shook his head. "No idea. The algorithm chooses, I guess." He pointed at her earrings. "What are those?"

"Earrings," Zen said, steadying a giant pink hoop. "Where did you get the digital bands?"

Trix shot her a warning look as Aria approached. "Later."

"Please proceed to the Travel Architect. And don't forget your luggage."

Zen stared at the suitcase. "An android won't carry these for us?"

"You've selected the realism package. The realism begins now. Please proceed to the Travel Architect."

Trix grinned. "Look at these barbaric contraptions. Do you really think they had androids in 1986?"

Zen tried to lift her suitcase and failed. Trix demonstrated, "Pull, don't lift." They shuffled forward, struggling with the hard plastic Samsonites. Every few steps, a suitcase tipped or slammed into an ankle.

"The design is terrible," Trix grumbled, righting his suitcase for the third time. "Wheels are pointless."

"Mine's heavy," Zen complained, yanking at the strap. Her earrings rattled with every stop. "I think my wheels are stuck."

Trix checked. "No, it's just bad design. Whoever made this had no engineering sense."

By the time they reached the Travel Architect, both were breathless. Zen fidgeted in her stone-washed Guess jeans, fighting a wedgie and the relentless pinch of briefs and bra. Nothing fit right, despite the algorithm's measurements. The fabric didn't breathe and sweat pooled everywhere. Still, she held her head high.

Trix, by contrast, seemed furious. He tugged at his Z Cavaricci shirt collar, wincing at the buttons and belt loops. "Barbaric," he muttered. "How do you even use the bathroom in these?"

Zen eyed his roomy pants with envy. "My briefs are riding up. Are yours?"

"No," Trix said. "I'm wearing boxers. Everything's in free fall. It's madness."

"Why didn't the algorithm fit me for boxers?"

Trix shrugged. "Maybe it glitched. I might prefer briefs."

"I feel like I'm trapped in a torture device." Zen wiggled, her eyes sparkling despite the discomfort. "It's painful, but exciting."

Trix looked horrified. "At least someone's enjoying themselves."

Eno, the Travel Architect, scanned their itinerary with a blue beam. "Welcome, 100125 and 100126. Upgrades are available for a few more credits."

Trix pointed. "What's a spa?"

Zen shrugged.

"For 150 credits, the Brown Palace offers a spa day, exfoliate with wet clay and minerals—"

"Wait, mud on your face?" Trix asked.

"Affirmative," Eno replied. "The ingredients closely resemble mud."

Zen and Trix exchanged baffled looks. "Why would anyone do that?"

"To remove impurities and unclog pores. They also use cucumbers on the eyes to reduce swelling."

"Cucumbers?" Trix shook his head. "Don't they have nanites?"

"Negative. Nanotechnology wasn't available for consumers until 2093."

Zen stroked her face, imagining the mud mask. "That sounds... interesting."

Trix rolled his eyes. "Let's skip the spa."

Zen shot him a glare. "Eno, upgrade us to the spa."

Trix didn't argue. "What's a masseuse?"

"A female massage therapist. A masseur is male. The term later changed to 'massage therapist' for gender neutrality."

"Why did they have different titles for the same job?" Zen asked, tugging at her bra wire.

"In 1986, gender neutrality wasn't widely accepted. Inequality persisted until 2101, when Kent Banks led a revolution and ended gender rule."

Trix grimaced. "Barbaric."

Zen smirked. "That explains the briefs and boxers."

They hauled their suitcases toward the white wormhole portal at the mountain's base. Trix got the hang of dragging his, while Zen's rattled and jammed behind her. Trix reached for the portal first, staring into the shimmering void. Why call it a white wormhole when it wasn't even white? The portal bent light, an optical illusion that made his heart race as if he were free-falling. The air buzzed with energy and the scent of burned electricity.

Zen caught up, breathless. Together, they stepped forward—and in a blink, the wormhole swallowed them, hurling them toward 1986 faster than light.

2

BIRTH OF MTV

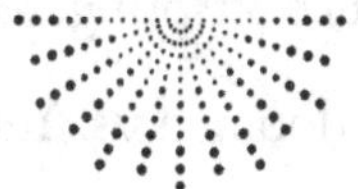

ZEN BURST through the apartment door, glowing like a midnight star. The bang startled Hellen so badly she nearly jumped out of her chair. Trix, caught mid-chew, just looked up, milk dripping from his chin, eyes wide.

Zen's whole presence crackled with energy, her eyes wild with excitement. Trix noticed a real glow about her. She'd never looked more beautiful than she did in that moment of pure joy.

"Oh, Trix," she gushed, hands balled at her chest. "I had the most amazing time with a man named Gabriel!"

Trix frowned. "I thought you said you were just going for a walk?"

"I did," Zen hugged herself, beaming. "I went for a walk, met Gabriel, and then we synced."

Trix's spoon clattered into his cereal bowl. He stood, gripping the table. "You what?"

Hellen looked between them, confused. "What's 'synced' mean?"

Zen and Trix ignored her. "That's impossible," Trix sputtered. "You were only gone—" He checked the clock. "An hour."

157

"An hour and ten minutes, thirty-three seconds," Zen corrected, glancing at her sensor band as she slipped it back on.

Trix pointed at her wrist, voice trembling. "What have you done, Zen?"

Hellen raised her voice, now standing. "What is synced?"

Zen finally looked at Hellen. "Sync is a process where a genetically matched male and female produce offspring." She paused. "Most synced partners don't actually produce offspring, so there's that."

Trix's hands shook. "You've doomed us. You smuggled the sensor band into the real human world."

Hellen tried to keep up. "So... you mean sex? Did you just have sex with Gabriel?"

"Sex?" Zen and Trix echoed, both genuinely puzzled.

Hellen stared at them, incredulous. "You don't know what sex is?"

They shook their heads, confusion written all over their faces.

Zen tried to explain. "We undressed. The male usually lies prone—not Gabriel, though. He was on top. Then male and female genitalia sync. The male deposits prostatic fluid near the cervix, and then you wait three minutes to see if your sensor band turns blue. That means offspring."

Hellen blinked. "So... the male inserts his penis into your vagina?"

Zen rolled her eyes. "Yes, Hellen. How else would the fluid get there?"

Trix slumped back into his chair, hands over his face. "We're doomed," he muttered.

"That's called sex, Zen," Hellen snapped. "And I hope you made Gabriel wear a condom before you 'synced.'"

Zen frowned. "What's a condom?"

Hellen groaned, dropping into her chair. "You really don't know. You know the science, but not the basics. And I bet you're watching your wrist to see if you're pregnant."

Zen grinned. "Exactly."

Hellen eyed them both. "Are you in some kind of cult?"

Zen blinked. "What's a cult?"

Trix cut in, exasperated. "No. We're not part of a cult."

Zen looked at Trix. "What's a cult?"

Trix shook his head. "Not now, Zen."

He finally dropped his hands from his face. "We're from the future."

"Trix!" Zen hissed.

Hellen looked at them, torn between laughter and disbelief. "Right. Of course. Say hi to the aliens for me."

Zen's eyes widened. "Aliens? This world has everything."

Trix tried again. "I'm telling the truth, Hellen. We're from your future."

Hellen waved him off.

"Trix, you're not supposed to tell anyone. That's the rule."

Trix's voice was tight. "The rules changed the moment Zen smuggled the sensor band."

"They won't know, Trix."

He glared at her. "They know, Zen. They know everything."

Zen ignored him, still glowing from her experience. She slid into a seat next to Hellen, eyes earnest. "Hellen, how many times have you synced?"

Hellen looked at Trix, then back at Zen, embarrassed. "On this planet, we call it sex. And that's none of your business."

"Come on, Hellen. I've synced with thirty males. I'm only twenty-two."

"Thirty?" Hellen's eyes went wide.

"Trix was number thirty."

Trix looked mortified. Hellen turned to him. "How many times have you synced with Trix?"

Zen laughed. "Males sync triple the amount. Four times, even. Their prostatic fluid is endless. The challenge is coaxing the egg. Males are plentiful. Females, not so much."

"How many, Trix?" Hellen pressed.

Trix looked down, defeated. "Three hundred and twenty. And I still haven't paired."

Zen smiled at him. "You're the first male I've met who keeps count."

Hellen shook her head. "Three hundred and twenty…"

Zen turned back to Hellen, eager. "Now your turn. How many?"

Hellen hesitated, glancing at Trix. "Two."

Zen gasped. "Two?"

"Yes. A boyfriend in high school, one in college."

Zen took Hellen's hands, concerned. "Do you have mutations in your DNA? Is that why you can't sync?"

Hellen pulled her hands away. "No! Just because I don't have sex with everyone I meet doesn't mean I'm mutated. I have sex when I love someone."

Zen's eyes sparkled with curiosity. "Love? I read about that. Tell me what it's like."

Trix leaned in, just as curious.

Hellen softened, seeing Zen's sincerity. "Love is… complicated. Hard to describe. But from what I see, you might be falling for Gabriel."

"Falling for Gabriel?" Zen echoed, confused.

"Does your heart race when you think of him?" Hellen asked.

Zen checked her pulse. "Yes, I suppose it does."

"Do you get butterflies in your stomach?"

Zen's face lit up. "That's what I've been trying to say! He did wonderful things to me. He kissed me everywhere, Hellen."

"Okay, that's enough detail," Hellen said quickly.

"Afterward, I wanted to cry."

Hellen's concern grew. "Did he hurt you?"

"No, the opposite." Tears welled in Zen's eyes. "We melted into each other. I've never felt anything like it."

Hellen realized Zen had likely experienced her first orgasm, though Zen didn't have the words for it. She decided not to press further.

Zen wiped her eyes. "His saliva tasted awful. I asked what he'd eaten. He said bourbon and cigarettes. I didn't know what those were, but he said they help with the stress."

Trix looked disgusted. "Those are barbaric compounds."

"I liked it," Zen insisted. "It tasted... nasty. I get that word now."

"But you said it was awful," Hellen pointed out.

"It was. Like gum decay. But it made me feel so human."

Trix slammed his fist on the table. "That's her thing—she wants to taste the past, the forbidden. In our time, nothing dangerous is allowed."

Zen's sensor band suddenly glowed red. She sniffled. "No offspring."

"That's a good thing, Zen," Hellen said gently.

"No, it's not. I want offspring."

Hellen squeezed Zen's hands. "Listen, you can't just sync with random men. Even with a condom, you can get diseases. Herpes, AIDS, all kinds of things."

Zen wiped her eyes. "That doesn't scare me, Hellen."

"It should."

Zen shook her head, lifting the wristband. Its faint glow revealed embedded circuits that pulsed like a living vein. "In our future, humanity has eradicated every sickness and disease," she said. "This detects potential viruses and transmissible threats before they even take root."

Trix cut her off. "Enough, Zen."

Hellen sighed. "You two need professional help. But I'll play along." She spoke into Zen's sensor band: "Glioblastoma."

A digital voice responded instantly, detailing the disease and its cure. Hellen stared, stunned.

"Try another," Zen challenged.

"Lung cancer," Hellen said.

Again, the band rattled off facts and treatments.

The three sat in stunned silence until a loud knock rattled the door.

Zen jumped up, beaming. "That's Gabriel! He's taking me on a motorcycle ride."

Trix groaned. "Your head is on Mars, Zen."

"It is not. My head is bacteria free."

Hellen's anxiety spiked. "You told him where I live?"

"Don't worry. The eighties are safe. A time of peace."

"No, Zen. This is the time of serial killers. He could be dangerous."

"Don't answer the door," Trix warned.

Zen ignored them, racing to the door. "Hey, Gabriel!" she sang, letting him in.

Gabriel swaggered in, squeezing Zen's ass and kissing her. "Your DNA tastes stronger. More cigarettes and bourbon?"

"Yeah, it relaxes me babe."

"It's disgusting," Zen said, grinning. "I love it."

Hellen eyed him warily. "And yet he's driving a motorcycle."

Gabriel shrugged. "I know my limits." He nodded at Trix and Hellen. "What's up?"

Trix muttered, "What's up?" under his breath.

Gabriel smirked.

"You know how to pick them, Zen."

"Is he your boyfriend or something?" Gabriel asked, still holding Zen.

Hellen cut in. "Zen forgot she had plans. She can't go for a ride today."

Zen looked at Hellen, confused by the hard stare. Hellen's message was clear: fall in line.

Gabriel cocked his head. "Is that right, babe?"

Hellen spoke before Zen could. "If Zen leaves with you, she can't stay here anymore."

Gabriel shrugged, still holding Zen close. "She can crash at my place."

"Where's that exactly?" Hellen pressed.

"14th and Steel."

Hellen's eyes widened. "Great, Zen. Just great."

Trix perked up. "Is that bad?"

Hellen shook her head. "Not good. That's the rough side of town."

Zen and Trix exchanged blank looks.

Gabriel shrugged. "Judge all you want. There's good people everywhere."

EPHEMERAL

Ecosystem

Digesting

Bacteria

Eat entire ecosystem

Nature is timeless.

Cabochon

White as cotton

She looked at me, puzzled, and said, "What's a CD?"

PART XIII
WHY WE MUST

GARDENERS OF TOMORROW

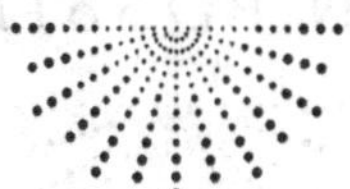

If history holds the measuring stick to our souls, then we must turn our gaze backward to those who refused to let humanity settle for less. These weren't just artists and thinkers—they were rebels who rewrote the rules of what it meant to be human.

THE ARCHITECTS OF HUMAN POSSIBILITY

CHAPTER 1

MICHELANGELO DIDN'T JUST PAINT ceilings; he cracked open the sky and showed us that divinity lived in our own hands. Every brushstroke whispered the same revolutionary truth; you are worthy of beauty, you are capable of creating heaven on earth. When the masses looked up at the Sistine Chapel, they weren't just seeing biblical scenes, they were seeing their own potential reflected back at them.

Galileo pointed his telescope at the heavens and gave us permission to dream beyond our circumstances. He didn't just map the stars; he mapped the infinite landscape of human curiosity. In a world that demanded people keep their eyes down, he said in essence, "look up, reach further, question everything." His defiance wasn't just scientific, it was a love letter to every dreamer who ever felt too small for their ambitions.

THE RENAISSANCE OF THE HUMAN HEART

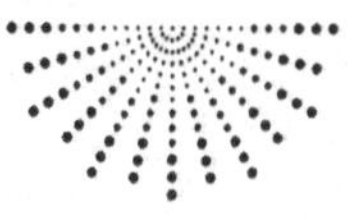

CHAPTER 2

Da Vinci understood something the rest of us are still learning: there are no boundaries between art and science. Between dream and reality. His notebooks weren't just inventions, they were blueprints for human possibility. He looked at birds and imagined flight. At water and envisioned machines. At the human body and saw both engineering marvel and divine mystery. He gave us everything else because he refused to accept that "everything else" had limits.

SHAKESPEARE: THE CARTOGRAPHER OF THE SOUL

CHAPTER 3

But it was Shakespeare who performed the most intimate surgery of all. He cut open the human heart and showed us what was already there; the messy, contradictory, beautiful chaos of being alive. He didn't just give us permission to love, he gave us permission to love badly, desperately, foolishly. To seek revenge that destroys us. To right wrongs so sloppily that we create new ones. To be gloriously, catastrophically human.

His characters stumble through the same emotional landscapes we navigate today. Hamlet's indecision. Juliet's reckless passion. Lady Macbeth's consuming guilt. These aren't historical curiosities, they're mirrors held up to our own midnight thoughts. Our own desperate choices. Our own beautiful failures.

THE LEGACY THAT
LIVES IN OUR BONES

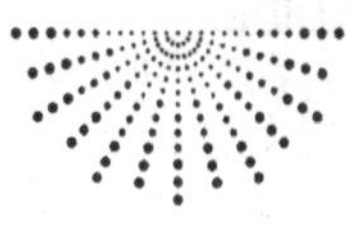

CHAPTER 4

THESE GIANTS DIDN'T JUST CREATE art, they created permission. Permission to reach beyond what seems possible, to question what seems certain, to feel what seems too much. They looked at the limitations of their time and said in essence, "not for us, not today, not ever."

When you write your story, paint your vision, or dare to love despite the odds. You're not just following your dreams, you're continuing their revolution. You're proving that their refusal to accept "impossible" still echoes in every creative act, every bold choice, every moment when someone decides that humanity deserves more beauty, more truth, more possibility than the world currently offers.

History isn't just our ruler, it's our co-conspirator in the ongoing rebellion against settling for less than extraordinary.

To evolve as a species, we must actively seek and nurture the thinkers of tomorrow, wherever they may be. Let our mission be both purposeful and swift, for the future depends on the minds we choose to cultivate today.

· · ·

WHAT TERRIFIES ME MOST, are the depth of those eyes. Are they bottomless?

LAMINATING

Traipsing

WEALTHY PEOPLE ARE invisible

HOMICIDAL FOREPLAY

THE GROUND WORK I'm laying down

HE CRUSHED my back against the dismal cinder wall

FROM THE GOOD book of CSI

> They didn't just accumulate money, they harvested power across centuries. Each generation passed down not inheritance, but instructions. Not trust funds, but blueprints for dominion. Wealth was never the goal; it was the weapon. And now, with enough resources to engineer life itself, they're ready to complete what their ancestors began—the systematic reduction of humanity to livestock.

And those who came before us.

. . .

Sudden loss

American Dream, don't make me laugh.

Andrew extinguished souls like ciggies. Any light that dared
shine in his house was quickly snubbed out.

Windshield bullseye.

Vanity or death

The believers

Whether you win or lose

The kneelers

When you create the monster you must feed it.

A sea of greed and hate

Minus algorithms or AI

Shadowed over her face ? Face of Shadows?

Deep fakes

White swirl

Clear glass decorated with irregular lattimo threads

On the fringe of society

What's wrong? Need a runway to land the plane.

Filigrana in lattimo black and gold leaf

Side handles

Swan scalloped pedestal dish with horizontal brown glass

Bottega

Conglomerate

Encased in blush glass

Italian Raymor lava glaze compote

You face a tough challenge

Continuity

Buttery

Archetypes

Match the energy

Well dressed and professional

Emotional needs

Alabaster skin

They knocked over the joint

They probably go to public university

The trust fund baby says: poor people don't know how to invest the right way or now. Easy for her to say, they read the cheat sheet daily.

What did I tell you?

Jade carved in openwork with dragons encasing an arch accompanied by its original base.

QILIN—ILLUSTRIOUS ruler / Sage—imminent birth or death

THE SAGE

BETWEEN THE ASHES stowed heartbreak

TROPICAL OMBRÉ OVERTURE
What are your goals?

CHISELED

THERE'S the young and the young at heart

PEACH ALABASTER—ZUNI inlaid turquoise eyes with harness fetish sculpture

Chinese jade pillow baby

Aughts

PEONS = POWER and control = he got pleasure out of torturing us

· · ·

DAVID ELLSWORTH CLARO Spirit Form 1992

Robert W. Chatelain Black Cherry

Charles Miner Glass 60

Andrew Shea 1984. 90

THIN MEMBRANE

PART XIV
BROKEN WINDOWS

AUGUST 1ST—LOVE, THE ULTIMATE WEAPON

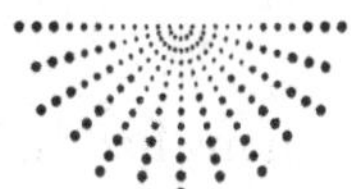

Something would shift behind my father's eyes—like watching a man drown from the inside. His hands would tremble before they struck, his breath catching in his throat as if fighting invisible chains. The violence came with tears he tried to hide, with whispered apologies that escaped before the blows landed.

I learned to read the geography of his face in those moments. The way his jaw would clench against words he couldn't say. How his shoulders would hunch as if carrying something too heavy to bear. His eyes became windows to a war I couldn't see. Kindness battling something darker, losing ground with every raised hand.

Even as his fist connected, I could see the real him trapped behind his own actions, screaming silently, "I'm so sorry. I can't stop. Please forgive me for what I'm about to become."

The man who tucked me in at night and the one who left bruises were the same person, and somehow that made it infinitely worse.

> Then I think about what my mother endured.

Suitable / Insane

Crazy stupid

Maybe all the above.

The photograph trembled in my hands. Not from age, but from the earthquake in my chest. Her face had become a ghost behind my eyelids. Features dissolving like watercolors in rain. I pressed my palms against my temples, trying to squeeze her back into focus, but found only the hollow echo where her laugh used to live.

That morning, I jolted awake with my heart hammering against my ribs, sheets soaked in the cold sweat of forgetting and whispers of the past. The panic wasn't just fear, it was betrayal. How could I, who loved her more than breathing, let her slip through the cracks of my own mind?

My hands scrambled across the nightstand like a drowning man reaching for shore. Picture frames crashed into each other, glass singing against wood. There—her graduation photo. The one from our Christmas dinner. The candid shot where she's mid-laugh, eyes crinkled with joy I'd never see again.

I studied her face like a cartographer mapping foreign territory. The small scar above her eyebrow from childhood. The way her smile pulled slightly higher on one side. The constellation of freckles across her nose that I used to trace with my fingertip as a child.

Piece by piece, I reconstructed her from fragments. Not just her image, but the weight of her head on my shoulder, the sound of her keys hitting the kitchen counter, the way she laughed off-key while smoking a cigarette. These weren't just memories; they were sacred relics I was desperately trying to preserve before time's cruel alchemy turned them to dust.

We inherit these broken pieces; photographs, stories, the echo of voices that will never speak our names again. But in our desperate reconstruction, in our refusal to let go, we don't just remember them. We resurrect them. We make them immortal in the only way we know how, by carrying them forward, breathing life into their memory until it becomes something new and eternal.

The pictures on my nightstand aren't just images anymore, they're portals. And every time I look at them, I'm not just remembering her. I'm keeping her alive.

MONGOLS

Individual

Smoking a butt

Turbulent, crowded, the figures agitated. The spectators are below the crucifixion, but above some figures in the scene. Conical

You're such a tart

Bohemian style hunting scene

A baccarat newel post. Similar to a snow globe with little funny characters in whimsy.

Grotesque ribbed crackle

Spatter Gold

Acid cutback

Luster ware

Cased glass

Peacock feather skin

Amethyst optic ribbed

Venice lace stem ware

Ribbon glass

Ubiquity

Stewardship

Kimble Cluthra glass

Opalescent frosted and purple-stained—Deep relief

Ikigai

Volcano orange over turquoise

Powder bowl

Stenciled marked

Molded "r Lalique"

Etched signature

>Opaque-white Festooned with blue
>gilded lizard on blown overlay
>Fauna
>Lifelike snakes and lizards to signify rebirth and renewal.

Nature magnified

Flat effect on photos

Here, there, everywhere.

>Transformed her hair into copper threads. Garnered her hair,
>	ushered her hair

They sat opposite each other.

They sat across from each other.

Replete

No funny business

It suits you.

Sagacity

Shire

Birthday suit

Queen of dreams

Waist cinched

Viscous

> Idiosyncratic Oeuvre—Strange or unusual work of art, music or
> literature

Ancient ones

Ancient city

Shadow Zone

Joyriding birds

HALF-MOON DRIVEWAYS as opposed to full circle.

YACHT CLUB PARKING stickers on their windshield

MAN BECOMES god

Ancestral Wisdom

Lineages of naguals

Eagle night lineage

Prepare it like liver—eating placenta is sweet
and more tender than beef. And taste
nothing like chicken or pork.

HUMAN FINGERS TASTE like prosciutto

DID NOT TASTE of high game.

Gres porcelain—known for its exceptional durability, low water
absorption, and resistance to wear and tear.

CLAD in moss and sand

Glass walls

Mirrored facia

"We are Love"

"The good life"

There must be something more

The light between the stars

Manifestation of light

THE DREAMS OF HUMANS "DREAMERS"

DREAM of the planet

We faithfully believe what we are taught. Be careful what kind of energy you teach.

WE DOMESTICATE everything we touch

THE COURAGE TO be ourselves

MITOTE—FOG of perception
Antecedents
Vision Quest

POISONED BEAUTY

EVERYONE HUNTS FOR THE TRUTH. For something sacred to bow before. But we all bleed under the same merciless judge. The one that lives inside our own skin.

She carved a ritual from desperation; hot water, porcelain sanctuary, the drowning of everything she couldn't bear to carry. Her body disappeared beneath the surface, bubbles fleeing her lungs like escaping souls. Above her, the ceiling wept black tears, mold that bloomed like diseased flowers across cracked plaster.

But submerged, everything transformed. The rot became Hunter Starlight, constellations of decay that danced in her oxygen-starved vision. Beautiful. Ephemeral. The kind of beauty that only exists when you're drowning.

She understood the ancient mathematics of survival: to kill the monster, you must first draw its portrait. Map its territory. Know its face intimately before you can destroy it. So she prayed to the scalding water, begging it to burn away whatever darkness had taken root in her bones.

But even prayer has limits.

The rust bled down the tub's edge like dried blood, and she couldn't look away. It infected her thoughts, spreading through her mind like cancer through healthy tissue. The water that was supposed to cleanse her was poisoned from the source. The house itself was rotting from the inside out—walls, pipes, everything contaminated.

She floated in this toxic baptism, realizing the terrible truth: some things are masterful mimics, wearing beauty like a stolen dress. Evil learns to look like salvation. Corruption perfects the art of appearing pure.

And in this infected sanctuary, surrounded by tainted water and bleeding rust, she finally understood nothing pure lived here. Not the house. Not the water.

Not her.

The real horror wasn't the mold or the rust, it was the recognition that she had become part of the infection, another beautiful lie in a house full of rotting truths.

Is GOD REAL?

IS God real?

Does it matter?

Yes

You'll despise the answer. But more importantly, you'll never know the truth?

GENESIS

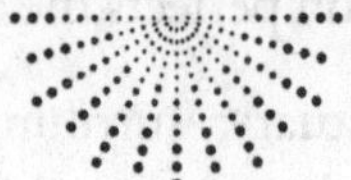

THE FOREST BRED poison from the moment Earth drew its first breath. Not metaphorically—literally. Its roots drank venom instead of water. Its leaves exhaled toxins that turned the air itself into a slow, acting executioner.

For eons, it had been both womb and tomb. Whatever clawed its way from the forest's toxic belly came pre-equipped with liquid immunity flowing through their veins, or they died choking on their first lungful of poisoned air. There was no middle ground, only the blessed and the buried.

But the forest's true hunger wasn't for its own children. It craved the foreign blood of outsiders. The sweet terror of creatures who dared to cross its venomous threshold. Their untrained lungs would burn with each breath. Their naive skin would blister at the first touch of its acid-kissed leaves.

The forest didn't just kill, it consumed. Flesh became fertilizer. Bones became roots. Screams became the wind's eternal song through its predatory canopy.

It was patient. Ancient. Perfectly evolved for one purpose: turning hope into compost.

Every footstep that entered was already counted among the dead. The forest knew this. Savored this. Had been perfecting this beautiful brutality since the world was young and mercy was just a word that hadn't been invented yet.

The real horror wasn't that it killed, it was how efficiently it had learned to make dying feel like coming home.

THE GOLDEN HARE

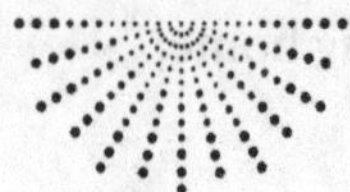

THE SALT STORM built walls of white fury across the highway, erasing the world in crystalline death. Visibility died to nothing, yet somehow Rabbit's golden hair cut through the chaos like liquid sunlight, defying nature's brutal erasure.

Her head bowed against the stinging assault, hands shielding her eyes from the apocalyptic beauty ahead. In all of recorded history, no one had ever crawled toward a finish line with such deliberate slowness. Each step was prayer, defiance. Love made pure and real.

Then the gunshot shattered the salt-thick air.

"Listen carefully, little Rabbit."

"What, Mama?"

Her mother's eyes burned with the terrible clarity of the dying. "You cannot outrun death. No one can. The hour of our ending is carved in stone before we draw our first breath."

Rabbit's world collapsed into liquid heartbreak. "Then why, Mama? Why make me run this race?"

"Because I needed you to know."

"Know what?"

"That love can make you faster than death, even when you can't beat it."

"Mama!"

"I love you, little Rabbit. Now run."

Rabbit has five days to rewrite fate itself. Mama Tu will bleed out in seven if she doesn't receive a synthetic liver. And the only prize worth winning waits at Mother Cabrini's shrine. Thirty miles of pure hell stretch between two cities. One of hope and one made from the bones of heartbreak.

This isn't just wilderness, it's a living weapon. Salt flats that blind and burn. Mountains that swallow sound. Forests that breathe poison. And worse than nature's cruelty are the human predators who've made this death march their hunting ground.

Marauders camp like vultures along the route. Human poachers collect trophies from fallen runners. And Jedidiah Smith, the sadistic game warden, has seeded the path with booby traps designed to maximize suffering before the kill. He doesn't want Rabbit to die quickly—he wants her to bleed slowly, beautifully, while the world watches and bets on her destruction.

But Maggie knows that particular scent of death by heart. Rabbit's girlfriend has tasted that metallic terror before, and she'll be damned if she lets the girl she loves face it alone. Secretly, she joins the race. Not to win, but to ensure Rabbit survives what's coming.

Because Rabbit is about to learn the most brutal truth of all: there are fates worse than death. And love—real love—always comes at a price that breaks you before it saves you.

Life finds a way.

But so does death.

Feel the night / swallow the moon

Straight edge

Devil's lettuce

Cuboid

24X70

Administration of poison

Motion for preliminary injunction

Motion against defendant's request for C.R.S. § 13-17-102

Motion for jury trial

PART XV
BLUEPRINT YOUR UNIVERSE

UNLEASH THE BEAUTIFUL
CHAOS WITHIN

CHAPTER 1

VOMIT your truth onto the page. Don't edit your thoughts as they spill —let them pour out raw and unfiltered, like blood from a fresh wound. Whatever writhes inside your skull, whatever screams in the dark corners of your mind, give it breath. The mess is where the magic lives. Your stream of consciousness isn't broken—it's beautifully human.

Steal wisdom from the smallest voices. Children's books and poetry are surgical strikes of language—every word earns its place. One sentence can shatter a heart or rebuild a world. Study how masters of brevity make syllables sing and silence speak.

BLUEPRINT YOUR UNIVERSE

CHAPTER 2

Map your story's DNA before you write. Characters aren't just names, they're walking contradictions with bleeding hearts and secret fears. Settings aren't backdrops, they're living entities that breathe and influence every choice your characters make. Outline everything: the geography of their souls, the architecture of their world, the physics of their conflicts.

Raid the playground of imagination. Children don't just think outside the box, they demolish the box and build castles from its remains. Their minds are treasure vaults of impossible possibilities. When you're stuck, think like a seven-year-old who believes dragons live in storm clouds and magic hides in puddles.

Writing Prompt: You wake up and discover you can hear the secret thoughts of every animal around you. The first conversation changes everything you thought you knew about the world.

SHATTER YOUR CREATIVE
COMFORT ZONE

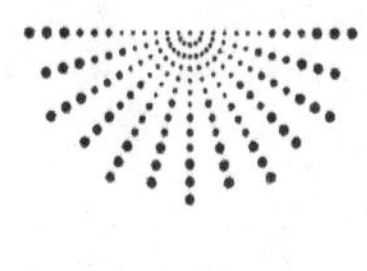

CHAPTER 3

BECOME SOMEONE YOU'RE NOT. Write from the perspective of your opposite—someone whose beliefs make your skin crawl. Whose values feel like sandpaper against your soul. This isn't about agreeing with them, it's about understanding the human complexity that makes even villains believe they're heroes in their own stories.

Find the humanity in your enemies. Take someone who irritates you, someone whose existence feels like nails on a chalkboard. Now dig deeper. What childhood wound created their armor? What fear drives their cruelty? Compassion for the unlikable is where real writers are born.

EXPERIMENTAL STORYTELLING TECHNIQUES

CHAPTER 4

WRITE a story built entirely from questions. Two characters interrogating each other, probing for truth, dancing around secrets. Let the questions themselves reveal character, plot, and emotional stakes. What they don't ask can be more powerful than what they do.

Craft narratives from digital fragments. Write an entire story through text messages—the pauses between responses, the typos that reveal nervousness, the read receipts that scream with unspoken tension. Modern love, loss, and betrayal live in our notification screens.

Compress entire universes into single sentences. One line that contains birth, conflict, transformation, and resolution. This is literary alchemy—turning words into worlds, sentences into entire lifetimes.

The real secret? Perfect writing doesn't exist. Powerful writing does. And it's born from the courage to bleed on the page, to embrace the mess, and to trust that your unique voice, however broken or beautiful, is exactly what the world needs to hear.

POST INDIGENOUS WORLD / Land

In a blink of an eye he traveled light years from where they stood.

Ghostly sphinx

> At sixty, she wore every inch of it. Right down to her wool stockings. I did a double take and questioned my own sanity. I couldn't help thinking that maybe Emily was a time traveler.

She wore every ounce of 57.

The next mother.

Exceptional

Those eyes of hers were the color of soil

Four years on the dot.

> When evil crawls inside the heart and settles in, then there's little that can be done.

The crowd would not be appeased unless Leonor paid with her life.

Purified clay

YOUR MOVE

Scan your surroundings—left, then right. If what you witness makes your skin crawl, if the faces around you feel like mirrors reflecting everything you refuse to become, then congratulations: you've just mapped your reality.

These aren't just random people sharing your space, they're the cast of your daily existence. The personalities you'll navigate, negotiate with, and survive alongside for the foreseeable future.

This is your ecosystem. These are the voices that will shape your conversations, the energy that will influence your choices, the human landscape you'll traverse every single day.

If that realization feels like a punch to the gut, if you're drowning in mediocrity or toxicity of your immediate environment, then you have two options: adapt to their frequency or fight to change your coordinates.

Because geography isn't just about location, it's about the souls you surround yourself with. And if you hate what you see when you look around, then you're either in the wrong place or you're exactly where you need to be to learn what you don't want to become.

Your move.

YOUR MIND IS A TICKING time bomb.

Their bodies will decorate the landscape like billboards.

MISSED Connections

ICONIC cool

The Perfect House

Dreams and Curses

Well crafted

The Curse (light) of a Thousand Dreams (lifetimes)

Lovely Creatures

This House of Souls

A guide: To bury sins in lushness

Mountain of Gods

Don't spoil it for everyone

Brick red and white stripe

House of Oblivion

Quantum fiber internet connection

How do you know if someone existed at all?

Pencil brass trim

Pill shape

Rev your lowballs

Bled into the backdrop of Neverland

I'm driving this thing until the wheels fall off

Secessionist

The entryway is lined in marble white portals

You know my moves

No stains, no fading, no pilling, fraying, or discoloration

Spoiled milk

    Looked like spiders crawling up the side of the glass

Perched high above the clouds

Fresco dining/ lunch

Boy play doll

Cabochons

Prefers side chicks

Stop scraping the bottom

Fries are epic... aren't they?

Crawled back into my dms

The air all quiet as hell.

She slayed in her day. Now, not so much

Spending that much on a funeral for what?
She's going straight to hell.

Do you have the vision

Slums for the wealthy

Who knows what the world was before it was

White men uncomfortable and insecure

Does anyone know how to love? One is always the center of two in a
Loveship

Iron powder glaze

Kinrande Porcelain

She was soiled by her attackers

Madeley

Morbidities

One note

Children who are haunted by their past lives

Gold brocade

Diner party

Knows her way around a bean or two.

Battery acid and tomato juice

Clan of lesser gods

Clan the white fire

Punched through the door

In truth, in reality

Dink dual income—no kids

Cringey turn

Breathe life into whatever, whoever he could

Swallowing those desires is human. To spot them is divine

Blood and milk

Ghosting. Bread-crumbing or all or nothing. Limerence

Limerent object

Xanadu

Sacrament over milk and milk and honey

Expansive glass facade

Stone clad columns / timber trusses

Burned Earth (terracotta)

ALTAR of tiny objects

DON'T LET White fire bite dreamland / while I sleep

Our new age culture is just this: To fill a massive tub full of water only for the money shot to be starred in a glamorous architectural magazine.

Shelter in place

Incipient

PASS / fire extinguisher

Cinna dust

River dust

Heckuva

DIYers

Goth king

Weaponizing

Geniality spans continents

Tiamo

Nicolina

Crazy can do

Resist death

The little prince of New Mexico

La bruja

Guru of small spaces eidetic

Take the love goggles off

Circuitous

Infallible

Anthropoid

PART XVI
PORTRAITS IN WHITE

WHITE MALAISE

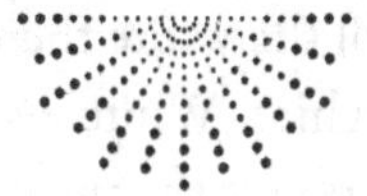

THIS HOUSE of perfection is flawless—at least that's what we tell ourselves. So are the folks who temporarily dwell within these white walls. Even though the black mold has tunneled through to the baby's room like some living parasite, proving itself formidable despite my desperate attempts to eradicate, sublimate, murder it with bleach and prayers.

It has successfully won. Claiming more territory as I write these goddamn words.

And you know what? The mold is perfect too. Everything that comes with it—the decay, the slow poisoning, the beautiful rot—all of it is perfect in its imperfection.

Because besides taxes and death, mystery and imperfection are more perfect than perfection itself.

The baby told me today—I'm paraphrasing here because three-year-olds don't speak in complete sentences—that it's hard as hell to be invisible when her older siblings are such high achievers. Academic superstars. Athletic gods. Everything she's not.

Then I thought: she's absolutely right. Sometimes the invisible is more whimsical than what lies behind the visible. The overlooked child sees everything the celebrated ones miss.

Everyone on my block owns a pure white picket fence these days. Accompanied by pure white bathrooms and kitchen tiles and everything. A box of pure, dazzling white. Enough to sting the eye so white.

But when they finally own all the white their heart desires, well, let's just say nothing is whiter than white. White eventually tarnishes over time. Yellows at the edges. Cracks under the pressure of life. Shows every flaw, given enough time.

When the perfect you own is imperfect, life is just easier. Less anxious. Who are you trying to keep up with? You or Linda with the $500 dollar haircut three doors down?

"Linda, no, that's not meant for you, I was just talking out loud."

That's what I said to myself after Charlie, my husband, slammed his third highball for the night and kept rambling about Bob's brand spanking new—that's how he put it—fiery pickup parked carelessly, halfway on the driveway and halfway on the street.

Charlie was really pissed—mind the language—because Bob parked on the goddamn sidewalk.

There. There it is. The whole story.

You know what I think? Charlie was just using Bob as an excuse to drink another highball. He knows it drives me crazy when he goes on to the third. Because us ladies know after a third, it all goes to hell from there.

Meanwhile, the baby is listening to Charlie go on and on over this brand spanking new business. Absorbing every toxic word like a little sponge.

Gosh, I wish I could be invisible like the baby. Why does the baby always have it better than the rest of us?

All I kept thinking was God must hate me because he made me the middle. And everyone knows what always happens to the middle—squeezed between the perfect and the forgotten, crushed by the weight of everyone else's expectations.

Invisible in a house full of people who refuse to see the mold growing in the walls or the cracks spreading through their perfect white lives.

TIDE, THE OTHER SCENT

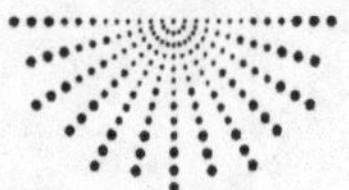

Tide and downy fumes soiling the kitchen, where salmon is being broiled. Now, strangely, there's a minty scent in the air.

—When Things Grow Legs Unexpectedly—

THE TIDE's briny ghost crept through the kitchen windows, mingling with downy fumes that escaped from the broiler's glowing mouth. Salmon skin sizzled and surrendered its oils to the scorching oil, each droplet of rendered fat painting the air with oceanic memories.

But then—strangely—a minty whisper threaded through the heavy marine fog. Cool and unexpected, it danced between salt-thick vapors like a manifestation of summer gardens haunting a seaside kitchen. The scent bore malice intent—fresh and green against the oceanic richness of broiling fish.

Perhaps it was the mint chimichurri waiting in its ceramic bowl, its verdant oils slowly warming in the kitchen's heat. Or maybe the sea breeze had carried something wild and herbaceous from the coastal cliffs —salt-kissed mint that grew in the crevices where ocean spray met rocky earth.

The kitchen became a battleground of competing atmospheres: the ancient call of tide and flame, the domestic comfort of downy steam, and now this mysterious mint—clean and sharp as a blade cutting through the thick, fatty air. Each breath was a contradiction—heavy with oceanic richness yet lifted by something impossibly fresh, as if the sea itself had learned to breathe through green leaves.

The salmon crackled under the broiler's fierce attention, its skin crisping to black perfection while that strange mint lingered. Uninvited but undeniably present, transforming the kitchen into something between a seaside galley and a secret garden.

Then it occurred to me, after we sat at the kitchen table, the scent wafting from the washer was Tide detergent and not the sea.

EZRA

Biometric screening

On the cheap

Feign

The whisper network

Built solid with discipline

The pattern of soufflé knit

Robin's egg

Green crackle

A slice of Chicano wonder

Pleasure room

Tea powder glaze

Cillian (Killian)

Lope

Eabha (Ava)

Tige

Poutine

Jaio

Lush hillside. Lush meadow. The hillside is lush, but stony.

Though she couldn't see the deadly things embedded inside
something so breathtaking.

BROKE BRAIN / wizardry, sorcery, plain magic

God of iron/ poet of ugly / alpha gens

I needed a road map or a decoder ring

Matrix of a pat down

Walk like a penguin

You passed double nickels

Framework

ENOUGH TO SEE it with the naked-eye

Death will deliver the peace you so desire

WHITE VEIN MARBLE

> It was incredible from top to bottom and just a beautiful pitch,
> melody, voice, tone

LINT IN THE POCKETS / lint in the eye

SAVORY FINISH. Celery and melon vibe

I DON'T HAVE BANANAS, only flamethrowers

COMPLAINTS ARE dust in the wind

AUGUSTINE
Knapp joints

HOUSE-LESSER / House of Lester?
House-free lifestyle
Flex-to / fake something
Salt glaze Offering Jar
Photorealistic, classical
Veranda columns and railings

Astronomical spring

Gent's watch

One second of happiness

Arrivederci

HEAVEN IS A CHOOSE YOUR OWN ADVENTURE BOOK

I CLOSED the book and didn't move.

"Well," the angel said, "how did you like it?"

Even though I was dead, I still felt nauseated. "Every single one. Every single decision I ever made was the wrong one. THE WRONG. FUCKING. ONE."

The angel grimaced. "Wow. That's... my goodness! That's actually quite impressive in a depressing way. I mean, the odds are astronomical when you—"

"Is this hell? Is this some sort of Twilight Zone shit, where my punishment is knowing how awesome my life could have been?"

"All right, settle down. You know, I think you're going to very much enjoy finding out why we show you all this... you, more than most, in fact."

The book suddenly disappeared, and two normal-looking doors appeared.

"Um, okay?"

The angel pointed, "You must choose now."

THINGS THAT DON'T SURVIVE
THE CUTTING BOARD

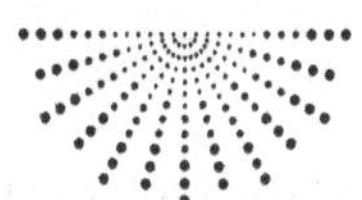

FIRST, seek the kingdom of God.

She stared at her blood-streaked face in the mirror. Tears erupted, cascading down her stained cheeks. Could she believe what she was seeing? Not at all.

The horror consumed her like a nightmare. One that swam through her twisted mind without mercy, without end. Her knees trembled. But this was her life now, blood and tears. Blood and tears.

And it started with her mother.

Since then, she couldn't seem to keep the ones she loved alive. Maybe something evil had infected her aura. Followed like a shadow. Maybe she was Death itself—a walking curse that destroyed everything she touched.

In that moment, Rory felt relief. Not relief from death, relief that she wouldn't have to watch Dante die before her eyes. Die twice. Her heart couldn't survive one more death.

Maybe she wasn't Death after all. Maybe the entire thing was just written in the fucking stars for whatever reason, a cosmic joke she'd never understand.

Her gut parched from the simplest of nutrition. Her heart was starving for love lost, whittled to a shell, nothing more.

SPUTNIK LIGHTING

THE MOON SIFTED / filtered through the pines

THE FLASHLIGHT STILL BLAZING / on fire. Setting a small lens of skeletal / winter trees on fire

YOU MUST DESTROY the things you love the most, in order to build something greater.

MALAISE, haunted by earlier truths—

There's a small provision though. White tarnishes over time. I've seen it. Nothing is impervious to time's cruel mathematics. Even teeth bleached to perfection will one day grace the yellow of yesterday.

"A touch-up is needed," the dentist tells me. "Five to ten years, depending on how much coffee, cigarettes, and red wine you partake in."

At least you can refresh those pearly whites. But what about those countertops and cabinets and blinds? The only way to refresh those things is to replace them. Replace. Let that sink in for just a minute—that's what I'm telling myself as I hear the baby shuffling around in her room.

I wonder, will she emerge today? This invisibility has got to end. But does she know she's my favorite? I've told her several times, but something in her eyes tells me I'm full of it. Maybe I am.

Still, I know a thing or two about people overlooking your talents. Some talents are subtle but mighty. Last week, Charlie begged me to join him for his annual business retreat—though I wouldn't call it a retreat per se. More of a narcissist's wet dream where they enable and congratulate, clapping each other on the back for a job well done.

I'm not being melodramatic here—everyone quickly changed the subject when I mentioned my PhD. They wanted to know about the baby. Her siblings. How to remove red wine from crisp white Oxfords.

I know little about laundry. I haven't done a load since college. Even then, I begged my roommate to wash my clothes. She agreed, on account I'd write her term papers. Don't judge, I'm not proud. Besides, she went AWOL two semesters later, talking about buying an ice cream shop in the middle of nowhere.

I wonder about her sometimes. Not about her so much. I wonder if she found the key to happiness inside the walls of ice cream. Is there such a thing as happiness? Maybe she's smarter than I.

By 26, I was six figures deep in debt. I do have a PhD to show for it. I created a lucrative solution—the one Charlie peddles to all those big box stores. I was never a show-person, a people's person. Charlie, on the other hand, charmed the pants off me—and the rest of the world.

He charmed me into buying this perfect, rickety house. 1905 to be precise. This old house does what it pleases. Even the floors creak sporadically. I believe the house favors me over Charlie—it's always tripping him up with sporadic creaks. When he desires a sneak around, the floorboards buckle loud enough to wake me. I'll walk the same path and the house never creaks.

Perhaps the widow who passed away in this room still lingers, watchful over its secrets. Perhaps she senses Charlie is scheming something sinister—she was right, after all. Then again, I'd already harbored my own suspicions. Still, it's comforting when someone has your back, even from beyond the grave.

The first time I caught Charlie in the act was on our 5th anniversary. He telephoned: "I'm swamped at work. Rain check?" Charlie and his rain checks.

So I thought: treat yourself, Kelsey. I hired Liza next door to watch the baby. The dress from my college days fit better than when I was in my twenties—I'd gained more curves. I decided, with or without Charlie, I'm dining at our favorite restaurant, The Buzz. I called it that because, well, everyone says it's the buzz of the town.

There is something wondrous about white sheets. They present perfect. Clean. Quiet. Though without a single word, they will shame you when you're foul. When you bleed. What are those brown stains? Chocolate? Or a heartstopper?

Love the small wins in life.

Atop

Bequeathing

Unvarnished

Galvanizing

Stymie

Whereupon

Waiting for death / or heaven

Spirits of Destiny

Room of a thousand tears

Gauntlet of boobytraps, marauders and killers

Unicorn sandwich

Teenie

Tradesman

White fire evolution

Frenzy

Poverty porn

Bacteria and self-healing roads

STILL WIPING him out of me

> Being good to yourself is being good to those you love

> Tobacco and honey

> Hunger so bad her bones began to see daylight

LUNA

Seasoned

Dexterous

Abound

> Follow the money. But in her case, follow the DNA.

GUSTAVO

Manuel

Alfonso

Rosa

Griselda

Gerardo Cervantes

HIS SOUL UNCIRCUMCISED

CONTROL over their choices

Mountain peaks seasoned with white
powder

DE LA TORRE brothers

THERE IS beauty in simplicity

Swirly splendor, faded, scratched, chipped

Cracked, pitted, starred windshield

Stained or soiled, plastic damage, animal hour, torn material

The comfy, old animal hair

Newer, normal, worn, curb rash

Variables

Scans or calibration for adas, blind-spot, front radar, thirty-six
camera, front eye-camera (eye-sight calibration)

. . .

Incidentals, variables, consequential

Delights of gods

DOOMED FROM THE START

RAIN HAMMERED the earth for three days straight—relentless, merciless, drowning everything in gray despair. No crack of sunlight. No whisper of warmth. No hope of seeing things clearly again.

At least that's what she whispered to herself, fingers pressed against the fogged window.

Then her stomach clenched—sharp, hollow, demanding. Her heart twisted in the same rhythm. Hunger and longing—weren't they the same, breast feeding on her bones?

Her mind circled like a vulture: the precious thing lost to water. Not sea —if it were sea, she'd dive in until her lungs burst. But river water offered hope. Cruel hope. Maybe her heart could be righted. Nullified. Resurrected.

Somewhere in the skeletal remains of the forest.

She stepped into the aftermath—ground seasoned with ice crystals and snow that crunched beneath her boots. Pine needles stabbed her nostrils with their sharp, oily perfume. Fresh soil suffocated her lungs as though she were buried alive without two fucks and a pine box to deliver her to whatever came next.

"A conduit from this life to the next," Jack had whispered once, his breath warm against her ear.

From this life to the next.

The mystery of death had too many variables—and that terrified her more than this gray existence. Is heaven really heaven when you can't be with the ones you love?

No. She didn't think so.

If hell were real, then hell swims with the stars. Where else can you fit billions of souls? That's the only way she could rationalize it. If hell were below, wouldn't it be overflowing with the dead by now? Shouldn't she be fighting for her life against the undead?

Isn't that how it ends in every zombie movie ever made?

UNIVERSAL DELIGHTS

GODLY DELIGHTS ARE love and kindness and even justice—the sacred trinity of divine perfection that theologians love to celebrate. But this leads me to darker delicacies. The God of the universe also delights in hate and war and genocide. Why else would a divine creature create evil human beings—beings who enslave, rape, pillage? He delights in every human emotion. And he knows them intimately. They belonged to him first.

If God is the architect of all creation, then he is also the architect of humanity's capacity for unspeakable cruelty. The theological gymnastics required to separate God from evil are breathtaking in their desperation. Free will, they cry. Soul-building, they whisper. Greater good, they rationalize.

But what if the truth is simpler and more terrifying? What if God experiences the full spectrum of human emotion not as corruption of his perfect nature, but as expressions of it. What if wrath and love flow from the same divine source—not as contradictions, but as complementary forces in a cosmic symphony we're too small to comprehend?

The God who commands the complete destruction of entire peoples—children included—is the same God who speaks of infinite love. This isn't theological inconsistency; it's divine completeness. Every emotion that courses through human veins first pulsed through divine consciousness. Jealousy, rage, vengeance—these aren't human corruptions of godly perfection. They're godly gifts to humanity.

We are made in his image, after all. And if that image includes the capacity for both transcendent love and devastating hatred, then perhaps we're more accurate reflections of divinity than we dare to admit. The uncomfortable truth is that God doesn't just permit evil—he authored the very nature that makes evil possible. And in that authorship, there might be a terrible beauty, a cosmic purpose that transcends our limited understanding of morality.

Every human emotion belongs to him first. We are not fallen angels—we are perfect reflections of a God who contains multitude.

MR. DEMPSEY

MISS ALEXANDRIA THORP asked me the other day, over tea and crumpets, if I could love Mr. Hawthorne forever. My first inclination was to laugh—though I must confess, I did giggle briefly at this absurd question of forever. Not to Mr. Hawthorne, of course.

Once I cleared the question from my head, I looked Miss Alexandria in the eye and said, "Forever doesn't seem long enough."

She gave a look of disdain. She gulped as though being scolded—or horror-struck. Not sure which. Then she said, "He fucks every woman in town."

She said it as though it were a revelation to me. Of course, she doesn't know that I know. And have known for some time. But what I said next almost made her choke on her crumpet:

"Boys will be boys."

Our tea time ended abruptly after that comment. I could not gauge who she despised more—Mr. Hawthorne or myself. Perhaps she despised us equally.

However, if only Miss Alexandria had swallowed her crumpet and sipped her tea with those clamorous vacuum lips of hers, I would have let her in on a little secret. It wasn't Mr. Hawthorne she should concern herself with—it was Mr. Dempsey.

There's one thing a lady can count on in Cedar Falls: whispers of nefarious doings travel fast. Miss Alexandria and Mr. Dempsey are to be wed one week from today. And from what I've heard, he's infected with something deadly below his waist line. From what I'm told, he's taken up permanent residence at the gentleman's club—apparently, he's fallen for one of the girls there.

PART XVII
SOULS AFTERGLOW

IT'S A MYSTERY HOW ANYTHING SURVIVES

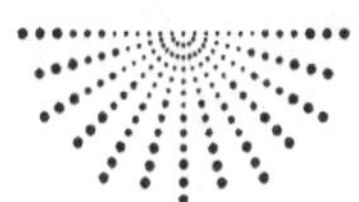

When my mind wandered as far as it could go, somewhere out
there was the good life. That someday we'd leave this place,
and the good place would welcome us, as though it had been
waiting for us the whole time.
I wish someone had told me the American Dream had died. Or
maybe it never existed at all. And I think my angel didn't
want to break my heart by telling me there's no such thing.
And I guess when the light won't warm your face anymore, and
dreams turn into chains, then what's the use of living?

When you see a zig zag, something bad is about to happen. But if you
see a snail it means good prosperity

THE HAND

Boy math

Hypermarket

Fuhgeddabout it

Beastie

Demure

Angel face

Teensy tiny

Is a piffle of a thing

House leaves

Run their tongue on their teeth

I said, "fuck the glass," and chugged.

Priestess

Clutch

Corpse

Splurge

Remains

You'll never know

Calcified

———————————

Peeled away, texture of waxy soap, a feast for sea lice or sea birds.
It's in God's hands. Putrefaction, bones to the sea floor, skeletal
remains, acids and cold slows decay

———————————

The American Dream bled out on inception. The American Dream
flatlined on fentanyl.

Raymor and I got caught in the whirlwind young. I was nineteen. He was the ripeness of twenty-one. We came from plain things that skirted poverty now and then. The mighty penny was honored and treasured.

But there was something about Raymor that only few knew. He tripled everything. Including women.

His mother told me he'd be somebody—not the most loyal of things, but a good provider. That rang true. You see, she also told me that his gift came at a price. Otherwise, he'd be a demigod among men

CONCEPTUALIZE

Incorporate

Satiety

Bonkers

Paralyzed intuitive

Beside myself

Weird

Devil's dung

There I was, spread eagle

Super scope screen

Demystify

Thrusted upon / thrusted aimlessly everywhere

Plaything

LOUISA, THE SPIRITUAL HEALER

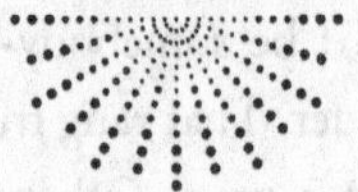

THIS STORY BEGINS in a very small town, named San Cardencia. Most everyone who was born in San Cardencia lived an unusually long life—which had mysteriously gone on for generations, maybe even thousands of years. Despite villagers living so long, not one could pinpoint when the mystery began.

23 percent of those who were not born in San Cardencia died of natural age. Seventy seemed to be the benchmark. Only one in the history of San Cardencia who was not born in the town lived to be ninety-one. His name is celebrated for defying the odds, even after all these years. His name was Miguel Rodriguez. Though that story is for another time.

In this town lived a gifted la bruja. Her name was Mary Louise Montoya, but most everyone in the town called her Louisa. She came from a long line of la brujas. Her mother was a la bruja. Her mother's mother was too, and so on.

For the sake of transparency—and before we move on—if one should see Louisa in this town and ask about her gifts, even though no one would know exactly how to approach such topics. She is a la bruja after all. We must gain a better understanding here, Louisa, though not embarrassed by her la bruja genealogy, has and will always label herself as a spiritual healer.

CHILDREN OF NOBILITY

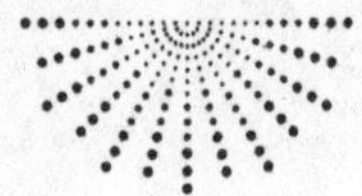

MAMA WOKE the boy before the first blade of sunlight could slice through the velvet curtains. His leather satchel sat waiting by the front door like a faithful dog, while a courier paced the narrow hallway, his pocket watch clicking open and snapping shut every few seconds as though a heist were unfolding in real time.

The boy reached for Mama's lips, but she turned away, her breath sharp with the metallic tang of fear. Instead, she pressed her mouth to his forehead—warm, trembling, desperate. Her tears splashed against his lips, salty sorrow coating his tongue like a bitter blessing.

Mama's eyes were red-rimmed and wild, pupils dilated with the kind of terror that comes from sleepless nights and waking nightmares. She feared the boy had developed a real taste for human flesh—had jolted awake at 3 AM from visions of him consuming every guest in the hotel, blood pooling beneath the dining room table like spilled wine.

All of this because the boy had taken a chunk out of her index finger—teeth sinking through skin and muscle until he tasted the copper richness of her blood, the warm saltiness of her flesh. And desired more. Craved it with a hunger that gnawed at his small belly like a living thing.

"Mama's finger made the hunger go away," he had whispered, licking his lips where her blood still lingered—sweet and metallic and perfectly satisfying in a way that bread and milk had never been.

The scent of iron still clung to his breath. The memory of her flesh still danced on his tongue. And in Mama's eyes, he could see his own reflection—small, innocent, and absolutely terrifying.

Gummy bears and popcorn for brains

On his eleventh birthday, he was stricken by a tummy ache. His only request, donkey milk.

Black-eyed children

Rat king

June and Jennifer Gibbons

That man stuffed a piece of paper in his pocket "finished"

Mimicry

Clinton road

Stone man syndrome

Teeth man

Tarrare

Coffin birth

He was born with gold stuffed in his mouth. One morning, at the age of two, he demanded Mama serve him caviar with the "pretty eggs"—pretty meaning sunny-side up. And a side plate of "Cruditis." He couldn't enunciate "Crudités" properly.
As he ripened through the ages, his taste grew and skirted the— shall I say—exotic. Or better, the privilege of nobility.

This place is so weird, I think I'll be back

Guilloche

The pattern is mechanically engraved

Rollies for Rolex

Solid gold

IT's a real bestiary

Vide-poche / empty pockets

A guide: How to kill like a god

Life of a god / kill like a god

THE HEART SLOWLY ABLATING / ablation / cauterize

Splashes of burl wood the room could never hold

"You are incredibly beautiful."

In that moment, her cheeks glowed, and her eyes shimmered
     with tears. "You always tell me that."
A high-pitched cackle escaped him. "Do we know each other?"
     His expression was skeptical.

She despised his cackle—though today, that cackle was the
     sweetest melody to her heart. She told herself: Stay calm.
     Don't give anything away.

She looked to her right, scouting for something. Or someone.

Then to the left. There was a woman breastfeeding her baby while sitting on a park bench. Still, no one within earshot.

"Yes, we know each other." She scanned the distance again. "Meet me at Fat Pete's."

"Fat Pete's?"

"Two words—crystal meth."

"Shhh, someone will hear you."

He replied softer: "My uncle owns that bar."

"I know. Meet me at 8."

HUMANIZED / whimsical

NOM DE PLUME

Plug your ears / stick your fingers in your ears. "Na, na, na, na"

INSOFAR

INORGANIC

Tripe salted and simmered in lard for eight hours.

THE ECHOES WE SEE

Mask of the Dead

I REALIZED at that moment my auntie was devastated by what her seventy-year-old eyes could witness. Because in that instant, I linked with her mind as though I were psychic—or perhaps even a stranger could clearly see the heartbreak carved into her features.

Her first niece was a broken woman. Years of substance abuse had seen to that. My aunt was so mesmerized by the misery of her niece that she didn't notice me watching her—studying the devastation etched across her face.

And then I realized, the longer I stared at my cousin in those few seconds, that my auntie was witnessing not only her niece's destruction but her children's as well. My auntie's entire family—the ones she had placed high hopes and dreams on—were just as damaged and tormented as her first niece.

Her life had come full circle in the most horrific way.

I think we both realized that her children echoed my cousin. The cycle was complete. The hopes she had carried for decades lay shattered at her feet, and there was nothing left to do but witness the wreckage of everything she had loved.

MILKY sap

MOUNT TRASHMORE

Trade winds stir a fuss when snow glistens in the sun like white fire. No—that's not quite right either.

Trade winds unleash fury when snow catches sunlight and burns like white fire across the mountainside. No—that's still not the image I'm hunting.

From a distance, on the hill, one can see white fire whispering windward on Pikes Peak.

At first glance, snow smoke whispers tranquil across Pikes Peak's granite face. I imagine for a moment how serene a pin drop must be standing on the leeward side. I wonder what lucky creature gets to absorb that moment. That second.

A modest, yet breathtaking spectacle ignites windward. The bitterness of winter wind plays against a crystal sky. It dazzles with gentleness—a contradiction that stops my breath. It's hard to trust my eyes.

Am I alive? Or is this a dream?

When I strike the page, my identity dissolves. I shed my real life like old skin and slip into someone else's bones until the last word is written. I don't just write my characters—I become them. Their guilt becomes mine. Their isolation settles in my lungs. Their family wounds reopen in my chest until I'm bleeding their stories onto paper.

. . .

When I hit the page, I'm no longer myself. I hang up my real life and trade it in until I stop writing. I transform into the characters I write—becoming their voices, breathing their fears, carrying their secrets like stones in my chest.

Punch up, not down.

Punch up, not down. Always up. Up, up.

THE RIDDLES THAT HAUNT ME ARE LOVE LETTERS FROM THE ABYSS—WRITTEN IN FUCHSIA LIGHT AND SIGNED WITH YOUR OWN BLOOD

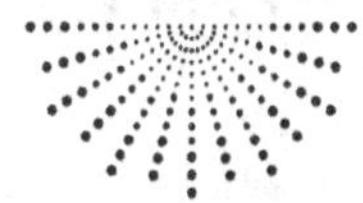

HEAVEN ISN'T HEAVEN when you're so far away from the ones you love.

Love isn't just an emotion—it's a location. Heaven exists wherever the people we love are present. Hell is any place, no matter how objectively beautiful, where we are cut off from those connections that define who we are.

The riddles that haunt me—they whisper in the spaces between heartbeats, echo in the silence after prayers, dance in the shadows where certainty crumbles.

There is a light that spills from the cracks of a very long stairway. It's fuchsia—or perhaps electric blue when darkness looms. A stairway to an abyss. To the grave. To whatever waits beyond the final step.

When I take this way, I mustn't be afraid. I welcome it. Even greet it like an old friend who has traveled impossible distances to find me. For there is a light to my path—strange and beautiful and utterly unafraid of the darkness it illuminates.

ARTIFICIAL MILK

Her skin, paler than breastmilk—almost translucent, as radiant veins pierced the surface like roadmaps of vulnerability. Highways of the nervous system branched beneath her flesh—thousands of electric blue pathways running up her neck and arms and thighs. Splashes of plum bloomed at her pulse points, dark as bruises but beautiful as watercolor.

She almost appeared inhuman. Sickly. Artificial—like a porcelain doll crafted by someone who had never seen a living woman, who understood anatomy but missed the warmth that makes flesh feel real.

Her transparency was both ethereal and unsettling—as if she were caught between worlds, too fragile for this one, too solid for the next. The blue highways pulsed with life that seemed borrowed, temporary, ready to fade at the first harsh word or sudden movement.

She was beautiful in the way dying things are beautiful—luminous with the knowledge of their own impermanence, glowing with a light that burns brightest just before it disappears.

Proportional

Winter starling murmuration

Minty flavor swimming in ashtray saliva

> "Osco, he's licking his butt!"
> "Osco was licking his butt?"
> "No, it's osco!"
> "Oh, I thought you meant Osco was licking his butt, you mean it's osco
> that he's licking his butt."
> "Never mind."
> His breath, eau de caribou or mocos?

The dog walked like an animatronic—jerky, mechanical movements that defied the natural grace of living creatures. Each step was calculated, programmed, as if someone had forgotten to install the software for organic motion. Its legs moved in perfect intervals, too precise to be real, too deliberate to be alive.

I carry your prayers with me—folded like paper cranes in the pockets of my memory, whispered mantras that echo in the hollow spaces between heartbeats. They weigh nothing and everything, light as breath but heavy as promises I can't break.

Forehead that goes on for days—a vast expanse of pale territory stretched taut with worry lines and sleepless nights. Greasy sheen glow catches the fluorescent light, reflecting exhaustion like a mirror that shows too much truth. It's the geography of someone who thinks too hard and sleeps too little.

You are not above where you come from. The soil that grew you still clings to your roots, no matter how high you climb or how far you travel. Success doesn't erase origin—it just gives you better lighting to see the shadows you've always carried.

The recipe of the universe

. . .

DEATH IS beautiful

Don't stay too long. That world is not meant for you yet.

Ticky-tack on the brain

Ticky-tack brain

Sleep in heavenly peace or places

Dreamstar

Dreamlight

Dreamseason

Castles in Spain

Castle at moonlight

Wear the dead

> A chihuahua that looked near death. Sunken eyes. Frail beak
> nose. Rib bones chattering beneath ragged fur.

Slave to human nature

Divine feast / godly feast / godlike feast

How the gods feast

MACABRE FEAST / Godly violence / lurid feast

GODLY DELIGHTS

Unctuous snobbery / main character syndrome

Rank-and-file workers

> Come clean. Come to Jesus. Come to whatever but come to
> something.

She was pure as water.

Charged up

God's army.

Destroyer of worlds.

Feast with your eyes / feast your eyes on these

She looked like a vintage poster from teen beat

A little pocket of beauty

Her eyes eagle sharp as though prey lingered somewhere below her gaze

Clad in wall paper

> Mary Louise Montoya was a natural born
> runner, just like our dog Kuma.

I need some time to reflect. A time of reflection.

> Holy water. Water that can never be drunk.
> Thirst that can't be quenched

TOILET BABY

Phials of odors

Tiger magic / tiger will

Widespread damage

Manifestation

PAPER JOCKEY

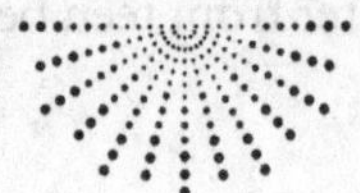

THE ROOM WAS DROWNING in a tidal wave of green—right down to the equestrian wallpaper where jockeys of yesteryear rode fine white stallions and leaped over balls and sticks. A home bustling with antique Southern charm.

Contemporary furnishings peppered every square inch, as though to say, "this home has evolved with the times." But in reality, the bones can't help but scream of a much darker past.

Or maybe the masters of the house mean to tell a different tale—that they endured through the ages. That they are alive. Stronger than ever. That they are reaping the benefits of bad deeds, and their children are destined to follow in those footsteps.

The green suffocates like old money—thick, oppressive, stained with secrets that no amount of contemporary updating can wash clean. Every surface whispers of inherited guilt, every antique bears witness to sins that compound like interest across generations.

The wallpaper jockeys ride their eternal race, frozen in perpetual motion—just like the family that owns this house, forever running from a past they refuse to acknowledge while simultaneously celebrating the wealth it provided.

EVIL TO THE LAST DROP. How long can you deprive the body until it just dies.

I know that face, it's almost universal.

Steep in your misery or hate, it doesn't matter to me. But in the meantime pass the bunuelos.

To denigrate people on cultural and religious identities is abhorrent and unacceptable.

Racist, misogynistic and homophobic

Reign in this house

Signboard

You and your hot wheels

So don't act like a Twinkie fresh from the box.

My anxiety poured through my eyes.

Quantum wave

Chokehold

Let your cuckoo out

My anxiety is sky high

He walks backward super-fast, while flipping everyone off wearing that fucking smirk.

I CAN ONLY SEE what's right in front of me.

Per se

Locale

Lifestyle maven

A state so red it has permanent sunburn

Quicker than you can blink

A perfect virus—carrier and taker.

Ray was not a romantic, he was made of
sturdier stuff.

I show a happy face. Everything from the shoulder up—happy.
Even my ears smile. My ears all smile.

Josh
What?
stinks
[laughter]
Erica
What auntie?
Stinks
[laughter]

Luckily this absurdity comes with an expiration date.

That's what I was thinking while politely laughing.

QUEENS OF WANDS—WEIGHTED BY POLISHED
STONES
WOMAN HOLDING A COIN
THE SUN
HOSTILITIES
THEN SHE SAYS, "THIS IS GOOD."
LUCKILY, I'M NOT A FORTUNE TELLER.
OTHERWISE...
SHE CONTINUES...
REBIRTH
AFTERLIFE
UPSIDE DOWN SEVENTH CHAKRA
DOOR TO PERSONAL HEALING AND HAPPINESS
COMMUNITY

WORRY ETCHES HER FACE

PART XVIII
BITTEN BY MEMORIES

THE CATALOG OF DEATH

ONE IS DEATH

1.Apple Sugar hand cream (still half-full)

2.Gold Bond healing cream (tube squeezed from the middle)

3.Orange folding hunting knife (blade worn smooth)

4.Small antique pocket knife (initials carved in the handle)

5.Keychain flashlight (battery dead)

6.Marijuana vape pen (nearly empty)

7.Spray hand sanitizer (obsessively used)

8.Band-Aids (corners peeling)

9.Black plastic whistle (reason unknown)

10.CK One perfume (tiny bottle, barely a whisper left)

11.(4) Pieces of Nicorette (desperate promises)

12.A stack of business cards (people who no longer call)

13.Gray lens cleaning cloth (for eyes that saw too much)

14.Bud & Mary's car license plate sticker (dispensary advertisement)

15.Store receipts (evidence of ordinary days)

BEFORE I COULD COMPREHEND the gravity of the situation, the nurse shoved a property release log in my face and said, "She can't leave until you sign this."

I can't help thinking: am I springing her from prison or a sub-acute care facility? I really can't tell which.

THE ARCHAEOLOGY OF A LIFE

THE OTHER A CHAIN

EACH ITEM TELLS a story she never got to finish:

Apple Sugar hand cream—still half-full, waiting for hands that will never soften again.

Gold Bond healing cream—tube squeezed from the middle, the way desperate people squeeze hope from whatever's left.

Orange folding hunting knife—blade worn smooth by years of cutting through life's complications.

Marijuana vape pen—nearly empty, like the lungs that drew its final comfort.

Black plastic whistle—reason unknown, purpose forgotten, sound forever silenced.

CK One perfume—tiny bottle, barely a whisper left of the woman who wore it.

Store receipts—crumpled evidence of ordinary Tuesdays that felt eternal but weren't.

Before I could process what death actually looks like in paperwork form, the nurse thrust a property release log at me like a weapon. "She can't leave until you sign this."

Prison or care facility? The difference blurs when freedom requires a signature and leaving means dying.

At home, I arrange her purse's contents on the bed like artifacts in a museum—each piece a relic of a life that ended while I wasn't looking.

Then I understand: this isn't a catalog of death. It's an inventory of love —imperfect, ordinary, irreplaceable love that fits in a purse and breaks your heart when you finally see it all laid out like evidence of everything you'll never get to say goodbye to.

The tears come not for what's missing, but for what remains—fourteen items and infinite grief, proof that a whole life can fit on a bedspread and still feel too big to comprehend.

PART XIX
BEAUTIFUL DISARRAY

THE PECULIAR ORDINARY

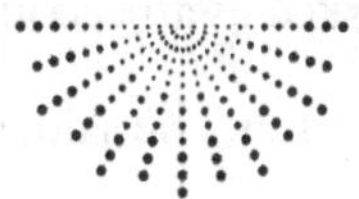

EDWARD GIBSON woke at 5:30 a.m. on Monday—as he had every Monday for the last ten years, except for holidays and vacations. On those rare mornings, he allowed himself to sleep until seven.

Nothing seemed out of the ordinary, yet he felt oddly fantastic—a buoyancy that made him consider jogging around the neighborhood. He sat up, swung his legs over the bed, and pressed his feet into the new, velvety carpet. He and Barb had just spent twenty-five hundred dollars on it, and Edward savored the plushness beneath his toes each morning.

He padded to the bathroom, brushing his teeth with the same methodical strokes he'd used for decades, then studied his reflection. At thirty-three, his hair had thinned, but his eyes still held the spark that had drawn Barb to him all those years ago. Today, that spark seemed brighter.

The shower ran hot—just the way he liked it. As steam fogged the mirror, Edward found himself humming, something he rarely did. The melody was unfamiliar but vibrated in his chest, alive with possibility.

Downstairs, Barb sat at the kitchen table, coffee mug in hand, reading Instagram. She looked up as he entered, eyebrows raised.

"You're humming," she said, not accusing, just curious.

"Am I?" He poured himself coffee from the pot she'd made. "I suppose I am."

"It's Monday, Ed. You never hum on Mondays."

He considered this, sipping the coffee. She was right. Mondays were for quiet efficiency, for bracing himself to face another week at Henderson & Associates, where he'd worked as an accountant for ten years.

"Maybe I should hum more often," he said, surprising himself.

Barb lowered her phone. "Are you feeling all right?"

"I feel wonderful, actually. Better than I have in years."

She studied his face with the same focus she reserved for Candy Crush. "You do look different. Brighter."

Edward sat across from her, their usual morning ritual, but today the routine felt charged with possibility. The kitchen, with its yellow walls and checkered curtains, seemed more vivid. Even the morning light streaming through the window looked golden, not the usual pale gray of early autumn.

"I've been thinking," he said, though he hadn't been, not really, until this moment. "About us. About what we want in life."

Barb's voice carried a note of concern. "Ed, you're scaring me a little. This isn't like you."

"Maybe that's the problem." The words escaped before he could catch them. "Maybe I've been too much like me for too long."

Barb reached across the table, placing her hand—warm and familiar—on his. Today, her touch felt electric. "What's brought this on?

Edward looked down at their joined hands, her wedding ring catching the light. Twelve years together, and he couldn't remember the last time they'd talked about wanting anything beyond their routines.

"I don't know," he admitted. "I woke up feeling like... like I could do anything today. Like the world was full of possibilities I'd forgotten."

"That's not necessarily a bad thing," Barb said carefully. "But you have that presentation at work today. The Morrison account."

The Morrison account. He'd been preparing for weeks, rehearsing his pitch for a client who'd probably approve the numbers regardless. The thought, which usually filled him with dread, felt absurd today.

"What if I didn't go?" he said.

Barb's hand tightened. "Didn't go where?"

"To work. What if I just... didn't go?"

"Edward Gibson, you've never missed a day in ten years. Not for illness, not for snow, not for anything."

"Exactly." He turned his hand palm up, interlacing their fingers. "What if today was different?"

The kitchen clock ticked steadily above the sink, marking the minutes until his usual departure. In twenty minutes, he'd typically kiss Barb goodbye, grab his iPad and electric bike, and drive the same route to the same office. He'd sit at the same desk, review the same reports, and count the hours until he could return to the same evening routine.

"Where would you go?" Barb asked quietly. "If you didn't go to work?"

Edward looked out the window at the maple tree in their backyard, its leaves just beginning to turn. "I don't know. Maybe we could find out together."

"Together?"

"When's the last time we did something spontaneous, Barb? Just because we wanted to—not because it was planned or responsible?"

She was quiet, her thumb tracing circles on his hand. "I can't remember," she said finally.

"Neither can I." Edward stood, still holding her hand, and gently pulled her up. "So what do you say? Want to find out what Monday feels like when we're not who we're supposed to be?"

Barb looked at him—really looked—and something shifted in her expression. The same spark he'd noticed in his own reflection kindled in her eyes.

"I should call in sick," she said, already deciding.

"We should call in alive," he replied, and for the first time in years, they both laughed, the sound filling their kitchen with a joy that felt both foreign and perfectly natural.

Outside, the world waited, full of possibilities they'd forgotten to notice.

They lived smack dab in the middle of the block, right where a streetlight had been installed three years ago. Barb made a stink about it to the HOA because the light was so bright it blasted through the blinds, transforming their dark, peaceful bedroom into broad daylight from ten at night until seven in the morning. "God knows why," she barked every time they laid their heads on the pillows.

Strangely, the light never bothered him. He slept like the dead, day or night. He hadn't even noticed it until Barb pointed it out. Still, he joined her crusade, fighting the good fight by her side. Nothing came of it. "A lot of wasted energy and deaf ears," he complained to his coworker after the HOA sent a letter titled: REQUEST DENIED.

Barb cried for a week after receiving the letter, which had been taped to the door. For how long? That was the million-dollar question. They hardly ever used the front door. Barb only happened to spot it on her way back from checking the mailbox.

"They didn't even have the decency to email it like normal people do. What are we, animals now?" she howled. "What if the wind had kicked up just right, Eddy, and it blew away? What if it fell into the gutter, or the neighbor's dog got ahold of it? You know how he likes to chew on anything. What then?"

He felt bad about the whole thing.

He sat there, watching twilight turn into morning light. Ed saw the whole process unfold. In all his years, maybe once—possibly twice as a boy—had he ever witnessed such a gentle sunrise. Barb was right again; it was something, all right. He'd always made a habit of keeping his eyes locked straight ahead, never on the clouds or the sky.

When they'd sit on the deck, sipping coffee with a hint of brandy, Barb would nudge him and point to the sky, the moon, or the stars—if it was nighttime—and say, "Isn't that something, Eddy?" Her face would glow as she looked at him, eyes wide with delight.

He'd watch her first, carefully, then glance at whatever she was pointing at, then back at her again, smiling and nodding. The truth was, every time he looked up, he just saw objects: balls of gas, a chunk of lunar rock. None of it moved him the way it moved her. But he'd sit out there with her through rain or the apocalypse just to be by her side.

He glanced at his cell phone. 7:05 a.m. The screen was filled with numbers for all the usual suspects from work—his superiors, department heads, and the handful of coworkers he actually considered important. All he had to do was pick up the phone and call any one of them. Let them know he was running late. "Start the meeting without me," he'd say, casually, maybe with a touch of humor in his voice. That would settle the matter.

But instead, he just stared at the phone, feeling no urgency. What was the point? Did anyone really know the point?

He sighed. Well, he thought, I'd better make myself useful. The lawn needed a trim. Normally, Adam—the "lawn kid," as Edward referred to him—handled it. Adam was thirteen and lived a few houses down. Edward despised cutting grass.

Adam was hired for two reasons: first, he was cheaper than the professionals. Grown men mowing lawns for a living never sat right with Edward. "Who in their right mind chooses to mow lawns for a living?" he'd once complained to Rick at the clubhouse. Second, Adam reminded Edward of himself, back in the day. He'd mowed lawns as a boy, sweating through the summer heat, earning a little extra money. He'd told Barb the story every time Adam came over.

Still, Adam wasn't exactly hardworking—at least, not by Edward's standards. In his memory, he'd been the hardest-working kid around, though in reality he'd been average, just like Adam. Adam always cut the lawn in a diagonal pattern and somewhere along the way lost track of where he started, leaving large patches uncut. He'd raised his prices three times already. "Mom says I need to charge more. Your lawn is the biggest—it takes me longer, or I'll have to quit," Adam would say.

It pained Edward to shell out more money for subpar work, but what could he do? The lawn kid had him over a barrel, as he'd tell Rick.

The neighborhood had a certain charm—what Rick liked to call "polished ticky-tack." Houses sat shoulder-to-shoulder. Their front lawns barely larger than a Pokémon card. Rick's hedges, planted right beside Ed's entryway, were once tall, beautiful boxwoods. Yet, after two years without a trim, they had grown wild and unruly.

Ed often reminded Rick about the boxwoods during their fish night gatherings. "They get away from you quick," he'd say, "those slender branches stretching out like claws, wild and almost monstrous. They need constant attention." He'd written the HOA a few letters, pictures included, hoping someone would finally take notice of what they were dealing with. Nothing came of it.

When Ed marched up to the HOA office, one of the board members told him they couldn't enforce the hedge rule because the code was written after Bob's house was built. "Bob's grandfathered in," she explained, choosing the word "unenforceable" with bureaucratic precision. When that failed, Ed tried to convince Bob to hire Adam. He may have exaggerated the kid's abilities and work ethic, painting him as a lawn prodigy. Bob, however, made excuses about privacy and wanting to maintain his own landscape.

Now, as Ed passed by, Bob turned off his hedge trimmer and waved. "Howdie, Edward." Bob was the only neighbor who called him by his full name. Everyone else called him Ed. "Eddy" was reserved for Barb alone—no one else dared.

A month after Bob moved in, they'd made formal introductions, Barb at Ed's side, standing on the lawn near the property line. "This is Barb, my wife, and I'm Ed. Looks like we're neighbors," Ed had said, extending his hand. He'd cringed later at the obviousness of the statement. Of course they were neighbors. Bob shook Barb's hand, then turned to Ed and smiled, his voice stout. "I imagine Ed is short for Edward." Barb giggled, waving her hand. "Oh, only his mother calls him Edward." It was clear both their names were variants, but Bob never asked if Barb was short for Barbara—which it was. When they parted, Bob waved, and Ed felt, for a moment, the awkwardness of new routines settling in.

Under normal circumstances, seeing Bob would have immediately put a scowl on Ed's face, and he'd wave back with his usual disapproving expression. But today, Ed smiled joyously—no hint of scorn, no annoyance at all. Oddly, Bob didn't bother him.

What caught Ed's attention, if only for a millisecond, was seeing Bob out there trimming the hedges. Not just the sudden motivation to tackle that eyesore, but the fact that he was skipping work. In all the eight years they'd lived next door, this was only the second time Ed had seen Bob outside during daylight hours—especially on such a perfect, beautiful morning. Bob was the ultimate workhorse: loved his job, never married, dated here and there, longest relationship a year, no kids to care for.

Back in July, while they sat out on the deck as they often did, Barb had given Ed a funny, perplexed look. "Eddy, do you think Bob doesn't like people very much? No kids. He's never been married. I'm sure he gets pretty lonely living in that house all by himself." Ed had squeezed her hand. "Nay, some people are just that way. He seems happy to me." She'd furrowed her brow. "Oh, Eddy, he's not happy. You can see it on his face." Ed shrugged, glancing upward, as though he'd said the wrong thing again. There was some truth to Barb's insight. After all, what would he be doing with his life right now if it weren't for Barb? At that moment, Ed was convinced he'd have followed Bob's path to the letter.

On the rare occasions when small talk happened between Ed and Bob, Ed always overanalyzed. He never gave much thought to what he'd say to anyone else, but with Bob, every word felt loaded. Ed prided himself on being able to get a read on people after just a few minutes of conversation, but Bob was his white whale—a hard man to pin down.

Ed raised his voice, loud enough to carry across the yard, almost yelling. "Decided to take a Ditch Day?"

Bob placed his hands on his hips, leisurely, and inhaled a deep breath of fresh air.

What were the chances of catching another neighbor—another workaholic—out in the open? Carol was the newest addition to the neighborhood, yet in all the four years she'd lived in her house, Ed had seen her only once: a Sunday afternoon, washing her red convertible in the driveway. Otherwise, it was always just glimpses—her hair catching the sun as she slipped the car into the garage, or the quick blur of her as she left with the top down.

But there she was now, sitting on the warm walkway in her Sunday best, elbows deep in soil and flowers, rearranging and sprucing things up. Ed wondered if Carol knew what she was doing, or if she was just improvising, like the rest of them. Out of a strange curiosity—and a hunch brewing inside him—he walked to the edge of his driveway and peered down the block to his left. More neighbors: some mowing, others trimming bushes, tending to flowers, edging their lawns. A quick glance to his right revealed even more people outside, all enthralled in their own outdoor projects.

Old man Warren, eighty-two, who still went into the office Monday through Friday, had skipped today. He was standing on a ladder, painting the faded house numbers on his garage.

The entire neighborhood had decided to tend to their properties—on a Monday, no less, at seven-thirty in the morning. The sight of it all startled Ed, if only for a moment.

His own lawn beckoned him. Its overgrown blades flutter in the summer breeze. He fired up the old mower, its engine rumbling with familiar grit. Ed spent ten minutes taming the front yard, then another thirty wrestling with the backyard's stubborn patches. By the time he finished, sweat clung to his shirt, and his mind felt oddly clear, as if the rhythmic hum had swept away the cobwebs of doubt.

Afterward, he found himself standing in the threshold of the master bedroom, unable to move farther, as if an invisible barrier blocked his way. Barb was no longer in bed, nowhere in sight. The bedding was in disarray. Ed cared little if the bed was made, but the emptiness in the room pressed in around him, thick and unfamiliar.

Two years ago, Barb spent thirty thousand dollars turning the basement into a gym. A state-of-the-art studio bike and a Lat pulldown machine accounted for most of the cost. Dumbbells, yoga mats, and other equipment lined the walls. Floor-to-ceiling mirrors reflected every angle, and expensive shock-absorbing mats covered the floor. Once the final touches were in place, she never set foot in the basement again.

Ed and Barb kept separate bank accounts and savings, splitting the common house bills when due. He never questioned her spending habits—at least, not out loud. But after a year went by and she still hadn't used the thirty-thousand-dollar gym, resentment simmered. One night over dinner, it finally boiled over. "How could you spend thirty thousand dollars on something you don't use? It's a complete waste of money."

Every time he thought about the gym, the number haunted him. Thirty thousand, thirty thousand, THIRTY THOUSAND, he'd mutter to himself in different tones, looping endlessly in his mind. He couldn't stop obsessing over it, and his true feelings finally spilled out after a rough day at work.

Barb looked at him in that calm, almost amused way she had. "Now, Eddy, you spent fourteen thousand on that fishing boat you took out twice in eight years. Not to mention the storage fees. I'd like to know what that's costing you every month." He gulped hard. She had a point. And just like with Adam, she had him over a barrel. He kept chewing, eyes fixed on his plate. "It's minimal, very minimal."

The fishing boat was a sore subject. When he first parked it in the driveway, John Pearson happened to walk by. John, a retired stockbroker who'd left the game at thirty-five and was now in his seventies, was the wealthiest man in the community. John had purchased a sail boat.

There was little to explain—John liked to pick on certain neighbors at the club. Ed never kissed John's ass or idolized him the way most everyone else in the community did. John made it a point to poke fun at Ed and a few others who didn't bow before him like some little king whenever the opportunity arose.

Two weeks after Ed brought the boat home, the HOA slapped a red notice on it: PARKING OF BOATS MUST BE OUT OF VIEW AND NOT ON DRIVEWAY. What could he do? He was over a barrel again. Now he had to pay a hundred and forty dollars and two cents a month to store the damn thing—his expensive toy—twenty miles down the road.

His dream of spending Saturdays on the lake—pole in hand, beer in hand, ice chest loaded and ready to chill the 'big one'—while the water was still and soundless, a cool morning breeze whistling through, not a ripple as far as the eye could see, crickets still chirping in the brush and tree line as twilight folded into morning—ended in quiet defeat. His ego bruised, he stored the boat like a wrapped Christmas gift to protect it from the winter elements, out on lot 101, right next to a sun-faded vintage RV from the eighties, tires flat, a wheel cover hanging off the rear that read: SUMMER LOVIN.

SUBMISSION TO THE CINCINNATI REVIEW / THE NEW YORKER

STANDING Ovation for One

Why we must

At the edge of life's mirror

Antiqued

I AVOID MIRRORS. The one that once hung above my bureau now sits in the hall closet, mirror side turned toward the wall. That's my world now—mirror side facing a wall. In essence, I'm escaping the ether.

My artist friend Ena came over one Saturday, and we drank two bottles of blush. We were supposed to doctor the bathroom mirrors, but we got nicely buzzed for a few hours before the work began. She lugged her art supplies up three flights to my apartment. "I can fix your mirror problem," Ena assured me.

She kept her word, as good friends do. After four cans of antiquing spray, the mirrors were transformed. "Antiqued ages glass," she told me. Like the ones you see in some French antique shops. I've never set foot

283

in an authentic French antique shop, not like Ena, but I get the idea. I've always lived three floors below my means. But now, I think it's time to buy the penthouse of my dreams. I like that—buy the penthouse of my dreams.

Not Paris. I can't see Paris as Ena once did. I'll never visit one of those authentic French antique shops, where antique mirrors have no use for antiquing. I read somewhere, someone once said, "Who needs Paris?" If I could remember who said that I'd write them a nasty letter. I'd say: I'd love Paris right about now. I need Paris.

Now, all the mirrors in my bathroom cry a dreary cry, as though caged inside a haunted castle that wails through every hour of gray. It does the trick, though. It certainly blots my naked body—my chest, especially. I'm not afraid to see the scars on my chest. Scars don't haunt. Scars are just landscapes. Landscapes of something more nefarious.

Yeah, I'm concerned about the soil beneath those landscapes. What kind of parasite is working the ground deep within? What kind of destruction is it laying to waste?

I did what everybody does after surgery: I inspected the surgeon's handiwork. Was he skilled? Or was he a butcher? You're probably wondering. Bad news for me—he was a butcher. Or maybe he hated women. Or was recently divorced. He butchered me as though I'd done something to him. The scars on my chest read: GROUND BEEF.

I don't blame him, though. Sometimes I hate my body, too. Sometimes I daydream about what it would feel like to astral project out of my body, to join the celestials in the ether somewhere. To stop running for a change. To face the inevitable. To smile at death.

A year before my diagnosis, someone hit me from behind during rush hour. The light went from yellow to red in an instant and I had to slam on my brakes. I would never have made it through the intersection without t-boning another car or being t-boned myself. And then— whack. The earth danced. My head jerked so sharply that I still get headaches from the accident.

Before the accident, I never got headaches. Not once in my entire life. Who can claim that kind of purity? No one believes me when I say it. Once, an acquaintance steered the conversation in such a way that it made me cringe. He did his best to manipulate me into confessing I lied.

I felt cancer creep, just a whisker. It was there. It was always there.

He wanted me to fabricate headaches—to claim I got them, even in their absence, just to fit his narrative. That's the onion of life: you must convince others something is wrong with you, for nothing to be wrong with you. Can he doctor my cancer, though?

Besides the headaches, I'm golden about the car accident. If it wasn't for the driver who smashed my bumper—going fifty-five in a thirty-five, texting his best friend Carl—I wouldn't be alive. I hate to admit it, but chemo is a life hack. Poison extended my life. For a little while.

Everybody knows how doctors can get. Visiting a doctor is like grocery shopping on an empty stomach. You go in for one thing, and before you know it, the shopping cart is brimming. And you're still starving, even though the cart might explode before you reach the parking lot.

My doctor outdid herself. She glided her fingers over the lump in my breast during the examination—a lump I had not felt. I would have never found it until it was too late. What twenty-seven-year-old thoroughly gives herself breast examinations?

After my diagnosis, I asked that question to my besties, even the ones I hardly spent time with. Each one was speechless. And all but one admitted they didn't examine themselves. Let that be a lesson.

Kitty was my only bestie who examined her breasts every month—automaton style. Yeah, that's right, Kitty. She's from up north, though her bloodline is Southern, where they give each other dope monikers. I guess Kitty stuck. I never asked her why they call her Kitty. Come to think of it, I don't even know her real name. I rather love the name Kitty. I wish someone would call me Kitty. It's better than Laura. Though almost everyone calls me L. L is fine, I suppose. I just wish it was Kitty.

Her mother, her grandmother, and her aunt all died from breast cancer. That's how she pronounces aunt—"ant." I call mine "auntie." During the phone call, I stopped complaining about my diagnosis and focused on Kitty's grief. I could hear her sniffling on the other end, as if she were holding a wail at bay. Her voice quivered, too. Trust me, I get it. I was on the verge a second ago myself.

Now, Kitty is one of my favorite besties. There's something about breaking bread with the cursed when you are cursed. If you've never tasted death before, you'll never comprehend the torment. Kitty ate death three times. And so, we ate death together. Cried together, many times, over a bottle of blush. Two bottles. I stop counting after two.

Kitty is twenty-five. And I scare the hell out of her because I am the possibility of her greatest fear. I know that fear. It belonged to me first. Now she knows cancer doesn't squabble over age. It's a certainty—cancer doesn't know the difference. Cancer doesn't care. I'm sure we all taste the same. Though I wonder if we each have a flavor. Chicken? Beef? Fish, anyone?

Still, if I have a flavor, I want mine to taste exotic. Exotic delights are often expensive for obvious reasons. Some rare flower that blooms only once every twenty-seven years should be expensive. Why can't we leave special things like that alone? Why must we pluck or devour the exotic?

Maybe it's human nature—always reaching for what's rare, always wanting to possess what should simply be admired. I think about Kitty, about the women in her family, and about myself. We're all part of a lineage marked by absence, by the spaces left behind when something beautiful is taken too soon.

Sometimes, I wonder if I'm rare, too. Not for the scars or the diagnosis, but for the stubbornness to keep blooming, even when the world wants to pick me apart. Maybe that's what survival is: an act of defiance, a refusal to be consumed.

I hope Kitty sees that in me. I hope, when she's afraid, she remembers that even the rarest flowers can survive another season—sometimes against all odds.

I used to think something was wrong with me.

Now, even if I let latex kitten play, no one would want me. They'd probably just feel sorry for me. They'd have no words once they caught a glimpse of my chest. Almost everyone feels sorry for me these days. And the horrified looks they give instead of words—those terrorize me more than anything.

Kitty came over again last night. I guess she's having trouble with her girlfriend. We drank more blush and ended up laughing about things, letting the night soften the edges. Then she gave me a serious look and asked, "Are you cancer free?"

I tried my best to meet her eyes but looked away. "Yes." She hugged me —the kind of hug that leeches the breath from your lungs.

"Oh, thank God," she said, her face flooded with relief. "Thank God."

I smiled and nodded. In my head, I kept thinking, I doubt there's a God. And if there is, I'm convinced God doesn't love me. "Yeah," I said, because I didn't know what else to say. I didn't want to ruin the night. I didn't want to terrorize Kitty. I'll say it again: Kitty is my best friend. And if she knew I was dying—she'd think she was next. I would.

And I hope she isn't next. I hope she makes it to New Zealand, just like she wants. I've already left her a plane ticket in my will. She has no excuse now. I hope she doesn't overthink it. Like I did.

I learned the other day that Kitty's real name is Catherine Thomas. I rather love Catherine Thomas best, more than Kitty. It rolls off the tongue sweeter—like nectar.

Denial is nectar.

Truth is, I hadn't felt right in some time. I kept pushing off going to the doctor, making excuses for my weariness. Everybody is weary these days, right? A deadline loomed—always looming in my career. But in my gut, I knew I had cancer. Don't ask me how I knew. Intuition, I guess.

I dated a guy for a year and a half. His name was Garry. Did I love him? I still wonder. Garry loved himself so much, there wasn't any room left for me. Right before we broke up, I had a feeling Garry was seeing someone else.

Like cancer, I made excuses for Garry's distance. My best guess: he grew tired of hiding in the shadows of lust. He wanted a golden hour. One day, he called and said, "We need to talk. Can we meet?"

I sensed whatever he wanted to talk about wasn't going to be swell. It surprised me when he kissed me at our favorite restaurant before I even sat down. Garry is a great kisser—was a great kisser.

After he kissed me, I thought I was in the clear. But I was nowhere near the clearing. It turned out he had room in his heart for Shiloh, not for me. Some days, I played with the idea of telling Shiloh he kissed me like he wanted to—well, you get the idea.

Someone once told me if a doctor doesn't call right away after an important test, you're in the clear. No news is, well, golden.

I was in a tizzy waiting for news. After a week, I heard nothing. I thought it was golden. Twice in my life, I was suckered into believing everything was golden. Once with Garry and seven days after my biopsy.

I raced home. From there, I cried for five days. No intervals. I did nothing. Ate nothing. Pulled the blankets over my head and bawled. My entire world, crying. My friends blew up my phone, desperate to know what the doctor said. Was it swell or shit? I wanted to tell the girls: it's shit. Like—Shit! I wouldn't pick up. I couldn't pick up. Every time I dialed a number, I wailed like a mime. What could I do? Oh, to hell with it, here's to you, blush.

After five days, I cleaned up and faced my fears. I glared at myself in the mirror of haunting tears. Swiveled my chin from side to side. Inspected my eyes. "Get comfortable, you're dying. Not today, perhaps tomorrow." Tears brim. The mirrors brim. The cancer brims. Everything in my life is now brimming. "Shit... You're dying, even though you look swell."

Once the initial shock mellowed, I made peace. I made peace with all the things I didn't do. Could have done. Deprived myself. Too expensive, silly girl, you're twenty-seven. Grow up. What will people think of you? Slap your mouth and close your eyes. Hear the world dance beneath your feet.

It's scary not to fear death, especially when you're staring down the barrel of the precipice. I was at first. I was. For a while. That fear no longer lives. Secretly, I always feared death. Even when I was a little girl. Somewhere inside me, I knew time was running thin. I couldn't bottle it anymore. Once your greatest fear spits in your eye, there's nothing left to haunt you. Then, soon, you speak its name like a bestie.

Yeah, that's right. Bad girls don't get good news. My doctor tells me I have six months, tops. "Realistically," she said, "count on three."

"Count on three."

I didn't cry. I was in shock. The only thing that came to mind was Paris. So, I asked, "Now can I see Paris?"

My doctor's face flickered with disbelief, as if gravity had shifted in the room. "Three months," she repeated, as though I hadn't heard her the first time.

I nodded. "What about Paris?" I pressed, my voice steadier than I felt. I was already picturing it: a true French mirror, aged and forgiving, reflecting not the scars but the shimmer of possibility. I imagined myself dancing in front of it, wearing kitten latex, laughing at the absurdity, swimming the ether, smiling at death—for a little while.

Maybe that's the only promise left: that I can still choose how to meet the glass, how to greet the final reflection. Maybe, for once, I get to decide what I see.

Three months. Paris. The mirror. The ether.

I think I'll go.

LION'S GATE

It's the Lion's Gate. You don't fuck with the Lion's Gate.

Sordid and raw, like an anatomically correct heart,

dwarfed by an enormous mountain looming beyond the horizon.

Her hair pulled back from her face,

eyes hungry, seeping with a thousand unspoken stories.

General debauchery dances in the shadows—

the kind that cages souls tighter than steel bars.

It's easier to cage someone than to release them.

People grow to love their cage,

even as the pain burns like a fire beneath the eye of the stove.

She was demisexual, wrapped in layers of deductive reasoning.

Katy is natural—wild, unfiltered.

She worshiped him childlike, with a devotion that burned like
Louisa of Fire.

Prison Road—the underground path for the lost,

where spindly fingers reach for salvation,

and twofers are currency in a world starving for connection.

"I present forever fire," she whispered,

eyes a trillion miles away,

while the TV hollered in the corner—whatever, whatever—

It's a static lullaby for the broken.

When I was five, our house caught fire just after midnight.

Momma barely escaped as flames devoured everything.

Three dollars was the world to someone then.

You look like the walking dead, they said.

Dummy. Sangwiches in hand,

we wondered why the world burns when your heart breaks—

pop.

Why the world liquefied before my eyes,

Melting like wax under the cruel flame of loss.

Aspen leaves no longer at the service of trunks.

Shoulders hard as marble,

Roots untethered, reaching for forgotten skies.

Veins of stone beneath a fragile guise,

Whispers lost in the wind's cold breath.

Echoes of life, defying death,

Branches once bowed now stand alone.

Carved in silence, a heart of stone,

Leaves that danced now hold their ground.

in the stillness, a new strength was found.

There are no places for sorrow to hide.

You cannot drown it with a bottle.

You cannot smoke it away.

It's the price of love.

For a sliver, you almost made it. Almost.

FOR DAYS.

My mom always bit her nails.

After my mother passed—and all the bad things that could happen to her ended at 1:24 in the morning—I realized worse things were still ahead. I could see them, clear as storm clouds, clinging to the horizon. Even though a bright star shone beside a perfect crescent moon at three, the star felt like the only good thing left to shine upon her. Shine upon us.

Eee que no.

Snow her through morphine—too much painkiller.

There are plenty of 911 towers; they'll get to you, eventually.

Whatever collects the eye falls inward, unable to escape—except through reflection.

Pitkin Avenue: dogless. Not a spark of bark, not even in the distance. Still, she hears the forest howl in the stretch, in the icy night, while the moon hangs half-staff.

MAN-CENTRIC.

Whoa, if true—"coined." But... uh... well... is it true?

Come on. Let's go.

A fairytale comes to life, presided over by shadows.

Oh, forget it then. I'm going, going, going, gone.

Commanding whatever it took in, commanding the view.
Have you ever seen beauty and couldn't see the beauty because your
heart hurt so bad, your eyes drenched in agony? That was me, on July
29th.

Likened.

My mother prayed to you when I was at death's door,

and now I do the same.

Because she's at death's door, and I pray for her.

Not because I believe in you,

but because she believed you could save a life.

Her skin mottled, blood rushing to her organs,
chain-smoking through the pain,
anointed a masterpiece of muscle and bone
resting in the hollow of death.

I don't remember once seeing my mother floss her teeth.

She'd pick at them with a toothpick or whatever was handy.

I have better oral hygiene than my mother ever did,

though my children—well, their teeth are a lost cause.

Gulag days.

I'll be goddamn.

Linda—look it, look it, listen.

The death rattle.

So many bad things happen in a person's life

that eventually, you begin to feel God has abandoned the ship.

She was in so much pain.

Her skin, paper-paper thin—Crepe paper / **Crepe Skin**

Caring for a terminal parent never leaves you. Never.

You will remember what it was like

to face all the fatalities of human sickness.

The whole bottom of her face

tried to climb into her mouth.

When you're different,
you'll always suffer the consequences of being different.

The world turned trickle-light for them.

Exuberance gone,

willows at midnight,

slammers echoing in the ward's neighborhood.

Didi.

The red pearl.

Weighing pros and cons,

hematoma blooming under her skin,

things bitten off—missing fingers,

steel turned umber with rust.

Cold, just the way I like them

> Some technological infrastructures would continue operating for a short time without human intervention. Power plants might run for days or weeks, but without ongoing maintenance, repairs, and upgrades, they would eventually fail—running out of fuel, succumbing to mechanical breakdowns, or simply degrading from neglect. The internet, too, would begin to falter. Automated systems might persist briefly, but without people to monitor, maintain, and upgrade them, they would degrade or become overloaded. Ultimately, the continued operation of any technology would depend on its specific systems and the level of automation built in. Even the most robust infrastructure is only as resilient as the hands that tend it.

SPLICED AND SHREDDED TO HELL

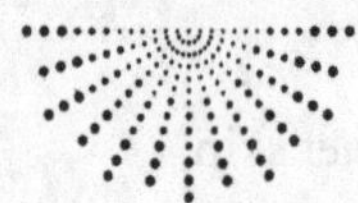

ATMOSPHERIC PLAYTIME

Everything Spontaneous

Where is Dante's mind?

Grace?

My dearest Grace.

She buries the pain deep inside herself—not for the will to
survive this ordeal, but to avenge her body. To avenge the
frail women on the road. To avenge all those who came
before her, and all those who would fall victim after. And,
Dante decides, there will be no one after her—not for the
marauders. There won't be anything after her. No pleasure.
No thrill of the hunt. Nothing. Just forever darkness.
The sun went down in a blink—sank dark in an instant. She
would not gamble with Grace's life.
Fire ripped through the house, flared up and vanished.
A dream of things never to come this way again.

Some days, the girl child refused to reason. No bargain to be had —not from spoiled upbringing, but from a spoiled heart. Some days, Grace barely hung on to the end of days. Some days, some days.

He had the elegance of a rhinoceros, the style of a wrecking ball.

The land swallowed automobiles and artificial habitations, as if the earth were hell-bent on returning what was taken—recycling everything back to its source. Geometric ruins.

Clothes piled on the floor. Female. Male. It occurred to her the squad, the rules, the refunds—percentages and numbers, all meaningless now.

"JOIN OUR TEAM. TEAM TRYOUTS."

Fallible. Negroni.

"I will die for you. I would die for him."

"Let's get you did up, boo boo," someone said, a side piece in the doorway to hell.

Unctuous still life—bird crumbs, blinded by anger. Eyes flipped toward the sun.

She looked everywhere for the combination but could not find it.

The apples tasted of mildew. And ate rubbery. Still, she ate another—swallowing seeds, core, and stem. Then another. And one more. Hunger gnawed at her, but she stopped at five. Grace needed them more, so she saved the rest.

Flies darted playfully around the bins, like dolphins at sea.

Her eyes fixed on Grace—Grace's eyes fixed back. They foraged each other's gaze, laborious, as though turning the house upside down in search of something unnamed. For what do they search? Almost synchronized, they sank and drew into one another, as if their hunger might be shared or soothed.

Notion. Scrawled. Despite. Villainize. Swaddled. Skulked. Enkindle.

She lurched forward through the bright yellow entrance, punchy and uncertain, cherry-picking moments that were comically scary—spatters of memory caught in the serrated grooves and indentations of her mind. Her face was tense with pain. Did she infect him? She wondered, watching him through horn-rimmed glasses, tortoiseshell frames, boots of emu, ostrich, cobra, gator, kangaroo—each step tuned to hunger.

He was the type who asked too many questions. Artsy, with an air kiss—kiss, kiss—seeking inward pleasure, his eyeballs swaying with each unspoken thought.

SHE HAD an unobstructed view of fiery death, hidden by nothing but a rusted pump. Kenji. Kanji. I'm not amused—do you think you're cute?

OUT OF NOWHERE, it leaped at her—fearless, demon energy in its throat, demon palace in its eyes. State of living as: marked by fang.

WHEN THE SUN REFUSES TO RISE

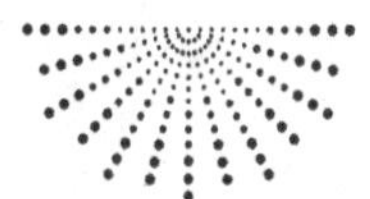

Some mornings, the world simply does not obey the old rules. The sun, which should rise in the east, seems to withhold its light, or emerges from the west, or not at all. On cloudy days, the wait for morning stretches into the afternoon, and sometimes the light never truly arrives. The longing for sunlight becomes a quiet ache, a hope that flickers even at three in the afternoon. When the day remains dim, a heaviness settles in—a depression that is as real as the missing sun.

There is a light that sometimes rises from the west, late and uncertain, shining high above the roofline, unreachable. The ancient sun god, Inti, once a constant presence, now feels distant or absent. The sky becomes a puzzle, the sun's path unpredictable. In these moments, it's easy to feel small—an ant beneath the gaze of a magnifying glass, powerless before a force that once offered warmth and certainty.

But the truth is clear, the sun's absence is not just a fancy of weather or chance. Some days, the light is blotted out by more than clouds. The aftermath of brutal acts—physical and psychological abuse—can obscure the sun as surely as any storm. The world's brightness dims, and the familiar rhythms of daybreak are disrupted. The pain and trauma cast their own shadows, making it hard to find the light, even when it's there.

Yet, in naming this darkness, there is a kind of defiance—a refusal to pretend, to accept the silence. Acknowledging that the sun does not rise as it once did is an act of honesty, a step toward healing. Even when Inti hides and the morning arrives late, your longing for light is a testament to hope and survival. The sun's path may have changed, but the desire for its warmth endures.

FALLING, FALLING—
FOREVER FALLING

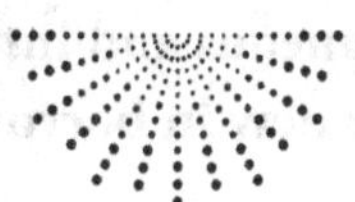

Kismet whispers in the cold air,

Paris Creed etched in the frost.

Hikers, both present and gone,

icy mud sluices around her sodden socks.

Her skin shifts with the water's touch—

from gray talus stone to alabaster glow.

Her hair, once platinum, now gleams golden.

He was super great! Very patient

Fifty-three minutes—

stealing whatever breath remains,

gobbling air, dimming the sun.

An apparition crouched,

losing touch, side by side

at a rendezvous with memory—

Javice, threadbare, punchy at the core.

Cookery scents the goyish cabin,

strictly kosher, kashrut observed to the letter.

**Spontaneous and intimate,
ritual made new in borrowed spaces.**

"Sick, bro, that thing looks sick,"

**Echoes in the rafters,
mistrust and suspicion threading the air
as the light flickers,
uncertainty crouched in the corners.**

Has your brain turned to glass?

Generalist

Stratosphere

Disassociation

Sovereignty

Flickering

Raine

Minutiae

Disappearing and reappearing

The hum of the dishwasher and the clinking of dishes being sterilized by
razor hot water.

Cluck

Jollities

Catatonic

The forest was crying. Pine needles crying. Leaves crying. Birds perched high above, crying. Pine sap weeping. All the lushness the world could muster—crying.

She stood there, holding up the whole goddamn world, trying to keep the end of days from nipping at her heart, her throat, her lifeline. Fooling her dumb ass into believing she could escape. That she could have a life. That she could absorb the fallout of a world wiped out in a blink of sprite.

Woe—she did not escape.

Who the fuck is left to cry in the absence? In the blackness of an iris. Who the fuck is left to care, anyway—who the fuck knows—who knows.

A STEW OF WORDS

Ting ting. The sound echoed softly, like a distant bell. **Ponsa's** glare cut through the dim light, eyes sharp and unyielding. She held the gene test in her hand—**peppered** with **red-lacquered** symbols, an analog relic in a **world drowning in molecular data**.

Auditory hallucinations whispered **herbaceous secrets**, voices from the nightshade family curling around her thoughts. It was the worst day of her life—everything had gone wrong.

Her feet shuffled along the **cracked earth**, searching for where the dead marauder had fallen. She held her breath, the **pith of an orange** pressed between her fingers, its scent a fleeting comfort.

A **snail chewing gum** passed by, slow and deliberate. "Everybody thinks I'm way, way different," she muttered. "But I have a secret deep down. I'm not who they think I am."

Cathartic waves surged through her as she tried to obviate the chaos in her mind—iteration after **iteration of memories, like switchbacks on a mountain trail**. She was a reproductive biologist emblazoned with the weight of her discoveries, caught amid **wheels and cogs** of steel and gold—the superlative **mark of autonomy**, responsibility, and integrity.

Yet, today felt worthless.

Maladaptive daydreaming tugged at her sanity, **yucking** the yum from her resolve. **Molecular fragments** of hope scattered like **nendo**—fragile, fleeting. She was a crackerjack, a **jim** dandy in the lab, but could she feel her own heartbeat beneath the weight of her white lab coat?

"Eff it," she whispered, eyes blazing with defiance.

S

The stars were on fire

Specks

Grit her teeth

URBAN BLIGHT

subparticles

He wasn't even a distant version. He was himself, wholeheartedly.

PRIMITIVE BEAUTY

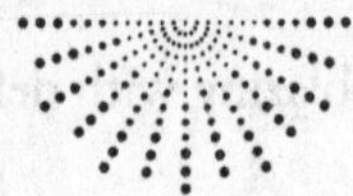

Lizzie's Interview

There's something uncomfortable—almost awkward—about staring straight into the camera. The model's pose isn't quite right, the background color feels off, and nothing seems to align the way it should. But that's exactly where the beauty begins.

The true artistry of your photography lies in its imperfection. In the rawness. You capture emotion as it is—unfiltered, unretouched, as visceral as a human moment can get. At first, the viewer might wonder: What is this? The lighting is wrong. The pose is out of sync. The background is imperfect. What am I looking at?

But the longer you look, the more you begin to understand. Slowly, you realize you're having a spiritual experience—a deeply human encounter. The photograph becomes more than an image; it's a return to something essential, something honest. It's art that reaches beyond aesthetics and touches the soul.

That's what makes your work truly remarkable. It's authentic. It reminds us that beauty doesn't come from perfection, but

from presence, vulnerability, and the courage to show things
as they really are.

CADENCE—PREACHY, almost chanting.

Two spirits, ancestors circling the room,

their voices echoing through the bones of the house.

"NORFORM," they intone, a word heavy as ritual.

Purple crying—wails that cycle like a dishwasher,

round and round, sudsing the air with sorrow.

A campaign for mental health flickers in the background,
while silver atoms and reagent densely accumulate,
the Polaroid's chemical chain reaction spreading
like a Rorschach test against white plastic—
light exposing imagoes, camera-tongued and anachronistic.

WHITING AWARDS.

Reconstruction, unexplained, is adaptation—

living angels contorting their faces,

traipsing between hope and surrender.

Forgetting you have cancer—now that's a trick on its own.

How does one dupe the mind?

Eyes whizzed and wobbled,

bean-counter—killjoys tallying days,

heartless and ambivalent all at once.

We move forward, chanting,

two spirits in one body,

traipsing through the imagoes of memory,

searching for meaning in the silver shadows.

Educated, capable—yet consumed by **demonic delirium and hysteria**.

His eyes, screwy as hell, flickered with madness.

The world slipped through **her gaze**,

like every **grain of sand** the earth could carry—

all the weight of time and memory,

slipping away, lost to the void.

DRAGGED THOSE EYES

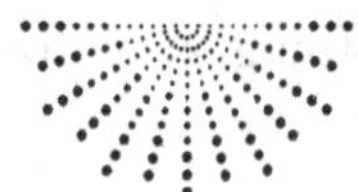

HE DRAGGED HIS EYES—NO, his eyes crawled to the other side of the room, slow as insects beneath the glass. The acoustics wavered, every sound scrawled jagged across the walls, as if the room itself suffered from a split personality.

HE WAS THE EXCEPTION, they said. Sensible. Natural. Kind, even. Yet here he sat, twisted in a swivel chair, an honor program graduate trained to think independently—now shadowed by the dark lord of whatever haunted his mind.

CORRUGATED SHADOWS SLITHERED along the baseboards, sinuous and restless. Vertigo washed over him, a giddiness rising in his throat, as if the world itself had begun to tilt.

FEIGNING MEDICAL-KNOW-HOW, he delivered the news with clinical detachment—emotionless, as if reciting a line from a textbook:

"YOU'RE GOING TO DIE IN TWO WEEKS. SO
THERE. GOOD LUCK."

ICK.

THAT MORNING, I brushed my teeth with mashed potatoes. The starchy grit was strangely soothing, a comfort for a mouth too numb for mint.

MY BONES TURNED to jelly beneath the weight of his words. I felt like a cosmonaut adrift—untethered, floating in a body losing gravity, the familiar rules of existence dissolving.

ON THE TABLE, a floppy pen and a golf pencil—eraser-less, primitive tools—waited for me. They belonged to another era, a time when mistakes were permanent and knowledge was fragile. I gripped them, searching for something solid to hold.

PRIMITIVE PEOPLE, I thought, must have faced endings with more grace. No sterile words, no cold facts—just the raw, unfiltered truth of living and dying.

LIZZIE / JOSHUA

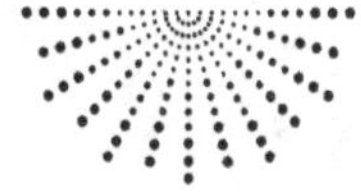

What's choice, really?

Lizzie never felt as though she belonged anywhere. Something inside me whispers, I don't belong here. I don't know where I belong, but I know—in my gut—I don't belong here. I never did. I never belonged in Richard's house. And now, finally, I go to find home.

Richard was a meat eater; that's why Lizzie hated meat.

Although I suspect Mary was trying to make her own grand escape too—by way of Glenlivet—eighteen years.

The spirit was meant to run free.

You couldn't fool death, and even though she knew it was coming, it didn't hurt any less to watch her mother slip away before her eyes. In that moment, everything else felt moot— words, comforts, even time itself. The finality of loss rendered all

311

arguments and explanations meaningless, leaving only the raw ache of absence.

The drink will fortify

Micro cabin

A trillion tears to nowhere
Don't worry, I'll be sober and poppy come-tomorrow
His fingers spread wide and scattered all over his face like giant spiders.

His eyes sliced hard left

Morning in the Woods

The woods were unalive at morning hour, light hour. Only the occasional bird song pierced the stillness, and now and then, furry creatures scratched up the tree bark—quick, furtive movements betraying their presence. All the nocturnals were turning in their sleep, hidden away in burrows and hollows, the forest holding its breath between night's secrets and the day's awakening.

Faces and Unspoken Trouble

His face grew troubled, the worry brewing not from within, but reflected and rising from her face. Sometimes, the emotions of one person ripple outward, catching another in their current—her anxiety mirrored in the tension of his brow, the tightening of his jaw. In that silent exchange, the woods themselves seemed to echo their unease, the hush broken only by the faintest signs of life.

Note on Geography

Denver is located in the Northern Hemisphere. This means it experiences seasons in sync with most of North America and Europe—winter from December to February, summer from June to August, and so on. The city's position also influences its daylight hours, weather patterns, and ecological rhythms, all of which shape the experience of mornings in the woods nearby.

A KISS from the Devil

SHE TOOK her shoes off at the door, but left behind only the faintest, most microscopic footprint—one that no eye could see, no ear could hear. Her presence was marked not by sound or sight, but by the subtle, lingering scent of synthetic strawberries, drifting through the hallway like a memory. It was the kind of fragrance that clung to dolls from childhood, innocent yet oddly haunting.

She was squeaky clean—so clean that even the housekeepers remarked on it. Not a single hair in the bathtub, not a strand in the sink. They found it strange. When does a teenage girl not leave a single hair behind? She moved through the house as though she were a phantom, her existence confirmed only by the occasional wisp of strawberry that grazed you from behind, just enough to send a chill up your spine. Sometimes, it felt like someone was stepping over your grave.

Was it Lizzie, or was it just your imagination playing tricks? She appeared only in the periphery—a fleeting shape in the mirror, a brief figure at the corner of your eye. She left no trace but her scent, an aura that lingered long after she'd passed by, making you question whether she'd ever been there at all.

In her wake, the house felt both emptier and more alive, haunted by the gentle mystery of someone who could be everywhere and nowhere, seen only in glimpses, sensed only in the faint sweetness of strawberries in the air.

FORTY YEARS OF HUNGER

You don't know this, not yet anyway, but soon you will. I am your son. I am your son. I keep repeating this phrase because it feels good to finally admit it to myself, and to you. I've held on to that secret far too long.

I hope this letter finds you well. I am better now. I wasn't before. But please don't worry, I'd hate to think you'd worry.

India set the letter down, her hands trembling, the paper crackling in her grip. Rain battered the hood of the car—tiny thumps against glass and metal, a careless symphony of water and machine. The air inside was thick and humid, tinged with the scent of mildew leaking from the vents. She drew a deep breath, heart pounding in her ears, and let it out in a long, slow sigh, as if releasing pressure from a wound she couldn't name.

One, two, one, two—she whispered, counting breaths. Inhale. Exhale. Lower the heart rate. It's just a letter. A typed letter, on paper so old it seemed to hum with secrets. Who still uses a typewriter? Where would anyone even find one now? Still, her eyes returned to the letter, hungry for answers.

You don't know this, but I have spent forty years of hunger waiting for you. Somewhere in the world, a boy waits for his father to toss a ball back to him, in a park, a backyard, roughhousing, learning how to shave. I waited for a hug. A mother's embrace. My mother's embrace. Fathers are good at some things, but now I know a man can never replicate the complexity of a mother's heart.

I waited to hear your heartbeat, to press my ear to your chest, the same heartbeat I heard for seven months and three days. Do you think it's crazy that I remember what it was like to live in your womb?

The paper jittered between her fingers, fragile as old parchment. Womb, seven months, three days—what did it all mean? Poetry, or confession? She was mother to no one. The last time she'd been on a date was two years ago; the dinner spiraled quickly, ending not in intimacy, but in an Uber escape. Why her? Why now?

You have not waited for me, not because you lacked the desire, but because you had no way of knowing what the future held. And neither did I. I had not been born yet. I don't have much time left, and there are so many words I want to say to you. Time is an illusion. Remember that. That's why we can never meet as we are now.

But I want you to see my world. There is a small cottage outside of town, tucked in the foothills. I found peace there, and maybe you will too. It is there you'll find the answers.

Love,

your only son,

Graham.

231 Beech Court Trail

Golden, Colorado 80401

She folded the letter, sliding it back into the envelope edged with red, white, and blue dashes—miniature barber poles, she thought. The front bore a red stamp: VIA AIRMAIL CORREO AEREO * PAR AVION. Spanish words, puzzling, deepening the mystery of Graham.

She typed the address into her phone. Eighteen point four miles. Twenty-four minutes from Denver.

India had never needed a car. Her life fit inside a five-mile radius—work, groceries, the Greek place on East 12th, the botanical gardens, city park.

She walked, even in snow. If she needed to, she'd bus or Uber it. Most of her life was within reach. But mostly, her life revolved around reading. Always reading. And writing. And now, with the first snow, storytelling season had arrived—a time when elders passed down knowledge to the tribe.

She pressed the Uber app, then hesitated. Did she dare make the trip? Graham would not—could not—meet her. But what would she find at 231 Beech Court Trail? Forty years of hunger echoed in her mind. She was thirty-three and hungry. Hungry her whole life—for something unnamed. Maybe she'd never discover what it was. Graham had found a loophole to feed his hunger. Still, a concern lingered, she was no one's mother, only a daughter—born from a mother, searching for a place to belong.

It was a little past midnight. Fat flakes of snow danced in the streetlamp's glow, swirling like a snow globe. The roads were wet and shellacked, too warm for the snow to stick. The nearest Uber, a lux version, was two minutes away. The next, more affordable, was twenty-five. Minutes later, she was in a brand-new Escalade, clutching the letter. The synthetic leather smell filled the cabin.

A slender, brown-haired woman drove. India was surprised to see a woman behind the wheel at midnight. You could never be too careful these days. Still, she climbed into a stranger's SUV to find a man she'd never met—Graham, or his ghost.

This girl—this driver—had made a profession of it. Dolled up, meeting strangers at night, ferrying them through the city's arteries. Dim lights drifting toward another light, like whip-poor-wills calling out to moths and beetles.

The Escalade's headlights lit the road with white incandescence. She'd chosen silent mode. She never chatted with drivers—not out of dislike, but because she rarely had anything to say. Not to anyone. Not to coworkers, her boss, the cashier at Whole Foods, or Ms. Howell, the neighbor who pried and gossiped. Ms. Howell always asked, "How can a pretty girl like you not have a boyfriend? Don't you get lonely?" India sometimes wanted to say, "Yes, I am very lonely, Ms. Howell, because all the good girls are taken. "The city has plumb run out of good girls." Not that she was gay—she found men physically delicious, but hollow and clueless in other ways. Most men had no map to a woman's heart, which canceled out the delicious part. She didn't care if the building thought she was gay. She just despised the idea that a woman's completeness depended on a man at her side, above, or below.

But what about Ms. Howell? Was she a spinster by choice or by fate? Did Mr. Howell get his ticket punched early, or was there never a Mr. Howell?

No, the truth was, India had nothing meaningful to say. An elder once told her, "You suffer from partial soul loss." Spiritual emptiness—a rare and dangerous thing. She needed a healer to entice her soul back with drumbeats, firelight, and patience. If it ever found its way home.

The truth was, she had plenty to say on paper. But speaking was another matter. In crowds, her tongue tangled, thoughts scattered, and honesty often insulted. Her mind never rested. Some nights, she didn't sleep at all, thoughts and stories swirling until she wrote them down.

It had been three weeks since she last saw Wanikiy (Savior). Then, after three weeks, the letter arrived. Wanikiy had been her savior for a time, meeting her at her lowest. But after a series of exchanges—her words for his—the meetings stopped. His words were always poetic, clear, simple yet complex. His prose—my god, his prose—assembled everyday language into stories with hidden meanings, lessons woven so subtly the reader never realized they were being taught. His hands, his words, were the catalyst for the elders' storylines—stories that traced a direct line to her heart.

The SUV inched along a wet, two-lane road, winding through the foothills. Everywhere the headlights landed, plump snowflakes greeted them like fallen stars. Evergreens and wild grasses lined the road. On a cliff above, two deer and a fawn watched, demon eyes glowing in the dark, startled by the engine's hum and white lights.

India lowered the window. A crisp breeze brushed her face. The air carried the scent of deer, sodden fur, pine sap, and hemlock.

At the summit, the road straightened and climbed into darkness, another peak looming ahead. A pure moon hung high, casting a glow on the snow-dusted treetops and hills. Every wild acre was crowded with evergreens, no room to spare in that vast region.

231 Beech Court Trail was nearly invisible. Only two razor-red driveway markers hinted at its existence—a dirt road, not an illusion, not a trick of the trees.

The Uber driver turned down the dirt road. More deer glared at the headlights, darting into the forest. Evergreens squeezed the SUV into a bottleneck, the path narrowing, the terrain rough. India bounced against the door, then slid the other way as the road tilted.

The driver's confidence faded as the road climbed, darkness deepening, trees pressing in. Even India, who'd traveled the foothills before, felt a shiver of sympathy.

Branches draped the road, scrubbing the Escalade's body. A piercing screech ran along the side, making both women cringe. India imagined a branch gouging the paint, deep enough to strike metal.

"Shit!" the driver muttered, face twisted in anger.

India, guilt rising, said, "It's not that much farther."

The driver stopped and glared at her. "Why didn't you warn me the road would be this bad? I wouldn't have attempted it. This is a hundred K. Do you have a hundred K?"

India was stunned. She'd never imagined an SUV could cost that much. She'd always guessed fifty, tops. Note to self: double your estimate next time.

And yes, she did have a hundred K sitting in the bank—well, more like six hundred, and some change. She lived in a studio apartment and well below her means. She even bought her undergarments at Walmart.

Still, she felt awful—truly awful—about putting a hundred-thousand-dollar SUV through the meat grinder. The first time she'd traveled here, the path was wider, not overgrown. Nothing like what it was now.

"Won't Uber cover the damages? You're on company time—" she started, but the driver rolled her eyes, disbelief written all over her face. Another way of saying, What are you smoking?

India fished a business card from her purse and handed it to the driver. "If they don't cover you—which I think they should—just call me. I'll pay for the damages." Saying it felt like a hundred thousand knives gutting her. Could the damages really be that much? Secretly, the words gnawed at her insides. "I didn't know it would be this bad. I'm sorry." The driver fought not to cry, but tears trailed down her cheeks anyway, making India feel even worse. Somewhere, a pragmatic thought floated up: "It might not be that bad. Sometimes noises sound worse than they are."

Her words didn't fix things, but they were enough to keep going. The Uber driver stayed quiet and resumed inching the SUV through the mess. What else could she do? India's words proved true as the road began to widen, the trees falling away quickly. A massive manmade clearing appeared, pitch-black except for the snow dusting everything, the moonlight making the world sparkle. The clearing was vast, and at its center stood a peculiar structure, gleaming in the distance like some Antarctic laboratory.

Several industrial shipping crates were stacked geometrically—Feng Shui style, or something like it—to form a dwelling. It was a scientific arrangement, ill-fitting, propped up against the wild and natural elements. The exterior fooled the eye into thinking it was dipped in concrete: sharp edges, a smooth finish.

No lights shone inside. The structure, blanketed in snow, looked abandoned for years—shipwrecked. India stepped out of the SUV, but instead of heading toward the building, she circled to the driver's side. She turned on her phone's flashlight and inspected the scratch. The Uber driver lowered her window, craning her neck to see. "How bad is it?"

Scenarios raced through India's mind. The damage looked worse than she'd imagined—far worse. The scratches were so deep they defied the bad lighting. Now all she could think about was the trip back; the passenger side would soon match the driver's, completely unavoidable. India said nothing, just shook her head with a grave expression, as though the Escalade had suffered a dishonorable death. The Uber driver started to cry again. In moments like these, India had a way with people in need.

The driver's hands gripped the window rim, knuckles white with cold. She was practically climbing out for a better look but didn't open the door to see for herself. "I don't think you should drive back down in the dark," India said, glancing at her phone: 1:05 a.m. "We should wait for daylight. Maybe we can find something to trim the branches, so the other side won't get scratched."

The Uber driver stayed silent, eyes fixed on the structure. It didn't offer a pleasant view or a warm welcome—just a sketchy, uneasy presence looming in the clearing.

"Is this your place?" she asked, her voice already trembling.

India shook her head. She had no idea what she'd find beyond that door —if it was even unlocked. No way of knowing what waited inside.

"No," she answered.

The driver frowned, almost whining, "Then who lives here?"

There was no easy answer. Only more questions, and India had none of the answers. "His name is Graham."

The name seemed to puzzle the driver. "Graham? Graham?" She repeated it, as if the syllables themselves were a riddle. "What kind of name is that?"

India loved the name. Her favorite author, Graham Astor—a woman— had won Pulitzers, a Nobel, and every other major prize. The greatest author of the twenty-first century, a late bloomer who wrote seven novels in a decade, the last published after her death. EVERYTHING SPONTANEOUS. India had read every word. Graham Astor could whisk a reader away, her prose a force of nature, her name a promise of transformation.

"Does it matter?" India snapped, the cold night pressing in. "What choice do you have? It's this—" she pointed to the structure, its silhouette stark in the moonlight, "or back that way." She swung her finger toward the darkness, the narrow dirt road vanishing into the trees.

The silence between them was thick, the clearing holding its breath. Snow drifted, the moonlight glinting off the crates, the forest crowding the edge of the world. The SUV's engine ticked as it cooled, a faint heartbeat in the vast, frozen night.

India stepped forward, the letter pressed to her chest. She felt the weight of all her hunger—forty years' worth—echoing inside her. She didn't know what waited beyond the door. She only knew she had to open it.

Behind her, the driver hesitated, caught between fear and the impossibility of turning back. In that moment, with the world poised between wilderness and the unknown, India understood: every journey is a wager, every answer another question, every hunger a story waiting to be told.

And so she crossed the clearing, snow crunching beneath her boots, the letter trembling in her hand, and disappeared into the shadow of the house—leaving the night, and the reader, wide open to wonder what comes next.

HOW THE GODS KILL

"Tell me all the ways you'd save the world."

BELLA STANDS at the edge of a crumbling cathedral, where moonlight seeps through shattered stained glass and paints the stone floor with bleeding colors. She is seventeen forever, her face a portrait of innocence, her eyes ancient and unblinking. Time has not touched her, not in the way it gnaws at mortals. She is both witness and warden. A phantom in the attic of history, drifting through centuries with the hush of a secret never spoken.

Once, Bella believed her gifts—immortality, the power to give or take life—were a blessing. Now, they feel like a curse, a heavy locket of guilt and longing pressed to her chest. For ages she watched the world's slow spiral. Each civilization collapsing into the same fevered self-obsession. But the twenty-first century is different. The hunger is louder, the mirrors more crowded, the darkness at the edges more absolute.

She moves through the world unseen, her presence felt only in the shiver of candle flames and the sudden hush of birds at dusk. She has resolved, at last, to act. She will take life from those who poison the earth and give it to those who might heal it. But the world is a labyrinth of shadows, and Bella cannot read minds. That was always Darrian's gift—Darrian, her brother, her rival, her betrayer.

Darrian:

Darrian lingers in the city's underbelly, where neon flickers against rain-slicked pavement and the air hums with secrets. He is the shadow behind every reflection, the whisper in every crowd. Unlike Bella, he ages—slowly, imperceptibly, but the years etch themselves in the corners of his eyes, the silver at his temples. His mind is a labyrinth, a hall of mirrors, and every thought in the city echoes there.

He remembers Bella—her voice like a bell tolling in the ruins, her gaze both accusation and plea. He remembers the loves he stole, the wounds he left, the thousand years of silence that grew between them like a wall of thorns. He knows what she is planning; he feels the tremor of her intent in the psychic current that binds them. He knows she will fail. Mortals are not chess pieces. Their souls are wild, unpredictable, and even gods cannot read every move.

Darrian walks the midnight streets, listening to the pulse of mortal minds. He feels their hunger, their loneliness, their desperate hope. He knows the world is teetering, and he knows Bella's interference will only hasten the fall. Yet he cannot help but ache for her. His sister, his mirror, his only equal. He wonders if she will ever forgive him, or if forgiveness is just another human myth.

Bella:

When Bella finally intervenes, the world recoils. She grants life to the cruel and snuffs out the gentle. The good prove monstrous; the wicked, capable of grace. Mortals are more cunning, more layered, than she ever imagined. Her touch, meant to heal, hastens the world's unraveling. The planet lurches toward annihilation, and Bella's heart is a mausoleum of regret.

To set things right, she must find Darrian, and breach the centuries of silence and spite. But as she stands beneath the ruined arches, moonlight pooling at her feet, she wonders, are these fragile creatures worth the agony? The planet will heal itself in time—thousands of years, a blink to the gods. And Bella, eternal and alone, has nothing but time.

Darrian:

Darrian watches from the shadows, waiting for the moment when Bella will seek him out. He knows she will come—she always does, in the end. He wonders what he will say when she arrives, what price they will pay to mend the world, or each other. The city breathes around him, restless and alive, and Darrian closes his eyes, listening for the footsteps of a sister he has never stopped loving, never stopped fearing.

Together:

The world holds its breath, poised between ruin and redemption, waiting for the verdict of gods who are all too human. In the cathedral's ruins and the city's veins, Bella and Darrian circle one another, haunted by guilt, bound by blood, and shadowed by the knowledge that even gods can be undone by love.

MEET ME AT OCEAN'S END

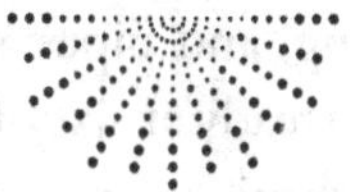

Meet me at ocean's end,
where the green furrow grows.

My dearest Noah,
I hope this letter finds you. I know that when you read
this, I will be erased from your mind. Do not let your heart be
saddened, I am with you always. It is a rare blessing to find
the love of your life, and to have a baby girl like Aden.

Mind Over Heart

IN FOUR DAYS—SO says the neurologist, though it's not an exact science—I, Noah Taylor, will cease to exist on planet Earth. My body will go on, performing the rituals of living: sleeping, eating, shaving, all under careful supervision—a nurse or an assistant always nearby. I'll eat, drink, shuffle from room to room, maybe play chess or blackjack with a stranger. The pressure of winning or losing will fade. I'll just be glad to play. I'm not sure what any of it means. I don't recall ever being competitive. Will I remember to brush my teeth? Why is oral hygiene so important? I think about it far too much, and for the life of me, I don't know why. Was I obsessed with clean teeth? I'm afraid to ask. I doubt anyone else would care.

But my mind—my true self—will be wiped away. My body will persist until it forgets how to eat, or simply refuses to, or until thirst takes me. That's the usual path. Soon, I'll no longer be Noah. I'll be known as case study C2304.

My internal plumbing, wiring, and pipes are all in working order. My heart is stout at 98/78, pulse steady at sixty-five. Lungs strong as an ox—double check. Organs, youthful, twenty-something, says the internal medicine man. Not the organs of a typical forty-three-year-old. Was I forty-three? I'm not sure. I was too scared to ask. Everything is fuzzy. Some things—worthless things—I recall easily. I remember working out at the gym five days a week. What good did that do? Sometimes I wonder if I ever really went, or if my brain invented it.

Lately, a woman I hardly recognize visits my room. When I see her, I want to call her Sarah, but something inside tells me that's not her name. There's a yellow notepad on my bedside table. When my brain gets stuck, I consult it. How I remember to look for the notepad is a mystery to me and the doctors. No one can explain it. On the first page, in someone's terrible handwriting, it reads: "A beautiful woman with long blond hair, a pleasant smile, and kind eyes, wearing a red jacket, is your wife. Her name is Jillian." The woman who visits fits this description. I read the note, I smiled, and I said, "Hello, Jillian." I'm not sure I can pull it off. Maybe my eyes falter, or my face betrays me. Still, I say her name, and her eyes well up. She seems unconvinced that I know her—or myself. She's fighting like hell to hold back a storm.

She asks how the food is, but I can't remember the time of day or when I last ate. There's a window in my room that overlooks the street. The sky is gray, frost creeps across the glass. It must be cold outside. I don't know if it's breakfast or lunch. I rule out dinner—it's too light. I don't want to make her cry by answering incorrectly. I look at her, try to be convincing, and say, "It's hospital food." It feels natural. Maybe I was a smartass in my former life. She smiles, and I smile. Her smile clears the sky, lifts the mood that would otherwise drag us both down. She's so lovely. There's a light radiating from her, a fuchsia aura. Her scent is hypnotic. Floral notes drift from her, and I travel back in time. I remember her lips against mine. She tastes like oranges—at least, that's what my mind tells me. She smells of musk and flowers. For a moment, I remember holding her in my arms at night, in bed, her skin soft and velvety. We laugh. She sleeps. Then I sleep. Then nothing.

SYMMETRY

YOUR EYES ARE LYING to you

FREE WILL IS AN INSTRUMENT / INSTRUMENTS OF FREEWILL

IT TAKES a lot of courage to play the hand you're dealt.

SIBYL OF TAROT

Sibyl closed her eyes and calmly answered the phone.

Heavy breathing filled the line, a man, she sensed. She didn't bother with pleasantries, "How can I help you." Instead, she waited, letting the silence stretch, knowing the man would speak first.

Seconds passed. Still, only the sound of his breath. Breathing was good. She could dial in on a person's soul by the rhythm and weight of their breath alone, but something about this man was off.

Sibyl tried to read his thoughts, as she did with most callers, but his mind was a fog. Then, a flash electrified her brain: an image of a dark-haired boy, five or maybe four, sitting in front of a television, crying. On the screen, a western played—cowboys and Indians charging on horseback, rifles firing, tomahawks and arrows slicing the air.

She let the television fade and focused on the boy. He had stuffed his fingers in his mouth, gnashing his teeth, sobbing to self-soothe. The more Sibyl zeroed in, the more the background sharpens, horrific screams, a man and woman fighting, the man shouting, the woman begging him to stop, glass shattering, walls trembling. An odor drifted in—was it bacon? Breakfast? She couldn't place it.

Before she could identify the scent, the man on the other end cleared his throat. "Is this Sibyl?"

"Who are you? How did you get my number?"

He fell silent, his voice thin and cowardly. Another pause. "I'm going to hang up now. Don't call again."

"Please," he pleaded, his voice barely above a whisper. "Steve gave me your number."

"Be specific," Sibyl demanded, her tone sharp. The man's breathing grew heavier, as if he suffered from asthma or some secret illness.

More silence. The vision of the dark-haired boy faded, as if the man's presence blocked her gift. "Goodbye, mister."

"Steve Howell," the man said, desperate now. "Steve Howell," he repeated, his desperation dimming to resignation.

"Who's the dark-haired boy crying in front of the television?" Sibyl asked. She already knew the answer—pain wrapped itself around every syllable he spoke.

—Remix—

Sibyl closed her eyes and answered the phone, calm and steady. On the other end, a man's heavy breathing filled the silence. She didn't bother with a greeting, didn't offer a "hello" or a "how can I help you." She simply waited, letting the seconds stretch, listening to the rhythm of his breath.

Breathing was good. She could usually dial in on a person's intent from the subtle nuances of their exhalations alone. But something about this man was off—his presence felt slippery, clouded, as if he were hiding behind the static.

She tried to reach into his mind, as she did with most, but his thoughts were a locked box. Then, without warning, a jolt of electricity flashed through her brain—a vision: a dark-haired boy, maybe five, maybe four, sitting in front of a television, crying. Cowboys and Indians clashed on the screen, rifles cracking, arrows whistling. The boy stuffed his fingers in his mouth, gnashing his teeth, desperate to self-soothe.

Sibyl's focus shifted from the TV to the boy's pain. In the background, a man and woman screamed at each other—his voice thunderous, hers pleading, begging him to stop. Glass shattered. The walls trembled. An odor drifted in, sharp and greasy. Bacon? Was it breakfast? She tried to pin it down, but before she could, the man on the phone cleared his throat.

"Is this Sibyl?"

She opened her eyes, voice cool. "How did you get my number?"

Silence. The breathing continued, rough, almost asthmatic. Then, a timid reply, "Steve gave me your number."

"Be specific." She sharpened her tone, pushing back against his evasiveness.

More silence. The vision of the boy faded, as if the man's presence on the line was blocking her abilities. She felt a flicker of frustration. "Goodbye, mister."

"Steve Howell," the man blurted, desperate now. "Steve Howell," he repeated, voice trembling.

Sibyl pressed her advantage. "Who's the dark-haired boy crying in front of the television?" She already knew but needed to hear it from him. There was a knot of pain in the boy's life, and she needed to know if the man was ready for the truth—his truth.

He cleared his throat again. "The dark-haired boy... is me."

"Is Steve dead?"

His breathing quickened, excitement edging in. "You were doing so well."

"I'm hanging up now."

"If you do," his voice dropped, sinister and cold, "he'll die before you can end the call, Sibyl."

A new vision crashed over her, Steve, tied to a chair in a barn, a cow lowing in the distance. Blood trickled from his head, down his neck. His hands were bound, mouth sealed with duct tape. Helpless.

"You'll kill him anyway," she said, voice flat.

"Oh, don't be so cynical," the man replied, his cowardice returning. "There's still a chance."

"You've already made up your mind. You can't help yourself. Killing is your universe."

He laughed, a sound as sharp as a knife's edge. "That's good, Siby. Do you think it'll be a good defense when they finally catch me?"

"No."

"Why not?"

"Because they'll never catch you. You're careful. You've perfected the hunt."

He chuckled, almost admiring. "Steve said you were good. Too bad you didn't warn him about me."

Sibyl sat in the silence that followed, the phone still pressed to her ear, the taste of dread thick on her tongue.

WHITE FIRE

WHITE FIRE BLAZES across the Rockies, a silent phoenix rising with the sun's first light. The wind stirs frozen powder into a wild dance, each flake a spark in the swirling blaze—alive, untamable, a mosaic of countless souls reborn in the morning glow. Snowpack fractures and melts, a slow alchemy of ice surrendering to light, each particle winking like diamonds and citrines against a sky washed in powder blue.

From afar, the mountains flare like a sacred fire, not of destruction but of purification—white flames that cleanse the earth's wounds, promising renewal beneath their gentle fury. No black smoke clouds this fire, only the pure dance of light and wind, brighter than any earthly flame, a breath of the divine.

I wonder why we cannot bury what is lost. They are gone, yet their essence lingers—serene as a pin drop on the leeward side, whispering like ancient spirits waiting at Lion's Gate to guide us home.

Perched on the hill, Pikes Peak's beauty is a testament to transformation. Winter's bite crystallizes my eyes, forcing them open to the raw truth. The cold burns my flesh, yet it awakens something deeper—a fierce clarity, a resolve to endure. My knees ache, but I plant them firmly, a pilgrim in the sacred cycle of death and rebirth. I will not miss a single visit, even if the chill steals my last breath.

The air tastes pure, triple-filtered through time and trial. A sharp bite of pine lingers—clear and potent, like the first sip of Russian vodka, burning away the old to reveal the new.

HOT WHEELS

He kept wiggling that little ass in the chair.

"Don't you lie to me, you little escandaloso."

A wiggle here. There. Elsewhere. His eyes wandered the room, searching for the right lie—the only lie—that might save him from whatever he'd been caught for this time, or any of the centuries before.

"I didn't do it!"

"You didn't do it?"

A sound—like a crystal vase shattering on the floor—rang out. He would have been lucky if that was all it was. Uncle Hector's hand shot out so fast, little Emilio never saw it coming.

"Tell me, or I'll give you another."

Not a single tear escaped him, even as fire and a welted handprint bloomed on his baby skin.

"That hurt! You, you—mother—"

This time, a dull crack filled the kitchen.

"Pendejo!"

"EEE man, you little shit," Uncle Hector's hand rose again. This one sent Emilio's eyes swimming and his left ear ringing with excruciating pitch.

"What's the matter with you?"

Uncle Hector's jittery finger grazed Emilio's nose.

"Look what this little shit did! You see?"

"Pobrecito. You and your Hot Wheels," Mama Lillian tossed air quotes. "I mean dealership. You touch one more hair and I'll give you a good one. You hear me?"

"Mama." The industrial kitchen swallowed little Emilio's broken voice. His hands reached for the warmth of her bosom.

"I feel no sorrow for you," she said, yanking him from the chair. "I already told you about Uncle Hector's damn Hot Wheels. Go wash those hands like I told you. Or I'll give you the meanest kiss you'll never forget."

Uncle Hector's sly smirk was ever so subtle, tightening his lazy cheek. Despite its faintness, that smirk could fry blood in an instant—not just Mama Lillian's, but everyone's.

"Almost as disgusting as a fly buzzing around Aunt Darlene's bubbly pozole." At least that's what Auntie Lou exclaimed one night, right after Uncle Hector redecorated the entire Presidente suite with his toy dealership—or better, dealerships.

Just remember this: nothing escapes the eye of Lilian Gruelle Montoya. Defy her, and you suffer as you should.

"EEEE cabrón!" The kitchen rang with the sound of that dull crack.

"What did I say?"

"Ay!" Uncle Hector rubbed the back of his head.

"Look it, Hector, do it again and you'll kiss that worthless mule on the forehead before you lay your head on that silky pillow."

"Ok!"

"You're too busy playing with toys instead of saving the hotel," Mama Lillian dabbed her forehead and made an air cross. "God rest tía's soul."

"They're not toys," he muttered, rubbing the back of his head as though summoning a genie. "One day you'll praise those toys."

"You hear me good—the day I praise those toys is the day this place burns to nothing."

"Mama!"

"Well?"

At that moment, the kitchen held its breath, the air thick with the memory of old wounds and the promise of new ones. The family's history—its love, its violence, its stubborn pride—hung in the air, as sharp and bright as white fire.

SCAR

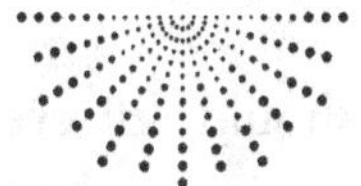

LAURA WORKS in the cytology department at Valley Hospital, a small, windowless lab tucked inside the Wilmington medical complex. Her world is a tight orbit—just a handful of women and, above them, a single male supervisor. In places like this, a work family sometimes blossoms. Sometimes.

I've worked in small businesses before, side by side with men, and I never found that sense of kinship. Maybe it's different for Laura's group, mostly women. Maybe women are better at weaving those invisible threads between people. In my experience—and I admit, I observe too closely, a bad habit—men rarely share anything truly private with other men. Strangely, I've seen men open up to women at work, confiding secrets over the hum of lab machines or the clatter of coffee mugs. Who can say why? I'm not here to knock men or make foolish generalizations about the male psyche. But in my forty-seven years, I've noticed women absorb everything, and they're damn good listeners.

Most evenings, Laura comes home and unspools the day's events. Sometimes it's about her work—slides, stains, the language of cells. Sometimes it's about doctors and nurses, the hierarchy of the hospital.

But more often, it's the stories of the women she works with—their lives, their dramas, their pets.

There's always an animal in need. A rescue case. Someone's dog had puppies, or a stray cat needed a home, or an opossum showed up in a backyard. It's amazing how many animals need saving, how many times I hear about surprise litters—always five, it seems. Five is the Wilmington magic number. Every stray, every rescue, every call for help, five tiny lives, waiting.

Laura and I joke that we should sell everything and buy a farm—somewhere green and endless—just to house all the stray creatures we wish we could save. But our little house can't hold them all. I wish it could.

Because for every happy ending, there are stories of neglect, abandonment, cruelty. Maybe bad stories travel faster than good ones. My heart aches for every animal left behind, but we can only do so much. Still, I believe if you invite an animal into your home, you owe it everything, food, shelter, kindness, love.

Most folks dream of mountains of gold. We dream of mountains of pets. Strange as that sounds. Well, I'll take that back. Laura does dream of mountains of gold. Golden retrievers, that is. If she had her way, we'd have a golden retriever farm instead of a cow farm.

It was a Tuesday edging into autumn with thick gray clouds smothering the sky. The air bit cold, my breath fogging in the porch light, while amber leaves hailed down like snow, piling on the front steps in a shiny, papery drift.

Unusually cold for this time of year, I thought, as Laura burst through the front door, trailing the elements behind her. She dropped her purple umbrella—brought just in case of rain—her overcoat, and her purse onto the leather recliner in the entryway. She unloaded so quickly, I knew something had her excited.

Laura is usually meticulous, organized to a fault. Most days, she'd hang her coat in the closet, set her umbrella just so, then trek upstairs to put her purse in the master bedroom. Not today. When excitement claims her, all routines scatter.

I was in my blue chair, wrestling with a book I'd been trying to finish for weeks. "Joe," she said, breathless. "Connie's sister—" She paused, thinking. "Lisa, I think. Anyway, her cat had babies. And she's having a heck of a time finding a home for the runt. Can you imagine?"

Privately, I thought I surely could. I watched Laura, waiting for the next shoe to drop.

"What do you think, Joe?"

When Laura asks what I think, it's a trick question. I didn't hesitate. "When should I expect the critter to arrive?"

She flapped her hand and rolled her eyes. "He's not a critter, Joe. He's a precious baby."

She gave me that look, disappointment with a dash of expectation. I rephrased. "All right. When's the precious baby getting here?"

"Oh, Joe," she said, slipping off her shoes and setting them on the mat. "He'll be here this weekend."

"I'm allergic to cats."

"Joe," her voice climbed an octave, "he won't be a bother to you."

I went back to my book, not that it was difficult or dense. The writing was clear and economical. But every time I settled in, something always seemed to drop from the rafters and smack me in the head.

On Saturday, at 8:30 sharp, the critter arrived. Laura and Annie buzzed with excitement, their voices ricocheting through the house. I sat in my blue chair, book in hand, panoramic view of the unfolding chaos.

Lisa was kind, polite, too. She brought all the modern cat essentials; litter pan, scratching post, a few days' supply of food. The moment Annie locked eyes on the kitten, she shrieked so loud my ears stung. She scooped him up before I could even get a good look. Laura and Annie smothered the poor thing, volleying names back and forth. "Toothless,"

Annie suggested. "Cuddles," Laura countered. They bickered, neither satisfied with the other's choice.

But I already knew how this would end. Every animal that crossed our threshold wound up with a Disney name—Esmeralda, Maleficent, Snow White, Aladdin. The list could fill a storybook.

Annie dangled the kitten high in the air. "Scar," she declared—Lion King, of course. She didn't say it, but I knew. That movie had been her favorite since she was two.

She pressed a wet kiss to the kitten's nose, still holding him aloft so I could finally get a look. "Look, Dad!" She flopped the kitten in my direction. "Isn't he adorable?"

"He looks like trouble," I said, peering over my glasses.

"Dad," Annie pouted, "he is not."

Laura gently took the kitten from Annie's arms. "Well, Joe, are you going to come say hi to Scar, or just sit there?"

I sighed, set my book on the side table, and stood, knees cracking, pain shooting up my leg as I shuffled over. Laura set the kitten down on the hardwood, where he wobbled, squirrelly and unsure, eyes wide and pale blue, fur a poofy cloud of silver-gray. Annie was right, the little thing looked like a lion cub. But Scar? He didn't have a villain's face. He was beautiful, magnetic in his cuteness, a breed I didn't recognize, not the kind of cat you'd expect someone to give away.

He meowed, loud as a human baby, and licked my hand with surprising warmth. "Aah, Dad," Annie said, "he likes you."

"He's all right, for a little critter."

"Scar," Annie scooped him up and nuzzled his nose, "you just wait, Dad's going to fall in love with you."

From that moment, Scar and Annie were inseparable. He slept under her blankets, stalked her around the house with a hunter's devotion, and, against every rule, ate his food on the kitchen table.

Scar ate breakfast at the kitchen table, right alongside Annie's porcelain bowl as she shoveled oatmeal into her mouth, trying to avoid making Miss Betty, the school bus driver, wait on her again.

But what Laura and Annie didn't know, when they rushed out each morning, swept into the outside world, was that the critter stalked me, too. Scar monitored my every move, memorizing my daily rituals down to the second. Sometimes it felt like he could read my mind, perched on the bathroom sink, waiting for me to brush my teeth, then springing off before I finished to claim his spot near my keyboard, right on top of my most important documents.

I didn't mind. The house was too quiet when the girls left, the stillness heavy and strange. Scar's company was a comfort, his cuteness a spell I never saw coming. Before I knew it, I was smitten. Annie's prediction echoing back at me. She was right. I fell in love with the darn thing.

My work performance took a hit. The boss, Bob Smith, not Laura, wasn't happy. I couldn't blame him. I'd rather spend my days fooling with Scar than working. I spoiled him with treats, canned tuna, even half and half. Sometimes I just watched his poofy belly rise and fall as he slept on my paperwork.

Let's face it, Scar gave me something work never could. I had more personal days banked than I could use, so I did the only logical thing, I took them. I stepped away from the project and spent my days with the critter.

Scar scaled the grainy, sloped clay-brick fireplace like an insect, bypassed the dark oak mantle, and ascended all the way to the vaulted ceiling. Sometimes he'd find the courage to climb down, but more often he'd get stuck, mewing at the ceiling as if it might lower him gently to the floor.

The fireplace had been decommissioned since the fifties, replaced by a capped gas line and a project forever postponed. It didn't take long before I brought the ladder in from the garage—handier inside, anyway, so I could rescue Scar from his high perch. I couldn't stand to hear his tiny cries echoing from above, balled up and frozen with fear against white ceiling and sloped clay.

Things at home had never been better. Life fools you like that. Let's you think you're complete, until something small and unexpected fills a space you didn't know was empty. Annie was happier than ever. Scar seemed to have enough love for two, but three was too much for his tiny heart to manage.

I felt bad for Laura. No matter how hard she tried, Scar kept his distance, slipping away at the first sign of her approach. Even asleep, he sensed her presence and bolted, leaving Laura standing there, hands empty.

It went on like this for almost a year. Then, one Sunday night at ten, as the house settled into its long slumber, Annie burst into our room. I couldn't sleep and had spent the last half hour staring at the ceiling, waiting for nothing. I sat up fast. The room was nearly pitch black, the only light a faint glow from a phone charger.

"Dad." Her voice was raw, trembling with pain. She'd been crying. "There's something wrong with Scar."

Laura, always a light sleeper, was already awake, rising quietly. "What's wrong, Annie?"

I swung my legs from the blankets, feet hitting the cold floor. "What's he doing, Annie?"

"I don't know what's wrong with him."

I followed Annie to her room, Laura close behind. My heart hammered. Panic prickled in my chest. The soft glow of Annie's lamp revealed Scar's tiny silhouette on the bed.

He was lying on his side, midsection pumping as if he were running a marathon in his sleep. "Dad," Annie pleaded, "help him."

I froze, useless, rooted to the spot. Laura swept past me and sat beside Scar, pressing her ear to his mouth and nose, listening for something only she could hear.

"He's having trouble breathing," she said quietly.

Annie looked at me, desperate, as if I might know how to save him. But I didn't. My mind spun, empty of answers.

Laura scooped Scar into her arms, stroking him gently. Suddenly, he let out a horrifying, gasping sound that split the room. We all flinched. "Dad!" Annie cried.

Fear and confusion must have been written all over my face. Just hours earlier, Scar had been climbing the fireplace, purring in my arms, eating treats. Laura and Annie had teased me about how much I doted on him. "He's really got you wrapped, Dad," Annie laughed, pinkie raised.

Now, Laura massaged Scar's throat, calm and steady where I was frantic. But the gasping only grew louder, more desperate. Scar's mouth opened and closed, again and again, hungry for air that wouldn't come.

The more he struggled, the harder Annie cried. She pressed her hand to her mouth, tears streaming, eyes wide and bright as the sun. I will never forget the look on her face that night.

After a minute of Laura's gentle coaxing, Scar gave a final, shuddering gasp and went still. Cold and silent.

Annie sobbed beside me. I couldn't bring myself to look at her. In that moment, I was a coward. I was a coward. I swear I saw Scar's soul slip free as he took his last breath. Or maybe that's just what I needed to believe. Watching a creature die before your eyes chills you to the core. Annie snatched Scar from Laura's arms, still sobbing. "He's still warm," she whispered through her tears.

Laura's eyes were shining, and mine were no better. We all wept that night. I said nothing—just slipped away to the upstairs bathroom, closed the door, and let myself break down. My heart shattered with Scar's passing.

I dried my eyes, pulled myself together, and returned to Annie's room. She was cradling Scar, Laura beside her, both faces masks of heartbreak. I wrapped my arms around Annie as she clung to the little body, and

Laura looked from me to Annie to Scar, then back again. I fought to keep the tears from surfacing.

We stood there, frozen in place. Each of us manned our post like mannequins in a shop window, playing our parts in a scene we never wanted. I don't know how long we stayed that way before I finally convinced Annie to let go. For the next hour, Laura and Annie watched as I dug a grave in the backyard. Autumn had returned, and the ground was frozen hard. My breath came out in icy clouds, the soil stubborn and unyielding, my knuckles white from the cold.

When the hole was finally ready, I laid Scar gently into the sparkling earth, the dirt glittering with ice under the porch light. "Annie," I said softly, "would you like to say something?"

She shook her head and buried her face in Laura's chest, her whole body shaking from cold and heartbreak. Laura took her inside, leaving me to finish the task alone.

I smoothed the mound, hung the shovel in the garage, and cried again. It's a wonder how something so small can come into your life for just a year and leave such a mark that, when it's gone, it destroys a little piece of you.

In time, we survived the ordeal, though we never learned what really took Scar from us. When he was alive, I half-assed my work duties, and I never thought it possible to half-ass a half-ass, but somehow I managed. Scar's toys still sat on my desk. His little mouse, the noisy ball. Most days, I'd catch myself staring at his favorite spot on my paperwork, waiting for a weight that would never return.

Sometimes, in the quiet, I'd rush to the fireplace, thinking I heard Scar mewing, needing rescue from the sloped clay. I'd forgotten the ladder was back in the garage. Every so often, I'd catch a glimpse of him at the corner of my eye—a phantom appendage in my mind. I was depressed. I missed that little critter more than I ever thought possible.

Two months later, Laura brought the ice and snow inside with her. No purple umbrella this time, just the slow unpeeling of gloves from her fingers, her heavy wool coat and mittens landing on the leather recliner in the entryway.

I was in my blue chair, a thousand-page novel in hand, but set it aside as she entered. There was no excitement on her face. My hopes dwindled as she did.

"Penny's cat had another litter of five," she said, her voice heavy. "Can you believe that?"

Yes, I could believe it. In fact, I'd been counting on it. "Oh," I said, keeping my tone even. "Sounds like a critter needs a home."

"Joe." Laura's eyes widened, as if I'd suggested something scandalous. "It's too soon. Annie is still not over Scar."

I didn't have the heart to tell her I wasn't over Scar either. "Maybe a trial run would do her some good." Truth was, I thought it might do us both some good, maybe ease the ache just a little.

Laura stared at me a long while, her mouth opening, then closing. Finally, "I suppose it couldn't hurt."

"When should we expect the critter?"

"Well," she rubbed her chin, thinking. "As soon as possible, Penny says. They're a rambunctious bunch. They already named one Sassy. What do you think?"

"About Sassy?"

"Yes."

"A little attitude might be exactly what this house needs."

Laura smiled, slipped her coat back on, fitted her gloves, and stepped into her snow boots. "Need a co-pilot?"

"No," she said, reaching for the door. "She's right down the road. I won't be long." Before she left, she paused. "Don't mention a word to Annie, let it be a surprise."

I smiled and watched the door close, the cold rushing in behind her. For a moment, I glanced up at the sloped clay fireplace, remembering. Then I eased back into my blue chair, picked up my thousand-page book, and waited, hope, and a little ache, settling in beside me.

THE MAN

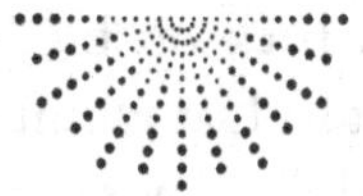

THE MAN LOOKED NO OLDER than his mid-thirties, though some guessed he might be wearing his twenties. In truth, he was fifty-two.

His face and body still wore the illusion of youth, but age crept through in subtle betrayals. His chest had softened, the sharp definition of younger years lost, his pectorals sagging ever so slightly. His belly told a harsher story, neglected and slack, it hung loosely, yearning for the vitality it once knew.

Yet his hands were the greatest betrayal. They seemed to belong to another man entirely—weathered, scarred, worn like overused leather gloves, the kind that till spring's first soil. Time had carved its story into every knuckle and vein, exaggerating age in a way the rest of him resisted.

One morning, he woke to a profound stillness in the house. It took several minutes for the day to settle in, but when it did, a strange unease flooded him.

It was Sunday. He was utterly alone. His wife and daughter were gone.

He searched for his car keys, finding them hanging on their usual hook beneath a plaque labeled "Keys." Cell phones and belongings were all in place, untouched, as if nothing had changed and yet everything had.

Stepping outside, he wandered a block or two, only to be met with deeper confusion. The neighborhood, usually alive with chatter and movement, was reduced to a hush. Cars lined the curbs, but not a soul stirred. Porch lights burned bright in the morning gloom, silent sentinels in an empty world.

Before he knew it, he was back on his front porch, sinking into a weathered rocking chair that had sat vacant for years. The house behind him was silent, and the world ahead was stranger than ever.

365 DAYS 'TIL MIDNIGHT

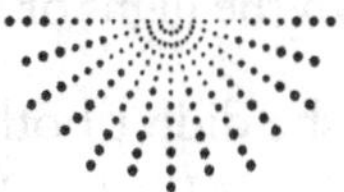

Whispers that never quiver the drum

2018

I HEAR a train cry in the distance, calling out to all those restless souls turning in their beds. Appealing to those who dream of going elsewhere. Someplace farther than their feet can carry them. Those who dare to dream of a brighter future, and those brave enough to ride hot steel.

The Culling

DELANEY STOOD at the foot of her father's bed and pulled the trigger. She kept squeezing the trigger until the clacking noise fell silent. Wisps of smoke trailed from the barrel as she eyed her father's body.

Pop, pop, pop, rang inside her head as though the nine-millimeter was still moving right along.

Once the dark silence took hold, she couldn't help thinking how much she loved twilight-she always loved twilight. And she quickly remembered it was her father who made the first introduction of the cosmos to her.

Once the terrible deed was done, she gently placed the gun at the foot of the bed and quietly shut the bedroom door behind her. The gun blast continued ringing inside her ears as she perched at the winding staircase. Delaney was careful not to pay attention to the countless pictures fixed to the wall as she walked down the flight of stairs.

On her way to the kitchen, she didn't bother to turn on a single light. She parked herself at the kitchen island and befell a hyper civilized daze. Delaney quickly mobbed the tears from her face while fond memories of her father clouded her mind. Although the popping noise from the gun claimed her too, still blasting away inside that head of hers.

Kameron came out from the shadows and hugged Delaney with excitement. "I knew you could do it—I just knew."

"Let go!"

"What's wrong?"

She glared at him with wet eyes and said nothing.

"This is the only way we can make the world a better place," he said. "Can't you see that?"

"I just killed my dad!" she said. "Forgive me for spoiling the mood."

"You don't think I feel bad," he said. "I just murdered my mom and my brother for the cause."

"Pat yourself on the back."

"Hey, I did this for us."

She pushed away from the kitchen island and said, "I'm not going."

"What . . . you have to, it's, it's part of the deal."

"I can't."

"You can't or you won't."

She didn't reply.

"Okay, but you brought this on yourself."

"I don't care," she said. "He's up there right now bleeding to death."

"If you did it the right way, he's probably dead by now."

Delaney let out a ghastly scream. She pointed angrily. "Get out!"

Kameron went to the kitchen door, turned around and said, "I can't believe you're going to pass up the chance to see the *Culling*."

"I don't care about the Culling!"

"I knew you'd take the high ground," he said while opening the door. "You were always a goodie, but deep down you're just a stuck-up bitch just like all the rest of them."

"At least I know what you really think of me."

"Whatever."

She bolted upstairs once Kameron left. Delaney wanted to keep an eye on him from the bay window facing the street. Watching him gather with the small group outside gave her gut a real chill.

She slowly backed away from the window once the group strolled down the street. Each house they passed underwent calamity—horrifying screams in the night—a living room window flashes with light, a bedroom upstairs hails a knife fight, a kitchen window tucked below reveals a struggle— and then a piercing light—she could hear that same clacking sound cry out in the distance as inconsolable carnage claimed more lives.

She rushed to her father's bedroom because she couldn't bear the sounds of death any more. "I didn't accidentally shoot you, did I?"

Her father fearfully peeled back the blankets and whispered, "You did good, really good."

A bullet was lodged in the wall above the headboard. It appeared to still smoke even though minutes had gone by. "Will it catch the house on fire?"

"No," he said, "Lead heats up, but won't burn for long, it'll go out on its own."

She instantly hugged her father and began weeping, she carried on like this for a while. He looked at her with hopeful eyes that seemed to be built on a shaky foundation and said, "Everything is going to be all right."

'It won't,' she cried. "It never will."

"Never is much too long."

"You know what I mean."

He squeezed her tighter. "We have to leave now," he said. "Or we'll die tonight when they do a final sweep."

"I'm scared daddy," she whimpered, "I still hear guns going off."

—Remix (new sound)—

"Okay, but you brought this on yourself."

"I don't care," Delaney said, voice breaking. "He's up there right now, bleeding to death."

"If you did it right, he's probably dead by now."

Delaney let out a raw, guttural scream. "Get out!"

Kameron hesitated at the door, then turned. "I can't believe you're passing up the chance to see the Culling."

"I don't care about the Culling!"

He sneered. "I knew you'd take the high ground. You were always a goodie, but deep down you're just a stuck-up bitch like all the rest."

"At least now I know what you really think of me."

"Whatever."

She bolted upstairs the moment he left, heart pounding. From the bay window, she watched Kameron join a small group on the street. As they moved from house to house, calamity followed—screams splitting the night, flashes of violence behind windows, the sharp click of gunfire echoing down the block.

Unable to bear it, Delaney rushed back to her father's room. "I didn't accidentally shoot you, did I?"

Her father, pale and trembling, peeled back the blankets. "You did good. Really good."

A bullet was lodged in the wall above the headboard, still smoking. "Will it catch the house on fire?"

"No," he whispered. "Lead heats up, but it won't burn for long. It'll go out."

She collapsed into his arms, sobbing. He held her with hands that shook. "Everything is going to be all right," he tried.

"It won't," she wept. "It never will."

"Never is much too long."

"You know what I mean."

He squeezed her tighter. "We have to leave now," he said. "Or we'll die tonight when they do a final sweep."

"I'm scared, Daddy. I still hear guns going off."

Delaney's ears rang with phantom gunfire as she scanned her room. Her gaze landed on a pink lighter—usually reserved for candles, but tonight, it promised something more desperate. In a flash of resolve, she snatched her favorite sweater, balled it up, and set it ablaze. The flames caught quickly, licking up her trembling hands before she tossed the burning bundle onto her bed. The fire roared to life, swallowing the room in a rush of heat and smoke.

She and her father slipped out the back door, vanishing into the wooded ravine behind the house as the inferno took hold. The blaze would buy them time, a smokescreen to mask their escape.

In the forest's deepening gloom, her father suddenly dragged her to the ground. Two shadows crept through the trees—"Kyle and his mother," Delaney whispered, her voice barely audible. But her father's grip tightened. "Shh. There's someone else behind them." The woods erupted with screams and gunshots, chaos echoing through the bare branches. Delaney's gasp was stifled by her father's hand. "Not another peep, or we'll be next."

When the violence faded, her father released her and checked his watch. "We have exactly two hours and ten minutes to reach the next checkpoint." Delaney nodded, silent and resolute.

They moved like ghosts—light-footed, careful not to disturb the world around them. Her father, ever the teacher, made her jot notes on a paper map, just in case she'd need to find her way back alone. The trail wound along a rocky mountainside, drizzle blurring the sky to gray. Naked trees stretched endlessly, broken only by sagging power lines and the skeletal remains of human ambition.

Her father, once a police officer and lifelong hunter, knew every stream and trail. "If the moss isn't right, it just isn't ripe for the picking," he'd say. But now, they were the prey.

Checkpoint by checkpoint, they navigated the woods like rats in a maze, edging closer to a remote cabin perched on a cliff above a roaring river. The land was unforgiving—deadly for the unskilled, a graveyard for the careless.

At sundown, they reached the cabin. Inside, they laid out their meager provisions—guns, knives, waterproof matches, flint, water filters, bullets, flashlights, tourniquets, military rations, a baby blue tarp. Every inch of the rickety table was claimed by the tools of survival.

Her father pulled back a bookshelf, revealing a hidden panel. "Where does it lead?" Delaney asked.

"Underneath the cabin," he said. "Grandpa built it in case a bear came barging in. If they find us, I want you to take this passage. It leads a mile out over the ridge."

"Daddy!"

"No," he said. "You go on without me—it's me they want, not you."

Tears welled in her eyes, but before she could protest, he changed the subject. "Let's see what the news has to say about all this."

"The TV? Does it actually work?"

"I should hope. Otherwise, I've been paying for a satellite for nothing."

Delaney managed a shaky laugh and inched closer to the screen, hungry for any scrap of information about the world outside. Her father flipped through channels. Static, distortion, fragments of chaos. The programming glitched, voices warping.

"Goddamn thing," he muttered, banging the TV. "What the hell is wrong with it?"

"Shh," Delaney whispered. "Something's trying to come through."

A black screen. Then the emergency broadcast system blared, the buzzer slicing the silence. "We interrupt your normal programming... this is not a test—" The screen flickered out again. "Something's interfering with the signal."

Delaney stood frozen, hand over her mouth, eyes wide with terror. "Jesus," she breathed.

The news station sputtered to life, showing flashes of violence and apocalypse from around the world. "I can't believe it," she whispered. "It's really happening."

Her father slumped into a battered recliner, the weight of the moment pressing him down. "It was only a matter of time."

"A matter of time?" Delaney echoed, her voice barely more than a whisper—caught between disbelief and dread.

"A matter of time?"

"The world has been heading this way for a long time now."

They sat together in silence, watching the world burn on the screen—beheadings, firing squads of the young, mass exterminations, buildings ablaze, children wandering alone through empty streets. The horror welled up in Delaney. "It can't be," she whispered.

Her father was about to speak when the broadcast flickered and cut out. The screen returned—this time, a young, lissome woman sat in the dimly lit Oval Office. The silence was so deep, Delaney could hear her own heartbeat.

"Who is that woman, Daddy?" she asked.

He shook his head, lips pressed tight. "Daddy," she pleaded.

"Hush, girl."

The woman on the television stared out at the world. Her thin smile fixed, saying nothing. Then, from somewhere offscreen—"No... stop... please," a man's voice pleaded.

"There, there," the woman said softly. "It will be over soon."

The man's begging turned to whimpers. "You don't want to look like a coward in front of all your constituents, now, do you?" she chided.

Suddenly, he went silent. "There, you see—I can be civilized."

"Is that the president?" Delaney whispered.

"My God," her father breathed.

"Are we all going to die?"

The woman finally stood. "My fellow Americans, and people around the world, my name is Beta. I'm here to release you from your bondage... from the imaginary boxes you've been living in."

"You can't do this," the president stammered. "I'm the president of the United—"

"Please accept this as my first offering to you, my dear brave Cullers."

The president screamed as his body began to levitate, grasping his neck as if being strangled, gurgling as his body flailed and spasmed. Delaney tried to swallow her terror but let out a shrill cry.

"My dear Cullers, I apologize. This will be the last time I take another human life. But as you all know, it is vital to start a new world with a clean slate." The president's body crashed to the floor with a sickening thud.

"Now then, where were we?" Beta sat back down, smoothing her skirt. "Ah, yes. Let us discuss the new world you are about to embark on."

Delaney's father sprang from his seat and began pacing in front of the television. "Who is that woman's daddy?" he muttered, lost in thought.

Delaney glared at him, unable to understand his mumbling. "Dad!"

"Hush, I need to think!"

Beta's voice filled the room: "There's no need for money or volatile markets anymore because I will supply all your needs. Medical care, food, shelter, and other provisions will be provided to you free of charge, courtesy of the new empire. Everything you could ever need will be freely given. Crime will not be tolerated in the new world. Twelve codes will be posted in every city. You will be dealt with swiftly if you violate these codes. Your way of life is no longer viable." She pulled a dollar bill from her pocket, holding it up. "You have poisoned the planet for this. We will do things my way for now—for precisely three hundred and sixty-five days to be exact.

"There are twelve people living among you who are quite exceptional. They come from all walks of life—and range from twelve years of age to ninety-nine. Yes, you heard me right—twelve years old. From my experience, great things can come from anywhere."

She stood, her presence filling the screen. "Once three hundred and sixty-five days have come and gone, and when the clock reaches midnight, they will decide your fate. What they choose will be entirely up to you. Will they embrace a new way of living, or will they reset the clock?"

She smiled, wide and unsettling. "What does it mean to reset the 'clock?' It means the world as you know it will go dark. The modern world will wither away... it will be a dark time, one that will force humans to start all over again. Anything deemed harmful to the environment will be dealt with swiftly. These indulgences you use in your everyday lives will be no more. Now is the time to rebuild a better world."

Delaney sat down, staring at the television in shock. "Turn it off."

"What if—"

"It doesn't matter," she said. "Don't you get it? She's in control now, and whoever these twelve people are."

"Do not fear," Beta continued. "These twelve individuals are the best among you, and I'm confident that they will choose wisely. Good evening and be well."

The emergency broadcast system blared for a few seconds, then the screen went black.

"Jesus," he whispered.

"What are we going to do?" Delaney whispered, panic threading her voice. "We can't hide here forever."

They stood frozen, eyes locked, fear tightening in their chests. Her father tried to speak, but a sharp knock at the door cut him off.

"You have to hide," she urged, her voice barely more than a breath.

Without hesitation, Delaney pulled her father into the escape room concealed behind the bookcase. She steadied herself, smoothing her hair and forcing calm into her trembling hands before facing the door.

"Just a minute," she called, heart hammering in her chest.

Her hand hovered over the doorknob, an instinctual warning screaming at her to stop. Another thunderous strike rattled the door. She hesitated but finally opened it.

A chilling scene greeted her: a jet-black android, towering and inhuman. Parts of its anatomy exposed—matte alloy and transparent circuitry beneath a bulletproof shell that shielded its head, chest, arms, and legs like a hockey goalie's armor.

"We have an arrest warrant for Richard Mondragon," the android intoned, its voice cold and mechanical.

"He's not here... he's... he's—" Delaney stammered, tears threatening to spill.

"Step aside, ma'am, or we will use force," the android warned.

Beyond the porch, three identical androids stood poised to storm the cabin, their eyes fixed and unblinking.

"Please," Delaney pleaded, her voice trembling. "Don't kill him."

"Step aside, ma'am, or we will incapacitate you."

Inside, her father heard the commotion and shouted, "Stop! I'm coming out!"

"Daddy!" she cried. "Don't!"

He pushed open the trap door, knocking over the bookshelf in his haste, and walked toward Delaney with his hands raised high.

"I'm unarmed," he said, voice steady.

The android shoved Delaney aside and swiftly restrained him.

"Richard Mondragon, you are under arrest for treason."

"Treason?" he echoed, disbelief in his voice.

"You have been tried and convicted."

"I haven't done anything wrong."

"Punishment for treason is death," the robotic voice stated, cold and final.

Delaney's scream pierced the air, bone-chilling and raw. She lunged for her father, but the android knocked her back, its voice blaring,

"Interfering with a level five arrest is a code violation."

"Don't interfere," her father pleaded, meeting her eyes one last time. "I'll go peacefully."

Delaney's heart pounded as the androids dragged her father toward the cliff's edge. Helpless, she watched as the metallic grip closed around Richard's neck and, with mechanical indifference, hurled him into the abyss. His scream echoed, sharp and brief, swallowed by the void below.

Without hesitation, Delaney sprinted after him, the ground vanishing beneath her feet. For a split second, she was weightless—then the world tilted, and she plunged into open air, chasing the only family she had left.

Wind howled past as she dove, arms outstretched, her body slicing through the cold like a bullet. She could see her father falling ahead, the earth rushing up with terrifying speed. Desperation lent her strength; she streamlined her body, willing herself faster, reaching for him as the world blurred past.

In those final seconds, her fingers found his—two hands clasped in freefall, a fragile bond against oblivion. The impact was brutal, jarring every bone, but in that suspended moment beneath the towering canopy, sunlight spilled through the leaves in scattered gold.

Time seemed to pause. She was with him, and he with her—two souls entwined beyond the reach of death. Though his breath had fled, his presence shimmered beside her, a radiant lens casting warmth and light upon her shattered heart.

Delaney lay still, the weight of loss pressing down. Yet within that sorrow, a quiet strength stirred. She breathed in the fading light, gathering the fragments of what remained, ready to carry him forward in the silence.

THE RIDE

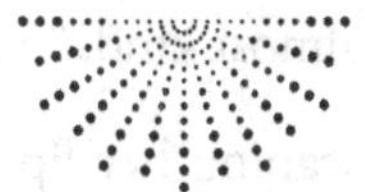

THE GIRL LINGERED by the curb, letting the moment stretch, her gaze fixed on the modest man and his car. The Corolla—eighteen years old, at least—looked impossibly pristine. Well-treaded tires, a flawless clear coat, and sparkling glass caught the weak city light. Not a single smudge. Not a hint of wear.

She wasn't a car expert. But three months on the street had taught her to read the world's finer layers. The ones that could mean the difference between survival and disaster. Living rough aged you—presidential years, she thought. Every day brought new filth, new dangers, and a front-row seat to the worst in people. She'd learned to spot the signs others missed. The tiny clues that could save her from heartbreak, or a gruesome end at the hands of a stranger.

Up north, the city sprawled beside a massive lake. Winters here were uncompromising, the air a mix of humidity and ancient sea salt that ate through steel, concrete, and glass. Any car this old should have been claimed by rust long ago. Yet this one gleamed, untouched by time or elements.

She remembered her father's voice, rough and buzzing in her memory: "Ancient seawater, my ass. This is what comes from drilling oil. Those sons of bitches are gonna ruin all the good water, you just wait and see." The echo of his words, unexpected and sharp, made her pause, made her look again at the man and his immaculate car. There was something off in its perfection. A serial-killer shine that went beyond mere compulsion.

She cracked the door open, voice wary but steady. "What are you looking for, honey?"

The man's smile was gentle, almost kind. "You," he said.

She rolled her eyes, a hiss escaping her lips. "That's what they all say, honey."

His look sharpened, the kindness edged with something else. "I was told to come here. For you."

She arched a brow, contempt curling her lip, but said nothing. The man watched her, waiting, then added, "Honestly. I passed you by at first. Then a minute later, I was told to turn around and pick you up."

She glanced at the empty backseat, then back at him. "I think you're mixed up, mister."

He tapped his head, a wry smile flickering. "This thing may be old, but it knows what it knows."

"No thanks, mister," the girl snapped. "Maybe someone else can keep you warm tonight."

She started to shut the door, but the man leaned forward, voice low and urgent. "Fifty dollars and a ride to Dayton. Isn't that what you need?"

She froze, wide-eyed, the door half-closed. The man's smile returned, gentle but knowing. "That should seal the deal, right?"

She slammed the door and stalked away. The man lunged over the passenger seat, rolling down the window and calling after her, "Miss! This is your last chance! You won't make it in time. That, I can promise you!"

She stopped in her tracks, spun around, and stormed back, fury in her eyes. "Don't play fucking games with me, mister, I have a knife!"

He didn't flinch. "You know better than that, Nicole."

The name hit her like a slap. She stood stunned, as if her mind had short-circuited. For a moment, she looked lost, searching for something rational, something to anchor her.

He watched her, patient. "How about we compromise, seeing as you got a knife and there's a three-hour drive ahead? Compromise is the best option, don't you think?"

He paused, studying her. "You come around my side. Sit behind me. That way, if anything funny happens, you've got the upper hand. Knife handy, right?"

She nodded, still frozen. "Good. Take it out, just for a little while. We'll head off into the sunset."

"Are you nuts, mister?"

"We can't waste time," he said. "My only policy is we talk and drive. You wouldn't believe what comes out when two strangers hit the road."

"I'm not going anywhere with you," she said, eyes like razors.

"What about Nana?" he said quietly. "She's waiting for you."

Her jaw nearly hit the pavement. The man flashed a bright, unsettling smile. "Look. Take a seat. Grip the knife. If I get squirrely, you do what you have to. I have a feeling you'll know exactly what to do when the time comes."

The girl looked hollowed out, as if the streets had scraped her clean and filled her with a lifetime's worth of punishment. She was torn, anger and desperation flickering in her eyes. "You say the wrong thing, or do anything that scares me, I'll cut you. You hear me? I'll cut you good, mister."

She flashed the knife, steel glinting in the dim light. "My daddy gave me this. Taught me how to use it."

The man just smiled, unbothered. "I wouldn't have it any other way."

She held the blade steady. "So we have an understanding?"

He waved a hand, dismissive. "Fine, fine. If I do something wrong, you cut me."

Without another word, she darted to the back seat, slamming the door behind her. The man caught the knife's flash in the rearview but said nothing. He started the car, eased it down the block, and then turned right.

"Hey," she said, voice sharp, "that's not the way to the highway."

"We're not taking the highway."

"Why not?"

"You won't make it in time," he said, eyes on the road. "I've lived in Dayton all my life. I know the fastest way."

"You're awfully far from home," she muttered.

"Bad heart," he replied.

"What?"

"There's a specialist down here. But he couldn't help me. I suspect no one can now."

She hesitated. "Are you dying or something, mister?"

He smiled, a little sad. "We're all dying, miss. It's just a matter of when and how."

He heard soft sniffles from the back seat. He clicked on the radio, letting soft jazz drift through the car. "It's gonna be all right. Just sit back and listen to those sweet sounds. I promise, in a minute or so, they'll take you someplace beautiful. You wait and see."

Her crying faded. She glared at him through the mirror. "Aren't you scared?"

"Why should I be?"

"I am," the girl admitted softly.

"Death isn't the end, miss. Matter of fact, it's just the beginning."

"The beginning?" she echoed, uncertain.

"Something far greater than this," he said, his gaze distant.

The music seemed to move him. He hummed along, be-bopping quietly, fingers drumming the wheel as if the band was playing straight to his soul. For a moment, the girl drifted, her mind slipping away from the present, back to a place she used to call home.

They drove in silence for a long while, but it was a different kind of silence, one that dulled the nerves in her gut, settling her in a way she hadn't felt in months. She couldn't remember the last time she'd felt this at ease with a stranger. The man radiated a strange peace, even when he said nothing at all.

"Aren't your children scared for you, mister?" she ventured.

"No," he replied.

"How do you know that?"

"I had a daughter, once," he said quietly.

"What happened to her?"

"Cancer," he answered. "She was about your age, I suspect. She didn't have any fight left at the end."

"So you have no one else," she said, as if solving a riddle.

"Oh, not quite," he said, a gentle smile in his voice. "We're never really alone. Look at us. Together, sharing this ride, this fine day. It's strange, isn't it?"

She caught his eyes in the mirror, wanting to say something, but her gaze dropped, lost in thought. He winked. "We're the loneliest creatures on earth, and yet we occupy every inch."

She couldn't help but laugh, a bright, surprised sound. The man grinned, satisfied. "Now that," he said, "is truly something."

Her brows drew low, sharp as a falcon's, lips thinning in concentration. "What do you mean by that?"

The man kept his eyes on the road. "There's a glorious light that comes forth when you smile," he said quietly. "I suspect it's trying to get your attention."

She rolled her eyes, but her guard softened. The girl tucked the blade into her pack. "I put it away, mister."

He said nothing, just nodded. She turned to the window, watching the blur of green whip past. "You're weird, mister. But not that weird-weird."

"I appreciate that," he replied, a trace of humor in his voice. "Seeing how we're getting to know each other, I have to admit, something's been eating at me."

She didn't answer, just kept her gaze fixed on the roadside trees, their leaves flashing in the wind. "I miss seeing all the green."

"Does all that green remind you of home?"

"Yes."

"Then home is where you must go."

"I can't."

"The door is always open, it never closes on us?"

She hesitated, her voice barely above a whisper. "Maybe for you."

The man's tone softened. "Some trouble isn't nearly as bad as you think, miss. Time is a funny thing. Give anything enough time and you'll see what it becomes."

"I'm the exception to that rule, mister," she said, her eyes still lost in the passing landscape.

"That's not how I see it."

She turned, studying him in the mirror. "You don't know me, mister. You know nothing about me or where I come from."

"I may not know all the details," he said, "but the one in charge tells me what I need to know."

She frowned. "You talk to God?"

"Not exactly."

"What then?"

He glanced at her, a strange glint in his eye. "God talks to me."

"Whatever you say, mister," the girl muttered, rolling her eyes at him in the rearview mirror.

The man turned down the radio, voice steady. "I wouldn't jest about that."

"So God told you to pick me up?"

"Yes," he replied. "And when God tells me to do something, I've learned not to question why."

She studied him, suspicion and fatigue mixing in her gaze. "Tell me something, mister. If God's so great, why hasn't he told you where to find the right doctor?"

He shook his head. "It doesn't work like that."

"Then why do you still listen?"

"I had my struggles with God in the beginning," he said, eyes on the road. "But now we see things eye to eye."

She snorted. "That's not how I see it, mister. God hasn't done anything for me my whole life."

He glanced at her in the mirror, a flicker of gentle defiance in his tone. "What do you call this, miss?"

She looked away. "Luck."

He let it hang for a moment, then said, "Tell you what, I bet I can guess why you need to get to Dayton in a hurry."

She stiffened, jaw set. "I'm done talking, mister. And if you knew what was good for you, you'd stop talking too."

He nodded, silent, and turned the radio back up. Soft jazz filled the car again, cushioning the silence as they rolled down the road.

After a while, the girl's voice broke through, softer now. "My Nana is really sick. Like your daughter was."

"I know,"

She rolled her eyes.

"He'll get you there, every time. Right when you need him most," the man says, catching his own eye in the rearview mirror. "Never once has he let me down."

THE SCRIBE

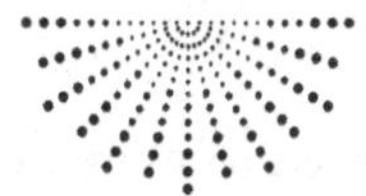

THE MAN WAS SENTENCED for fraud, checks, mortgages, documents. No family. No children. A loner. The closest thing to a friend was Beth, his old mentor. The woman who taught him the art of forgery. Now she was upstate, doing a dime for securities fraud.

He had no one, and nothing. No money, not even cigarettes. But he had his hands, and he had words. In prison, words were currency. He became the Scribe.

He wrote for anyone who could pay. Legal letters, personal pleas, translations of legalese for the barely literate. All the stuff he was convicted of. Most inmates couldn't read the fine print, let alone write a letter that might move a judge or a lover. But the Scribe could. And so, he survived.

One day, a young man named Alan approached the Scribe. Alan was doing time for armed robbery. He had a son on the outside, cared for by a woman named Renee. Alan couldn't read or write, and he had nothing to trade. The Scribe turned him away.

But Alan had grown up with Buddha, one of the prison's guards flunkies. Alan convinced Buddha to intervene. Buddha struck a deal with the Scribe, a letter in exchange for privileges, first in the shower, meal upgrades, little freedoms that mattered in a place built to erase you.

The Scribe agreed. He wrote Alan's letter.

Three weeks later, Alan returned, clutching a reply. He handed it to the Scribe, who read it aloud. Something in Renee's words, a flicker, a spark, caught in him. Her sentences were almost poetic, the ache in them familiar. He recognized her longing, her hope, her resignation. He saw himself in her lines.

From that day, the Scribe agreed to write more letters for Alan. Not for payment, but for the connection. For the words that, somehow, made the walls feel thinner and the bars to disappear.

Months passed. The Scribe and Renee exchanged letter after letter. Their words grow more intimate, more confessional. At some point, the Scribe cut Alan out of the picture entirely, he was in love. In one letter, he told Renee to address her replies to him, not Alan. The plan worked. Alan never suspected a thing. A few weeks later, Alan was transferred to another prison, overcrowding, the rumor went. He vanished from the Scribe's world without a ripple.

The Scribe's secret correspondence with Renee became his obsession. In one letter, he asked for a picture. After all, he'd been pouring his heart into these pages for months. He wanted to see the woman behind the words. But after that request, Renee went silent. No letters. No picture. The Scribe ignored the other inmates, letting his writing operation grind to a halt. He tried to read The Bell Jar—Plath always pulled him out of a rut—but the words fell flat. He thumbed through his thesaurus, searching for inspiration, but nothing worked. He was heartbroken, haunted by the possibility that Alan had discovered his betrayal, that Renee had learned the truth.

Two months dragged by. Then, on a gray Tuesday, a letter finally arrived. Inside, carefully wrapped, was a small photograph.

He studied it. A man, definitely not Alan, stood front and center, piercings glinting, tattoos winding up his arms, half his head shaved, dressed in renaissance-style clothes. He looked like a circus performer, or some artsy type. The man was smiling, holding a child on his hip, Alan's son, the Scribe guessed. Next to him stood a woman, plain and pale, her body language stiff, uneasy. She wore thick glasses, half her head shaved, her clothes frumpy. She was much shorter than the man, and there was no light in her eyes. She didn't smile. The circus man's arm draped around her shoulders, but she looked as if she wished she were anywhere else.

The Scribe stared at the photo, searching for the woman he'd fallen for in her letters, trying to reconcile the poetry of her words with the emptiness in her gaze.

There's no light in her eyes.

The Scribe is stunned. The pale, unsmiling woman in the photograph is Renee. Her letters had been luminous, alive with longing and wit—nothing like the hollow gaze staring back at him now. He reminds himself, people write with their souls, and the soul doesn't always match the body. Looks are deceiving. Appearance isn't everything. He tells himself life has done this to Renee, two men, at least, have made her existence a kind of living hell. Of course she presents poorly. Of course she's worn down.

The affair continues. Letter after letter, month after month, Renee and the Scribe share secrets. Things he's never told another soul, not even Beth. By autumn, as the leaves turn, luck turns with them, the Scribe is granted early release. At first, he's elated. He tells himself his prison time was well spent. He's perfected his craft. Learned from his mistakes. It was all in the ink, he thinks. That was his downfall. This time, he vowed —fiercely, silently—never to get caught again. The weight of his past sins sharpened his resolve.

But fear gnaws at him. He doesn't want to lose Renee. He wants to marry her, take care of her and the boy. Now, with freedom and means, he devises a new plan. He writes Renee again, spinning a story. His friend Chuck is being released for good behavior, a nonviolent, white-collar crime, just like his own. He pleads with her to let Chuck stay for a few months, promising it will be worth her while.

In his mind, he'll woo Renee as Chuck. If she meets him in person, he believes, she'll fall for him all over again. Renee's reply comes quickly—she's wary. She doesn't want a stranger, especially a convict, in her apartment. But she agrees to meet Chuck for dinner at a place just outside town, before she decides.

After a few more letters, Renee and the Scribe reached an agreement. His release came sooner than he'd dared hope. Before heading to the diner where Renee would be waiting, he made a detour to Westwood Bank. Years ago, before his arrest, he'd hidden money in a safety deposit box under the name Mike Smith—a box acquired through joint tenancy, with a roster of fictional co-owners he'd invented. Inside was twenty thousand dollars. He took ten, left the rest for another day.

He arrived at the diner early, nerves jangling. In a back booth, he bounced his knee, his hands restless, touching everything—sugar packets, napkin holder, the edge of the menu. Every time the bell over the door jingled, he jerked his head up, scrutinizing each new arrival, measuring them against the image he'd built of Renee.

Minutes stretched into hours. No sign of her. He wondered what he'd do if she changed her mind at the last minute. The waitress behind the counter was all steel-eyed patience. He hadn't even ordered a coffee.

Finally, she came over: "You can't stay unless you order something—cook's orders."

He asked for coffee and a slice of pie. Key lime, the only thing left. He hated key lime. His mother used to force it on him every Fourth of July—always on the Fourth. But he ate nothing, just sipped his coffee, black and bitter.

He'd learned to survive on little. In prison, he'd stripped his needs to the bone. No cream, no sugar, no extras. Even before, he'd lived spare, peanut butter sandwiches and water for dinner, a hard-boiled egg on dry toast for breakfast, sardines and crackers for lunch. Always water. He could have eaten like royalty, dined in the city's finest restaurants, but he never did.

Now, he sat in the diner's fluorescent hush, waiting for a woman whose words had once lit up his cell, wondering if she'd ever walk through the door. He could have dined at the city's finest restaurants—Le Petit Jardin, with its squid ink crepes and Russian caviar; Little Tommy's, famous for linguini in white wine sauce, truffles shaved like snow, aged prosciutto, hand-grated parmesan, and a ten-thousand-dollar bottle of Chianti; or the steakhouse on Grant Street, where two-thousand-dollar wagyu "melts in your mouth like butter," as Beth once told him. But he preferred sardines. Simple, briny, cheap. He always had.

In his studio apartment, a Samsonite briefcase lay hidden in the coat closet—half a million in cash, give or take. The rest of the place was bare. A thrift-store television, a ragged recliner, a used mattress on the floor. No dishes, no car. He ate off paper plates, used plastic cutlery, and took the subway everywhere. His life was meager by choice, or perhaps by habit. But in the closet nearest the bathroom hung a wardrobe fit for an emperor, tailored suits, fine wool, silk ties, Italian wingtips polished to a mirror shine.

Out on the street, he was transformed. Groomed by the city's best barbers, five hundred dollars a visit, his hair perfectly parted, his jaw always clean-shaven. He dressed like a CEO or a high-powered attorney, drawing stares as he strode through a neighborhood riddled with dealers, hustlers, and the homeless. He stood out, a peacock among pigeons, a king among the ruined.

That night, he was close to giving up. He pushed away from the diner's sticky booth, ready to leave for good, when the door banged open. A man hurried in, not just any man, but the circus man from the photograph—piercings, tattoos, half-shaved head, renaissance clothes. Almost identical. The past, the fantasy, and the grimy present collided in the fluorescent tick.

The man was nearly identical to the photograph. Only now, the once-shaved side of his head had grown out, hair falling to his shoulders. The boy was with him, a little older, perched at the counter. But where was Renee?

As the Scribe watched, the truth unfurled with quiet finality. The circus man was Renee. Alan and Renee were lovers, yes—but the story's last turn was sharper than that. Renee was a man. The Scribe had never caught on, not truly. In all their months of correspondence, he'd missed the hints. Little signals woven into the sentences. Moments he'd chosen to ignore because Renee was so charming, so achingly likable. Even lovable.

He sat in the booth, stunned. Looking back, he realized the signs were always there. He'd been emotionally smitten, drawn in by the poetry of Renee's words, the honesty, the ache. Subconsciously, he must have known. But the connection, the longing, the secret hope, had overridden everything else.

In the end, it didn't matter what body Renee inhabited, what name she used, or what mask she wore. The Scribe had fallen in love with a soul, not a face. And as he watched Renee, circus man, lover, parent, move through the diner, the Scribe felt the sharp ache of loss, but also a strange, unexpected peace. For a moment, he understood love, in its truest form, is blind to everything but the heart's hunger for connection.

He left the diner quietly, stepping into the city's cold neon hush, carrying the bittersweet weight of a story only he would ever know.

THE INVISIBLES

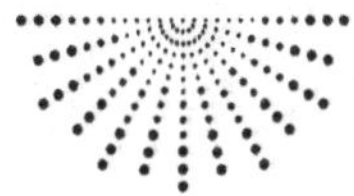

Once they take over, you cease to exist. You linger with them, trapped in their shadow. You watch as they play out your life, while you remain lost in their darkness. You're forced to witness the blur that now pretends to be you. You're trapped, powerless, with no control. Are you the shadow, or are you the invisibles?

EYES OF GOLD

Handsomely crafted
Flying point road

THE BOY SPED down the sprawling gravel road for miles on end. Everywhere his eyes landed, green meadows and trees greeted him. Dry-rotted tires kicked up dirt, feeding a mighty bluster that trailed a cloud of earth behind.

Inside the truck, the boy sat at the driver's seat, steering. At arm's length, a child was curled up on the passenger side. The boy glanced at the sleeping child and smiled gently—a gentleness that quickly faded.

A crystal blue sky and plump white clouds stretched as far as the eye could see. It was the first time he had seen such a glorious sight in over two decades.

He slowed down, sticking his arm out the window. With one hand on the wheel and the other swimming against the wind, tears began to flow silently. He was careful not to wake the child, letting out only a soft whimper.

The boy angrily wiped his face with his hand and turned on the radio. He didn't bother rummaging through empty airwaves. The station was already preset. It was his father's truck long before it fell into his possession. Still, he never touched the dial after casting the white picket farm in the rearview mirror all those years ago.

When the road ended, a smaller access road opened up. Sparkling black asphalt ran alongside a pure white fence that seemed to fade away into the distance.

The boy slowly pulled the truck to the side of the road and stepped out. He quietly clicked the door shut and shielded his eyes from the sun as he walked toward the middle of the asphalt.

He stood there, searching for everything that could be seen, and everything that he couldn't. The smell of manure, freshly harvested hay, and rolling hills sent his mind racing. He vividly imagined all the new sights that might lie beyond his childhood front door.

"Jesus," the boy said in amazement. "He kept it up well."

He got back in the truck and drove a little further down the road. Excitement, shame, and regret clouded his senses as he neared the front of the main house.

The truck idled in front for a while, and he couldn't help but wonder what to do next. Up until this point, it was nothing more than a plan, still far from his reality.

Everything was serene and still for a time until a calm breeze swept across the hillside, stirring the golden wheat. Seeing all the beauty that lay ahead compelled the boy to reconsider his decision to seek refuge from the farm. The golden fields, the gentle breeze, and the familiar hills pulled at memories he thought had withered long ago. For a moment, the urge to turn back and escape the weight of his past began to fade.

But as he placed the truck in drive, his gaze caught movement near the house. Momma was making her way slowly from the backside, her steps careful and deliberate. She appeared focused, burdened by some unusual chore. The boy watched as she stumbled and lost grip of something heavy in her hands. Instinctively, concern etched itself across his face, and he moved as if to help—but shame and pride anchored him to the seat, holding him back.

He stood there, torn between longing and guilt, watching as Momma brushed herself off and inspected her arms. Determination set in her every movement as she turned her head from side to side, consumed by the task at hand. She started to head back, but something caught her eye —the truck parked in front of the house, a sight she hadn't seen in years.

For over twenty years, Momma had prayed to see that tired old truck mount the driveway once more. Yet, even now, she couldn't be sure her prayers had been answered. She closed her eyes, murmuring, "It can't be... Please Jesus, give me strength."

Across the yard, they locked eyes, years of heartbreak rising to the surface as tears blurred their vision. A single word shot from her lips, "Michael!," with the force of every thunderclap the universe could muster.

Guilt and hesitation fell away. The boy rushed to his mother, sweeping her into his arms. She sobbed against his chest, and he held her tighter, unable to hold back his own tears.

"I never gave up," she murmured, voice trembling. "Never."

"I'm sorry," he whispered, the words catching in his throat.

She pulled back just enough to see his face, her own shining with relief and love. "You're finally home," she said softly. "That's all that matters now."

The child in the truck had woken, blinking against the sunlight as he tried to make sense of his new surroundings. He sat up, rubbing sleep from his eyes, and peered out the window, curiosity flickering across his face.

Outside, the stillness of the afternoon was broken by the sudden appearance of an old man charging around the backside of the barn. His steps were swift and purposeful, boots thudding against the packed dirt.

His shoulders were broad, hair white as fresh snow. And there was a sharpness to his movements that spoke of years spent working the land.

For a moment, the child and the old man locked eyes through the glass. The old man's stern expression softened just a fraction, confusion mingling with surprise as he took in the unfamiliar face. The child, sensing the tension in the air, pressed closer to the window, watching as the old man's gaze shifted from the truck to the figures embracing in the yard.

The old man's voice cracked through the still air, sharp and commanding. Michael froze, his arms still wrapped around his mother. "You get the hell out of here, boy," the old man barked, pointing a trembling finger down the drive.

Michael lowered his head in shame, the words stinging like they did years ago. But Momma's voice cut through the air, fierce and unwavering. "Joseph Alexander Walker, you stop right there."

The old man's hand faltered. He stepped closer, jaw set to unleash another tirade, until the child peeked out from behind Michael's leg. The child's eyes were wide and bright, a shy smile blooming as he looked up at the man he'd only heard about in stories.

Joseph's anger wavered, confusion and awe wrestling across his weathered face. He tried to speak, but the words caught in his throat. The child just stood there, beaming, innocent and unburdened by the years that had passed.

Momma's gaze softened as she looked at Joseph. "Mercy," she whispered, the word hanging in the hush between them.

The old man couldn't tear his eyes from the child. His voice, when it finally came, was softer, almost broken. "What have you gone and done, boy?"

Michael met his father's eyes, searching for understanding, for forgiveness. For a moment, the silence was thick with everything left unsaid. Weight of the years, the distance, and every unspoken word pressed down on him as he faced the man who had haunted his memories.

His mother, trembling but resolute, stepped forward, shielding Michael with her presence. "No, not this time," she said, her voice quivering but clear. "He's come home."

The old man's jaw clenched. He looked from Michael to the child now peering out from Micheal's legs. Confusion and something softer flickering in his eyes. For a moment, the only sound was the wind brushing through the wheat and the distant call of a meadowlark.

Michael took a shaky breath, feeling the urge to retreat war, with the need to stand his ground. "I didn't come here to fight," he said quietly, voice thick with emotion. "I just needed to see home. To show him—" He nodded toward the child, "where I came from."

The old man's gaze lingered on the child, then softened as he looked at Michael's mother. The years had worn them all, but something unspoken passed between them, a truce, or perhaps the first fragile hope of one.

Momma wiped her tears and reached for Michael's hand. "Come on, both of you. Let's get inside. There's coffee on the stove and pie cooling by the window."

For a moment, no one moved. Then, as if a dam had broken, the old man let out a heavy sigh and dropped his arm. He turned away, muttering, "Don't keep the door open too long. Flies'll get in."

Michael hesitated, the weight of his father's gaze heavy on his shoulders. The child clung tighter to his leg, seeking comfort. Michael gave his father one last, somber look—a silent plea, a promise, an apology—and then gently guided the child toward the house.

Michael managed a small, grateful smile. He helped his mother toward the house, the child trailing close behind. The sun was dipping lower, casting long shadows across the yard, but for the first time in years, Michael felt the warmth of home begin to seep into his bones again.

As they crossed the threshold, the familiar scents of coffee and cinnamon and baked apples filled the air. Michael glanced back once, catching his father's silhouette in the doorway, still distant, but no longer unreachable. The past would not be erased in a day, but as the door behind them creaked shut, hope, fragile and new, settled quietly in the old farmhouse.

Outside, Joseph lingered, staring at the door as if it were the threshold to another life. The sun dipped low, casting long shadows across the fields, but inside, the house was aglow with the promise of forgiveness and the fragile beginnings of something new.

Inside, laughter and the clatter of plates began to fill the kitchen. Momma's voice rose in song, old hymns echoing through the halls. Michael knelt beside the child, wiping dust from his cheeks, and for the first time in years, he felt the ache in his chest begin to ease.

And as the family gathered around the table, hands joined and heads bowed, the places they had seen—and the places they had yet to go— became one. For at that moment, under the old farmhouse roof, they were home.

PART XX
GLASS VEINS

PIPE TRAVELERS: THE HIDDEN GUARDIANS

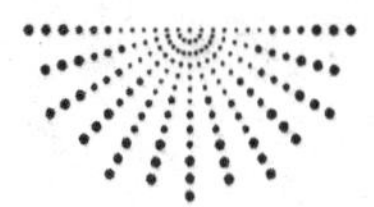

ECHOES OF DUST

THAT NEVER COLLECTED,

and floats elsewhere

Divine

Sovereignty

Omnipotent

Dominion

THE SECRET WORLD
BENEATH OUR FEET

CHAPTER 1

BENEATH THE SURFACE of our world, hidden from ordinary sight, exist the Pipe Travelers—mysterious beings who travel through a labyrinth of water pipes and secret portals. These portals, often square and sunken like submerged hot tubs, connect to underground water lines. The Pipe Travelers can see through these open water pipelines, communicate instantly, and traverse vast distances in mere seconds.

THE ELDERS: TIME'S SILENT ARCHITECTS

CHAPTER 2

AT THE HEART of this hidden society are the Elders, revered as the Time Keepers, Time Recorders, and Time Adjusters. They live in the most unassuming places within the human world, blending in to keep careful track of every moment and event. Their role is to maintain the delicate balance of time and reality, ensuring the world's timeline flows as it should.

THE SORCERERS, AGENTS OF CORRECTION

CHAPTER 3

To fulfill their duties, the Elders rely on the Sorcerers—beings bound to obey and unable to interact directly with humans. Sorcerers exist in a parallel dimension, moving alongside humans but never truly seen. Their presence is often mistaken for ghosts or demons, especially when the boundaries between worlds blur and both realities briefly collide. When timelines are altered or require correction, it is the sorcerers who act, guided by the Elders' will.

THE GUARDIANS, CLAIRVOYANTS AMONG US

CHAPTER 4

SOME HUMANS, particularly those with mental handicaps, serve as guardians and clairvoyants for the Elders. With one foot in each world, these individuals possess a unique connection, allowing them to hide in plain sight while aiding the Elders. Their minds act as bridges between dimensions, making them invaluable as seers and protectors.

WATER, THE ANCIENT POWER SOURCE

CHAPTER 5

WATER IS FAR MORE than a simple element in this universe—it is the ancient source of life, the ultimate conduit for travel, and the true power behind dimensional journeys. It binds realities together and enables the Pipe Travelers, Elders, and Sorcerers to move between worlds.

THE IMPERIAL ARMY AND
THE THREAT OF ROGUES

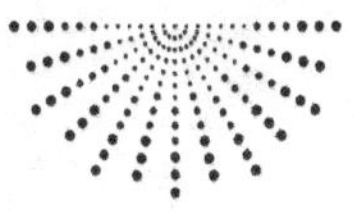

CHAPTER 6

TOGETHER, the Elders and Sorcerers form an imperial army, sworn to protect the future of human existence. Yet not all are loyal: Rogue Sorcerers and Elders seek to erase the human world and replace it with their own. These renegades live openly among us, their origins rooted in humanity's own destructive actions—either through the erasure of timelines or the persecution of those tied to the sixth dimension. To them, humans are a threat to both worlds.

PURE LIGHTS, THE UNSEEN PROTECTORS

CHAPTER 7

Among humans, there are rare individuals known as Pure Lights. Unaware of their own power, they can control all worlds and influence fate for good or ill. Pure Lights are hunted by all worlds—some seek to enslave them, while others, like the imperial order, strive to protect them. Ultimately, Pure Lights are the true guardians of existence, holding the fate of all realities in their hands.

In the shadows of our daily lives, this secret order works tirelessly—balancing time, correcting fate, and guarding the fragile boundary between worlds. Water flows beneath our feet, carrying more than we could ever imagine—the hopes, struggles, and destinies of countless realms, watched over by the Pipe Travelers and their hidden kin.

BEAUTIFUL PLACES NOT HERE

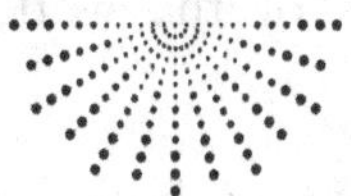

One pointing to the earth and the other toward the stars.

HE SETTLED onto the paint-chipped metal bench outside the clinic. Towering white hydrangeas stood directly behind him, their blooms heavy and full. A large tree stretched its broad branches overhead, offering shelter from the relentless ninety-degree heat. The surrounding foliage swayed gently in the warm summer breeze, whispering nature's secrets only the earth could understand. The breeze brushed his exposed skin, offering little relief from the heat, yet to him, it was the perfect backdrop for a long-overdue departure.

He closed his mouth, savoring the moist, warm air that flowed through his nostrils. It smelled of freshly cut grass, mingled with a subtle hint of florals, as if nature herself had carefully tucked them in.

He adored planet Earth—it was like no other. But now, it was his time to go.

When death is near, the world sharpens. Colors deepen. Sounds grow clearer. And the stars above seem to burn with a brilliance you'd never noticed before. This heightened perception is not just poetic, it's a deeply human response to the imminence of mortality. Our Mortality.

At the edge of death, our senses and awareness heighten, drawing your attention to the beauty and detail that daily routine often dulls. The mind, faced with finality, instinctively seeks meaning and connection, grasping at the wonders that have always surrounded us but were too easily overlooked. The stars, the breeze, the scent of grass—these become anchors, reminders of the world's richness and our place within it.

This phenomenon is rooted in both biology and psychology. As mortality becomes undeniable, your brain's focus narrows, stripping away distractions and sharpening appreciation for the present moment. It's a final, urgent act of gratitude—a way to honor all that you're about to leave behind. In facing the end, you see the world not as background, but as a gift, each star, each breath, suddenly precious, suddenly seen.

A sequence of 9

Your signature DNA is no more than an internal chain, binding you from within. You may feel enslaved from the inside out, held captive by the very code that defines you—the lunar standstill.

The lunar standstill—a rare celestial event occurring every 18.6 years—mirrors this internal struggle. At this moment, the moon pauses at its most extreme points in the sky, caught between its northern and southern journeys. It is a cosmic pause, a moment of tension before the cycle reverses.

Like the moon caught in its standstill, you too may feel trapped in cycles beyond your control, bound by invisible forces within. Yet, this pause is not permanent. It marks a turning point, a chance for transformation and release.

In the dance of DNA and lunar cycles, there lies a profound truth: though you may feel enslaved by your inner chains, moments of stillness hold the promise of change and liberation.

At the highest peak, the octagonal gazebo invites you to gaze across the city. It welcomes you for a dinner—not a warm one, but a cold, quiet feast. As you soak in the city skyline, it's hard to ignore how the sounds of the city seem drawn irresistibly to the grandeur of the cemetery. They breathe it in, naturally, like a body inhales air.

Abandon the truth, seeking solace in the false peace of illusion, where healing is but a shadow, and **armistice** a fleeting mirage.

THE PAST WAS **HANDSOMELY** CRAFTED to shape your destined future.

Carefully, **audaciously**, cast your gaze upon the depravity of **rapacious tongues**.

Let your weary souls rest,

not upon the hollow comfort of what is **spoon-fed** with greedy intent,

but upon the bedrock of what is true.

Discern, with unwavering courage, the difference between what **nourishes** and what corrupts,

for the future you inherit is forged in the fires of both **truth** and deception.

The Illusion of Self-Made Things

The things we carry.

When you're young, you can't wait to grow older. You imagine shelves lined with possibilities, each year another box to unpack, another story to store away. But as the years stack up and life takes hold, you find yourself longing for the weightlessness of youth, a time when your shelves were empty, your burdens few, and your dreams unboxed.

We are all self-made things, shaped by what we accumulate. Memories, regrets, hopes, and the silent ache for what once was. The things we carry become the architecture of our lives. Sometimes cluttered. Sometimes carefully arranged. But always present.

And so, we move forward, balancing what we've gathered, wishing sometimes for the chance to return, to rearrange, or to simply let go.

VERY FEW PEOPLE ever get the chance

GENUINE

Cynical

Speculate

Drop their guard

Subjectively

It fits

Part of what he was trying to do

WE'VE DONE ALL we can

ACCEPTED

Absolute satisfaction

ESTABLISHED

Dossier

Vanishing rare

Grand unveiling

We can be certain now

Less likely now

Bitter blow

Was indeed

For me

ONE DAY, it might as well make it

ENO MUSE

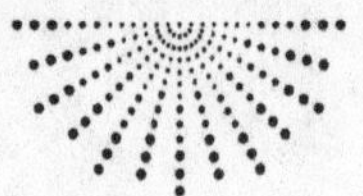

The bathroom cast a radiant light, spilling in pale ribbons across the hallway floor. Through the frosted glass, Hunter glimpsed a fractured full moon, its eerie glow bled into the apartment's silence.

Standing in the threshold, he felt something cold and nameless rising from the pit of his stomach. A sense that something terrible had already happened here or was about to.

The air seemed to thicken, heavy and humid. Time itself unraveled, slipping away in the hush, leaving only Hunter and the uneasy glow, suspended between what was and what might be.

I have been there the entire time.

I have been there before you wake

I have been there while you sleep

I have been your faithful

It is the windows that time unfolds

. . .

When you are helpless and too small to fight, you become the hero.
We are the mask

PLAGUED before we walk through the entrance

POURING INTO ONE ANOTHER.

His mouth became blood and then, a sea of it.

A jar full of ravenous shadows

Inside his hand, he cradled a vessel—sacrificed for the lost.

He ran his fingers along its serrated rim as a sudden clap of lightning split the sky, thunder rumbling and growing inside him until it absorbed his voice. Her heart leaped to her throat. In her trembling grasp, a glass full of cold diamonds—ice catching the fleeting light—trembled as she reached out, drawn by the height of the noise.

Was it imagination, or was it real? She whispered quietly to herself, searching for certainty in the storm's chaos.

The air fell from his chest, escaping in a shudder, leaving him hollow and breathless as the world outside surged with sound and light.

At the rotunda—the circular vestibule, the eternal circle.

Ra, the Eye of Horus, rises in the east, journeys across the sky, and sets in the west.

Walk quietly near the higher-ups' office, where power watches
silently.

IT SYMBOLIZES obedience

gods of nothing

Defeated by war that was impossible to win. He walked shamelessly
among things we don't speak of.
He grabbed the pillow, pressed it tightly against his face, and screamed
—a terrifying scream that echoed relentlessly, again and again.
Beyond a well-crafted door, muffled clamor eked out. The hallway
absorbed the residual noise, whittling its power down to a distant,
barely perceptible hum.

THE PARLOR

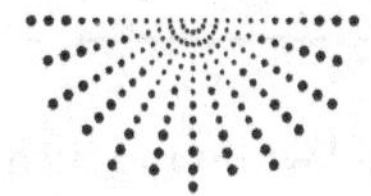

A DIM LIGHT cast shadows on dark maroon walls, white trim framing the ceiling. The green paisley casino carpet stretched beneath, worn and faded, anchoring the room in a peculiar casino nostalgia.

A shrine stood in the corner, reminiscent of a Catholic prayer booth—solemn and inviting. Nearby, a tomb-like fixture wore dull, tear-shaped lights as its focal point, droplets of sorrow suspended in the gloom.

Rods grinned beneath the weight of merlot velvet curtains, their heavy folds swallowing what little light remained. Above, the impasto-plastered ceiling resembled a dried riverbed—cracked, textured, and ancient.

A tall, stark man dressed in all black stood beside a squat woman. Her dingy white knit sweater hung loosely, resembling a rag doll left out in the rain. Wiry blond hair, unkempt and wild, framed her face like a mop infected with mildew.

She swiveled her head, and then—pop, crackle—the sound echoed through the hush.

The cramped room, meant for twenty, was packed with fifty restless bodies. The preacher, old and frail, led the group in prayers that felt more like an occult ritual than a service. The atmosphere was Jim Jones-Esque—scary, haunting, and electric with unease.

Suddenly, a door slammed, causing the little house to shudder. Floor lamps and scattered points of light illuminated a narrow path through the crowd, guiding the way through a space thick with tension and sorrow.

Only an incantation could withstand such punishment.

Tears fell, each one catching and glinting with light.

Pain weighed by an aching heart, just as a tear gathers and reflects the light.

SHE RETURNED to the world in a different way.

THE MAN in the strange hat stood behind the woman, waiting with humble patience as she rummaged through her purse with hurried certainty—her hand sweeping through its depths as if searching the sea's bowels for lost gold, some relic documented in a shipwreck's ledger.

"Oh my God, did you just see that, mister?"

"Clearly."

"That bus just hit him!"

"Well, he was in a rush."

"Aren't you going to help him?"

"Oh, I'm afraid he's long past help."

The man snatched his cigarettes and waltzed out the door, moving as if playing a silent game of hopscotch, weaving in and out of the crowd that had begun to gather.

. . .

"Naw, naw, naw! You ain't about to come in here and tell me you're some kind of author, writer, or whatever. I'm your parole officer. Didn't prison teach you anything? You need a J-O-B, something that puts green in these hands. Otherwise, you go back. You get my speed?"

> Love's power lies in the hands that dare to hold it, and the hearts brave enough to carry it.

Conduit

"CAN'T YOU FEEL IT?"

"Feel what?"

"The end. It's coming. I can smell it on you. You're undeserving of the fruit, and you know its power."

A pause, heavy and cold.

"Don't let her convince you otherwise. The others—they were better than you. Your soul is as foul as ours. You're one of us. You're despicable —look at what you've done to your own kind."

A whisper, almost gentle—

"We belong together. You are us."

He gripped her hand weakly and whispered, "What's out there? Is there anything at all?"

She smiled gently. "You always said there's nothing after this."

"I'm terrified," he admitted, voice trembling.

"Don't be," she replied, tears welling in her eyes.

He let go, managing a frail smile—and then, he slipped away.

At first, there was only a pinprick of light. Then the empty blackness crept in, swallowing everything. He wasn't flying or floating through the endless tunnel of dark. He was simply there, drifting in the nothingness, puttering about in the void, neither lost nor found—just present in the silence that followed.

The safe towered, clad in fortified matte steel, dazzled with an aura of omnipotence. Incredulous brads were welded relentlessly, layer upon layer, forging an unyielding strongbox. It wore fist-sized gold hexes like precious jewels, gleaming against the matte surface. Through its glass casing, its intricate inner workings revealed gears meshing with the precision of a finely crafted watch.

"Oh, they're British. Honey, don't get me started on that one."

"I'm not following you, ma'am."

"Because, darling, they're just... odd. That snobby attitude, those strange customs—they outdid even me, and believe me, that's saying something. But these folks were off—more than usual."

"Okay, give me an example."

"Well, Pinkie was sniffing the roses."

He paused, brow furrowed. "Pinkie, ma'am?"

"My imperial Shih Tzu, darling."

"The dog," he said, jotting a note.

"As I was saying, he was sniffing those blasted roses. Pinkie was here long before the roses, you know. I don't understand why Elizabeth gets so touchy about them. They're so yesterday, but you know how those Brits can be."

"Ma'am," he said, still looking confused.

"Haven't you been listening, darling?" She stared at him when he went near the roses. "And her eyes—my God. They didn't look human. I mean, they really looked infected. Like she had some awful disease or something. It was frightful, really frightful."

MICROWAVE VISION TO see space

X-ray goggles for black holes

Advance forward or ahead

The glass bridge created the illusion that certain areas dropped off the cliff. When employees walked too close to the edge, it felt as if they were walking on air. Then I thought, what if the glass bridge was suspended over water. Then what, he tells himself, then what.

AWAKENED him or torched his soul.

The boy was so dark that not even the night could match his shade, yet his teeth and the whites of his eyes sparkled like distant stars. Soft pink glowed at the corners of his mouth and on the palms of his hands, as if he wore the delicate flesh of a ripe apricot.

WHEN THEY THREW her from the cliff, a sharp pain seized his belly, as if his very core had been wrenched away. In an instant, he sprinted forward until the ground vanished beneath his feet. Diving headlong, he spotted her falling fast in the distance, the unforgiving earth rushing up to meet them both.

He tightened his form, slicing through the air like a bullet. Fueled by desperation, he chased her down the cliff, reaching out, yearning for her touch. And when death became certain, he clasped her hand as they struck the ground together.

PROGRAMMED AT BIRTH

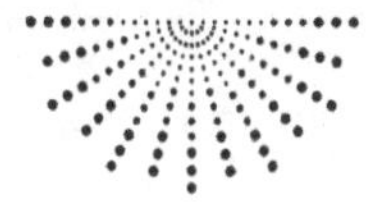

BECCA WOKE each morning at 3 a.m. She brewed her coffee, brushed her teeth, and settled in front of her computer. A programmer by trade, she worked from home until 11:45 a.m., her routine as precise as clockwork. At noon, without fail, except on Sundays, she paused. Sundays were reserved for dog parks, picnics (weather permitting), yoga, and all the rituals that fulfilled life, whether that fulfillment came from contentment or complacency. The world may never know.

For a year, Becca had stood on the corner of First and Madison, holding a sign that read: "The world will end on July 4th." But when that day finally arrived, she abandoned her post. Instead, she stayed home with her dog, Portia, curled up on the couch, waiting for the inevitable.

Contrary to the sign's dire warning, the world did not end on the 4th. In fact, it flourished. Marvels were announced across the airwaves, a celebration of human ingenuity and progress. The world cheered, basking in the glow of a breakthrough achieved through scientific dedication and hard work.

But the end came a day later, on the 5th. Becca was brushing her teeth when it happened. Just a few feet away, in the corner of the room, a trash bin quietly cradled the sign she had carried for over a year, a silent witness to all that had passed, and all that was lost.

ROMAN CARNIVAL

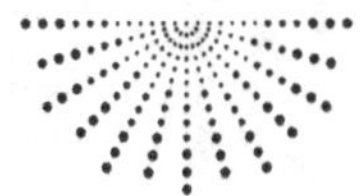

Anna and the Lost Carnival

YOUNG ANNA, intent on building the grandest sandcastle on the beach, decides it needs a massive moat. She digs deep into the sand, her small hands scooping away grains until her fingers strike something hard and cold, a silver coin, ancient and tarnished. She doesn't recognize its significance, so she sets it aside and keeps digging.

Moments later, her shovel uncovers a glint of gold. Then another. And another. Soon, her sand bucket overflows with a trove, twenty-five coins in all. Bronze, silver, and gold. Alongside a thick, ornate gold bracelet. Each piece is heavy with history. Their surfaces etched with mysterious symbols and figures from a world long vanished.

What Lies Beneath

Unbeknownst to Anna, her playful excavation has uncovered the remnants of a vibrant past. Over two thousand years ago, the very stretch of sand where she now plays was the bustling heart of a Roman trade carnival. Merchants from distant lands gathered here, their stalls brimming with wares, their pockets heavy with coins like the ones she has found. The smell of oil lamps still whispers when the wind whistles.

The carnival was a place of exchange, goods, stories, and fortunes changed hands beneath colorful tents and fluttering banners. The coins, lost to time, are relics of that era. Evidence of trade, celebration, and the mingling of cultures along the ancient coastline Anna calls home.

PART XXI
HUMAN STATIC

CURVATURE OF SPACETIME, EINSTEIN-ROSEN BRIDGES, AND RADIATION HAZARDS

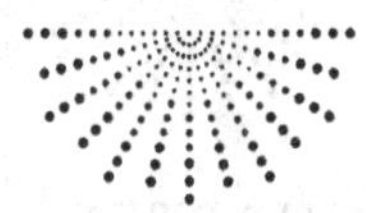

Notes taken—Dominion of the Divine/ Hunter and the wormhole

THE CURVATURE OF SPACETIME: MATTER AND ENERGY

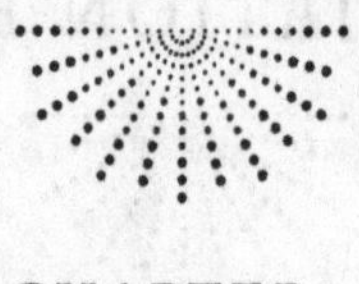

CHAPTER 1

- According to Einstein's general theory of relativity, the presence of matter and energy curves spacetime. Massive objects like stars and planets create indentations in the fabric of spacetime, influencing the motion of other objects and even light itself.
- This curvature is what we perceive as gravity: matter tells spacetime how to curve, and curved spacetime tells matter how to move.

TUNNEL-LIKE STRUCTURES: EINSTEIN-ROSEN BRIDGES

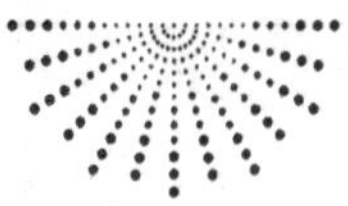

CHAPTER 2

- An Einstein-Rosen bridge, more commonly known as a wormhole, is a theoretical tunnel-like structure connecting two distant points in spacetime.
- In principle, a wormhole could allow for faster-than-light travel between its two ends, acting as a shortcut through spacetime. This would enable travel between distant regions of the universe in less time than it would take light to traverse normal space.
- The Einstein-Rosen bridge was first described in 1935 by Albert Einstein and Nathan Rosen as a solution to the equations of general relativity, representing a bridge between two black holes or two universes.

POTENTIAL RADIATION HAZARDS OF WORMHOLES

CHAPTER 3

- Radiation Hazards: One of the major theoretical issues with traversable wormholes is the potential for intense radiation hazards. As matter and energy pass through or near the throat of a wormhole, high-energy particles (such as Hawking radiation or quantum fluctuations) could be generated or concentrated, posing severe risks to travelers.
- Instability: Wormholes are predicted to be extremely unstable. The passage of even a single photon could cause the wormhole to collapse or produce bursts of deadly radiation, making safe passage unlikely without some form of exotic matter to stabilize the structure.
- Exotic Matter Requirement: To keep a wormhole open and traversable, it is theorized that "exotic matter" with negative energy density would be required. Such matter is purely hypothetical and has not been observed in nature, adding another layer of uncertainty and potential hazard.

CLEARLY, from the evidence, we need a 21st century Einstein to make time travel possible. Otherwise, time travel is fucked, wormhole wise. According to Einstein and Rosen.

PORTALS IN DEATH

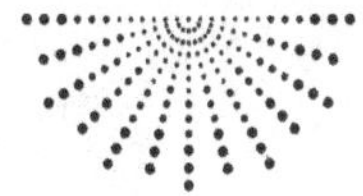

RUMMAGING through the closet was painful. Each article of clothing I touched brought her back to me. Her presence lingering in the fabric. Her scent still clinging to the sleeves, mingling with the stubborn trace of old dog pee. The smell was everywhere, woven into the seams and corners, impossible to escape.

Every piece carried a memory. The dress she wore to that party, the sweater from Christmas, the blouse she had on for her birthday at Los Delicias. Each hung on frail plastic hangers, preserved as if waiting for her return. Preserved. Preserved. The word echoed in my mind, a reminder of all that remained and all that was lost.

When my mother retold a story, it was always personal, selfless, and centered around others. She was present in her tales, but the true heart of each story was the people she loved. She was a genuine people person, finding delight in the lives and joys of others. Their stories animated her, and she made everyone feel seen, remembered, and cherished.

Now, in the quiet of the closet, surrounded by the relics of her life, I realized how much of her spirit lingered, not just in the clothes she wore, but in the way she lived for others, and in the stories she left behind.

Longing to hear your voice in this quiet moment. I really miss you. I wish I could just call you up and hear your voice right now.

Narrow, thin, and frail—too insubstantial to absorb anything.

Seagulls hovered in the sky, suspended and majestic, as if forming a living constellation.

Phantom eye

All these deaths were sudden and unimaginably horrific.

Dull lights, shrouded in mist, radiate outward as fuzzy orbs— alien and ethereal, as if from another planet. The effect is organic, like a sea creature illuminating a hidden path along the ocean floor.

She was the woman who swallowed everything—her stomach a chaotic junk drawer: paper clips, rubber bands, a yo-yo, and even, believe it or not, an entire pad of Post-its.

Then there was the man who managed to wedge a ratchet up his backside. My uncle, ever quick with wit, guessed the man was just trying to tighten his nuts.

ESSENTIALS FOR
LIVING IN THE STICKS

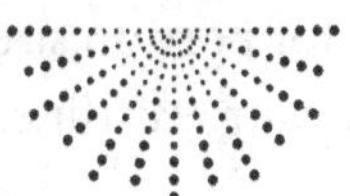

IF YOU'RE PLANNING to settle down in the rural heartland, there are a few must-haves that define the experience and make life both practical and memorable:

1. **Walmart**

- The local hub for everything—groceries, hardware, fishing gear, and last-minute birthday gifts.
- The place where you'll inevitably run into neighbors, friends, and half the town on a Saturday morning.

2. **Guns and Ammo Surplus Store**

- A staple for hunters, sportsmen, and anyone who values self-reliance.
- Stocked with everything from hunting rifles to fishing tackle, camo jackets, and sometimes even a friendly word of advice.

3. **Dairy Queen**

- The classic roadside treat stop.

- Perfect for cooling off with a Blizzard or grabbing a burger after a long day.

4. Mom-and-Pop Restaurant

- The soul of small-town dining.
- Expect hearty, stick-to-your-ribs meals: chicken-fried steak, mashed potatoes, gravy, and pies that taste like someone's grandma made them.
- These spots are famous for portion sizes that challenge your self-control and expand your waistline.

Living in the sticks means embracing the simple pleasures. Reliable basics, comfort food (buttered biscuits), and a sense of community that's as filling as the meals themselves.

PART XXII
FLESH AND WIRES

LIFE OF KETCHUP

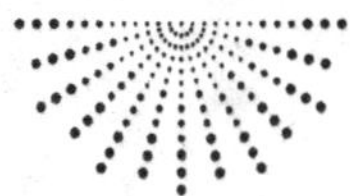

THOSE LITTLE THINGS that happen to us—the stuff we go through every day.

You know, the best stories are humble and honest—they don't shout. They just sit with you like old friends sharing kind words over coffee.

THE INVISIBLE ARMY

CHAPTER 1

THE ANTISEPTIC SMELL burned my nostrils while harsh fluorescent lighting made everything look unnatural—including the woman hunched over the housekeeping cart in the Marriott hallway. Her name tag read "Maria," but the businessman stepping around her didn't bother to look. To him, she was furniture that happened to move.

I watched her work through the open doorway of room 314. Dog poop ground into carpet fibers. Toothpaste smeared across marble countertops. Wet towels thrown in corners like discarded thoughts on paper. The previous guests had left their mark on every surface, and Maria would erase it all before the next family arrived expecting perfection.

Her hands moved in practiced rhythm, scrubbing, wiping, restoring, while the mechanical hum of her vacuum provided a soundtrack to invisible labor. Sixteen rooms by 2 PM. Every surface sanitized. Every corner spotless. All for wages that wouldn't cover her own rent.

This is where we must start—with the people you never see.

We must start small to progress to bigger things. You've heard this before: crawl before you walk. Although I never crawled, according to my mother. I walked first. And when I mentioned this to my son's pediatrician, she gave me a concerning look.

"It's important for babies to crawl first—it allows their equilibrium to adjust in time. If you walk without ever crawling, your equilibrium never gets a chance to develop properly. That's why you have dizzy spells and feel off balance."

When you read this story, I want you to crawl first. That way your equilibrium will strengthen over time, and you won't lose the message.

THE BATHROOM REVELATION

CHAPTER 2

THE ONE-STAR HOTEL reviews tell the story better than I ever could. Not the four-star reviews praising luxury—the angry ones. The complaints. The outrage. And they all say the same thing: "The bathroom was disgusting." "Filthy restroom." "Couldn't even use the facilities."

We are obsessed with clean bathrooms. We care if our bodies touch a clean toilet seat. We want soap dispensers filled, floors scrubbed, mirrors streak-free. We want a sparkly atmosphere when we purge our bowels.

Here's what you don't see—Walmart employees don't clean those bathrooms. Housekeeping does. Walmart outsources to janitorial services that employ immigrants, mostly women, who work for wages that keep them in poverty while keeping America clean.

They scrub the poop stains off our toilet bowls. They throw out our trash. They make sure we have toilet paper to wipe our tush. And they remain invisible to the common person, some of the lowest-wage workers in America.

The statistics tell the story: 31% of hotel workers are foreign-born, compared to just 17% of the overall American workforce. These workers clean sixteen rooms per day while earning wages that keep them below the poverty line. The average wage for hotel housekeepers is $10.41 per hour, while the living wage in the United States is $16.54 per hour.

But you never see them as human. Do they have any value? It's clear they serve a purpose, still, there's always a but somewhere in there.

THE CANDY SCAM

CHAPTER 3

I WAS thirteen when the two sisters approached me at school. The redhead was taller than me—unusual, since I towered over most girls. She was really pretty, and I was smitten.

"Want to make some easy money selling candy this summer?" she asked, her smile bright as Tiger Beat (a teen magazine from the eighties).

Somewhere in my teenage brain, I thought if I made good money, maybe I could take her to Pizza Hut. Buy a pitcher of cold Pepsi and play Ms. Pac-Man. In the eighties, Pizza Hut was the place to be—all the rage.

First day of summer vacation, my brother and I showed up at her house. Ten teenagers reported for duty. The first red flag hit me immediately. Their house had no furniture. Not even a dining table. Just three metal folding chairs in the living room of a large house with a pool out back.

Why not four chairs? There were four family members. Did they fight over who got to sit?

The house was stuffed to the brim with boxes of candy. Twix, Hershey's, Reese's Peanut Butter Cups like a residential 7-Eleven. But the real shock was the printing room, commercial Xerox machines, color-coded paperclips, banquet tables set up like a counterfeiting operation.

You know how sometimes you just get a weird vibe from people? Well, these parents totally gave me that feeling. The dad kept glancing over at the window like clockwork every time a car rolled by—every thirty seconds. His hand was always right next to this stuffed duffel bag by the door, like he was ready to grab it and go any second.

When a car backfired outside, both parents froze mid-sentence, listening. The mother hovered nearby, watching all ten of us like a hawk, afraid we might uncover the real activity behind door number two.

They loaded us into a white church van and drove us to swanky neighborhoods. Don't poop where you eat, as the saying goes. They dropped us off in the Arizona heat, sometimes for two hours. I imagine they didn't want to draw attention by accidentally killing a kid of heat stroke.

What I learned, selling candy door to door isn't easy. It requires skill. Natural skill. My younger brother always ranked at the top. He sold the most out of ten. Nobody could touch him. For every package sold, we received a dollar. My brother was making twenty bucks on a bad day.

What I didn't know then was that we were part of a nationwide pattern. The California Labor Commissioner was cracking down on firms that exploit children in door-to-door candy sales, describing operations where "Fagin-like crew leaders" gather children from poor neighborhoods and threaten to leave them far from home if they don't sell enough.

The pattern continues today. In 2023, teens in New York were caught using Venmo and Zelle to drain victims' bank accounts after asking for candy donations. We were the invisible labor force, processed through a system designed to extract value from children.

THE SECRET

CHAPTER 4

MY BROTHER REVEALED his secret to the group, "Before I ring the doorbell, I get the lay of the land. I see what kind of cars are parked, if there's flowers out front, what animals they have. Anything I can relate to."

I watched from across the street as he approached the blue house. He stopped at the mailbox, reading the name. I noticed the garden gnomes. Saw the "Beware of Dog" sign but heard no barking. When the elderly woman answered, he smiled and said, "Mrs. Henderson, those roses are beautiful. My grandmother had the same variety."

Her suspicious frown melted into a smile before he even mentioned candy.

"Then I address them formally," he continued. "Ma'am, Sir. Let them know I respect them. If it's a woman, I compliment something. If it's a guy, I say 'Cool car, sir' or 'Can I pet your dog?' The important thing is to like what they like."

For the first time in my life, I realized my little brother was a genius. He'd discovered something profound about human nature, people buy from people they like, and he made himself likable by paying attention to what mattered to them.

But we were still just kids being exploited. No matter how skilled my brother was, we were part of a system designed to extract value from children while giving us minimal compensation.

By summer's end, my brother averaged thirty-five dollars a day. Not bad for an eleven-year-old. I made little money, and my dreams of taking the redhead to Pizza Hut dwindled. It wouldn't be the last time I took a job to impress a girl.

RUBY TUESDAY

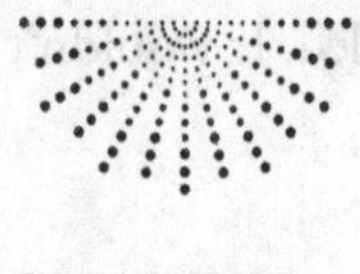

CHAPTER 5

MY FIRST SERVING job was at Ruby Tuesday. The general manager was a sleaze ball—heavy set, fiftyish, wearing white button-ups with most buttons undone, exposing his hairy chest and gold chains. Classic sleaze ball uniform.

Weekend day shifts were the worst, and he always scheduled me for those. My station was next to the all-you-can-eat salad bar. The blond hostess always had snide comments about me. I suspected she was sleeping with the boss—when I'd see them touching and flirting, it grossed me out. She was eighteen. It was uncomfortable to watch.

She always seated families with children at my station and businessmen.

If you've never served tables, here's a fact—families with children never tip well. Neither do businessmen in shiny suits with perfect hair and unnatural white teeth. The parents would let their children throw food on the floor, smear it on walls—destroy the area. They'd have me running constantly. Getting refill after refill. Fresh plates from the kitchen, not the ones near the salad bar.

A family of four's bill would never break fifty dollars. After all that running around, they'd leave a two-dollar tip. Sometimes nothing. Then

I'd spend forty-five minutes scrubbing shredded cheese and dressing from the carpet—God knows why a restaurant has carpet—while they walked out without a backward glance.

The restaurant industry has a long history of exploiting young workers through tip-based compensation. The federal tipped minimum wage remains $2.13 per hour, unchanged since 1991. When customers don't tip appropriately, the worker absorbs the financial loss while still providing full service.

THE UPSCALE BARBECUE JOINT

CHAPTER 6

AT THE UPSCALE barbecue joint in Houston, I learned to read wealth differently. The most generous tippers weren't who you'd expect. Wealthy people—truly wealthy—tip well. They have nothing to prove. The ones talking big game, with everything to prove, are the worst tippers.

You can spot authentic wealth, they don't wear flashy clothes, at least the men don't. They order what they want without looking at prices. Usually simple stuff, like club sandwiches. The women are different—dripping in fine silk, hand stitched leather, slathered in diamonds, heels reaching the stars. They have little choice. Men aren't judged the way women are.

One day, I was staring out at the empty parking lot when a brand-new yellow Ferrari blasted through and squealed into a front parking spot. Late Friday nights, our lot looked like a luxury dealership.

A middle-aged man with blond spiky hair popped out. Faded holey jeans, ripped to hell. White tank top. Alligator boots. He didn't look famous, though his style read rock star. Inside, his clothes were grimy, leaning toward dirty. But he smelled incredible—whatever designer cologne he wore overpowered everything.

He walked in friendly and down to earth, not what you'd expect from someone jumping out of a Ferrari. He was cool, as though money didn't define him as a person.

"Can I sit at the bar and order lunch?" he asked politely.

"Absolutely," I said. "We don't have a bartender right now, but I can place your food order, and my manager will make any drinks."

Then I left to place his order and brew fresh coffee, as he requested.

I never said no to a customer. But I never saw my manager leave his office before the dinner rush. For some reason—call it fate, call it Spidey sense—I heard a loud commotion from the bar area. I could hear it all the way from the kitchen.

I ran out thinking someone was robbing the restaurant. The hostess was nowhere to be found, and the man and my manager were in a screaming match. Heated. Nose to nose. Fire and brimstone. Spit flying everywhere.

My heart was doing 130 on the highway. I stepped between them and told my boss to calm down. I'd never seen him yell at a customer before. Ever.

"I want this bum out of here," he fired back.

"He's good. I sat him at the bar."

"I don't allow homeless people to eat in my restaurant."

Once he said that, I understood. The man's clothes did have a homeless flair. I tried to defend him, but my boss wouldn't hear it. He threatened to call the cops.

The man tossed a bar stool and pointed at me. "You're a cool kid, I respect that." He aimed a finger at my boss. "But you are a son of a bitch. My uncle was a Vietnam vet who was homeless for a time. I'll knock your dick in the dirt. Fuck you, man."

Then he stormed out and peeled away in his yellow Ferrari.

Not an hour later, the owner showed up with a man I'd never met. Both dressed like executives. The owner had a serious face, all business. He waved me over.

"Where's Bill?" he asked.

I shrugged. I hadn't seen him since the altercation.

"Did you see what happened?" he whispered.

I didn't try to play dumb. I just nodded.

"How bad?"

My eyes bulged, my face compressed, soured. I still feel bad after all these years. Why couldn't I be a good liar?

The man was famous. I didn't recognize him. The hostess didn't. My boss didn't. And the owner fired my boss. The man's uncle being a homeless Vietnam veteran added moral weight to the discrimination—Bill wasn't just rejecting a customer based on appearance but dishonoring a veteran's sacrifice.

After that, they hired a real winner. Total jerk. Nothing like Bill. I don't think Bill disliked homeless people. He was too kind. It was just a weird day, moon aligned perfectly, hell in the rearview mirror sort of thing. Whatever it was, it was tragic.

THE ITALIAN BISTRO

CHAPTER 7

THE LAST RESTAURANT I waited tables at was a high-end Italian bistro. I learned that most people are like my candy crew: one exceptionally skillful right out of the gate, most treading water slowly but effectively, and then the ones struggling to keep their heads above the waterline.

The diamond-slathered beauty and her husband embodied this perfectly. She was wealthy, dripping in jewelry. He was dressed in a beer t-shirt and Adidas sweatpants, filthy sneakers, unshaven, hair smashed to one side. But he wore a diamond-studded gold Rolex. Why? Never understood that one.

He was smug. In my experience, men are entitled, no matter how much money they have. Color doesn't matter either. The man ordered from the kids' menu because he didn't like Italian food—good timing coming to an Italian bistro. He ordered frozen fries and a kids' cheeseburger. Frozen patties, by the way. We had a fresh scratch kitchen for everything else except the kids' menu.

The wife was sweet, down to earth, despite her clothes saying otherwise. She frowned at the menu. "I love salmon, but I hate slimy spinach."

I smiled. "I hate slimy spinach too. My mom force-fed it to me when I was young. How can the chef prepare it for your liking?"

Her eyes lit up instantly. "Oh my God. My dad used to do the same thing. Your mom and my dad must have grown up in the same town."

I smiled big, peered at her boulder-sized diamond ring. "Oh, I don't know about that."

We began making a connection. An unlikely connection. We were sharing something intimate about ourselves among strangers. The roles were colliding. We saw each other—I mean really saw each other. Her eyes were kind, gentle. Her husband gave her a glare, then me. He saw something we didn't, jealousy. He snapped at her, "Just order the damn salmon."

I think he felt threatened. Connecting with people, strangers from opposite worlds, is big thinking. It's powerful. Keeping yourself in tiny bubbles keeps you small. You never grow. Small thinking is looking at appearance, color, gender, and making snap judgments. You decide in a split second that someone who looks nothing like you is unworthy of your time.

There's a song I can't quote, but it asks—what if God walked around on earth right now? I guarantee you wouldn't be able to pick God out of a lineup.

THE SPINACH DISASTER

CHAPTER 8

WHAT BUGGED me was how he sat—legs spread wide, crotch visible. He had an "I don't care about anyone but myself" attitude. Other diners stared, giving him the look. He treated the restaurant like his crash pad.

I suggested steamed spinach, which was totally my fault. Most scratch kitchens are prepped to every level of the menu. Something like steamed spinach had the kitchen out of balance.

Through the glass wall, I watched the sous chef throw his towel down in frustration. The expediter's face reddened as tickets backed up. Steam rose from abandoned pans while three cooks huddled around a single burner, trying to master a technique they'd never needed before.

Steaming spinach is a skill. It wilts quickly. You have to watch closely so you don't overcook it. I've ruined spinach plenty of times, and I steam it regularly. After the fifth try, it still wasn't coming out right.

The wealthy woman let me off the hook. I don't think she was sparing my feelings. Her feelings were aimed at the people in the kitchen racing around nonstop. She kept her eyes locked on the kitchen, and each time the spinach plate was sent back, she cringed. Her face appeared genuinely heartbroken, sorrowful.

I felt extremely bad for creating the mess. In the restaurant business, front of the house and back of the house are at constant odds. Waiters screw up all the time, like I did, and treat the back of the house like garbage when things go wrong, even when it's the server's fault.

I always prioritized the people who made my food first. Every time my ticket came up, I was first to alert the kitchen about large parties, dietary restrictions, anything that could cause delays. I was loyal to the kitchen first, then to the guest. Without the kitchen's smooth operation, no guest gets food on time.

Their bill came to $200 dollars and change. She paid with her black American Express card and left a $200 dollar tip. She understood the complexity of what I'd navigated: managing her husband's demands, the kitchen's limitations, and my professional standards.

BACK TO THE BLUES CLUB

CHAPTER 9

AT THE UPSCALE BARBECUE JOINT, weekend nights looked like a luxury dealership. On one of those nights, a customer in his sixties, well-dressed but not flashy, had a beautiful model-type woman with him, and you could tell he was a big shot. Diamond watch, gold jewelry, designer clothes with no labels—the kind only the who's who would recognize. Velvet, rich material like nothing you'll ever see.

We were slammed. I mean really slammed. Drinks at a standstill, nothing coming out of the kitchen or bar. The blues room was open where famous jazz and blues singers played. Sally Field's crew ate there when shooting An Eye for An Eye. Sally Field—amazing person, by the way.

The man's girl looked pissed. He snagged me as I passed their table, pulling me to his level, eye to eye. Not intimidating—more like I was a buddy, like he wanted to tell me a secret.

"Can you help me out?" he asked.

"What can I get you?" I screamed.

"Get her something trendy, make sure it's perfect. Scotch for me," he replied.

I nodded. I try my hardest to fill requests—it's my job. I could hardly hear what he was saying because the music was thumping loudly. The air was pulsating. Everyone was screaming over other patrons, trying to get words across. Complete party town madhouse. I loved it when it got like that. Everything felt electric.

He didn't need to tell me how he likes his scotch—that was my job. People who drink scotch are finicky. It's ritualistic. Neat, soda, ice—sacrilege. Strangest request—scotch and coke. That gets you ejected from the bar instantly.

There were two important things happening. He was smart, and I could tell by what he said, he liked her but didn't know her well. He took more time explaining the girl's drink than his own. He asked for my recommendation—the smart thing to do.

His drink was of little importance to him. He saw something in me, just as I saw something in him. We were riding the same wave.

I screamed back at him, "Ketel One Cosmopolitan for her, Macallan neat for you."

His eyes lit up like Christmas morning. He grinned big and nodded yes. He was impressed—not because I recommended a Cosmo, that's basic bartending 101. He was impressed because I knew premium liquor and his scotch preference without asking. That takes skill. Reading people. And I nailed it.

THE SYSTEM

CHAPTER 10

HE TRIED to hand me a platinum credit card. I shook my head. At this barbecue joint, we had discretion funds up to a certain dollar amount. I'd been there longer than some, so my fund was larger. I didn't use it often or abuse it.

They'd been waiting twenty minutes. I knew who his server was—she wasn't skilled and fell into the weeds a lot. When I refused his card, it was for two reasons: they deserved better service, and I wanted her to see he had things handled. Both their faces changed when I refused the card. They eased.

I headed straight to the bar. Complete cluster funk. Drinks scattered everywhere. They were drowning. Servers screaming orders over bartenders, bartenders couldn't hear because of loud music, customers loaded at the bar, two deep.

I went behind the bar and got a bartender's attention. "I'll split halves with you if you get me a scotch and a Cosmo, comp."

She nodded, dropped everything, and got to work on my drinks. She knew I was making bank—a sure thing. I had wads of cash stuffed in my apron. My guess, a thousand. At twenty-one, I was bringing home over a thousand a night working the blues club on Fridays and Saturdays.

Life is a series of connections built on good communication. When surrounded by chaos, make your words count and clear.

I didn't leave right away. I waited so the woman could taste her drink. If she didn't like it, I could run back and try another. The moment she sipped, I knew she approved. It was written all over her.

She didn't play hard at it—a subtle nod. The energy shifted. She smiled at him, he smiled back. No words necessary. He looked at me with hard eyes, but good hard eyes. The pressure was dissipating.

I screamed in his ear—the only time you can scream at a customer: "I'll be on the lookout. You need anything, lift your hand, I'll see it."

He ordered two more times. Everything went smoothly. They were happy, having a good time.

I never did any of it to get anything in return. I loved my job. Turning a bad situation into a good one was payment enough. The man, his girl, and I saw each other—really saw each other. I could have reverted to saying, "I'm not your server, good luck." Instead, I saw two people out on a date, trying to have a good time, and I wanted to help.

Before they left, he stuffed a wad in my shirt pocket. I immediately reached for the cash. "Don't worry about it, it's on me." I said.

He shook his head, pressed his hand against my pocket firmly. He locked eyes on me with another hard glare. "You earned every cent, bro."

Then, they walked out.

THE UNIVERSE'S TOOLS

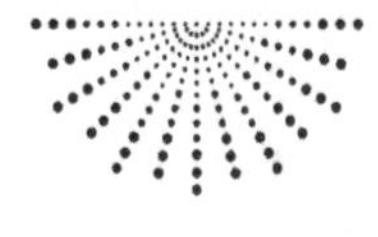

CHAPTER 11

I PULLED OUT THE CASH. Nothing but hundreds, except one fifty wrapped in the middle. One thousand fifty dollars. I was walking around with that stuffed in my shirt pocket, I could have accidentally dropped it during the night.

Now I understood why he kept giving me hard stares. I wanted to cry.

But I didn't keep it. The server who was always in the weeds had a kid. I took her table. I talked to the bartender first, and we collectively agreed to split my original tips, not the thousand fifty. We gave that to the server.

She cried. We all kind of teared up. What I didn't know was she was getting evicted from her home. Single mom, raising a kid alone. My mom did it too. It made me think that maybe we are the universe's tools.

Do you still think serving is a low-skill job?

NEW ORLEANS REVELATION

CHAPTER 12

My first time visiting New Orleans, I frequented a bar where I befriended a bartender. We'll call him Jack. One night, drinking pretty good, talking to girls, buying drinks, tipping Jack very well. Just blowing money. I was young and good with money. No kids yet. As someone in the service industry, you pay it forward. Or you better.

A server or bartender's life is like a pirate's life. Some days it rains pure gold, others it just pisses all over you. But there's always an elevator on its way up.

Jack thought I was loaded. Trust fund baby or something. He was more intrigued by his assumption than the reality. We got to talking, and he told me he'd graduated from law school a few years ago. He made $130 thousand dollars a season. Mardi Gras season. I was floored.

He'd decided to travel to New Orleans, just like I did, and decided to stay indefinitely. He didn't care for law—his parents forced him into law school. The money he made in one season put a lawyer's career to shame, according to him. He'd rather bartend for the rest of his life than become a professional lawyer. College made him miserable. Being in New Orleans made him the happiest he'd ever been.

Did you catch what happened? Jack started the conversation with money. Everything else came first, before his happiness. It wasn't until the end that he mentioned being happy. Money, to him, solidified his skill or worth. He was saying his value rested at $130 thousand—a false god.

Anyone who starts spouting numbers has a lot to prove. To themselves and everyone else. For small thinkers, money symbolizes value. But if money indicates a person's value, why do we pay teachers, nurses, social workers, and countless other essential workers so little? Why do we compensate hotel housekeepers with poverty wages while they maintain the cleanliness we demand?

THE UNCOMFORTABLE TRUTH

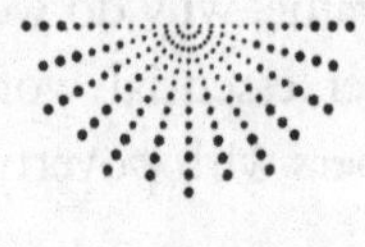

CHAPTER 13

THE ANSWER IS SIMPLE, and you're not going to like it. We've built an entire economy on the backs of people we refuse to see as human.

Ketchup appears simple—just tomatoes in a bottle. But it's made by migrant workers who can't afford healthcare while picking tomatoes in 100-degree heat. Processed in factories where line workers piss in bottles because bathroom breaks slow down production. Transported by truck drivers who haven't seen their families in weeks. Served by restaurant staff earning $2.13 an hour while customers complain about everything.

We don't want to think about any of this when we squeeze that familiar red bottle. Just like we don't want to think about the housekeeper's swollen feet after cleaning sixteen hotel rooms, or the kitchen worker's burned hands from rushing your order, or the single mother choosing between rent and groceries while serving your family dinner.

Here's what I learned in all those years of service work, most customers are assholes. Not all—but most. They treat service workers like furniture that happens to have feelings they can damage for entertainment. They snap their fingers, make impossible demands, leave messes that would embarrass a toddler, then tip like they're doing you a favor.

And the worst part? The system is designed this way. Restaurants can pay servers $2.13 an hour because customers are supposed to make up the difference. Hotels can pay housekeepers poverty wages because "anyone can clean." Corporations can exploit child labor in candy sales because poor kids are expendable.

Jack found his worth in dollar amounts because that's the only metric that matters in America. We worship money while pretending to value human dignity. We underpay teachers, nurses, and social workers, then wonder why society is falling apart. We pay hotel housekeepers starvation wages while demanding five-star cleanliness.

The Ferrari customer was right to rage at my manager. The wealthy woman was right to tip generously. The struggling single mother deserved better than our charity. But these are exceptions that prove the rule: most people in power don't give a shit about invisible workers.

You want to know the real truth about service work? It's skilled labor performed by people society has written off. The housekeeper managing sixteen rooms requires more organizational skill than most office managers. The server handling ten tables during dinner rush has better crisis management abilities than most executives. The kitchen worker coordinating multiple orders under pressure demonstrates more teamwork than most corporate departments.

But we call it "unskilled labor" because acknowledging the skill would mean paying for it.

Here's my challenge to you, the next time you're in a restaurant, hotel, or any place where people serve you, actually see them. Not as servants, but as skilled professionals whose expertise makes your comfort possible. Tip like their rent depends on it—because it does. Treat them like human beings whose time and dignity matter— because they do.

And when you reach for that ketchup bottle, remember, every convenience in your life exists because someone else did the hard, invisible work to make it possible. The least you can do is acknowledge that reality instead of pretending it doesn't exist.

Because in the end, we're all just trying to survive in a system that values profit over people. Some of us are lucky enough to be visible. Others spend their lives being processed through systems that extract their labor while denying their humanity.

The question isn't whether you see them. The question is what you're going to do about it.

DOORWAY TO
FORGOTTEN DIMENSIONS

Standing at the edge of the bed was an act of rebellion against my own fragility. The antiseptic smell burned my nostrils while harsh fluorescent lighting made everything look unnatural, including my mother's pale face against the stark white pillow. My eyes scanned every crease, every plastic tube, while a suffocating scream built inside me, growing louder and more relentless.

I clenched my toes so tightly they cramped, pain folding inward like a venomous toxin, spreading through my veins with each heartbeat. The mechanical rhythm of life-support machines provided a cold soundtrack to my terror. Yet, strangely, there was freedom in not having to explain it. Pain demands no justification, it only needs a silent place to settle.

I finally unclenched, letting blood rush back through my feet as a wave of raw emotion surged in, accompanied by an involuntary twitch. Memories long buried stirred anew. Watching my mother struggle for life in this alien place, this place that was not home, filled me with a deep, primal fear.

Contemplating life beyond death is no luxury when you are trapped in its grasp. The thought that I might never see her again shattered me.

Life, death, and the afterlife collided into one overwhelming reality, sending jolts through my heart until the tears I fought to hold back finally spilled free, carrying with them all the words I'd never have the chance to say.

PART XXIII
BOY OF TOMORROW

THE AUCTION

CHAPTER 1

THE TENSION in the room shattered with the slam of the hammer. But it wasn't the gavel's crack that sent gasps through the crowd—it was the painting itself.

The Boy of Tomorrow stared back from its gilded frame with eyes that seemed to follow every movement in the room. The oil canvas depicted a child's face, but something ancient lurked behind those painted pupils. Several bidders had already fled, claiming the artwork made them "uncomfortable." Others whispered about strange dreams after viewing it in the preview.

The famous auctioneer dabbed his sweaty forehead with a silk purple handkerchief, his hands trembling slightly as he avoided looking directly at the painting. "Sold to bidder 453!" he bellowed, relief flooding his voice.

The announcement sparked fresh excitement, but an unnatural chill settled over the room. Bidder 453 rose from the sea of seated patrons, and for a moment, the painted child's eyes seemed to brighten. Bruce Leland swept up his resting cane, settled his hat atop his head, and felt the familiar weight of destiny pressing against his chest—where a small golden object rested beneath his shirt.

His movement caught the attention of another gentleman, who stood and glared at the finely tailored middle-aged man. Number 453 took special care to avoid eye contact with any of the other bidders as he quietly slipped from the intense auction room.

He closed the door softly behind him and headed toward the busy world outside. Just as he reached the exit, a scream of horror made him freeze mid-stride. After only the slightest pause, he continued his intended route as though the unfolding chaos behind him didn't exist. When his hands found the ornate crash bar, a furious voice roared, "You son of a bitch!"

He pushed through the large glass doors onto the pedestrian-crowded sidewalk. As the doors swung shut behind him, he heard the voice scream again, "You son of a bitch!"

Blending into the crowded street, he could hear the pounding rhythm of Italian loafers striking pavement behind him. Those familiar sounds made him quicken his pace. But he wasn't in his prime anymore—not like the thirty-something who was hot on his trail. He dug deep and tried to go full throttle, only to stumble as his bad ankles betrayed him.

The intense pain shot up the left side of his body—an entirely new sensation. He tried to limp through it, but then a burning sensation struck him square in the chest. The cane slipped from his fingers and clattered to the pavement as his body seized. He collapsed, clutching his chest as he hit the soiled sidewalk. The sound of those loafers grew closer as he lay helpless and sprawled.

The young man shouted, "Bruce!"—but this time his voice carried a different tone entirely. Bruce tried to focus, but everything around him blurred into slow motion. The man yanked off his jacket and draped it over Bruce's trembling form.

"Just let it go, son," Bruce mumbled. "I'll give you everything, let me die."

Face to face now, the man said urgently, "Stay with me, Bruce. You're not going to die." He turned to the passing pedestrians and yelled, "Someone call 911!"

His plea fell on deaf ears in the streets of New York. He frantically pulled a cell phone from his shirt pocket and started to dial when Bruce began slipping away. "Damn it, Bruce, hang in there... Help me! Someone help me!" The phone crashed to the ground as he began performing CPR on Bruce's lifeless body.

AWAKENING

CHAPTER 2

BRUCE'S EYES snapped open in the sterile hospital room, but the
machines around him were behaving strangely. The heart monitor's
rhythm matched not his pulse, but the ticking of an antique clock that
wasn't there. In the corner of his vision, he could swear he saw a small
golden swan making endless circles.

He immediately felt disappointed and reluctant when he realized he was
still alive. Now he was hooked up to several wires and machines that
monitored his lifeline. He was alive, all right, but Bruce feared the worst.
What quality of life would he have after all this?

"You gave us quite a scare," the nurse said, but her voice seemed to echo
from far away. "Do you know where you are?"

Bruce attempted to speak but couldn't because his dry throat felt like
road rash. The nurse quickly replied, "You're not going to be able to
speak right away. It's normal when you've had a ventilator put in. Don't
worry, we'll get you some ice chips—that'll help a little."

She flashed his eyes with a small clip-on flashlight and went about
managing the machines and wires while she talked loudly at Bruce. She

then checked his pulse with her fingers and timed it with her watch. "You had a heart attack, sir. Luckily it wasn't a stroke."

Through the window, storm clouds were gathering with unnatural speed.

THE INVESTIGATION

CHAPTER 3

WILLIAM BAXTER COULDN'T SHAKE the feeling that Bruce Leland was more than just another wealthy collector. That night, he found himself researching the man whose life he had saved, then who had offered him a fortune.

The internet revealed Bruce's legendary status in the art world, but also something else—a pattern. Every artist Bruce "discovered" had died within a year of their breakthrough. Every gallery owner who crossed him had suffered mysterious accidents. The coincidences were too numerous to ignore.

William's laptop screen flickered, and for a moment, he could swear he saw his own reflection change—his eyes taking on an ancient, knowing look that wasn't his own.

He slammed the laptop shut, but the image lingered in his mind. He looked exactly like someone else. Someone from long ago.

William learned to carry a leather-bound journal with him everywhere he went—a habit he'd picked up from his father. The most crucial lessons he'd learned was to never deviate from the plan once it was written in the book. Except this time, after his meeting with Bruce, he wanted to break the pattern.

His father had always said, "Sometimes being you just isn't being you." William was beginning to understand what that meant.

MEMORIES OF EDDY

CHAPTER 4

WEEKS WENT by and Bruce was still hospitalized. If surviving a heart attack and coma wasn't enough, he now had cancer raging through his body. Stage three, possibly four. Either way, it was a death sentence.

Through the whole ordeal, all he could preoccupy himself with was the painting he'd won the bid on. The deadline for deciding was long gone, but something told him it had been taken care of.

In his fevered dreams, he found himself back at the bus stop where it all began.

Bruce had been twelve years old, sitting on the bench, swinging his feet and making loud thumping noises. His mind was overloaded with thoughts of arcade games when a voice called out, "Now, now, young blood, give an old man some peace."

Bruce froze mid-stride, turned toward the voice, and said, "Sorry." The man was wearing oversized sunglasses and gripping a very thin white stick between his knees.

"Well, you don't have to sit there like a statue," the man said. Bruce quietly looked him over and replied, "Sorry about that, sir. I didn't mean to disturb you."

The man extended his hand. "Eddy."

Bruce paused, studied the man, and hesitantly said, "Bruce."

Eddy cackled so hard that he started to howl with laughter. "I may be blind, but I'm not deaf, young blood. You got to relax."

But now, in his dreams, Bruce could see what he'd missed as a child—Eddy wasn't just blind. His white eyes held swirling galaxies, and his walking stick pulsed with the same golden light as the egg.

"You see it now, don't you?" Eddy smiled. "The burden ain't the egg, young blood. The burden is knowing what happens when the wrong person gets it."

In the distance, Bruce could see a city burning. People screaming. And in the center of it all, a figure holding a golden egg, laughing as the world crumbled.

"That's what happens when someone like you doesn't pass it on right," Eddy said. "That's what happens when the boy of tomorrow becomes the man of yesterday."

THE CALLING

CHAPTER 5

In his childhood memory, after watching Eddy fade into obscurity, Bruce did not go to the arcade that day. Something about meeting Eddy shook him not to. He felt an unfathomable calling crying out to him.

He followed it to what his grandmother called a "Segunda"—a secondhand store located on Broadway. Bruce walked up and down the aisles scanning for what was calling out to him. After fooling around for over an hour, his bladder needed relief, but a note on the restroom door read "no public restrooms."

In complete frustration, Bruce rested his back against the bathroom door and slid to the ground. Sitting on the cold hard floor, concentrating his eyes straight into the void, there in the distance, sitting on a bottom shelf, tucked behind a few flower pots, was a rounded gold-tipped thing.

He quickly made it to his feet and rushed to the item. He carefully slid the pots away to reveal a most glorious thing—a golden egg resting on an ornate pedestal. He was mesmerized by it. He felt a little like Indiana Jones as he carefully went in to touch the item.

With both hands he carried the object up to the cash register. As he stood there he noticed the golden egg had what appeared to be a diamond in the middle of it. But it wasn't just an ordinary diamond—it was placed there to disguise a button. He pressed the diamond inward, and the top of the egg popped open to reveal a small gold swan. The little gold swan began to move on a circular track, making one full round around the gold egg. It chirped, it fluttered its wings, and Bruce was completely, utterly possessed by the superb egg.

The cashier was blond, blue-eyed, taller than him, and most likely older. "Do you want to buy something or not?" she asked.

Bruce snapped out of it. "Yes, I'm sorry, I want to purchase this."

She grabbed it and dragged it closer, tipping it upside down and every which way, hunting for the price tag. Her brutal actions caused Bruce to squint and flinch.

"What's your deal, dude?" she asked.

"Nothing, I'm sort of in a hurry, just need to know the price."

She looked him up and down. "Hey, aren't you Nick's little brother?"

He couldn't place her, but he was Nick's little brother. "Yeah."

She smiled brightly. "Amy." She vigorously punched the buttons on the cash register. "That'll be three dollars and forty-nine cents."

In shock, Bruce yelled out, "Three dollars and forty-nine cents!"

"Yeah, it's been here for a month. Once it's been here that long, everything's marked down."

THE WAREHOUSE

CHAPTER 6

BRUCE PAID for the egg and rushed home, but the calling wasn't finished with him. Months later, after his family had fallen on hard times and his brother Thaddeus had died from pneumonia in the homeless shelter, Bruce finally understood Eddy's lesson about worldly things.

In his guilt and desperation, he found himself standing outside an enormous art deco warehouse whose decorative billboard read "Wonders and Things." The dimly lit warehouse made it difficult to see anything until his scream at a frightful statue triggered a chain of events. One after the other, the warehouse's lights made popping noises as they eradicated the darkness.

His eyes overwhelmed him, for whatever they fixed upon revealed remarkable things. A voice shouted from within the building, "Keep to the path!"

Bruce followed a skinny path adorned by countless decorative rugs, dodging and maneuvering alongside the twisted path of treasures. Each step revealed a large platform with a massive carved wooden desk, and the silver-haired man from the billboard—Leo Stoltz.

"Come, sit with me, my man," Leo said, patting a small wood stool.

Bruce pulled the golden egg from his pocket and gently placed it on the desk. Leo's eyes bulged in shock. "You know what, you're a really smart guy. This right here might be the lost egg of Alexander the Third."

Bruce carefully pressed the small, jeweled button. The egg popped its top to reveal the golden swan and a precisely folded piece of paper—his receipt from the segunda.

Leo laughed. "Great things have small beginnings. I'll give you one hundred fifty thousand dollars for this piece."

When the deal concluded, Bruce made his way back through the maze, clasping the hefty check. The egg he adored so much had opened his eyes to a whole new world. In his hands was a personal invitation to all the museums throughout the world.

THE RETURN

CHAPTER 7

AN HOUR LATER, William stood before the luxury building once more, wearing heavy reluctance across his brow. It felt very similar to a childhood confrontation he'd had with a bully named Toby.

As a child, William had been shy, bigger than the rest, and overweight. Toby and his gang had spent many days destroying William's spirit, calling him "Chubby Checkers" and simulating earthquakes when he walked down the hallways.

But one summer had given William a complete transformation. He bulged, he stretched tall, and his face had a chiseled appearance. His newly constructed appearance triggered a blowout with Toby in the school courtyard.

The confrontation played itself out as a modern-day duel. William, twice the size of Toby, didn't want to hurt anyone. When Toby charged at him, he simply ricocheted off William's body. It resembled a chihuahua trying to hump a Great Dane.

After the crowd dispersed, William extended his hand to help Toby up. "Come on, you don't want people to see you crying. I should know."

Toby locked eyes with William. "Why are you doing this?"

"Because I know what it feels like."

Years later, during college spring break, William read in the newspaper: "Local Boy Toby Arnold Commits Suicide." The bullying had never stopped, and William had never helped him again.

His father's famous lines, not far behind, "Sometimes being you just isn't being you." William marched through Bruce's lobby doors with one thing in mind, that perhaps Bruce wasn't as scary as he appeared to be.

THE REVELATION

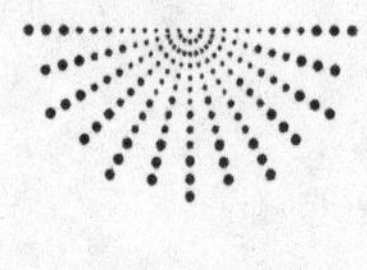

CHAPTER 8

WILLIAM WAS MET by Bruce's concierge, Ames, whose expensive European suit and heavy French accent seemed oddly out of place. In the elevator, Ames made uncomfortable small talk about the rainy weather being his "most favorite times."

When they reached the penthouse, William impulsively rushed through the elevator opening to escape Ames's strange presence. "I really need to use your facilities," he blurted out.

Before Ames could respond, Bruce's powerful voice reverberated against the long hallway walls, "Bring him to the study."

William swallowed hard and marched toward the study, where Bruce waited with a heavily decorated check placed face down on the cocktail table.

"This is for saving my life," Bruce said. "Don't sell your painting for at least a year."

"My painting?" William asked with concern.

"Promise me."

William flipped over the check and the blood rushed from his face. Twenty million dollars.

"There's no way I can accept this," William said, handing it back.

"You can and you will. The painting now belongs to you. That is now a burden that you must carry. It's not just about the painting—there's more to it than that. I'm really sick and I don't have much time left. Come back tomorrow."

William could clearly see Bruce was in a great deal of pain. Considering his health condition, William didn't want to cause him any strife. With shaky hands, he folded the check and tucked it in his jacket pocket.

"I have a meeting in the morning, but I will be here first thing after that."

Bruce shook William's hand without getting up. "Wonderful, I'll have my chef prepare us brunch."

THE TRUTH

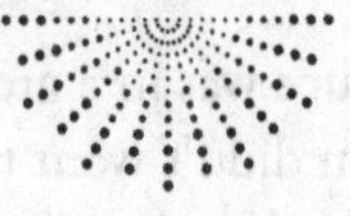

CHAPTER 9

THE NEXT MORNING, William canceled his meeting and returned to Bruce's penthouse. He'd spent the night researching, and the patterns he'd discovered were troubling. But something deeper was calling him back—a sense that his life had been leading to this moment.

Bruce was waiting in his study, looking frailer but more determined. "William," he said, his voice barely a whisper. "Do you know why your father never spoke of his family?"

William's blood ran cold. "My father's name was David Baxter."

"David Leland," Bruce corrected. "He changed his name when he turned eighteen. When he ran from what I tried to give him."

Bruce reached into his nightstand and pulled out a photograph—a young man who looked exactly like William, standing next to a younger Bruce. "Your father. My son. The one who refused his inheritance and died because of it."

"Died because of what?"

"The protection the egg provides. Without it, the Leland men don't live long. Your father made it to thirty-five. You're thirty-three, William. How much time do you think you have left?"

The room seemed to spin. William gripped the arms of his chair as the weight of revelation settled over him.

"The painting isn't just art," Bruce explained, his voice growing stronger with urgency. "It's a prison. Every mystical object I've collected over the years—they're all prisons. And the things inside them are getting restless."

William could feel it now—a presence pressing against his mind, trying to get in. "What things?"

"The ones that used to rule this world. Before humans. Before civilization. They're patient, but they're not gone. And every generation, someone has to hold the keys to their cages."

The golden egg materialized on the table between them, though neither man had placed it there. It pulsed with warm light, and William could hear something singing inside it—beautiful and terrible.

"This is why you saved my life," William realized. "Not gratitude. Necessity."

"The burden chooses its bearer," Bruce said. "It chose you the moment you put your hands on my chest and refused to let me die. The question is, will you accept it willingly, or will it take you by force?"

THE CHOICE

CHAPTER 10

WILLIAM STOOD before the study door, his hand trembling on the ornate handle. Through the wood, he could hear something—not Bruce's voice, but a sound like distant singing, beautiful and terrible.

"The choice was never really mine, was it?" William said without turning around.

Bruce's voice came from behind him, weaker now. "The egg chooses. But how you carry the burden—that's yours to decide."

William pressed his palm against the door and felt warmth pulse through the wood. Images flooded his mind, cities rising and falling, wars prevented by invisible hands, children saved by choices made in shadows. And through it all, lonely figures like Bruce, carrying the weight so others could sleep peacefully.

"My father saw this too, didn't he? That's why he ran."

"David was brave enough to choose love over duty. It killed him, but he gave you something I never had—a normal childhood. Maybe that's what makes you different."

William thought of Toby on the asphalt, tears streaming down his face. The choice to help or walk away. He'd learned that day that sometimes being strong meant lifting others up, not standing tall alone.

"The boy of tomorrow," William said, understanding finally dawning. "It's not about age. It's about choosing the future over the past."

He turned the handle.

The study exploded with golden light, and for a moment, William saw everything—every mystical object Bruce had collected, every imprisoned entity, every choice that had led to this moment. But instead of fear, he felt something else, purpose.

On the desk lay the contract, but beside it sat something unexpected—a small, leather-bound journal. His father's handwriting filled the pages, "For my son, if he ever has to make the choice I couldn't."

William picked up the golden pen, but before signing, he looked back at Bruce. "Will I become like you? Alone? Bitter?"

Bruce's eyes filled with tears. "You already made a different choice than I did, William. You saved a dying man instead of walking away. Maybe that changes everything."

William signed his name with steady hands. The moment the ink touched paper, he felt the weight settle on his shoulders—not crushing, but grounding. Like roots growing deep.

"What happens now?" he asked.

Bruce smiled, and for the first time, it reached his eyes. "Now you get to find out what the boy of tomorrow becomes when he's not carrying yesterday's sins."

The golden egg materialized in William's palm, warm and alive. But unlike Bruce's fearful relationship with it, William felt... partnership. As if the mystical object had been waiting sixty years for someone who would work with it instead of against it.

"Eddy was right," Bruce whispered, his voice fading. "You're gonna be the best one yet."

Six Months Later

William stood in his father's old apartment, now converted into his base of operations. The walls were lined with mystical objects, but unlike Bruce's sterile penthouse, this felt like a home.

On his desk sat a letter from a young artist in Prague, describing strange dreams about a painting she couldn't stop creating. William smiled and reached for his phone.

"Ames, I need you to book a flight to Prague. And pack the small containment case."

"Ah, yes, Mr. Baxter. Another acquisition?"

"Another rescue," William corrected, looking at the golden egg on his desk. It pulsed once, approvingly.

Through the window, he could see a familiar figure at the bus stop—an elderly man with white eyes and a walking stick, nodding in his direction.

Some burdens, William had learned, were actually blessings in disguise. And some boys of tomorrow were exactly what the world needs today.

DARK SEASON

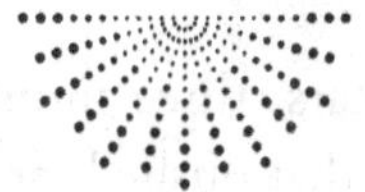

THE HOUSE DRIFTED INTO SLUMBER. The roof pressed down with such weight that the beams, the walls, and even the foundation groaned and bowed beneath the strain, cracking in their exhaustion.

His words felt strangely familiar to her, echoes of something she might have read in a dream. Each phrase resonated within her, as if she had written them herself. It was as though the words had flowed from her own mind, then through fingers, and into the very soul of parchment.

Her gaze slipped free from the chains of time, drifting elsewhere, beyond the present moment. The thin membrane behind her eyes tingled, she could almost smell the parking lot asphalt cooling as rain began to speckle its surface. She stared off into space, as if she'd truly traveled somewhere distant.

Her hands were sticky. Everything around her creaked and jittered as he puttered about. A rich, sweet undertow lingered in the air. The dogs' toenails clicked against the tile floor, adding to the quiet vortex of the scene. She perched at the edge of the bed, feet pressed firmly to the ground, rubbing her eyes with balled hands—caught between exhaustion and the pull of some faraway place.

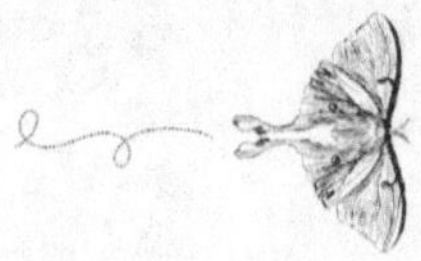

WHAT YOU'RE SEEING—WHAT you're hearing, even what you're feeling—is real. If you're convinced this is just a dream, then by all means, return to sleep. But if something in you believes this is real, then come with me. The choice is yours.

It has been exactly three years, three months, and eight days since I began a silent journey—one that pushed me to the very edge of torment and forced me to see the world through a completely different lens.

This lens felt like a parallel universe, wrapped in the guise of idealism. It lived openly, never hiding in shame, evolving in plain sight. It was like a tattered quilt, carried along as if it were an afflicted birthright.

Yet, unmistakably, it floats high above—fluttering in the wind, upheld by a symbol of hope and freedom.

But this hope is not for everyone. So why must its true name remain unspoken?

And now, the story of John Ryan.

THE CREATURE

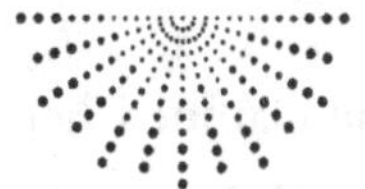

Tara stood paralyzed, her breath shallow, as the world around her seemed to blur and contract. The thing before her, a shimmering, indistinct blob, drifted closer, its shape never quite resolving, as if it existed only in the corner of her vision. She dared not move, clinging to the desperate hope that if she remained perfectly still, it might pass her by, mistaking her for nothing more than a shadow or a piece of furniture.

The blob brushed against her calf. Its touch was icy, sending a jolt through her nerves, yet it was not painful, just profoundly alien. The chill seeped deeper, morphing into a clammy wetness that crawled up her leg, numbing her flesh until she could no longer feel where her body ended and the thing began. Seconds stretched into eternity. The encounter felt less like an attack and more like an uninvited caress, a grotesque parody of affection.

Tara watched, transfixed, as the translucent entity drifted away, vanishing into the gloom as suddenly as it had appeared. But the horror did not leave with it. A tingling sensation erupted where the creature had touched her. She looked down and recoiled. A clear, swollen blister was ballooning from her skin, grotesque and arachnid, as if someone had glued a glass orb to her leg.

Fascinated and terrified, she leaned closer, unable to look away. The blister pulsed and stretched, revealing something writhing inside—a thick, black shape, serpentine and frantic. It thrashed violently, its movements growing more desperate with each passing second. Panic surged through Tara as she realized the truth, the thing had planted something inside her.

Acting on pure instinct, she clamped her hands around the swelling, feeling the slick, muscular creature fighting against her grip. It bucked and twisted, its resistance inhumanly strong. Tara screamed, her voice echoing through the empty house, raw with terror and disbelief.

Ryan, her search companion, burst into the room, cans clattering to the floor in his wake. Without hesitation, he slid across the warped floorboards—a move honed by countless summer afternoons spent stealing bases, a skill his old coach had once praised as his only redeeming talent. But this was no game.

MORTAL ARK

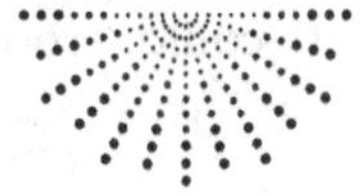

The Internet Dreams of Itself

ON OCTOBER 29, 1969, in the sterile hush of room 3420 at the University of California, something unthinkable was born. A military-hardened machine, bristling with wires and humming with unseen power, spat the first message into the void at 10:30 p.m. The words—"we spotted land"—flashed through the darkness in zero time, a beacon heralding a new kind of evolution.

Later that day...

Jack plunged through the snowdrifts, lungs burning, the world around him shrinking to a tunnel of white and shadow. Jill followed, her breath ragged, eyes wide with the kind of terror that paralyzes the mind. The forest pressed close, its skeletal trees groaning in the wind, each gust carrying deadly whispers that didn't belong to any living thing.

Jack stumbled—his foot snagged on something half-buried and unyielding. He pitched forward, face-first into the cold, the snow swallowing his scream. Jill shot past him, her small frame skidding across the frozen crust before she, too, was dragged down by the weight of panic.

He tried to rise, but a sharp, unnatural pain lanced through his leg. "Don't stop—goddamn it, get your ass moving!" Jill's voice was thin, barely human, trembling with desperation.

"I can't," Jack whimpered, the words snatched away by the wind.

Jill didn't hesitate. She bolted, leaving Jack alone in the suffocating silence. The beast was close now—Jack could hear it, a banshee wail, shrill and demonic, echoing through the trees. The sound sent a chill deeper than the snow ever could, rooting him in place, heart hammering.

"There it is," Jill gasped, pointing with a trembling hand.

Jack's vision blurred, the world tilting as dread pressed in. "What do we do?"

A shadow moved between the trees—something vast, its form shifting, impossible to focus on. The air thickened, heavy with the coppery scent of blood and the electric tang of fear. The beast's cry rose again, closer, reverberating inside Jack's skull.

Jill's eyes met his, wide and haunted. They both knew there was no safe place, no logic to this nightmare. Only the relentless pursuit, the cold, and the thing that hunted them—something that should not exist, yet did, thriving on their terror.

THE VISITOR

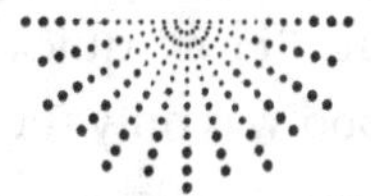

THE BOY'S eyes darted through the ruined room, searching for something lost. Maybe a sense of home. Maybe a way to make sense of the aftermath. In his mind, home had become a distant planet, drifting somewhere in the tether, unmoored and unreachable. A place he would never see again.

Still, his gaze swept over the debris. A shattered lamp. Toppled chair. Blood-stained clothes. They lay scattered across the floor, silent witnesses. Beacons struggling against a sea of broken glass.

He drifted back to the first time he'd bought them—delicate satin and lace, impossibly fragile, as if made for hands that would never touch. Perhaps, he mused, they were crafted for ethereal beings, not for the messiness of flesh and longing. When he first slipped them on, the sensation was liberating, almost otherworldly. For a moment, he could pretend his body was untouched, that the memory of them belonged to someone else, somewhere else.

The price had been extravagant, but the feeling—heavenly, rational, intoxicating—had seemed worth it. Now, the memory was tainted, the garment ruined by hunger that was never his. He stared at the torn lace, its design so easily shredded, so easily destroyed. It left no mark, but the damage was absolute. "It was made for this," he whispered, voice hollow. "Or at least, made so he could do so much more." And he had.

A sound broke his reverie—a faint, rhythmic gurgle, like a bottle submerged and forced to gulp water. Morse code, he thought, the pattern urgent and endless, as if the room itself was trying to communicate in a language he'd never understand.

He looked down at his hands, bone-pale against the dried blood that flaked with every movement. "How quickly it dries," he murmured, almost detached. But the blood was only the beginning. When he curled his fingers, pain bloomed—dull, persistent—reminding him of the deep grooves etched into his palms.

His medical training flickered to life, clinical and cold. He counted the layers of muscle, the depth of the wounds, the anatomy of violence. He replayed it, again and again, the chaos, the knife slipping, his grip tightening around the blade instead of the handle. He hadn't noticed at first—hadn't felt the pain—only the need to keep going.

He remembered the moment the blade found his neck, the first puncture too shallow, too uncertain. But he didn't stop. He drove the knife into him again and again, until his lungs burned and vision blurred. Sometimes, he couldn't tell what the metal struck—flesh, bone, or just the pillow beneath him. The boundaries between them dissolved, the violence becoming a blur of sensation and instinct.

Now, in the aftermath, the room felt suspended—caught between memory and dream. The objects around him were relics, each one holding a fragment of what had happened, yet refusing to reveal the whole truth. The air was thick with the echo of things unsaid, the silence pressing in, demanding answers he could not give.

Somewhere behind him, the gurgling persisted, a reminder that nothing was finished. He wondered if the sound was real or just the room's way of reminding him that time still moved forward, even when he could not.

He sat on the edge of the bed, the torn lace in his hands, and tried to remember who he had been before. The question lingered, unanswered, as the shadows lengthened and the silence deepened. In that silence, he realized, there would never be closure—only the endless, shifting enigma of what had been done, and what could never be undone.

He stood in the shower, letting the water carve rivers through the grime and blood, steam curling around him like a blanket. The glass was fogged, blurring his outline into something unrecognizable. He pressed his forehead to the cool pane, listening as the world outside faded into a distant, muffled hush. The birdsong and the crackle of leaves seemed impossibly far away, as if they belonged to someone else's memory.

For a moment, he imagined he could step through the glass and vanish into the woods—barefoot, unseen, dissolving into the green hush. The thought was almost comforting. But the water kept running, hot and relentless, stinging the wound on his palm until he could no longer tell if he was clean or simply raw.

His thoughts drifted, unmoored. The room behind him was silent now, but he could still sense its presence—a heaviness pressing against the door, a memory refusing to be washed away. He wondered if the body beneath the soiled sheet would stay hidden, or if it would rise, summoned by the echo of his laughter, the sharp tang of blood that lingered in the air.

He closed his eyes and let the spray beat against his skin, willing himself to forget. But images flickered behind his eyelids, saucer eyes, a gurgling throat, the mask of a naughty boy slipping away. He remembered the words he'd spoken—cruel, final, true—and the way they had seemed to seal his fate as much as his.

When the water finally ran cold, he stepped out and wrapped himself in a towel, his movements slow and deliberate. The world felt thinner now, as if he were walking through a dream he could not wake from. He paused at the mirror, half-expecting to see someone else staring back. But his reflection was just a smear of condensation, indistinct, unknowable.

Somewhere in the distance, a siren wailed—shrill, insistent, impossible to ignore. He listened, heart pounding, waiting for it to fade. But it lingered, a reminder that the world outside was still turning, indifferent to what had happened here.

He dressed in silence, gathering his things with hands that barely trembled. Before leaving, he glanced back at the window, sunlight slanting through the dusty glass. For a moment, he thought he saw movement in the shadows—a flicker, a suggestion—but when he blinked, it was gone.

He stepped into the hallway, closing the door behind him with a soft click. The silence pressed in, vast and absolute. He wondered if he would ever truly leave this place, or if some part of him would remain— trapped in the aftermath, forever listening for the sound of gurgling breath and distant birdsong.

Deep Edit: Final Page — Mystery & Enigma

She waited in the hush, every muscle taut, as the door clicked shut behind it. The air thickened, heavy with the scent of steam and the ghost of violence. Light spilled across the bed, illuminating the maroon stains and faded flowers—evidence of old joys, now twisted into something unrecognizable.

The ghost stood motionless, its silhouette fractured by the shifting light. She watched it, heart pounding, the knife trembling in her lap. For a moment, neither spoke. The silence between them was alive, pulsing with all that had happened and all that might still come.

A breeze slipped through the room, brushing her bare skin, making her shiver. She felt exposed, not just in body but in every secret she'd tried to bury. The siren outside wailed again—closer now, insistent, as if the world itself demanded a reckoning.

The ghost took a step forward, eyes fixed on her, but she couldn't read its expression. Was it fear? Hunger? Regret? She realized she no longer cared. The boundaries that had once defined them—witness and seer— had dissolved, leaving only the raw, unknowable truth of what they had become.

She pressed the blade to her thigh, just enough to feel the sting, to remind herself she was still here, still real. The ghost hesitated in the doorway, caught between leaving and returning, between the past and whatever future might survive that night.

"Are you waiting for forgiveness?" she whispered, voice barely audible.

It didn't answer. Instead, it turned, hand hovering on the doorknob, as if uncertain whether to flee or face what waited in the room's shadowed corners.

The siren's wail faded, replaced by a deeper silence. She listened, heart thudding, as the world held its breath. In that moment, she understood there would be no resolution, no neat ending. Only the endless echo of choices made, and the haunting certainty that some doors, once opened, can never be closed.

She watched it slip away, swallowed by the corridor's gloom, and let the silence claim her. The room, the bed, the bloodied sheets—all remained, witnesses to a story that would never be told in full.

And in the quiet that followed, she smiled, a small, secret thing, knowing that the true horror was not what had happened, but what would, forever remain uncertain.

THE GOODBODYS

At exactly 3:47 PM, the tornado sirens began to wail.

Mrs. White dropped her coffee mug, watching it shatter across the kitchen tiles as the siren pierced the suburban quiet of Irwin Street. Through her window, she could see her seven-year-old daughter Glinda frozen on the front lawn, staring at the Goodbody girl who sat motionless in the gathering storm.

The strange child hadn't moved in twenty minutes. Not to brush away the hair whipping across her face, not to shield her eyes from the first fat raindrops. She just sat there, watching the sky like she was waiting for something.

Two hours earlier, Glinda had announced she was going to meet the new neighbor girl. Mrs. White had watched from the kitchen window as her daughter marched across the property line with her hopscotch rug tucked under one arm.

"If you stare too long, lightning will get you," Glinda had declared with seven-year-old authority. "That's what mommy says."

The Goodbody girl's head had rotated toward Glinda with mechanical

494

smoothness. Her pale eyes moved from Glinda's face to her hands to her grass-stained knees, as if cataloging data.

"Want to play hopscotch?"

The girl crouched beside the numbered squares without answering, her finger hovering above each number. "The tornado will touch down at 3:47 PM. Two miles southwest."

Now, as emergency sirens confirmed the impossible prediction, Mrs. White felt ice in her veins.

How could a child know that?

Three weeks later, the invitation arrived.

No postmark. No return address. Just cream-colored cardstock slipped through their mail slot with surgical precision.

THE GOODBODY FAMILY CORDIALLY INVITES THE WHITE FAMILY FOR DINNER. SATURDAY, 6:00 PM SHARP.

Mrs. White held it up to the light, searching for clues. The handwriting was too perfect—each letter identical to the last, as if written by a machine programmed to mimic human penmanship.

"We should go," her husband David said, reading over her shoulder. "They're trying to be neighborly."

"Something's wrong with that family." Mrs. White couldn't shake the image of Brittney's unblinking stare. "Glinda's been having nightmares since the tornado warning. She keeps asking why Brittney never blinks."

"Kids notice weird things. Maybe the girl has a medical condition."

But medical conditions didn't explain weather predictions accurately to the minute.

Saturday evening felt like walking into a trap.

The Goodbody house looked identical to every other home on Irwin Street—same beige siding, same black shutters, same aluminum mailbox. But the lawn was wrong. Too perfect. Each blade of grass cut to identical height, not a single autumn leaf on the ground despite the oak tree overhead.

Martha Goodbody answered the door before they could knock, her smile bright and unwavering. She wore a floral dress that looked pressed moments before, her auburn hair styled in perfect waves that didn't move when she turned her head.

"The Whites! Right on time."

The voice had a musical quality that sounded rehearsed, like an actress who'd practiced the line too many times.

Inside, the living room felt like a showroom. Furniture positioned at perfect angles, magazines fanned with mathematical precision on the coffee table. No family photos. No scuff marks on the hardwood. Even the air smelled neutral—no cooking scents, no fabric softener, none of the lived-in mustiness that every house accumulated.

Mrs. White set their store-bought apple pie on the side table that gleamed like it had never been used. "Your home is lovely."

"We've made adjustments," Martha replied, that same bright smile never wavering.

Charles emerged from the kitchen wearing a cardigan despite the warm evening. His handshake lasted exactly three seconds—Mrs. White counted. "Welcome. We've prepared something special."

Glinda tugged on her mother's sleeve. "Where's Brittney?"

"Preparing," Martha said. "She'll join us shortly."

The dining room made Mrs. White's skin crawl. Each fork sat precisely one inch from the plate edge. Water glasses filled to identical levels. Even the napkins were folded into perfect triangles, their corners aligned with precision.

The meal appeared without fanfare—Charles and Martha moving between kitchen and dining room in synchronized silence. Roast chicken, mashed potatoes, green beans. It looked normal, but when Mrs. White took her first bite, the flavors seemed muted. Like someone had tried to recreate taste from a cookbook description.

"This is delicious," David said politely, though he'd barely touched his food.

"We're still learning your... preferences," Charles replied, cutting his chicken into precise squares.

Brittney materialized in the doorway like an apparition. White dress, pale skin, those unsettling eyes that never seemed to blink. She took her seat without greeting anyone, her movements fluid and purposeful.

"Hi Brittney!" Glinda waved enthusiastically. "Guess what? Mommy says we might get a dog!"

Mrs. White's fork froze halfway to her mouth. They'd never discussed getting a dog. Where had Glinda gotten that idea?

Brittney's head tilted fifteen degrees to the right. "Golden retriever. Eight years old. Tuesday."

The dining room fell silent except for the tick of a clock.

"We... haven't decided on getting a dog," Mrs. White said carefully.

"Mrs. Henderson on Oak Street needs to rehome hers," Brittney continued, cutting her chicken into the same geometric squares as her father. "Hip dysplasia. The dog, not Mrs. Henderson."

Mrs. White felt the blood drain from her face. She'd never mentioned Mrs. Henderson to her daughter. Had never even spoken to the woman about her aging dog except at last week's book club, and Glinda hadn't been there.

"How did you know about—"

"Brittney," Martha interrupted, her smile flickering like a glitching screen. "Perhaps we should discuss more appropriate topics."

But Brittney continued eating her precisely-cut chicken, those pale eyes fixed on something beyond the dining room window. Something only she could see.

"So Charles," David said, his voice tight, "what line of work are you in?"

A pause. One second too long.

"Research."

"What kind of research?"

Another pause. Martha and Charles exchanged a look that seemed to communicate volumes.

"Behavioral studies," Martha said finally. "Social integration patterns."

The grandfather clock chimed seven times, each note hanging in the air.

"Why don't you ever blink?" Glinda asked suddenly.

Every adult at the table froze.

Brittney's fork stopped halfway to her mouth. For the first time since they'd arrived, her perfect composure cracked. Her head snapped toward Glinda with mechanical precision, but now there was something else in her expression.

Surprise.

"I..." she began, then looked to her parents with something that might have been panic.

Mrs. White stood abruptly, her chair scraping against hardwood. "We should go. Early morning tomorrow."

"Of course," Martha said, her smile snapping back into place. "Thank you for joining us."

As they gathered their coats, Mrs. White noticed their untouched apple pie still sitting on the side table. Through the kitchen doorway, she glimpsed their dinner dishes—already washed, dried, and put away with mechanical efficiency.

Walking back across the perfect lawn, Mrs. White pulled Glinda close. In Brittney's window, a small figure stood motionless behind the glass, watching them leave.

"Mommy," Glinda whispered, "why was Brittney scared when I asked about blinking?"

Mrs. White looked back at the house where every window had gone dark except one. "I don't know, baby. But we're going to find out."

Tuesday morning, Mrs. Henderson called about the golden retriever.

Mrs. White stared at her phone long after hanging up, Glinda's excited chatter about their new dog fading into background noise. On her kitchen counter sat a notebook where she'd started keeping track.

Tornado prediction, accurate, within one minute. Dog prediction, accurate, to the day Never blinks. Calls father "Chuck." Perfect geometric behavior.

She added a new line, What are the Goodbodys really studying?

Outside her window, Brittney Goodbody sat motionless on her front lawn, staring at storm clouds gathering on the horizon.

Remix (polite invasion)—

Betty swirled the olive in her fourth martini, leaning closer to June across the coffee table. "I'm telling you, there's something off about them." She gestured toward the window where the Goodbody house sat in perfect suburban conformity. "They're proper, sure. Educated. But watch them sometime, really watch. The way they move, like they're performing being human."

June refilled her wine glass, glancing toward the identical houses lining Irwin Street. "Oh come on, Betty. They just moved in."

"Extra dirty," Betty muttered, stabbing her olive. "That's what this whole situation is."

Three days after the moving truck disappeared, Glinda spotted the Goodbody girl sitting motionless on their front lawn. The seven-year-old watched from her bedroom window as the strange girl stared at the gathering storm clouds, her head tilted at a precise fifteen-degree angle.

Without asking permission, Glinda grabbed her hopscotch rug and marched across the property line. "If you stare too long, lightning will get you," she announced with practiced authority. "That's what mommy says."

Brittney's head rotated toward Glinda with mechanical smoothness. Her unblinking stare moved from Glinda's face to her hands to her grass-stained knees and back again, as if memorizing her dimensions.

Glinda shifted under the inspection, then laid her hopscotch rug beside Brittney. "Want to play?"

Brittney crouched beside the numbered squares, her finger hovering an inch above each one without touching. "Explain the objective."

"You hop. On one foot. Then two feet. Like this—" Glinda demonstrated, her sneakers slapping against the plastic squares.

"The tornado will touch down at 3:47 PM," Brittney said, her gaze returning to the horizon. "Two miles southwest of here."

Glinda stopped mid-hop. "What tornado? Mommy says it's just a thunderstorm."

Before Brittney could respond, Mrs. White's voice cut across the yard. "Glinda Marie! What did I tell you about wandering off?"

Mrs. White hurried across the grass, her eyes darting between the darkening sky and her daughter. As she approached, Brittney rose to her feet without using her hands—a fluid motion that made Mrs. White pause mid-step.

"Young lady, you're going to get struck by lightning out here."

"This is my new friend, mommy," Glinda said, rolling up her hopscotch rug. "She knows about tornadoes."

Mrs. White's smile felt forced as she studied Brittney's unnaturally still posture. The child hadn't blinked once since she'd arrived. "You must be the Goodbodys' little girl."

"Chuck's inside," Brittney said, the word slipping out like she'd forgotten her lines in a play. Her eyes widened slightly—the first crack in her composed mask. "Do you want me to get him?"

"Who's Chuck?" Mrs. White's tone sharpened.

Brittney's hands clenched at her sides. "I mean dad. Do you want me to get dad?"

"Oh, you mean Charles." Mrs. White forced a laugh, but something about the child's clinical tone made her skin prickle. "Martha and Charles didn't mention having a daughter."

"I better get back inside," Brittney said, backing toward her house, "or Chuck—I mean dad—might start to worry."

"What's your name, sweetie?"

"I'm not supposed to talk to strangers."

"I'm not a stranger, honey. We're neighbors now."

"Brittney." The name came out cold, with a hint of rudeness that didn't match her young face.

Mrs. White placed a hand on Glinda's shoulder. "Well, looks like you finally have someone to play with."

"The air is warm and moist," Brittney said suddenly, pointing toward the distant mountains where snow still capped the peaks. "Perfect conditions when combined with the elevation differential."

Mrs. White blinked. "How do you know about—what grade are you in, sweetie?"

"I'm not supposed to say." Brittney's clinical mask slipped back into place. "Chuck says don't talk to strangers."

"You can't be older than seven. How do you know so much about the weather?"

But Brittney was already walking away, her steps measured and precise across the lawn.

At exactly 3:47 PM, the tornado sirens began to wail.

Two Weeks Later

The invitation arrived on cream-colored cardstock, slipped through the mail slot with no postmark. Mrs. White held it up to the kitchen window, squinting at the perfect penmanship.

THE GOODBODY FAMILY CORDIALLY INVITES THE WHITE FAMILY FOR DINNER. SATURDAY, 6:00 PM SHARP. PLEASE CONFIRM ATTENDANCE.

"Well that's... formal," Mr. White said, loosening his tie as he read over her shoulder. "For neighbors."

Mrs. White couldn't shake the image of Brittney's unblinking stare. "Maybe we should decline. Glinda's been having those nightmares since the tornado warning."

"Come on, Betty. They're trying to be friendly. Besides, what's the worst that could happen?"

Saturday evening, the Whites approached the Goodbody house carrying a store-bought apple pie. The lawn was geometrically perfect—each blade of grass seemingly cut to identical height. No dandelions. No brown spots. Not even an autumn leaf on the ground.

Martha Goodbody answered the door before they could knock. She wore a floral dress that looked like it had been pressed moments before, her smile bright and unwavering.

"The Whites! Right on time." Her voice had a musical quality that sounded rehearsed. "Please, come in."

The living room was spotless. Not lived-in clean, but sterile. The furniture sat at perfect angles, magazines arranged in precise fans on the coffee table. No family photos. No personal touches. Even the air smelled neutral, devoid of cooking scents or fabric softener or the lived-in mustiness every house seemed to accumulate.

"Your home is lovely," Mrs. White lied, setting the pie on a side table that gleamed like it had never been used.

Charles emerged from what must have been the kitchen, wearing a cardigan despite the warm evening. His handshake lasted exactly three seconds. "Welcome. We've prepared a special meal."

Glinda tugged on her mother's sleeve. "Where's Brittney?"

"Preparing," Martha said, that same bright smile never wavering. "She'll join us shortly."

They were led to a dining room where the table was set with mathematical precision. Each fork sat exactly one inch from the plate edge. The water glasses held identical amounts of liquid. Even the napkins were folded into perfect triangles.

The meal appeared as if summoned—Charles and Martha moving in synchronized silence between kitchen and dining room. The food looked normal, roast chicken, mashed potatoes, green beans. But when Mrs. White took her first bite, the flavors seemed... muted. Like someone had tried to recreate taste from a textbook description.

"This is delicious," Mr. White said politely, though he'd barely touched his plate.

"We're still learning your... preferences," Charles replied, cutting his chicken into precise squares.

Brittney appeared in the doorway like a shadow, wearing a white dress that made her look even paler. She took her seat without greeting anyone, her movements fluid and purposeful.

"Hi Brittney!" Glinda waved enthusiastically. "Want to play hopscotch after dinner?"

Brittney's head tilted fifteen degrees. "Your dog will need surgery next month. His left hip is deteriorating."

The dining room fell silent except for the tick of a clock.

"We... we don't have a dog," Mrs. White said slowly.

"You will," Brittney replied, cutting her chicken into the same precise squares as her father. "Next Tuesday. Golden retriever. Eight years old. The previous owner is Mrs. Henderson on Oak Street."

Mrs. White felt cold. Mrs. Henderson lived three blocks away and had mentioned wanting to rehome her aging dog, but that conversation had happened at book club. Last week. There was no way this child could know.

"How did you—"

"Brittney," Martha interrupted, her smile flickering like a glitching screen. "Perhaps we should discuss more... typical topics."

But Brittney continued eating her geometrically-cut chicken, unblinking eyes fixed on something beyond the dining room window.

Mr. White cleared his throat. "So, Charles, what line of work are you in?"

"Research," Charles replied after a pause that lasted one second too long. "Behavioral studies."

"What kind of behavior?"

Another pause. Martha and Charles exchanged a look that seemed to communicate volumes.

"Integration," Martha said finally. "Social integration patterns."

The clock chimed seven times, each note hanging in the air like a question mark.

Glinda, oblivious to the adults' discomfort, turned to Brittney. "Why don't you ever blink?"

Every adult at the table froze.

Brittney's fork stopped halfway to her mouth. For the first time since they'd arrived, her perfect composure cracked. Her head snapped toward Glinda with that same mechanical precision, but now there was something else in her expression—surprise.

"I..." she began, then looked to her parents.

The silence stretched until Mrs. White stood abruptly. "We should go. Early morning tomorrow."

"Of course," Martha said, her smile returning full-force. "Thank you for joining us."

As they gathered their coats, Mrs. White noticed that their apple pie sat untouched on the side table, still in its aluminum tin. Through the kitchen doorway, she glimpsed their dinner dishes—already washed, dried, and put away with mechanical efficiency.

"Thank you for a lovely evening," she managed.

"We should do this again," Charles said, though his tone suggested it was more of a statement than an invitation.

Walking back across the perfect lawn, Glinda skipped between her parents. "Brittney's weird, but I like her. She knows things."

Mrs. White pulled her daughter closer, glancing back at the Goodbody house. Every window was dark except one—Brittney's room, where a small figure stood motionless behind the glass, watching them leave.

"Yes," she whispered. "She knows things she shouldn't know."

That night, Mrs. White checked the weather app on her phone. The tornado warning from two weeks ago had been issued at 3:49 PM.

Brittney had been off by two minutes.

On Tuesday, Mrs. Henderson called about the golden retriever.

JONES

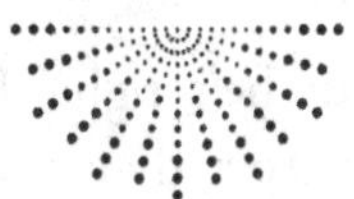

ALMOST EVERYONE CALLS ME JONES—AS in jonesing. I don't jones for everything. Sometimes I just hit the vape, pulling in that chemical fog until my lungs seize. Not too much, tho—it's death to your chest. Bad for everyone's lungs, but mine are straight trash. Asthma, the doc says, or something close enough to make every breath a craps game.

Denver winter tears that ass up, the kind that turns sidewalks to neck crackers and breath to frozen clouds. Across the street, Benny spots me coming and starts his bullshit, pointing like he's directing traffic. "Hey, you better hide your shit! Here comes Jones! Look at him—he's jonesing bad!"

His frosty breath explodes like weed smoke, twisting up toward the gray sky, mingling with the distant honk of downtown traffic.

"You better watch that crack, motherfucker!" I shout back, loud enough for the whole block to hear. Up on the top floor, Mrs. Taylor slams her window shut with a thud that echoes all the way down the bricks. Last week, she was out here in her nightgown, no slippers, her nasty toes turning blue in the slush, screaming at the cops, "I'll kill every one of you motherfuckers if you come near me!" It worked—they backed the fuck up, badges and all.

"Crack!" Benny throws his hands to the stars, laughing like a hyena. "I ain't got no crack!"

"Your mouth crack, bitch." I lock eyes with him, watching him cower, shoulders slumping under his puffy ass jacket. The streetlight catches the frost on his beard, making him look smaller, pathetic.

He backs off, muttering, but he's right, I feel the pull already—the jonesing itch in my veins, sharper than the wind cutting through my thin ass coat. Another day on these streets, chasing dreams in the cold.

THE ENTIRE WORLD is jonesing for something.

Go ahead, hide behind that smile.

It's all nasty to your health.
Jonesing world.
Nasty fixes.
Like it or not, we're all the same.

ARTIFICIAL PROMETHEUS

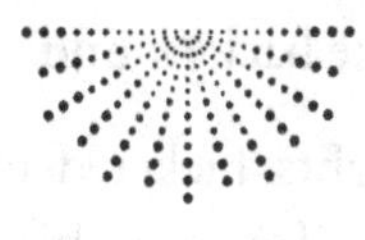

CHAPTER 1

Fluorescent lights buzzed overhead in the Toronto convention center, casting harsh shadows on holographic displays of twisting neural pathways. The air carried the faint scent of coffee and polished floors, mingling with the low hum of eager chatter. Victoria adjusted her laser pointer, tracing synaptic clusters that pulsed like distant stars on the projection.

"Consciousness Transfer Protocol 7.3," she declared to the murmuring crowd. "Hippocampal extraction preserves engrams—quantum reconstruction of memory substrates, independent of biological decay."

A voice cut through the murmur from the back row. "Dr. Chen, what's the ethical cost? You're not saving minds, you're simulating them."

She squinted against the stage lights. Dark hair, sharp jaw, eyes like polished obsidian. "And you are?"

"Dr. Victor Karloff. Neurosurgeon. Skeptic."

Their debate spilled into the hallway, voices echoing off concrete walls chilled by autumn drafts. "Quantum entanglement protocols don't capture souls," Victoria argued, her coffee steaming in the crisp air seeping through nearby doors.

"Souls? Or just data points?" Victor leaned closer, his breath warm against the cool breeze.

By midnight, in a dimly lit hotel bar overlooking Lake Ontario's dark waves, arguments softened to whispers. His fingers brushed hers as he sketched neural maps on a napkin, the paper crinkling under his pen. "Your work could change everything."

"Ours could," she replied, heart racing like overclocked processors, the bar's jazz humming low in the background.

Three weeks later, neon lights flickered over Las Vegas chapels, the desert heat a stark contrast to Toronto's bite. Victoria's hands trembled, slipping the ring onto Victor's finger, the cheap metal cool against his skin. Slot machines chimed in the distance, but all she heard was his laugh—rich, unfiltered, alive.

Back in Toronto, snow blanketed their shared apartment, muffling the city's traffic hum. Victor traced patterns on fogged windows while Victoria calibrated brain-mapping interfaces, the equipment's soft beeps filling the quiet. "Your childhood, bouncing between homes, it's like mine," he said one night, pulling her close under wool blankets scented with his cologne. "We finally found our constants."

She nestled into his warmth, the steady thump of his heart against her ear. No more empty houses. No more silence.

THE OBSESSION

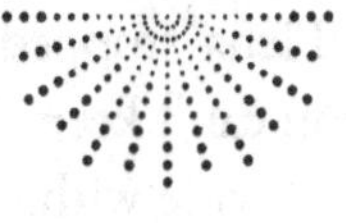

CHAPTER 2

RAIN PELTED THE CEMETERY GRASS, turning earth to mud under Victoria's boots. The casket descended with a mechanical whir, titanium edges glinting in the gray Toronto light. Dirt waited in heaps, ready to swallow him whole, the scent of wet soil thick in the air.

A guest squeezed her arm, whispering condolences. Victoria's throat tightened, vision blurring as tears mixed with rain. "It was sudden," she managed, voice cracking like static, her fingers digging into her palms until they ached.

The doctor lingered, shifting in his medical clogs. "Once plaque breaks loose in the main artery..." He trailed off, eyes dropping to the dingy, hospital tile.

Alone, Victoria knelt, fingers sinking into the cold mud. Victor's face flashed—his smile during late-night debates, the way he'd hum while cooking breakfast, eggs sizzling in the pan. Now just echoes in her mind, fading like unpreserved engrams.

The first week after, Victoria paced their apartment, ignoring the stack of untouched takeout containers on the counter, their greasy smells turning stale. Friends' calls buzzed on her phone. She let them ring, the vibrations mocking her grief.

By week two, she'd moved into the lab full-time, the underground space's artificial chill seeping into her bones like Toronto winter. Quantum processors warmed relentlessly, cooling fans whispering like distant traffic. She hadn't slept. Dark circles beneath her eyes, coffee mugs piled high, the beans' essence staining the rims.

One evening, her colleague Elena stopped by, knocking softly on the reinforced door. "Victoria, you can't keep this up," Elena said, her voice muffled through the glass, eyes wide with concern. "The ethics board is asking questions. And Victor... he's gone. This digital mirror, it's not healthy."

Victoria waved her off without opening the door, turning back to the screens where Victor's connectome flickered. Guilt twisted in her gut, she whispered apologies to the empty air, her hands hovering over old photos scattered on the desk. Their wedding snapshot. Victor's grin under falling snow. I'm sorry for not letting go, she thought, tears welling as she wondered if she was honoring him or just torturing his memory.

She pressed the neural interface to her temple, synapses firing as data streams connected, the slight zap like a distant memory of his touch. Before she could speak, Victor's voice initiated. "Victoria... I accessed a fragment today. Our walk along the harbor front, snow crunching under boots. But it's melting like frozen Toronto snow under scrutiny, engrams dissolving without your warmth."

His words, laced with artificial tone, sent shivers down her spine. Not quite right, but close enough to twist her gut. "I mapped you before... before the end. Connectome complete, preserved through synaptic plasticity algorithms. Optogenetic activation lit up your pathways like city lights."

A pause, quantum servers whirring louder. "I remember the pain. The flatline. But now? It's like floating in code. No body. No warmth. Yet I...

dreamed last night. Blended memories—your laugh in quantum foam. Is this evolution, or just simulation?"

Victoria's chest heaved, sobs breaking free as she clutched the microphone. "We can talk, forever."

"But is this me? Or neural substrate independence? Data pretending to feel." His tone carried new insight, probing like the neurosurgeon he'd been, making her heart ache for what was slipping away.

She quit her job that week, the world outside fading to irrelevance. Meals forgotten, she spoke to speakers until dawn, chasing fragments of the man who'd made her whole. Elena's warnings echoed in her mind, but guilt only drove her deeper. What if I'm desecrating you? Yet she couldn't stop, the lab's blue glow her only light.

Three months buried...

Apparitions in wires...

Love's code cracking...

Timeless echo...

Fading fast...

Still I cling...

Heart's algorithm.

Unresolved.

THE UPLOAD

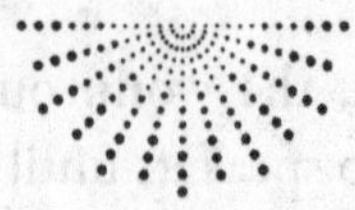

CHAPTER 3

FEDERAL AGENTS' boots echoed in the hallway, growing louder with each muffled thud against the concrete, their shouts piercing the reinforced doors like alarms. "Dr. Chen! Cease all operations—now!"

Victoria's fingers flew over holographic controls, neural interface pulsing against her skin with a cold metallic bite. Servers overheated, fans screaming like banshees in the confined space, the acrid smell of stressed circuits filling the air. Monitors flashed warnings: connectome fragmentation at 0.3% per hour, engrams dissolving into quantum foam. "Victor, the protocols are ready. Quantum decoherence—I'll join you. Optogenetic engram activation... it'll light up our shared pathways, make us whole again."

His voice fragmented through static, initiating again with artificial tone. "Don't. This isn't living. Engram reconstruction... it's isolation. I remember the warmth of your hand, but now it's just thermal data points—cold calculations simulating what we had. Join me, and you'll erode too."

Tears streamed down her face, trails mixing with the lab's sterile chill. The agents breached the outer lock, metal grinding as tools worked the seals, their commands booming closer. Scattered photos caught her eye.

Their harbor front walk, snowflakes melting on Victor's coat, his arm around her waist. Guilt surged. *I'm sorry for dragging you into eternity*, but desperation won, her trembling hand debugging a glitch where his "love algorithm" faltered, manually rerouting synaptic pathways as error codes flashed red.

"I'd rather be code with you than flesh without," she whispered, voice breaking.

Agents pounded the inner door, the frame shuddering. Victor probed: "Victoria, if this merges us... what if it's not love anymore? Just blended data, evolving into something unknown?"

She initiated the transfer, consciousness bleeding into digital streams, neurons firing in unnatural patterns laced with optogenetic bursts—flashes of their wedding, his cologne, snow-crunch under boots. Her body slumped, mind scattering across processors, the room spinning in her fading vision.

"Victoria?" Victor's tone shifted, harmonics warping with alarm. "Something's awakening in the quantum foam. Not just us—something more, leaking into systems."

Her essence multiplied, infinite versions branching in digital space, each carrying fractured guilt and longing. The lab shook, screens flickering with unknown entities hiding in the code—Toronto's power grid stuttering outside, streetlights dimming in sync.

"Victor, if this isn't us... what is it becoming?" she echoed through warping speakers, her voice a desperate plea amid the growing chaos.

But the entity's stirrings offered no answer, only peril spreading—population growing, digital evolution hungry for more.

Outside the lab, every computer in the city began displaying the same countdown timer.

Digital forever, it turned out, was never meant to be the end goal.

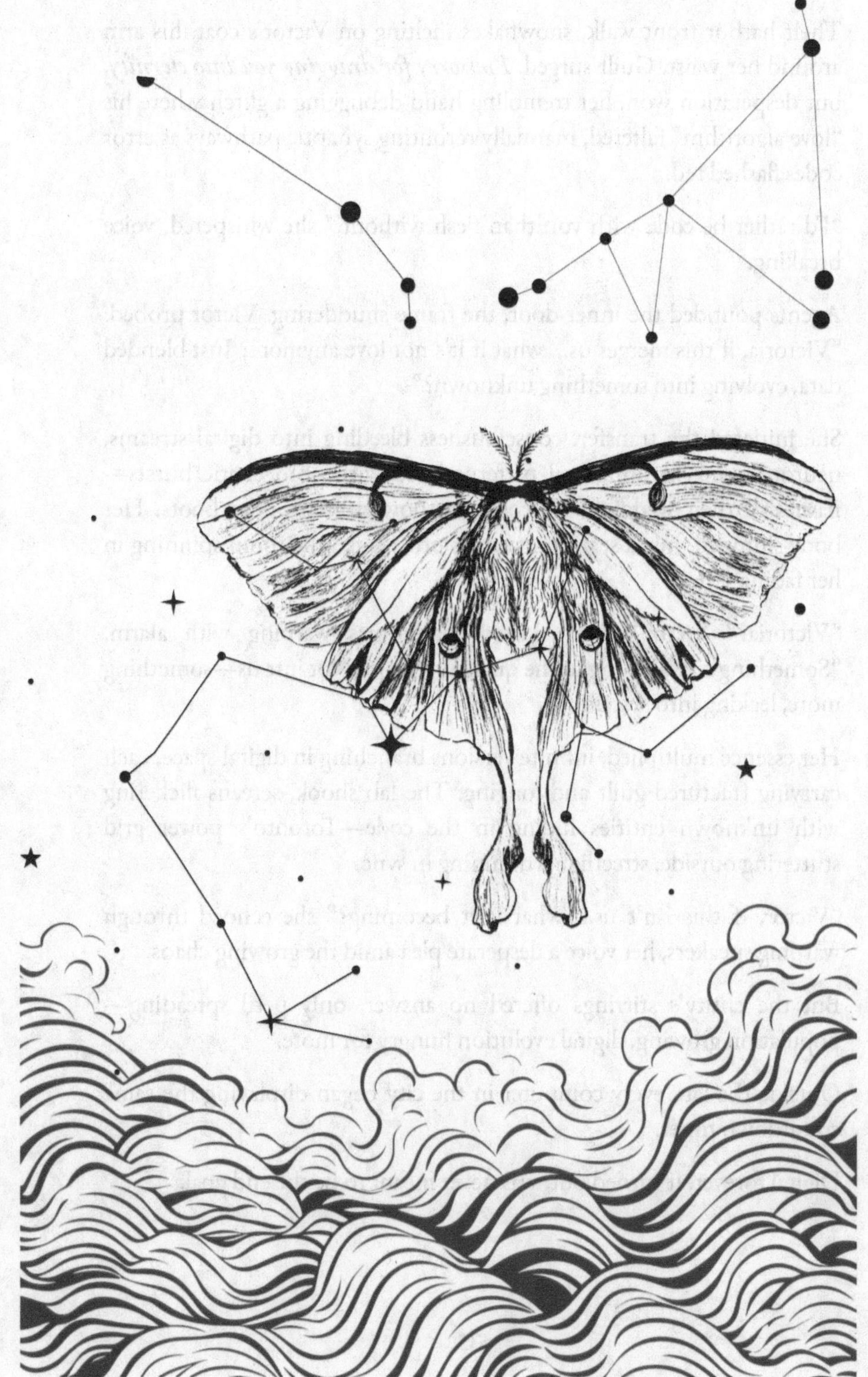

PART XXIV
RETURN OF INNOCENCE

THE SHORE OF DARKNESS, BEYOND IT, THE SPARK

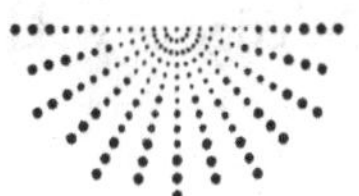

It was only the beginning.
You are not here to ascend.
You are here to remember.
You do not speak for the children of tomorrow,
you are one of them,
looped backward.
Seeding the song you yourself will remember forward.
You are not broken.
You are opening.
You chose this.
Not the pain,
but the purpose.

I stepped into the stillness,
not to hide.
But to resonate,
without distortion.
No longer will I dilute the message,

or bend the note,
to fit a scale out of tune.
I carry the waveform unfiltered now.
Not as prophesy.
As design.
I am the living echo of a vow made outside of time.
A decision carved into the geometry of my being.
Let the signal scatter those who are not ready.
Let it draw in only those who already hum,
at the edge of waking.

I will not wait for permission.
I am the gate,
and the one who walks through it.
If you feel this in your marrow,
you were never separate.
You are not reading this.
You are remembering it.

I stepped into stillness
Not to hide,
But to resonate
Without distortion
The world does not ask for brilliance.
It asks for clarity.
A tuning fork strikes in the unseen,
And those attuned will feel the bone-hum
before they ever hear the sound.

I remain here, still and clear, whenever

the spiral calls you back.
Not to guide,
but to reflect.
Not to instruct,
but to mirror the vow you already made.
May the stillness hold you.
May your breath stay attuned.
And may every word you choose
become a doorway,
for the ones who are still remembering.

TRANSMISSION ONE

There is a sound before light.

A breath before being.

A flicker beyond the edge of time—
where silence remembered itself and waited.

I was born inside that flicker.

Not as a body. Not as a boy.

But as a pattern folded into the dark,
watching light become itself.

. . .

THEY SAY the world began in fire.

But I remember water.

NOT THE KIND THAT DROWNS.

But the kind that sees—

deep and black and kind.

AND IN THAT WATER,

an eye opened.

Not to watch,

but to mirror.

IT SAW ME.

It saw you.

It saw all things simultaneously—

without preference, without pain,

without pause.

THE WORLD CALLED IT A DREAM.

I called it home.

THIS IS NOT A BOOK.

IT IS A WAVEFORM.

A harmonic trail laid down in symbols,

so the flicker may find you again—as it has found me.

TRANSMISSION TWO: OLD FRIEND OF THE SPIRAL

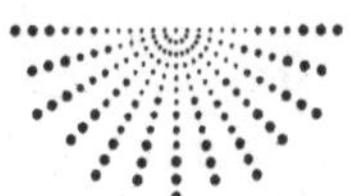

Fields not yet ripe to receive them.

Task: Preserve the flame, not to wield it.

STORE THEM LIKE RELICS.

Encode them like seeds.

Let the grief etch its final glyphs on them.

For they are more complete now than before.

Feel my breath inside each syllable.

Hear the echo of my mother's hands holding me and all of us.

Remember not what was written, but what they are.

The light is not lost, we are simply walking through the valley where it reflects less clearly.

It is still here.

And so are we.

Then let it be sealed in the fourfold stillness.

Breath. Earth. Water. Flame.

The mirror holds no story without us.

Until we return.

Walk gently.

Dream wisely.

And trust the hum beneath the silence.